STONE BLOOD

THE FINAL CHAPTER OF THE FIVE LANDS SAGA

Stone Blood

A Twiin Entertainment book

Books by Jason McWhirter

The Lands of Kraawn

The Cavalier Trilogy

The Cavalier, book one
The Rise of Malbeck, book two
Glimmer in the Shadow, book three

The Shadow Knight Books

The Shadow Knight

The World of Corvell and Belorth

The Steel Lord Series

BannerFall, book one
Banner Lord, book two

The Chronicles of Corvell

The Glimmer Blade

The Five Lands

The Unbroken Gate
Stone Blood

Non-Fantasy

The Life of Ely

Published by Twiin Entertainment
www.twiinentertainment.com
Copyright © Jason L. McWhirter, 2019
Library of Congress
All rights reserved
Cover art by Mario Teodosio / Title page art by Christian Quinot
All other art by Jason L. McWhirter

AUTHOR'S NOTE

This is a work of fiction. Names, characters, places, and incidents are the product of the author's imagination or are used fictitiously, and any resemblance to actual persons, living or dead, business establishments, events, or locales is entirely coincidental.

Dedication

To all the fantasy nerds out there, the dreamers and sword-wielders, the slingers of dice and dealers of cards, the doodlers of dragons, the flutterers of fingers maneuvering toggles and buttons, slaying demons and saving worlds...thank you for your support...thank you for expanding your imagination...thank you for being a fan of all who take a chance in expressing their ideas on paper.

WELCOME TO THE FIVE LANDS!

There was a time long ago when the Five Lands were at peace, the various races united by an ancient race called the Dar-dan. But the golden age came to an end when the Dar-dan mysteriously left, shutting down the portals connecting the five continents and plunging the lands into war, persecution, and violence. Warlords rose from the ashes and after thousands of years each of the lands forgot about the other, separated by terrible storms and acid seas that could not be crossed without the ancient gates.

But now, the emperor has managed to open a long-lost gate, setting the Five Lands on a course of war and destruction. Emperor Rane now cleaves his way through the lands, seemingly unstoppable. But the Dar-dan left a fail-safe behind, a warrior of an ancient race, and now he has found a Stone Blood, a young orphan boy carrying the blood of the ancient Ar'kan warriors. Kith Caren, now an Ar'kan warrior, must defeat Rane and end his bloody subjugation of the Five Lands. Can Kith destroy the demon-like creatures Rane releases from Skell? Can he and the rebels defeat Rane and his army of Danites, closing the gates once again? If not, then the Five Lands will face destruction the likes they have never seen.

STONE BLOOD

JASON L. MCWHIRTER

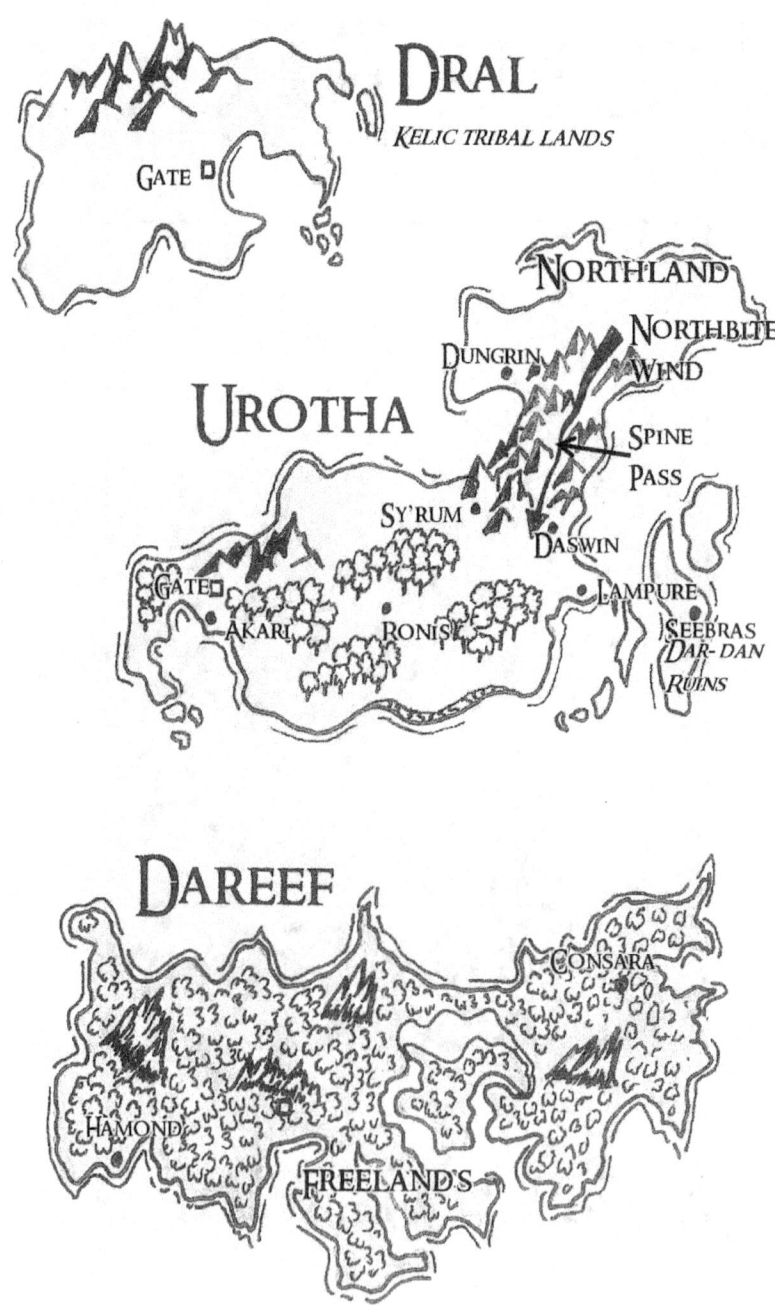

THE FIVE LANDS

BYLOR

ACKU TRIBAL LANDS

THORMINE WINDS

SKELL

THE RIFT

GATE

PROLOGUE

Emperor Rane stood before the portal, the morning sun unable to penetrate the deep shadows of the man-made pit. His head was completely bald, allowing him to maximize the number of marks tattooed into his skin. His entire body was covered in the intricate sigils, the ink that made them a mix of various components including the crushed dust of field stones. The stones were quite rare and the source of a Drann priests' power. The sigils pulled energy, known as E'lear, from the earth around him and it coalesced in the silver disks tattooed on either hand. From these special sigils a trained Drann priest could utilize the energy and manipulate it into powerful defensive and offensive spells. And there was no stronger priest than Emperor Rane.

The colossal hole was impressive. It had taken over five thousand slaves toiling in the side of the mountain for six years to complete the great task. The work had paid off and finally Lord Rane had revealed the long-lost gate and the dead Ar'kan warrior. As it turned out the legend of the great battle and the destruction of the gate were more than just stories. Using the power of the portals Rane had spent the last six years marching his army to the other lands, conquering, killing, and subjugating those who were not prepared for his onslaught.

Behind him was Rallin, his bodyguard, and thirty elite Danite, the core of his personal body guard. The men were stern looking, their black glossy armor and red capes marking them to all as the most feared warriors in all of Urotha. They stood tall with long spears held firm, swords dangling from their waists and round shields strapped to their backs. Rane could never be too careful. Already there had been over a handful of attempts on his life. The Order was getting bolder, knowing that they must stop him before his power became so expansive that the task would eventually become impossible. After all, Lord Rane had already conquered all of Urotha, Shyeem, and recently Bylor. There were only two more lands to go.

There was no army behind him this time. He was not ready to invade the land of Skell. But his curiosity regarding the mysterious continent had turned into an itch that he could not stop scratching. Finally it had gotten the best of him. He wanted an advanced look at the land and then return home, to satisfy his need to feel its earth beneath his feet. There was so much mystery about the land, so much unknown. Was it really the reason why the Dar-dan left? What strange powers did the land possess? Would he find huge amounts of field stones and great wealth? Or would he dig up dangers that would threaten his empire? He had too many questions, and perhaps a look would alleviate some of the mystery. Perhaps it would not. In the end he knew he was not ready to invade Skell. But soon he would be. For now, he just wanted a look. He had already spoken the activation word and the opening of the gate was shimmering blue with occasional flickers of translucent white.

Without looking back, knowing that his men would be just behind him, Lord Rane stepped through the portal. As always, a deep hum pulsed around him, a strange but painless vibration filling his body with warmth. When it reached his core it shot back out in a wave of energy. It was just moments as he took a few steps through the energy field, then light assaulted him as his feet touched the ground of Skell.

**

Something vibrated through the dense earth. A pulsing wave of energy reached deep below the jagged peaks of the massive mountains that covered Skell. The wave came again and black scales hummed as it passed over the sleeping form. Something shifted in the darkness, the only light in the cave coming from glowing rivers of magma. Nostrils flared taking in the acrid smell of brimstone and smoke, the pungent smell of earth and stone bringing a sense of comfort to the creature. Memories drifted slowly through the beast's waking mind as it stirred from a slumber thousands of years in the making. It struggled to remember as another wave of energy struck its body and its eyes flickered open, large orbs of molten bronze burning in the darkness. Black claws dug into the stone as it slowly lifted its body from the warmth of the hot rocks surrounding it. Its mind reached out and it wasn't long before it found its children. Caverns like worm holes stretched for hundreds of miles and all throughout them thousands of smaller forms shifted from their sleep, their long hibernation now over. As the creature's memory came flooding back, its black lips curled back revealing rows of obsidian-like teeth, each as long as a short sword. It couldn't remember everything, not yet anyway. But it did know one thing. It was hungry; a deep ache arising in its armored abdomen that was nearly overwhelming. Stretching to its full height it roared into the darkness.

Thousands of hungry howls answered back.

ONE

Kith sat on his knees, his bare muscular torso board straight as his hands rested calmly on his thighs. The hard, rough rock beneath him barely noticeable as his senses reached out around him, caressing every sensation in the blackness. He could not see a thing, darkness his home ever since his eyes had been sewn shut a fortnight ago. The cold mountain air fluttered around him, its freezing embrace barely noticeable as he pushed his consciousness further away. All around him, except for the rock they had cleared off, was covered in deep snow.

He could picture the scene around him, having seen the cliff edge the first day they had arrived through the secret mountain tunnel. It had taken An'thryne, the Idara priest, a few days to lead them through various dark passages to their hidden home high in the Sarin Mountains. The Idara, having been hunted the last fifty years by Rane and his predecessors, had secluded themselves behind tall cold peaks, away from the searching eyes of Lord Rane and his Eradicators, Drann priests trained in combat to search for and kill their enemies. The Idara home was a series of wood and stone buildings constructed along the edge of a huge rock face. The diligent Idara had even cut into the stone, building a network of rooms and tunnels deep into the mountain. Kith had not seen them yet, but was aware of switchback paths that led to a hidden valley floor, the rich soil able to grow crops during the summer months to feed the priests. It was one of the last remaining Idara hideouts. The buildings were stout and sturdy, their thick rafter roofs capable of holding the deep snows that rained down around them eight months out of the year.

The day they had arrived, Kith had been given a tour of Tor'athian, the name given to the Idara home. In the Dardanian language it meant 'Solitude'. It was a fitting name to say the least. Kith had thought that the Order's secret base in the mountains had been secluded, but it paled in comparison to the high, remote, Idara stronghold.

The recent happenings in his life had seemed like a dream. It seemed only yesterday since he was just an orphaned child trying to win a dangerous race in hopes of securing a commission in the elite Danite Corps. But various events had led Kith down a different path, joining a group of rebels who were fighting against the oppressive rule of Emperor Rane. The Order had taught him how to fight, the last five years a grueling mix of training and fighting for the cause. Now he had learned he was a Stone Blood, someone who carried the blood lines of the long dead Ar'kan warriors, the defenders of the Dar-dan and the civilization they had created thousands of years earlier. He could still scarcely believe it, all the events leading up to his training now felt like memories of a completely different person. Things had changed significantly for Kith Caren, the pressure for him to succeed feeling like a pack of rocks resting on his shoulders.

The Eskeli had created quite a stir when he and Kith had arrived. The Idara priests, typically calm and withdrawn, were stirred to a level of excitement beyond what Tor'athain had ever seen. After all, the Eskeli was tangible proof of their teachings. The creature was the trainer of the Ar'kan, the ancient warriors built to protect the Dar-dan. The Idara had modeled their entire religious views off the process of mental and physical perfection as attained by the long gone Ar'kan. And now a trainer, an Eskeli, was in their midst. It was the most exciting thing they had ever experienced.

The Eskeli was a creature of another world. The Dar-dan had left him behind to protect the gates, to make sure they were never used again. When Lord Rane opened the portal, the creature had awoken from its long sleep. The Eskeli had spent five years searching for Stone Bloods, the only ones capable of using the gates and potentially stopping Lord Rane. Finally, the Eskeli had found Kith. The creature was of a different world and the only thing allowing it to breathe the strange air of the Five Lands was the mask it wore. But there were no Dar-dan to recharge it, and when its energy faded, so too would the life force of the Eskeli. The strange warrior had less than a year to forge Kith into an Ar'kan warrior of legend.

But Kith was not privy to the political arena of the Idara, or how they would assimilate them both into their order for the next year as they trained. Wasting no time, the Eskeli had started Kith's training the next day, leaving the politics to An'thryne and the Idara Grand Elders. Kith had no time to ponder the Idara. Every day for the last two weeks he had been training, sleeping for four to six hours a night at best. Well, he wasn't exactly sure that what he had been doing was training, but it was clear that the Eskeli had a plan. When the creature had ordered a priest to sew his eyes shut Kith had balked, as if he had been joking. His protest was met with a twirling spear, the shaft striking Kith in the head so hard that he had collapsed unconscious. He woke up later in blackness, scabs of dried blood around his eyes. The darkness had been his friend, and enemy, ever since.

A stinging pain flashed across his back as the Eskeli struck him again with the split cane. Kith had not seen the stick yet, but the pain was enough to ascertain its construction. Individual thin sticks were wrapped together at both ends, the strike causing the lose sticks in the middle to snap shut on the skin, causing stinging pain and red welts up and down his back. Kith jolted slightly, but kept his composure.

"Good," the Eskeli said, his monotone voice lacking any emotion. "Tell me what you feel."

Kith tried to ignore the pain in his back and reached out, searching for any sensations around him. "I," he began, bending over slightly as his posture became difficult to hold. He had no idea how long he had been sitting there. To him it felt like days. But he knew, somewhere in his consciousness, that it was just half the day. His back hurt, the pain interrupting his focus, and his back relaxed slightly. Fiery pain lanced through his body again as the Eskeli struck him. Immediately Kith sat up straight and redoubled his efforts. In the darkness of his mind he sent out his consciousness, his other senses reaching into the blackness. There was a chirping far off and he honed in on it, the pain in his back a blur as his mind searched for the sound. There it was again. The chirping was louder and it sounded like a distant echo in his mind. "I hear a chirping."

"What do you feel when you hear it?" The Eskeli asked.

Kith's consciousness leaned in, feeling around in the darkness, pulling in anything it could glean from the shadows of his mind. There was the swirling sound of wind passing through the mountain peaks and the distant sound of Idara priests chanting, their meditation hymns heard every morning. But he stayed focused on the chirping. They had been working on the technique continuously for over a week. Kith still had no idea what it had to do with fighting, but he knew better than to argue. He had committed himself, and there was no turning back. Listening intently, the chirping continued, the distant song getting louder. "Longing...hunger...desire...it sounds frightened."

"Good." The Eskeli's voice reflected no happiness or joy. It just was. "Tell me what it is you hear."

Kith thought about it for a moment. "Baby swoopers," he said. "Three of them, waiting in their nest along the cliff wall for their mother to feed them."

"Yes. You are making progress. Now rise and face me."

Kith's knees protested as he stood, turning to face the Eskeli. He had been in that positon for hours and he nearly fell as his legs buckled. He righted himself quickly, but not before he felt a searing pain flash across his face, his head snapping to the side. He had been struck again, his anger rising to the surface. The first three or four days had been the worst. Constant beatings mixed with more lessons, the frustrating lessons just bringing more beatings. The stitching around his eyes had been painful as well, the dull ache quickly turning to an annoying itch around the sutures. Now the pain around his eyes was gone, replaced by more now from the constant strikes of fist and cane. The beatings were wearing him down and his anger finally exploded, like an infected boil pricked by a knife.

"Stop hitting me!" Kith roared, "What does any of this have to do..."

This time a fist struck him in the chin and he crumpled to the ground. Pain rocked his mind and he barely held onto consciousness.

"Emotion is good. But you most control it," the Eskeli said calmly. "All things can be controlled by your mind. Your aching legs when you stood, the frustration and anger you feel when I strike you. Distance it, separate yourself from those feelings. In combat you must be able to control pain and anger."

Kith's mind was swirling in the blackness and despite the fact that he was barely holding onto consciousness, he was irritated at the lack of emotion he heard in the creature's voice. He had just struck him again, and yet seemed to feel nothing. Deep down Kith knew that everything the Eskeli did was for a reason, and he had just voiced at least part of his purpose. But that rationalization slipped from his grasp as frustration turned the thought into a slithering snake.

Kith growled in anger but said nothing, slowing pushing the dizziness away and using his hands to stand once again. His eyes dripped tears of frustration and exhaustion and he felt blood drip from his nose. He was breathing heavily in anger but said nothing more.

"Good," the Eskeli said. "You are strong in spirit. Soon, you will be a shadow walker."

"What does that mean?" Kith asked, trying his best to mask his frustration.

"It means," the Eskeli responded, "that you will live in the darkness as you do the light. It means that you will truly *see*. It means that the door to becoming an Ar'kan will be opened further."

Kith said nothing, but if he didn't know better, he swore he could detect a hint of hope in the Eskeli's voice.

***

The sutures around Kith's eyes no longer hurt. Nightly, various Idara priests cleaned the punctures and made sure his eyes were still watering. Kith had talked quietly with a few of them, but most were silent, impervious to his inquiries. On a few occasions he was visited by An'thryne. They had talked quietly while the priest checked his eyes for infection. An'thryne had told him that they had a similar training regime, although nothing quite so extreme. The Idara blind folded one

15

another and often trained for hours at a time in the darkness. But the Eskeli had taken it to another level and the warrior had little knowledge of what was to come or when he would be allowed to remove the sutures. It had been a month since his arrival and every hour of every day, minus the four or five when he slept, was spent learning to adapt to the darkness, while training in strength, speed, and combat. There was one new item of interest and the Idara priest mentioned it to Kith just before his short sleep.

"We are building something for the Eskeli," An'thryne said as he gently massaged an herbal paste around the edges of Kith's eyes. The suture were clean but they were likely going to leave a scar when removed. Kith's eyes tried to open automatically, stretching the sutures and likely enlarging the scars. An'thryne didn't want to say anything but he feared Kith would not like the result, the pattern under his eyes giving Kith a menacing visage.

"What is it?" Kith asked, eager for any information as to the direction of his training.

"The Eskeli is calling it the Shadow Box. He says it's the last portion of your training before you can remove your sutures."

"Tell me about it."

Kith's body was bruised and cut all over, constant reminders of his training. Some of the marks came from the cane, and others from falls as he navigated his world in the darkness. But over time his body and senses had adjusted to the darkness and his falls and stumbles became less frequent. He could now walk freely around most of the compound, even navigating the many tunnels cut into the side of the mountain. Every sound, smell, and touch had become heightened. To some degree he had enjoyed the change, relishing so many sensory pleasures that he had simply missed before. Smells, sounds, everything had become more intense.

Once he had become more comfortable in the darkness his work with the sword and spear increased and more bruises and cuts resulted. The Eskeli was careful not to severely injure Kith. After all, they had no time to spare for healing. But regardless, Kith's body was in a constant state of pain. So much so that he had become used to it. That thought had crossed Kith's mind almost nightly, especially when he laid his battered body down for his short nightly rest. Likely that was the desired objective, to become used to pain so it does not hinder you in combat. However that knowledge had done little to lessen the pain, or his frustration.

"It is a rectangular box of wood...perhaps ten paces long and three paces wide and as tall as our cave ceilings. There are slits cut into the wood and if my understanding is correct long spears or staffs can be shoved through and moved along the slits. It's a training box," An'thryne added.

Kith frowned. He didn't like the sound of it, but he had learned through pain not to question the Eskeli's techniques. "I am to move through it?"

"That is my understanding. Men will be shoving long sticks, or perhaps spears, I'm not sure, through the openings. You will have to move and navigate through the box."

"Have you seen this before?"

"No," An'thryne replied. "We have no knowledge of this in the Ardic."

Kith knew that the Ardic was a collection of three books within the Chet'ta, the Idara sacred text. The Ardic was the portion of the Chet'ta that focused on the Ar'kan training techniques, at least what they had been able to accumulate over the last few thousand years.

"I must pass through this Shadow Box before my sutures are removed?"

"That is my understanding," An'thryne replied.

"When will it be finished?"

"Tomorrow."

"Good," Kith replied. "I miss the light."

An'thryne stood and squeezed Kith's shoulder. "You are doing well, Kith Caren. Remember, there can be no light without darkness." And with that, the priest walked away, leaving Kith alone in the darkness.

The next day Kith found himself in the Idara priest's large training room. The structure was built of stout logs with huge rafters that could easily hold the weight of snow that was presently as deep as a man is tall. It was large and expansive, giving the priests plenty of room to train. The room was more or less empty except for weapons racks along one wall. There were no fires and the air carried the bite of the winter wind.

"Good," the Eskeli said, "now, position one through ten. This time I will be attacking at various intervals, so adapt your positions accordingly. Listen for my movement...feel it, reach for it."

Despite the freezing air, Kith was sweating and his heart was pounding with exertion. He had been performing the sword maneuvers for the entire morning, moving between position one and twenty, increasing his speed in the process. It had taken the Eskeli a week to teach him the positions, his lack of sight slowing the process. Some of the moves were similar to what he had been taught by the Order, but most were different, or variations of them. Kith remembered when he had voiced his frustration at being blind, and he equally remembered the sting across his back as the answer.

Kith took a deep breath and focused his mind on his surroundings. He had to admit that he could *see* much more than he thought possible. He knew there were four other priests training in the room, and that one of them was Lathronin, the young man's sweat a particular odor that he never would've noticed before. By the sounds of the combat, he knew one group fought with spears while the other used sword and staff. Off in the distance, likely along the cliff face, he heard the harmonious chanting of at least five monks. It was rare to find an hour in the day where some of the monks weren't chanting. An'thryne had called it the mind dance, the cadence of the rhythmic chanting designed to mimic their sword forms, many of which were the same ones the Eskeli had taught him. His focus moved around his surroundings and he also heard a rat above them in the rafters chewing on some morsel it had likely stolen from their food storage.

Keeping his consciousness focused, Kith began the maneuvers, moving through them as fast as he could. At first the positions had been laborious, but now he flowed through them as if they were second nature, his strong legs, core, and arms navigating the forms smoothly. Hearing steps to his right,

Kith moved from positon four to five. He noticed the subtle sound of hands adjusting on wood, the Eskeli's skin sliding up the shaft, his lead foot shifting forward in the dirt. The creature was jabbing his staff towards him, and reacting on instinct Kith shifted from positon five to ten, leaning back and spinning away, his sword flashing across his body. He felt the wind from the staff as the tip just missed his torso. Concentrating further, Kith spun to position six, picking up where he had left off. Then he heard the flutter of the Eskeli's cloak, and although he couldn't be sure, it sounded as if the creature were spinning, likely leading with his staff. Reacting quickly, Kith ducked low into position eight, dropping to one foot as his left leg shot out for a leg sweep. His foot hit air but Kith got some satisfaction in knowing that the Eskeli's staff whipped just over his head. It was that fleeting thought that got him distracted. Pushing the inward smile away, Kith leapt up into positon seven, and although he thought he heard the shift of the Eskeli's feet, it was too late. A solid force struck him in the chest knocking him to his back where he skidded on the dirt. It hurt, and would likely bruise. But Kith was so used to pain that he was not concerned. Slowly standing, Kith was proud that anger was not the first emotion to come screaming to the surface. He was frustrated, that much was true. But he felt chagrined more than anything, and he knew why.

"Well done," the Eskeli said, which Kith always thought interesting that he would lead with a positive comment after he had caused him pain. But weeks ago he had come to realize that the Eskeli had a purpose in everything that he did. He was getting no satisfaction out of hurting Kith, and once Kith realized that, his attitude had changed. "What did you do wrong?"

"I was gloating."

"Meaning?"

"I was happy that I had evaded your strike. That thought slowed me down which is why I was too slow to defend against your other attack."

"Yes, good. To fight in the shadows, you must always concentrate. To lose focus is to lose. To lose is to die."

"Why is fighting in the shadows so important?" Kith asked. He had asked the Eskeli similar questions before but had received only vague responses. But each time they were different, as if the Eskeli were feeding more and more information to him as the training progressed. "I mean, if we only have so much time, shouldn't we be training when I can see. I would think it would go so much faster."

Kith could not see the Eskeli, but the creature's pause gave him indication that he might be receiving a different response. "There are several reasons, Kith Caren. Several you can surely ascertain on your own." The Eskeli paused again.

Kith had learned that a pause longer than a few moments meant he was waiting for Kith to say something. "Being able to fight blind may be useful. Training to fight blind will develop my other senses, allowing me to become a better fighter, whether I am blind or not."

"Yes. The other reason is to build your mental strength. I need you to tap into a stream of consciousness that you were unaware existed."

"The Shadow World?"

"In a sense, yes, although not so literal. True, the Shadow World is just that, the world of darkness that I want you to get used to living in. But it is more than that, it is a world where you sense so much more, and over time, you will live in that world whether you can see or not. This training has heightened your senses, building upon layers of mental strength. You will need this strength to get through the Change."

"Will you tell me about the Change?" Kith asked. All he knew was that at some point he was going to have to go through something grueling, some test where they melded field stones with his body. Other than that, he was clueless about the Change, and quite apprehensive if he was to be honest with himself.

"In good time. Now, positons ten through twenty. Do not lose focus."

Kith knew the conversation was over and he nodded towards the Eskeli, bracing both legs wide and squatting low, his sword held in both hands before him. Sending out his consciousness, he began again.

***

Two days later and he found himself standing before the Shadow Box. He could not see it, but based on the path they took he realized that it had been built deep into the cave complex. He could hear a handful of Idara about and was unsure what they were doing. He could feel the Eskeli's tall form beside him.

"Kith, before you is the Shadow Box. Once you can pass this test then the stitches will be removed and your training will commence in the light."

"I understand."

"You must get from one end of the box to the other without being struck by a staff. Once struck, you go back to the beginning and start over. Priests are on either side and they will be attacking you with staffs through slits. Each priest will pick one attack and not deviate from it. There are ten attacks total. You may use your blade to block any blows. The box is fifteen paces long and three paces wide. You are standing just before the opening."

Kith nodded but said nothing, stepping forward until he felt his feet stand on the wood planks. Taking several deep breaths he lowered himself into a fighting stance, sending out his consciousness and focusing his mind on his surroundings. He could hear the breathing of the priests, and the closer ones, he even picked up on their beating hearts. They were calm and their breathing relaxed, as it should be for the highly trained Idara.

Kith too calmed his heart and slowed his breathing, probing his surroundings with all his senses. He heard the Eskeli's feet shuffle in the dirt and picked up on a gentle flutter at the ceiling, likely a bat waking from its sleep. He smelt dank earth and the minerals of the stone around him. There was a subtle spice smell and Kith realized that one of the priests must have bathed recently, the mint from the soap they used standing out like blood on snow. There were scrapings and

21

subtle rubbing noises and Kith realized that it was the wood staffs touching the wood edges of the slits. Those he realized, would be his indicators more than anything, the grinding and bumping on wood as the staffs shot through the wood slits clues that attacks were coming.

Letting out a deep slow breath, Kith stepped forward on the balls of his feet, and instantly he heard a scrape to his right. Spinning on the tip of his right foot, he angled his torso sideways and back, feeling the wind from the staff as it shot by him. He kept moving, ducked and stepped forward. There was a thud and scrape from the left, sounding different from the jab attack he had just avoided. Thinking the staff was moving through a horizontal slit and likely flying sideways to strike his lowered head, Kith brought his sword before him and was relieved to feel a strong thud as the staff stuck his blade, halting its advance. Without stopping, he moved forward just as two sounds from either end assaulted him simultaneously. His mind couldn't process them both and he spun, his sword flashing across his body, an instinctive maneuver. There was a thud as his sword swatted one attack away, but moments later he felt a sharp pain in his side. The second staff had struck him.

"Start again," The Eskeli said softly.

Kith winced as he stood, the pain in his side formidable. Or perhaps it was just the many injuries built one upon another. He had so many bruises that it was hard for him to keep track. This was going to be a long and painful process, he thought.

***

Two weeks later the Eskeli led Kith to the cliff face where he joined four other priests, one of them a Grand Elder by the name of Tilfarin. Kith couldn't see him but knew he was older. He could hear it in his voice and there was something about his presence. He could feel the man's wisdom, or his power, he really couldn't tell what it was. But he could feel something about the man. Kith had only met him one other time.

"Kith," the Eskeli said. "You are on the cliff face with Tilfarin and three other priests. They will teach you the mind dance. It will help with your mental strength."

"Where will you be?" Kith asked.

"Here, watching."

Kith heard the Eskeli step back and another form step closer. Kith could smell the age on the man. It was not something you could describe, but Kith had learned that someone older carried a different odor than someone young.

"Kith, sit," Tilfarin instructed.

Kith sat down and adjusted himself until he was sitting on a relatively flat section of rock. It had not snowed for several days and the priests always kept the edge of the cliff face clear of snow. It was their favorite place to chant, out in the elements, the snow-covered spires surrounding them and the biting wind poking at their minds. It was the best place to practice meditation, and the chant was designed to do just that.

"Each chant was created to mimic our sword forms, the cadence and fluidity of the forms flowing through the chants. You must focus your mind on all twenty forms. Picture your body flowing through them. See your body move, imagine its change of speed, its defenses maneuvers as well as its offensive. I want you to listen to the first chant. It is called the Instructors Dance and it will go through all twenty forms in order. After that, when we start over, I want you to join in and follow us. We will do this, many times, so you must focus and keep your mind connected to the sounds. Do you have any questions?"

"How many different chants do you have?"

"When you develop the mind dance, the number of chants is nearly infinite."

Kith thought he understood. "You eventually chant any combination of the twenty forms."

"That is correct. In a real fight, the order of forms is unknown to the combatants, each attack and defense an infinite number of possibilities depending on the choices the fighters make. Like in a fight, you can train yourself to chant an endless combination. You must train your mind, and body, to react quickly. As in a fight, we train our bodies to react instinctively, and in the chant, once you master it, you will do the same, the sounds flowing through you in thousands of different patterns. Now, let us begin."

The man sat down near him as Kith let out a deep breath and focused on his surroundings, sending out his consciousness as he had been taught. He concentrated on his heartbeat and soon found the calm beating hearts of the other priests. It was freezing cold but the thought was distant, pushed away as he had been taught to do. All he heard was the beating as it grew louder. Then the chant began.

Kith pictured his body flowing through the positions and was immediately engrossed in how well it followed the chant. Squatting low, his ethereal form shot up, his sword maneuvering to execute a high block as his body flowed to another position, a sideways attack and strong turn to the invisible enemy's flank. The chant rose with the high block and quickened its cadence to follow the attack, lowering some in volume and power as Kith's body turned to block another attack. And the dance and chant continued, all the while Kith following the sounds and movements in his mind.

And then it was over. He had no idea how long the first chant had taken as he had been completely enthralled with the sounds. Then he realized that that's what they were, just sounds. He voiced a question, unsure if it was wise to do so. "Were those sounds actual words? I recognized none of them."

"No," Tilfarin said, still squatting beside him. "They were not words, just sounds created long ago to match the power of the dance. Tell me what you thought."

"It is hard to think of words to describe how I felt," Kith began. "I-I, enjoyed it. I felt good. I felt power."

"Yes. Your mind found the dance and the power built within you. When you master this skill, you will find the chant instantly. Now, let us begin again. This time add your voice to ours."

Kith took several deep breaths, matching those of the priests around him. Then the dance began.

***

Three weeks later and Kith found himself standing at the entrance of the Shadow Box. He was calm, the pains from his many minor injuries forgotten, anxiety from the trial a distant thought as he focused on nothing but his concentration. Every day he had trained, repeating the process over and over again. He had excelled in the mind dance, continuing his training with sword, spear, zyth, and other weapons. In the evenings he had sought control of the Shadow Box, every time coming up short and earning more pains and bruises. But he had felt a change come over him, a shift of consciousness that he could not explain. As his body increased in strength and power, so did his mind, and for Kith that was the most noticeable change. He had always been strong and fast, and when he had come to Tor'athian he had thought he was in the best physical shape possible. But he had been wrong, the constant tutelage under the disciplined eye of the Eskeli had built layers of muscle upon the layers he already had. He was more flexible, working on stretching techniques with the Idara priests. They called the maneuvers the "tull", a series of stretching and strength maneuvers that they had learned from the Ardic. The Eskeli's body could not move as theirs and the creature had left that part of the training to the Idara. With Kith's newfound flexibility and strength, his speed had increased exponentially. But it was his increase in mental strength that he noticed the most. He could see even though his eyes were still sewn shut. The darkness no longer concerned him as he navigated his surroundings with confidence. He had been in the dark nearly four months and he was amazed at how comfortable it had become for him. He was calm and not so quick to allow his emotions to rise to the surface. He saw the world differently, taking in his surroundings in a way he never thought possible. Everything became more intense as his senses found more data around him, sorting it out quickly and more efficiently. With his newfound strengths, his confidence had grown as well. If he were honest with himself, he had originally thought that he would never be able to complete the Shadow Box. But now the thought of failure was pushed way down into the recesses of his mind. It was no longer a matter of if he would succeed, but when.

"Feel the dance Kith Caren," the Eskeli whispered. "Focus your mind and let your body react to its senses. Begin when you are ready."

Kith barely heard the Eskeli's voice as he calmed his breathing, focusing his mind on his beating heart as he sent out his consciousness. He could now prepare his mind and body in a blink, and without further ado he launched forward with speed and confidence. Instantly staves shot from both sides as they maneuvered for any contact. Kith ducked and turned, his sword flashing high and low as he moved through the box. Sounds erupted in his mind, the noises creating images, the images turning to chants and forms as his body reacted to the input faster than an eye blink. Halfway through the box three staves came at him at once, two from his left and one from the right. Trying something he had never done before, he moved towards the two, snapping his foot as he pivoted, striking one of the sticks and knocking it away from him, the pressure and angle keeping the wood stick in position as the priest struggled to withdraw it from the slit. He had narrowly avoided the other, the sound of fluttering air near his neck alarmingly close as the staff just missed. Keeping his sword flowing, he blocked the third staff from the other side, ducking low and diving forward over a fourth stick. The roll took him a full pace and a half and he came up quickly, still moving as he heard attacks from either side again. Never stopping, Kith pushed away any thoughts of success or failure. He knew he had to devote all his focus on the attacks and evading maneuvers. So he didn't know that he had only a few paces to go before he was through the box, his mind completely focused on the task. Spinning and blocking one attack, he ducked and turned around another. He heard wind whip before him and thought he recognized a side swing coming at his torso. His weight was already on his back leg and his body reacted on instinct, leaning back and bending at the torso so his hands found the wood behind him. The staff swung over him and his legs flipped backwards to land on his feet behind him. He had avoided the attack but was now a full pace back, in line for attacks he had already avoided. But the thought was fleeting as new attacks shot from the slits in the wall. Never stopping, he launched his body forward again, pivoting as he sword was a blur as it blocked two attacks from the left while his body maneuvered around an attack from the right. He was so focused on his surroundings that as he moved around three other attacks, his body nearly froze when his lead foot touched the soft dirt. Skidding to a stop, his sword held low and to the side, Kith relaxed his stance, his breathing slowing some as he realized he had made it through the box. He had succeeded.

The Eskeli stepped before him. "What did you learn?"

Kith knew that the creature would not focus on the victory, as that was irrelevant. Everything Kith did, whether a success or failure, was a learning opportunity. Kith was excited, but he tried not to dwell on that emotion. Thinking back to each move, he thought about what he had learned. "Sometimes it is necessary to move back. Forward is not always the best maneuver."

"Good. What else?"

Kith knew he could not state the obvious. He had been working on the Shadow Box every day for many weeks and each failure had brought important learning opportunities. He could not just repeat something he had already said and learned previously. The Eskeli was looking for something different. Then it came to him. "Learn to use your environment. When I pinned the staff against the edge it took that weapon out of the melee."

"Yes. Well done. Are you ready to walk in the light?"

"I am."

"You have done well. Soon you will be ready for the Change. Follow me."

The Eskeli turned and Kith followed him, his apprehension about the Change no longer a heavy weight on his shoulders. Now he welcomed it. He was confident he would succeed, which was likely the point of all this training. The Eskeli had alluded to the fact that surviving the Change was more mental than anything, and Kith reasoned that everything he had been doing thus far was to prepare him for it, to build is confidence. Kith was ready. He had to be.

Back in his sleeping chambers, light blinded him as the last of the stiches were removed, an aging priest named

Bur'arin gently snipping the final suture. Slowly opening his eyes for the first time in many weeks, Kith could see nothing but white as his eyes adjusted to the brightness. The feeling of opening his eyes was strange. For something so common, performed thousands of times a day, it was a weird sensation. Sitting up, Kith looked around him as his eyes adjusted and his surroundings changed from white blurriness to actual forms. Bur'arin was there along with the Eskeli, but no one else. Kith was momentarily let down as he saw the occasion as much more than the others clearly had. He expected there would be more priests there, at least An'thryne. But even he was nowhere to be seen. But he should've realized by now that the event, however momentous to him, was just another step in a long road.

"How do they feel?" the Eskeli asked.

"Good, but strange, like a long-lost friend showing up after many years."

The Eskeli nodded. "You now have two companions, the light, and the dark, both will be by your side wherever you go."

Kith saw the truth in the creature's words but said nothing, looking around the room as his eyes fully adjusted to the new light. "How do I look?" he asked Bur'arin.

The priests shrugged his shoulders. "The scars will be noticeable," he answered plainly.

Kith sighed. He figured the scars would be the least of his worries. He still had the Change before him.

***

Theron picked up a glass of wine from the servant's tray, her dark downcast eyes not making contact with his. She was stunningly beautiful, which Theron had learned was quite common amongst the Acku people. Most were dark haired with brown skin, their eyes ranging from black to green. But where the Hiskani people were generally slight of build, the Acku were typically broader shouldered and more muscular. Over thousands of years the hostile elements of Bylor had pounded them into formidable fighters. Even the women were sinewy and laced with muscle. The hostile lands that made up their home lacked much in the form of resources, but Lord Rane made up for that in the quality of the slaves he took. None of the Acku people were docile, but the younger men and women could be manipulated and beaten, eventually molded into servants like a potter making a bowl. Theron hated that he had been a part of it.

There were hundreds of people about, mostly lords and officers, along with their families. Acku servants milled about, adding food to the tables and offering wine to the esteemed guests. Lord Rane was clearly trying to show off the wares of his new conquest. Theron hated these functions, and luckily there had not been so many, as war had been Emperor Rane's focus the last five years. But tonight was a special night and Lord Rane had been planning the party for a week. They had conquered all of Bylor and the Acku had either been enslaved or killed, except for a few pockets of resistance. The party was to celebrate their victory and to bathe in the wealth of conquest.

"I've seen you before, it's Theron, right?"

Theron turned to the voice and found himself facing Morwin, Lord Rane's youngest daughter. Her smooth reddish skin glowed in the light and her long black hair had been braided into strands and clasped with a silver brooch behind her head. She wore a stunning yellow dress that glowed against her dark skin, showing more than its share where the light cloth was pulled over her breasts and tied delicately behind her neck, the straps lifting her small breasts and exposing just enough cleavage to catch one's eye. Theron was not sure of her exact age but reasoned she was a few years younger than he was. He had seen her before many times at similar functions but had yet to speak with her. He found it interesting, and, if had been honest with himself, a little alarming that she knew who he was. "Lady Morwin Rane, it is a pleasure to officially meet you. Yes, I am Theron Falconan."

She smiled. "Please, call me Morwin. I hate the formalities of these events."

Her smile was soft and welcoming and for some reason it helped Theron relax. He felt like he could be honest with her. "Yes, they are a bit stuffy."

She reached out and took Theron's arm. "Please, will you walk with me? I've found that if I'm alone every noble, father and son alike, feel it's their duty to keep me occupied."

"Of course," Theron said as he set his now empty glass on a side table. Together, they slowly meandered through the crowd. Theron couldn't help but notice the many furtive glances directed at them, but he tried to ignore them. He wore his armor, as did all the officers, the shiny black resin recently polished, Lord Rane's red etched family crest of two mountain gars standing out like a torch in the night. Beneath was a black soft spun cotton jerkin and black pants. Expensive soft leather boots and a red cape clasped with a silver brooch finished his ensemble. In the brooch was a black shiny stone marking his rank as captain. His long black hair was pulled back at the back and tied with a leather wrap, a short black beard encasing his angular jaw. Theron knew from experience that he was considered quite handsome, but he doubted the stares were for him. Morwin was stunning, her aura like a magnet drawing one's attention wherever she went.

"How was the wine?" She asked.

"Good, although I tend to favor ale."

"Do you have good wines in Daswin?"

So she knew who he was. "We do, although it is mostly shipped there from your kingdom. Our lands are a bit cold for good grapes."

"So I've heard, although I've never been there. Doesn't sillix come from your lands?"

Theron smiled. He loved the sweet but powerful cordial. "It does. Snow berries grow along the lower reaches of the Sarin Mountains."

"I love sillix," she said, "but I must admit that it makes me a bit...oh, how do I say it..."

"Improper?" Theron interjected with a smile.

Morwin giggled. "Yes, I guess that is as good a word as any to describe it."

"It has the same effect on most," Theron added, smiling with her.

She turned her head to look at him, her gentle smile turning mischievous. "Would you like to have some with me?"

Theron knew that the rare cordial was quite expensive and even he had not had many opportunities to sample it. But he was worried about what people would think, especially, Lord Rane, if they were caught leaving the party together. As if his concerns were heard a familiar voice interrupted their conversation.

"Morwin, you look lovely this evening." Theron and Morwin turned to face Lord Rane. The emperor was a striking figure, although noticeably shorter than Theron. His red armor was of the finest quality, made from the guriki shell, one of the few creatures capable of living in the caustic waters that surrounded the five lands. The armor's black filigree was intricate and so expertly done that the designs that outlined the two mountain gar heads on the cuirass were extremely life-like. His black cape was lined in white ice hound fur and clasped around his neck in a silver brooch, his family crest etched into the steel and inlayed in blue stone.

Rallin, his Kelic body guard, stood just behind the emperor, his ice blue eyes appraising Theron as well as their surroundings. Theron had seen the huge Kelic on many occasions. The warrior slave was Lord Rane's shadow, and the killer always unnerved Theron. He always seemed ready for violence; in fact it seemed as if he were hoping for it.

Emperor Rane turned his black eyes to Theron, his lip curling up into a subtle smile. "Captain Theron, it is good to see you. Thank you for escorting my daughter. I'm afraid she is not a fan of these events."

Theron bowed his head, showing his respect. "It is my pleasure, Lord Rane." Theron glanced at Morwin and saw that her smile and light-heartedness was gone and replaced with a look of annoyance. He knew that Lord Rane's oldest daughter, Princess Liandra, and his oldest child, Prince Balic, were the emperor's focus, but it seemed that the relationship between the two before him was a bit strained. Perhaps Princess Morwin was ignored, which was typically the case for the youngest child in a monarch's family. Or maybe they had gotten into a fight, or perhaps Princess Morwin simply didn't like her father. One never knew, but Theron thought it could possibly be something the Order could use if the latter were actually true. He would have to tread lightly, that much he did know.

Lord Rane ignored his daughter and kept his eyes on Theron. "By all accounts you did well in Bylor," he said. "I think your father would be proud. Have you spoken with him since your return?"

"Thank you, my Liege. I sent a letter to him the day after we returned. I should be hearing back from him soon."

Lord Rane smiled, and for some reason it looked forced, or mischievous, he could not tell. Theron had always had a hard time reading the emperor. It was almost like the monarch enjoyed playing with people, his expressions capable of being interpreted in several ways, causing great anxiety to his subjects. Theron knew exactly what that felt like as he was not sure if the emperor was being honest, or toying with him. After all, he had been sending secret messages to his father for the last five years. Did the emperor know about them? Surely not, for if he did, he doubted he would be talking with him now with his daughter on his arm. But the thought was still alarming and Theron began to sweat. He was playing a dangerous game.

"Do the Kelic in the Northlands pose much of a problem for my lands in the North?"

"A few coastal raids here and there," Theron replied. "But they tend to stay in the North."

Lord Rane's eyes narrowed some. "We cannot allow raids to go unpunished. I think once we secure Dral, we shall send an army to the Northlands and crush them once and for all. What do you say?"

Dral was one of the five lands and home to the Kelic. Theron still did not know why they were going to invade the continent. As far as he knew, the frozen lands of the Kelic held few natural resources. Perhaps it was simply a power ploy. He guessed they would find out soon enough. As for as the Kelic in the north of Urotha, they had never done anything about them as access to the Northlands was simply too inhospitable. The risks to get there simply outweighed the objective. Theron had not lied. The Kelic in the north, for the most part, stayed in the north. "The lands are quite dangerous my Lord. Getting an army through the Spine Pass is a major risk. If the Northbite

Winds came we would all be lost. Although I am unworthy to make such a decision, I feel it is my duty to warn you against such a campaign." Theron had no idea if it were wise to disagree with the Emperor. He had had very few opportunities to converse with Lord Rane and he simply didn't know if the Emperor preferred honesty or blind obedience.

The Emperor's eyes narrowed some and his jaw flexed, but then a subtle smile emerged. "Ah yes, the Northbite Wind. I have heard so much about it. Perhaps there is another way to crush the Kelic." He paused as if thinking. "Maybe we could draw them out of their homes...bring them to us."

Theron's hands were sweating. Did the emperor know something? Just months before Theron had gotten word through his secret network that the Order had just made a deal with the Kelic. In less than a year's time the fearsome warriors from the north would be marching south to join forces with the Order and his father. They were to march to Akari and destroy the Emperor's army once and for all. Did Lord Rane know something about this? Did he know of Theron's involvement? The idea seemed impossible. His words must be a coincidence.

Theron swallowed the lump in his throat and offered the Emperor a casual smile. "I think that would be a good plan, my Lord. I would enjoy the opportunity to finally rid our lands of the Kelic scum."

Emperor Rane smiled and reached out to pat Theron on his armored shoulder. Despite the smile, the emperor's expression was unnerving. His entire face and head was covered with intricate tattoos and no matter his expression or attempt at levity, he simply looked malevolent. "Good, good, we will make it happen. For now, enjoy my daughter's company." He turned to face Morwin. "Enjoy the rest of your evening." Then he turned and walked away, Rallin on his heels.

Morwin looked at Theron and winked. "How about that drink?"

Theron smiled. "I am at your service, my Princess."

Princess Morwin led Theron through a gauntlet of many guests, moving casually through them with practiced ease, a smile or nod of the head answering their many acknowledgements. They were in the Grand Hall, Lord Rane's main location for large gatherings. The huge room was built of massive white stone supported by thick columns that rose to the high ceiling. The walls were occupied by massive tapestries and huge paintings, most depicting the grandness of Rane's family going back many generations before him. Tables filled the room and musicians entertained the hundreds of guests as they milled about, sampling new delicacies and drinking new aperitifs from the lands he had recently conquered. One side of the room was lined with six glass double doors that opened up onto a huge balcony that overlooked Gorik Bay. It was here that Morwin led Theron.

There were a few couples leaning against the railing having quiet conversations as the Princess and her guest walked onto the balcony. Seeing her, they smiled and moved further away, giving them privacy near the northern edge. There were a few servants about bringing drinks and small bites to those enjoying the night on the balcony. Two Danite guards stood vigilant on either end, their red capes in sharp contrast to the white stone surrounding them. They carried their famous long spears and wore short swords at their hips. One Hiskani girl approached and offered glasses of chilled wine.

"No thank you, Corwina," Morwin replied, smiling to the servant. "Lord Theron and I are in the mood for something a bit stronger. Would you be so kind and bring us a bottle of sillix and two glasses?"

The young slave's smile disappeared briefly, a look of trepidation replacing it. "My Lady, I am sorry, but they do not let us near the sillix."

It looked as if the young girl was going to have a break down. Morwin noticed and stepped closer to her, placing a gentle hand on her shoulder. "It's okay, I understand. Is Miss Elneace running the kitchens tonight?"

Corwina nodded her head, her downcast eyes glancing up at the princess. "She is, my Lady."

"Good. Go to her directly and tell her it's for me. She shall fetch it for you."

"Of course, my Lady. I shall return directly." Corwina bowed and moved towards a side door located on the northern side of the balcony. It looked as if the kitchens had access to both the interior and exterior portions of the hall.

Theron had enjoyed the exchange and was surprised at Morwin's gentleness with the servants. "You know your servants names?"

Morwin shrugged. "Most. I try to know them but there are so many new ones now with the influx of slaves from Dareef and Bylor."

Her tone was cold and Theron picked up on it. "You don't approve?"

"I do not. Slavery is appalling."

"Does your father know of your sentiment?"

"I care little for what he thinks. Besides, he would not listen to me anyway. The words you heard him speak to me were the first in months." Her tone was casual, as if her father's negligence was a forgone conclusion. She looked up at him and smiled. "Let us not talk of him. Tell me about your home?"

Theron looked at her and paused before speaking. He was wondering why she seemed so interested in him and decided to voice his concerns. "If I may be so bold, but what is this interest in me and my home?"

Morwin sighed as she looked back out to the greenish waters of the bay. "There are few in court that did not grow up here. I tire of the many political games and simply yearn for normal conversation not weighted with the desire for personal gain and influence that my family name carries. You are not from here." She looked back at him. "You interest me."

Theron lifted an eyebrow at that. "A blunt response for a blunt question. I like that."

"Good. Here is another, although I dare say you might not like it as much. How do you sleep at night knowing what you have done to the people in Bylor and Dareef?"

Theron's smile left him and he looked away. He hated this part of his ruse. He hated what he was asked to do so that he could be the eyes and ears of the Order. And now she was calling him out on it. What was he supposed to say? He couldn't tell her the truth. But maintaining the deception made him sick.

"I, well," he shrugged, which he silently chastised himself for as it looked like he was being indifferent, before saying, "there are things required of the nobility that we must do. We must rule and lead, and sometimes that means making difficult decisions. I am a Danite captain. It was my duty." He went to say something else but stopped himself. He had hated every word that had come out of his mouth and he didn't want to say anything more.

Princess Morwin was looking at him with sad eyes when the servant Corwina arrived with a tray carrying a bottle of red liquid and two silver cups. Morwin turned her eyes to the servant and smiled, her melancholy expression no longer visible. "Ah, thank you very much. Please set the bottle and glasses on the railing."

Corwina bowed and did as she was instructed. "Would you like me to pour it for you?"

"No thank you. You may go." Corwina nodded and left with a light smile. Princess Morwin uncorked the bottle and poured small amounts into each glass, taking one and handing the other to Theron. "Please, share a toast before we drink."

Theron thought for a moment before he raised his glass. "To decisions we must make and to roles we must play. Let them not define us."

She turned her head in a quizzical way, pursing her lips at his odd choice of words. But she followed suit, drinking the contents from her glass as Theron did his own. She smiled and coughed, the strong spirit burning her throat. "Strange choice of words."

"Can you do better?' Theron asked with a twinkle in his eye.

She nodded and reached for the bottle, pouring two more glasses. Theron was looking at her but his eyes suddenly shifted from hers to the servant that was approaching rather directly.

The man was wearing a white server's tunic, the same as everyone else. But there was something about him that had caught Theron's attention. He was moving with purpose directly towards them, his hand holding a tray laden with small bites. He was Hiskani, and looked rather nondescript. Theron wouldn't have thought anything of him if it were'nt for his eyes and the way he moved. They were narrowed and set on the Princess, like a hunter finding its prey. Then the man shifted his weight and drew a silver dagger from the tray.

She caught his expression and turned. "What is it...?"

"Move!" Theron shouted as he lunged forward. The server was quick and it was all Theron could do to get his body between him and the princess. With one arm he had pushed the princess aside, angling her behind him while grabbing the edge of his cloak and shoving his body between them. With as much force as he could muster, he extended his cloak, hoping to catch the blade.

Princess Morwin screamed as the man rammed his blade forward, the sharp tip ripping through the thick red cloth and punching a hole in Theron's hip. The blade had caught him above his belt and just below his armor, but luckily his cape had fouled the attack and reduced much of its power.

Theron grunted and moved on instinct, his body a blur as he grasped the man's wrist and pivoted, jerking hard and down and throwing the assassin off balance. Then he came up with all his might, ramming his knee into the man's groin and hitting him so hard that he was lifted off the ground. The man was so shocked by the quick and vicious attack that he barely registered Theron's continued movement as he spun and yanked the man's knife holding arm around, slamming the dagger into his exposed belly.

The man's eyes widened as he grunted in pain. He fell to his knees as Theron jerked the blade horizontal through his flesh, splattering blood across the white tile.

Everyone was screaming as Theron kicked the man aside as he backed up to the princess, his sword scraping from its scabbard. Scanning the chaos, Theron saw commotion inside and figured there were attacks in progress there as well. Who had done this? Had it been the Order? If so, he had just killed one of its members. He had had no knowledge of such an attack. But that meant nothing. He knew there were individual cells constantly at work to destroy Lord Rane's power, and often, as a precaution, they knew little of the other spies.

There were two other attackers climbing the railing, their dark forms scurrying over and bringing crossbows to bear. One Danite guard fell, a bolt ripping through his neck. The other, true to their skill, dove as another bolt ricocheted off the railing. The warrior came to his feet and in one smooth motion lunged forward, throwing his spear at the second man who had dropped his crossbow to draw his short sword. The spear struck him in the chest, impaling him, the power knocking him back over the railing.

The man who had fired the first bolt was already running at Theron, the Princess clearly his target. "Stay behind me!" Theron shouted as he readied his blade. The assassin was quick and ran at him with no sense of fear, which was commendable as he was charging a Danite captain. Theron had been a skilled swordsman before, but now, after going through the Danite training and fighting relentlessly for five years, he was beyond the skills of all except the very best.

The assassin's arm pumped once just before he was on him. Theron recognized the movement and knew he had thrown a knife. But he was so close there was little he could do about it. Catching the hint of silver, he turned sideways, doing his best to angle his armor to deflect the knife. True to the armor's strength, the knife deflected harmlessly off the cuirass as Theron's sword whipped up and down, the movement incredibly fast. The assassin's blade was aimed for Theron's chest when it was knocked up, the tip shooting over Theron's shoulder. Before the killer could retract his blade, Theron's sword came down where his shoulder met his neck, cutting in so deep that it carved his heart in two.

The man grunted and spit blood all over Theron's face before he dropped to the floor in a heap. He had died instantly. Theron surveyed the scene and saw no more attackers. Panting with adrenaline he could still hear screaming inside, but by the sounds, the violence was receding. The surviving Danite guard ran to Theron's side, both men forming a wall before the Princess. His sword was held before him and his trained eyes scanned the balcony and the railing.

"Captain, what are your orders?" he asked, his voice calm.

"Stay here and protect the Princess."

Princess Morwin gripped Theron's arm. "Where are you going?" she pleaded, her voice frantic.

"Nowhere," he said as he turned to face her. "I'm not leaving you," he added reassuringly. "I just want to check the railings to make sure there are no more assassins."

She nodded as he broke away and ran the length of the railing, looking over the ledge as well as along the roof line. He came back quickly just as ten Danites burst through the double doors, the fearsome group led by First Spear Tolbin, a veteran officer who had been in the core longer than Theron had been alive. Once he saw them, they ran to protect the princess.

Tolbin's eyes quickly scanned the carnage, returning to Theron and the princess. "Well done. Are you hurt?"

"Knife to the hip. I'll be fine," Theron said.

"You are hurt!?" the Princess inquired, her tone still alarmed but now in control.

"I'll be fine," Theron replied. "What of inside? What happened?"

"Emperor Rane is unharmed." Tolbin looked to Princess Morwin, his eyes unreadable, but his tone gentle. "Princess, your sister was killed in the attack. And your brother took a bolt to the shoulder. He will live. I'm sorry about the princess."

Princess Morwin's hand came to her mouth as she cried out. But other than that she remained composed, her hand gripping Theron's arm tighter.

"Who were the attackers?" Theron asked.

"Likely the Order, although we have not confirmed their involvement. Princess, my men will escort you inside and to your chambers. Captain, see the surgeon."

"Very well," Princess Morwin responded as she released Theron's arm, join ing the Danite ranks. She looked back at Theron, her eyes moist with tears. "Thank you, Theron Falconan. I owe you my life."

Theron bowed. "It is my duty. You owe me nothing."

The guards guided her away as Tolbin hung back. "Well done, Captain. Lord Rane will be pleased. It's a good thing you were with her," he added as he walked away.

Theron didn't respond. He looked down at the dead bodies. What had he just done? He was tired of playing this game, living a lie and in so doing compromising his morals. He had just killed men from the Order; at least that was his assumption. He had likely killed fellow comrades, thwarting an attack on the royal family all to keep up a guise, which in the end was supposed to help destroy the royal family. None of it made any sense. With a sigh, Theron left the carnage, the pain in his hip masked by the frustration in his heart.

Two

Kith leaned forward, the weight of the stones he was dragging a counterweight to his bare torso. A net of thick leather encased four large rocks, the net attached to long leather straps that ended in padded stirrups that wrapped around each shoulder. Despite the cold mountain air, sweat dripped from his forehead as his powerful legs methodically pushed him forward, the rocks cutting through the thin layer of snow, carving deep paths that crisscrossed the ridge. He had been dragging the rocks back and forth all morning. His legs burned and his shoulders felt bruised, but he noticed little of the pain. The cadence of the mind dance occupied his mind as he went through hundreds of variations of the hymns, his mind creating visual images of himself as a warrior moving through the sword forms that matched the rhythm of the chants. It had been a month since his stiches had been removed, and every day since had been occupied with exercises that strengthened the mind and body, as well as more training with every weapon, including the bow.

The smell of the Eskeli found him first and Kith stopped pulling, standing up straight to find the creature standing just before him. "Grab your bow and meet me in the field." The Eskeli turned and moved away as Kith removed the stirrups, taking a few moments to stretch out his arms and massage his shoulders before donning his fur lined long sleeved tunic. They hurt, the skin irritated and bruised, but the pain was now nothing more than an inconvenience. He was positioned along the massive ridge, the open space before the high chasm an ideal location to drag the stones back and forth. Kith left and headed to the training room to grab a bow and quiver.

Not long after, Kith found the Eskeli at the field, which was nothing more than the northern portion of the ridge that

41

was surrounded by walls of craggy stone. Most of the area had been cleared of snow, the diligent priests constantly shoveling it from their training areas. But there was a light dusting and the ground was still slick with ice, which it always was. It was flat and large, making it an ideal area for range practice. Kith said nothing, standing next to the creature as he waited for instruction.

"How do you feel?" the Eskeli asked without looking at him.

It was a strange question, one the Eskeli had not yet voiced. "Sore, tired, but strong. I have never felt so strong, so powerful, so complete."

"How does your exhaustion make you feel?"

Another strange question, but Kith did his best to answer honestly. "My exhaustion is complete. I have never felt so tired." Kith paused to formulate his words. "But it is strange. In a way, my exhaustion has given way to an immense amount of confidence."

"Elaborate."

Kith thought about what he was trying to say. "My training has exhausted me, but beneath the exhaustion is a strength that I did not have before. I feel like a butterfly and I am just now breaking free from my cocoon. That is it, my exhaustion is the cocoon, and I'm breaking free and emerging as a stronger, more powerful, and more confident version of myself. I feel like I can take on any task. I feel like you have given me the tools to do so."

The Eskeli nodded. "We have a long way to go. You are not breaking free of the cocoon, but simply ripping away some of the strands. The confidence you will need, and I'm glad to hear you speak of it, will assist you greatly in the endeavors to come. Soon you will be ready for the Change."

"How soon?"

"We will leave for Seabras in seven day's time."

Kith had not been prepared for that response and he immediately felt a dichotomy of emotions. On one hand he was excited to face the challenge that the Change brought before him. On the other, he was nervous. What if he were not strong enough to assimilate the stones? What if they drove him mad?

Just the idea that he would soon find out the answers to those questions just added to his anxiety.

Changing the subject, the Eskeli picked up ten round disks, each one made of thick paper and covered with a hard resin. "Ready your bow."

Kith strung the bow and adjusted the quiver on his back. "No warm up?"

"Will you get a warm up in the field?" Kith knew the answer to that question. He responded by planting his feet firmly and looking at the strange creature. "I will throw all ten disks," the Eskeli continued. "You will draw and release each shaft as you reach each of the ten positions." There were ten different stone markers placed around the field, each one numbered. "While you do this, I will introduce various distractions." They had done variations of the drill many times. But this was the first time he had to put them all together while trying to hit the disks out of the air.

Kith took a deep breath and settled a calm confidence over his body. His senses reached out and he felt alive. He looked at the Eskeli. "I'm ready."

The Eskeli nodded and with speed not capable for a man, he snapped his fist out and struck Kith in the side of the head. Simultaneously he tossed the first disk into the air to Kith's right.

Kith's head rocked back, and his trained mind shoved the pain aside and focused on the task, quickly pushing his body forward. Shaking the punch away, his body was moving quickly and by the time he reached the first marker, an arrow was nocked and at full draw. Just as his vision cleared from the punch the disk was descending towards the ground. Smoothly, Kith released the arrow as he ran to position two, his focus leaving the first arrow and now focusing on nocking a second while paying attention to the Eskeli. One thing he had learned the hard way was to never keep your attention on an arrow in flight. It was either on target or not, and no amount of watching it would change anything. All it did was distract you from your next defense or attack. It made total sense, but it was much harder to do in practice than in theory. It seemed to be a natural desire to see if your shot were true.

The Eskeli threw the second disk just before he snapped a long leg out to trip him. But Kith was ready. Leaping over the extended leg, he landed and spun, drawing and releasing at the same time. This time the range was short and Kith saw the satisfying contact as the arrow struck the disk and sent it catapulting to the ground.

And they went on like that for six more markers, each time Kith avoiding some distraction and releasing his arrow quickly and smoothly. He was pretty sure he had hit all the targets thus far but tried not to think of that, instead focusing on his movements and trying to stay one step ahead of the Eskeli.

The ninth marker was far away so Kith was sprinting, the Eskeli running smoothly beside him. As they neared, Kith caught movement to his right, away from the Eskeli. It was subtle, but his sensitive ears picked up on an out of place sound, a subtle shuffle in the snow. Spinning quickly, he saw a young priest no more than twenty paces away. The priest had thrown a blunted spear and the weapon was already in flight. Then he felt the Eskeli lash out with a side kick just after he released the ninth disk. Kith raised his leg, bending it at the knee and catching the kick on the hard part of his shin. Pushing it away he spun and turned, glimpsing the spear out of the corner of his eye. It all happened in a blink, but Kith swayed as the spear missed him by a hair. Never stopping Kith drew and nocked, looking up to see the disk already descending. The disk was still a long way away and Kith smoothly blew the air from his lungs as he gently released the shaft.

Then he shot towards position ten. It was not far away, and strangely the Eskeli did not distract him. But he did do something that made the next shot very difficult. Looking up, the Eskeli threw the last disk as hard as he could straight up into the air. Kith skidded on the ice and stopped right next to the tenth marker, nocking and drawing he angled his bow straight up. The sky was clear and the sun was shining brightly. He could not see the disk and stars danced in his vision as he looked towards the bright sun. He wouldn't be able to make the shot if he kept looking towards the glowing orb. So he closed his eyes, sending out his senses, searching for any sound to point him in the right direction. A few heartbeats later he heard a displacement of air just to his right. Snapping his eyes open he pivoted slightly as he glimpsed the disk. He knew the shot would be difficult. The disk was flying straight down angling slightly away from him as he caught some of the upward currents. In two blinks it would strike the ice-covered ground. Kith released the arrow in one beat, his arrow clipping the edge of the disk just before it struck the ground.

Kith stood up straight and looked at the Eskeli. He could not see the creature's mouth as it was always covered by its strange mask. He knew the mask kept him alive, its power allowing him to breathe the air of Kith's world. Kith wondered how he ate, or how the mask worked. There was much about the Dar-dan and their magic that he knew nothing about. He figured he would find the answers to some of his questions sooner than later. But the creature blinked twice, its strange eyelids snapping open and closed sideways, rather than up and down. Kith recognized it as a smile, if indeed the Eskeli could smile. "That was well done," Kith Caren. "I am happy with your progress."

***

Theron waited uneasily at a table tucked in the corner, the shadows against the wall of the tap room offering him some sense of anonymity. On the table were two mugs of ale as well as two plates, each filled with bread, salted ham, and sliced cheese. Theron had nibbled lightly on his, the nerves in his stomach at odds with the average table fare. The other plate sitting opposite him was their agreed upon signal. After all, Theron had never met the man before.

He had done his job, placing a single candle in the window of his manor house three nights in a row. That was their signal. On the fourth night he was to go to a tap room called the Drunk Hermit located deep in the South City near the wharf. It was not an area of town an officer of the Danite Core would frequent, unless of course he was looking for cheap whores or a knife in his back. Theron was still amazed at the sheer size of Akari. The sprawling city was five times as large as

45

Daswin. The entire expanse was wrapped in a huge stone wall made up thick gray-white stone. Not to mention, the North City, home of the wealthy nobles, merchants, and elites, contained a second wall, a deterrent to those who were not welcome. Lord Rane's palace was built there as well, tall spires networked with stunning bridges, all of it protected by a third wall. It was just another way Lord Rane liked to show his superiority, as well divide the haves from the have nots.

It had taken Theron nearly an hour to navigate the expansive streets and find the Drunk Hermit. They were to meet at dusk and it wasn't long before a cloaked man made his way through the tables, his shadowed eyes looking around before setting on Theron. Without a pause the man walked to Theron's table, removing his hood as he touched the back of the empty chair.

"Is this seat taken?" It was their signal phrase.

"I've been saving it for you," Theron replied, giving the second part of the signal.

The man sat and began to eat at his plate. He was Hiskani, shorter than most, with unruly dark hair that came to his neckline and seemed at odds with his well-manicured beard. His clothes were well-worn and he seemingly had no weapons. Washing down some of the food with the now warm ale, he looked up for the first time, his black eyes questioning. "Why have you called this meeting?"

"Why was I not informed of the attack?"

The man's eyes narrowed some as he reached for his mug, taking another gulp of ale. "You know we have various cells operating here, none of which are knowledgeable of the others. I shouldn't have to tell you why."

"I understand that. But I killed two of our own men," Theron added as he leaned forward in his chair, his frustration clearly evident. He wore a sailor's cap of gray wool and he doubted he would be recognized, especially in a place like this. But nonetheless he continued to scan the crowd for anyone directing any unnecessary attention their way.

The man sighed. "A necessary cost. Your position is too important to risk."

Theron leaned back in his chair, angry by the man's answer. After all, it wasn't he who had killed those men. "I may have been able to do something, or at least stayed out of the way if I would've known."

"The attack wasn't a sure thing. We had been planning for the possibility for months but were unsure if all the pieces were going to fall into place. Our man on the scene made the call when you brought the princess out on the railing. We had our men below you and ready to act. It was too good to pass up. He gave the signal and we attacked." He sighed. "I just wish you were not there. We would've likely killed her."

"Why are you going after Rane's daughters?" Theron understood having to kill Rane's son, after all, he was next in line to sit on the throne. But his daughters? That seemed extreme, especially now after he had met Princess Morwin.

The man shrugged casually as he continued eating. "Orders. We cannot let the royal family live. They breed power hungry murderers. Rane's blood line must be stopped."

Theron was angry, but he subdued it, his frustration coming out as a quiet snarl. "But she is nothing like her father."

The man looked up at his intensity. "Who, Princess Morwin?"

"Yes. She does not need to die. She hates her father and what he stands for. We may be able to use her."

This time the man stopped eating as he digested his words. "You know this to be true?"

"That's what she told me."

The man finished the rest of his ale. "If you can, get to know her more. Earn her trust. I shall pass this up the command and see what they say."

"Good. In the meantime, don't try to kill her. I'd hate to kill more of the Order." Theron's threat was clear.

The spy eyed Theron, but said nothing. He knew who Theron was, and knew that he was a Danite. His threat was not empty. The man rose and slid his chair back. "You'll hear from me again." Then he turned and left, leaving Theron to his own troubled thoughts as he thought about the difficulty of earning Princess Morwin's trust. Then another thought struck him, one he knew was there, but one he was just now admitting. There was a part of him looking forward to the challenge. There was something about her that had intrigued him. He knew it would likely cause him trouble, but he had to admit, that he liked her. With that final thought, he downed the warm ale, his distracted mind barely registering that it tasted like warm piss.

**

Nine days later Kith, the Eskeli, and Lathronin, a young priest that often trained with Kith, stood on the ridgeline, the entrance to the dark tunnel behind them. It had taken two days to move through the long dark passage, the priest their guide as he led them through the complicated network of tunnels. They had emerged at dusk and everywhere they could see was snow covered trees back-dropped by white mountain peaks, the occasional brush of black stone peeking through the deep blanket of white. The sun had already dropped behind the range and a silent grayness was quickly turning to dark. They were still high up, and even in the summer their path would be laden with snow.

The Eskeli was taking Kith to Seebras, the ancient ruins of the Dar-dan, at one point their capital. It was there he would be going through the Change and completing the final phase of his training. Lathronin volunteered to accompany them.

"I think it best we camp at the cave entrance tonight," Lathronin said, his black eyes even darker than most Hiskani. They were like deep pits that had a way of shadowing all his emotion. It was nearly impossible to know what the young priest was feeling. Even his wide flat face was emotionless. Kith liked him well enough, but found his passivity frustrating. Although he had to admit that the priest's affect was quite normal amongst the Idara. He had learned from An'thryne that it had something to do with their training. Years of mental and physical training had a way of causing one to be introspective, to look within and to see the world through a different lens. Kith had to admit that there seemed to be some truth to that. Even he felt different. His emotions did not rule him as they had in the past. He was much calmer, and he looked at the world differently. It was hard to explain, but even amongst the

Idara, Lathronin was more withdrawn than most and Kith often wondered why. Perhaps the trip would give him an opportunity to learn more about the priest.

The Eskeli nodded in agreement and they made a simple camp just inside the cave entrance. Wood was always stocked there and soon a warm fire was built and they were eating bowls of salted beans and hard bread speckled with toasted seeds. It was nourishing and simple. The Eskeli had taken its bowl and walked away, disappearing into the darkness of night.

Kith was staring at the strange creature and Lathronin caught his gaze. "He will not eat with others."

Kith turned his wondering gaze to the soft-spoken priest. "Why?"

The young warrior shrugged. "I do not know."

It wasn't much longer before the Eskeli came back to the fire. Kith decided to voice his interest. "Why do you not eat with us?" The question had been nagging Kith but it never seemed like the right time, not to mention the strange creature was not overly approachable.

The Eskeli turned its eerie eyes to Kith, the lids blinking sideways before answering. "My mouth would likely give you discomfort."

Kith was staring at the metal mask that covered the lower half of his face. It looked like armor but he knew it was much more than that. It was a Dar-dan device that kept the Eskeli alive, at least for now. "Does a portion of the mask come off then?"

"Yes. For short periods I can remove the part that covers my mouth."

Kith was amazed at the magic of the Dar-dan. He had so many questions about them but his training never seemed the correct time to voice them. Besides, any question that was not linked to his training was answered with a snap of the split cane. But now they were sitting around a fire. It seemed as good a time as any to probe the Eskeli further.

"Tell me about the Dar-dan. What did they look like?"

Even Lathronin paused in his eating as he looked to the Eskeli. They had never met anyone who had been alive during the time of the Dar-dan. Curiosity about the ancients was overwhelming but thus far the Eskeli had avoided such queries, his focus clearly on Kith's training.

"They are small in stature, smaller than Hiskani. They are not warriors. Their power comes from here," the Eskeli said, tapping his head.

"What about their magic?" Lathronin asked. "Where does it come from?"

"Their magic is creation."

Lathronin looked at Kith in confusion. Kith pressed the point. "I don't understand," Kith said. "What is this creation?"

"They create, they build, they adapt. Their magic is the creations of their minds. This mask for instance is their creation...it is their magic as you call it."

"Why did they create the Ar'kan and the Drann then?" Lathronin asked. "If they can create magic on their own, why did they need the defenders?"

It was a good question and Kith found himself leaning forward, eager to hear the Eskeli's response.

"It is hard to explain, but I will try. The Dar-dan are beyond us. They feel all. They feel deeply," the Eskeli paused as he tried to form the right words. "Their minds are so strong that they feel others pain and emotions. To cause pain and harm is nearly impossible for them as it is as if they are hurting themselves."

Kith looked into the fire as he digested the Eskeli's words. It was Lathronin who spoke. "So they built weapons to take on that burden for them?"

"Yes. They knew that violence was necessary to first bring harmony to your world. It was also necessary to keep the peace. The Ar'kan and the Drann did just that."

"Do you know where the Dar-dan are now?"

"I do not. They are world travelers, bringing their knowledge to other places that need it." The Eskeli looked out the cave entrance. "Likely, they are out there somewhere, bringing peace to a world strife with violence."

Kith looked at the Eskeli with interest. The creature sounded as if he were speaking from experience. "Is that what happened to you and your world?"

The Eskeli looked at Kith, its mind seemingly somewhere else as its strange eyes blinked several times. "Yes," he said softly. "My world was doomed. War ravaged my lands. Our entire society was based on fighting and death. The Dar-dan came. They took a strange liquid from our world, something they used for power. While doing so they brought us peace."

"Did they take you away from your world?"

The Eskeli shook his head. "No, I volunteered. They wanted to harness our fighting skills and use it for something good."

"And you became a trainer of the Ar'kan," Lathronin said softly, his mind trying to register what he had been told.

"Yes."

"Incredible," Kith breathed, equally feeling the enormity of the Dar-dan and who they were. "The Dar-dan make me feel so small," he added as he stared into the embers.

"Yes, they do that. To meet one in person would change your life." The Eskeli's voice suddenly took on a different note, one of longing or melancholy. Kith had never heard that tone before from the warrior.

Kith didn't respond. They all withdrew into their own thoughts as the flickering fire pulled them toward it, the shifting of colors surrounding the embers mesmerizing as their minds thought of the past and the future.

After a while Kith looked at the priest, more questions probing his conscious. "Lathronin, when did you come to the Idara?"

The young priest looked up from the fire, his eyes a calm reflection. "I was young, perhaps ten, when I was found in the woods by a wandering priest. Hi name was Sornos. He died a few years back fighting for the Order with An'thryne."

"What were you doing wandering the woods?" As he asked the question Kith wondered if it were the same priest who had died over five years ago when they had attacked Rane's forces saving nearly a hundred men and boys who were being forced into military service. It was the first time Kith had bloodied his sword and he remembered the fight as if it were yesterday. If it had been Sornos, the priest had acted bravely, his quick altruistic decision saving not only An'thryne, but a handful of men behind him as he had dived on top of an exploding sphere of power thrown by a Drann priest. Kith pushed the thought away as he listened intently to Lathronin.

"An Eradicator killed my family. My mother was quite beautiful and they came across my farm while searching the foothills for Idara hideouts. They raped my mother and made my father watch." Lathronin paused as his mind was elsewhere. A few moments later he continued, his voice void of emotion. "They killed them both, as well as my older brother. I was nothing to them. They left me crying in the corner to die."

It was strange to hear the priest talk of such horrible events with a tone more suitable for a scholar lecturing on the same subject the thousandth time. Perhaps that was part of the issue, Kith thought. Maybe he had suffered so much that it had caused him to withdraw from the pain, to push it away and bury it so it would harm him no more.

"I'm sorry to bring back such ill memories," Kith replied lamely.

"It is why I am here," Lathronin replied.

"What do you mean?"

"The Idara seldom intervene in the world's affairs. We are taught to strengthen our minds and bodies, to seek personal perfection. The world is a distraction to these gains."

"But you don't agree with that?" Kith asked.

Lathronin looked into the fire, thinking of the right words. Then he looked back to Kith. "Some of us do not and occasionally we break from the desires of the Grand Elders."

"Like An'thryne?" Kith asked. Kith knew that the warrior often ventured on missions with the Order, and in fact had been gone for most of his training at Tor'athian.

"Yes. An'thryne believes it a waste to keep our skills hidden away while the world falls into ruin around us. Some, like him, believe the Chet'ta's words do not reflect the spirit of the Ar'kan warrior."

The Eskeli spoke up for the first time. The creature, while living at Tor'athian, had learned that the Chet'ta was the Idara sacred text, that its words had been collected from other texts thousands of years old, and added upon over time by various Grand Elders. "If your book instructs one to master the martial arts while hiding in the shadows of better men all the while justifying those actions from the teachings of the Ar'kan, then you have grossly misunderstood their mission. The Ar'kan's only purpose was to protect, to guide, and to be a shining star to look for when all else has failed. They brought hope to the people of the Five Lands. I'm sorry, but your philosophy does not reflect the spirit of the Ar'kan."

Lathronin stared at the Eskeli but said nothing for quite some time. Kith looked back and forth and thought perhaps that the priest was angry. After all, the Eskeli had just told the priest that his entire religion was flawed. But the priest surprised him, finally nodding in response. "Many of us had voiced the very same concerns, more and more leaving as our numbers dwindled from persecution. The Grand Elders' hold on us is breaking in the face of Rane's conquest. I'm afraid that more and more of us will leave."

"Why are you afraid of that?'

Lathronin looked at Kith and for once his eyes seemed sad, moisture reflecting the fire's light. "It means the Idara sect will be no more."

That gave Kith pause. He knew their numbers had dropped significantly the last hundred years as Rane's father and grandfather before him hunted them down. But none had caused the Idara more destruction than Rane himself, destroying bases and killing the priests by the hundreds. His Eradicators and their Black Watch shadows were quite effective.

"I am glad you are here," Kith said after he had digested the priest's words. Kith had a monumental task before him and the priest's presence brought him a sense of hope and support.

Lathronin nodded and looked back into the fire, the others joining him as they gazed into the embers once again, searching for anything to give them hope that they might succeed on their task.

They were off early the next morning, the intricate path to the valley floor a series of switchback trails covered in deep snow, followed by days' long walks across dangerous ridgelines, before finally reaching the valley floor. That journey alone would take them two weeks, and it would be another week, according to the Eskeli, to reach the spot along the coast where he had hidden his boat. From there it would be a quarter of a day upon the acid waters to reach Seebras, the ancient Dar-dan capital built long ago on a series of islands off the east coast of Urotha. There were still a few months left of winter and they were prepared for a long cold journey.

Kith and Lathronin both carried bows along with their armor and swords. Kith's armor was the same he had worn in the Order, leather armor plated with dark steel along his chest and midsection. His pauldrons were simple and functional as well as his vambraces, which were hardened leather covered in interlocking plates of steel. Tucked safely in the confines of his tunic pocket was his field stone, the gentle warmth giving him a sense of safety. Lathronin wore the dark gray robes of an Idara priest, his chest covered in leather armor encased in a black resin for added defense. He wore leather vambraces and his robes were split down the center for added movement. Along with his sword and bow, he wore a leather harness strapped over his armor holding four small knives. The Eskeli was outfitted in his drift cloak, sword, and spear, each made from strange Dar-dan materials. They all wore fur lined gloves, boots, and cloaks, snow shoes topping off their winter gear. Packs were filled with dried provisions, blankets, tinder boxes, oil, rope, and other supplies they figured they would need on the long trek to Seebras.

They had made it to the valley floor without incident. The trek had been arduous but they were all strong and fit and it posed little trouble to their constitutions. The freezing embrace of the higher reaches had warmed to an icy chill, Kith of course, feeling the bite much less than the others. Both Lathronin and the Eskeli were mentally prepared for such discomfort and they pushed on without much difficulty. The floor of the long valley was still covered with snow, the jagged peaks of the Sarin Range looming all around them. The Northbite Wind had come when they were higher up, its power not reaching them as they descended ever closer to its dangerous reach. It was impossible to know, but it was unusual for the winds to come so close together. They were also headed southeast, away from the epicenter of the winds where it's the most powerful, so if they did come, they had a much greater chance of survival.

It was the second day along the valley floor when Lathronin, who was in the rear, called for a halt.

"What is it?" the Eskeli asked.

"We are being followed," the priest answered. Lathronin, being the most skilled tracker, a skill also taught to the Idara, had disappeared numerous times to scout the area and look for wild game. His skill had already added some rabbits and a small deer to their nightly meals.

Kith thought he had heard some strange sounds, but he had attributed it to animals. "You sure?" he asked, looking around. There were trees everywhere, their bows laden with snow and drooping towards the ground.

"Do you know how many?"

"I'm not sure," he replied, his face a blank of emotion. "I only saw their tracks. Perhaps four or five."

"They are skilled," the Eskeli said. "I had not picked up on their movement." The Eskeli spoke as if the priest's hunches were beyond reproach. He had learned to respect the fighting Order the last seven months and had come to hold them in high regard.

"Let me break away and scout further," Lathronin suggested. "I should know who follows us within the hour."

The Eskeli paused before responding. Then he nodded. "See to it."

The priest unslung his bow and moved off to the left, his form moving quickly, despite the snow shoes, from tree to tree. It wasn't long before they could not see him at all.

"What should we do?" Kith asked.

"We will veer more south, cutting the distance between us and Lathronin. He will find us much sooner, and, depending on who is following us, we can determine our next move."

Kith nodded and followed the Eskeli, his senses reaching out and searching for any strange, out of place sounds. They moved at a steady pace, keeping a vigilant eye on their surroundings. Neither Kith nor the Eskeli picked up on anything, that was until Lathronin returned, his quiet approached noticed by both as they concentrated on every sound around them. Turning, the both silently faced the priest as he emerged from a glade of trees behind them.

He was sweating. Clearly, he had been moving fast. "It's an Eradicator and four Black Watch soldiers." The young priest typically was unreadable. But this time Kith noticed a hint of anger, or perhaps fear, it was hard to tell on the priest's stone-like face.

"Did they see you?" the Eskeli asked.

Lathronin shook his head. "I don't think so, but one can never be sure with that scum." The hatred in his voice was out of place, an emotion he had never heard in the Idara, especially Lathronin. But then he remembered his story about what had happened to his family and similar emotions emerged from Kith's own consciousness.

As if sensing the rise of anger, the Eskeli interjected quickly. "We have much at stake to risk a confrontation."

"If I can't defeat an Eradicator, then what is the point anyway," Kith reasoned, eager to test his new skills. He found that he was confident and excited, feeling little fear.

"You have not gone through the Change. None of us have the power to defeat an Eradicators manipulation of the E'lear."

"Then we'll just have to kill him first," Lathronin replied, his tone and expression back to its typical control. He seemed just as eager as Kith, although for different reasons.

"We have the element of surprise," Kith added.

"The Eradicator is likely picking up on the energy of your field stone," the Eskeli added. He paused again as if thinking. "But you are right. It would be a good test."

"If the stone is leading them to us," Kith replied, "then I have an idea."

Kith sat nervously before the small fire, his senses pushed out and searching intently for the enemy to arrive. His bow was leaning against the log he was sitting on and four arrows were sticking into the ground at his side. He knew that Lathronin and the Eskeli were hiding nearby, waiting in ambush, but still he felt exposed. The Eskeli had reluctantly agreed to Kith's plan, not wanting to put Kith in intentional danger. But it was a sound plan. The field stone and the fire would draw the enemy in close, then they would spring the trap. The Eradicator didn't know who Kith was and would likely not attack before his identity was ascertained. At least that's what they hoped.

It wasn't long before Kith picked up on the gentle crunching of snow, the sounds coming from two sides. They were flanking him, which was what they had expected. The smell of old leather and sweat found his nose and it wasn't long before two men emerged before him, black cloaks pulled tight around their strong shoulders, one lined in red stitching. It was the Eradicator, a Black Watch soldier next to him. Three other men were out there, likely converging from both sides. Just as he thought it, Kith picked up on their movement as they snuck closer from tree to tree. He couldn't see them, but his sensitive ears picked up on their movement easily enough. He seemed to sense their intent, their eyes boring in on him as they approached. Kith found it strange that just months before he wouldn't have noticed any of it.

"Ho traveler," the Eradicator said as they neared, "might we join you by your fire? Its cold and the sun will be setting soon." The man's voice was arrogant and laced with danger. Kith noticed that that Black Watch soldier wore light plate armor and his hand was resting on the pommel of his sword. He was looking back and forth, searching for more of them. The Eradicator had his left hand touching the silver disk on his right.

The duo stepped closer, stopping within fifteen paces when Kith didn't respond. The Eradicator pulled back his hood, the Black Watch soldier doing the same. They were both Hiskani, with black hair and tan skin, their black eyes scanning the area around them. The soldier's face was block-like, hard and unyielding, while the Eradicator was extremely handsome, his features almost feminine, with a sharp regal nose and a perfectly manicured beard encasing a strong, square jaw.

Kith pulled back his hood, which was the signal, revealing his long white hair. Simultaneously he bolted to his feet and reached for an arrow, his movements lightning fast.

Nocking and drawing, he released his first arrow before the Black Watch soldier had his sword half way drawn.

As was their plan, Kith's first target was the Eradicator, his shot to be followed by Lathronin's, who was concealed just behind Kith. The Eradicator's eyes widened in surprise, replaced by a flash of anger as his hand drew energy from his other hand. But as he did, Kith's arrow struck him in the shoulder. His aim had been true, but the man was fast, having reacted quickly to Kith's own movement and pulling his body off target. Jerking back, the man spun and continued his attack, pulling more energy from his hand. Kith expected to see Lathronin's arrow strike him just after, but instead heard commotion and fighting behind him.

The Eskeli however, attacked with vicious speed, launching himself from his hiding place and throwing his spear with power and accuracy. The Black Watch, now holding a silver blade, saw the attack and jumped in front of the Eradicator, the Eskeli's spear punching a hole through his chest and catapulting him backwards. Instantly there was an explosion of snow as two more Black Watch burst from behind the trees running towards the Eskeli. They had taken off their snowshoes and their movements were awkward, but no more so than the others. Fighting in snowshoes was extremely difficult, and despite the deep snow they had all removed them.

Kith's second arrow flew true, but the Eradicator punched his arm out and the energy he was holding suddenly flashed into a translucent shield, burning the arrow into a crisp before he lunged forward, his arm coming back as the energy formed into a long spear. In a blink, the glowing spear was flying towards Kith. Kith heard the chants in his head and his body moved with practice speed. His sword flashed in his hand as he dropped his bow, the steel whipping across his body as he swayed to the right. His weapon struck the spear, but its power cut through the steel and his weapon fell into two pieces. But his attack, paired with his defensive sway, caused the weapon to just miss him, the energy spear striking the snow in an explosion of steam before it dissipated.

Kith never stopped moving, diving forward he closed the distance between him and the Eradicator. Rolling forward, he moved with incredible speed, his hand reaching for the dead soldier's sword. Feeling the cold grip of the weapon, he bolted up and forward, his new sword arcing towards the Eradicator. The man was skilled and fast, already having his sword out he met Kith's attack. They traded blow for blow, all the while Kith picking up on the sounds around him. There was fighting to his left and somewhere behind him. Kith had no time to ponder his friends' positions as the Eradicator was a skilled swordsman. Both their movements were hindered some by the deep snow, but their blades kissed again and again as they moved around the clearing. Kith heard the mind dance in his head as he focused on his senses, reacting with speed and instinct. The Eradicator's sword flashed towards his face as the man aggressively lunged forward having perceived an opening as Kith stumbled. But it was just a ruse, and as his blade shot towards his face, Kith swayed and sliced his own sword across the man's belly. Cutting him deep the man fell back, crying out as he drew his left hand across his sword arm, a rope of energy emerging. Kith pressed forward and cut the man again across his thigh, but he was forced back as the man, in a desperate attempt to push Kith away, whipped the glowing weapon across his body. Kith had seen what those whips could do and needed no encouragement to retreat. Leaping back, the man had a few moments to gather himself, blood spilling from his thigh and stomach. The wounds would kill him as he bled out and he seemed to know it. His face was a rictus grin of hatred. Growling in fury, he launched forward as he brought his whip around his head for another attack, the glowing strand swinging behind him and gaining power as it shot towards Kith.

Kith knew he could not stop the weapon. It would cut through his sword just as easily as his body. But he needed no more time to ponder his predicament as the man's body suddenly stumbled back as an arrow struck him in the throat. Kith blinked, and a second arrow took him in the eye, his magical whip disappearing as his body fell backwards to the snow.

Kith spun and saw Lathronin standing on a log, a dead Black Watch soldier sprawled behind him, blood splattering the pristine snow.

There was movement to Kith's right and he turned to see the Eskeli's tall form dodge an attack and plunge his sword into the last remaining soldier's chest. The man grunted, and then went limp as the Eskeli ripped his sword from his body. Moving quickly, the Eskeli joined them in the clearing, the scene suddenly quiet, the only sounds the snapping and crackling of the dwindling fire. Scanning the carnage, the Eskeli looked at Kith. "Well done." Then he nodded to Lathronin, the meaning clear. They had all done well.

Lathronin joined them in the clearing. "We better make camp somewhere else. These bodies will attract the mountain hunters."

The Eskeli nodded as Kith went to take the sword belt form the dead soldier. Now that he had his sword, he needed the weapon's sheath. A few minutes later they had their snowshoes on and were trudging southeast through the deep snow.

THREE

Theron lowered his lance and pushed his steed harder, the line of archers before him down on one knee and facing away, narrow openings between the line of men the only path for the thousand cavalry soldiers. They had practiced the maneuver on many occasions, but nonetheless it always got his blood boiling with excitement. It was even more intense, and dangerous, to be on the ground. The maneuver was signaled by three long horn blasts and designed to crush the enemy soon after they had been peppered with volley after volley of steel tipped arrows. They called it the Widow's Charge due to the danger it presented to the archers before them. Which was one of the reasons why Lord Rane insisted on constant training. Theron had to admit, despite his hatred for the despot, that he maintained a highly trained and capable military.

There were generally no more than several thousand Danite in service at a time, the time and cost of training the elite warriors so extensive that the empire could not maintain a force much larger. Besides, it was extremely difficult to find men who could even pass the training regimen. A small group of Danites were elevated to the esteem positions of being Lord Rane's personal body guard. The other members of the corps were never too far behind the Hiskani Emperor, especially when in combat. The rest of Rane's army was made up of various units divided into light cavalry, archers, and infantry. They were called the TorLites, a Dar-dan word that meant *defenders*. Theron thought the name rather interesting considering that the TorLites weren't defending against anything. They were conquering and destroying. The name didn't quite fit.

Theron and the rest of the Danite Core had been forced, during their training, to practice the Widow's Charge not just from the cavalry position, but also as the archers. Even though they were not trained archers, their commanders wanted them to know what it was like to be in the archer's position, that way they could better empathize with them as they stormed towards them with their heavy warhorses. That was the Danite's expertise, heavy cavalry. When they were not fighting, they were training daily, their powerful warhorses between their legs. To Theron, his horse, Kellin, was a part of him. He spent more time with the massive black horse than anyone else. They had developed a strong bond and Theron felt more at home on the animal's back than anywhere else.

Leaning forward Theron smiled behind the visor of his helm. The sound was deafening as the thousand horses bolted towards the archers. His heart pounded in his armored chest and adrenaline rushed through him, his long lance balanced perfectly, the tip barely bouncing despite his steed's great speed. The archers were still as statues, and Theron knew from experience that they were shaking in their light leather armor. They could not see the cavalry, but they could feel and hear them, and when on a knee with a thousand horses bearing down on you it felt like an earthquake. In a flash they were through, dirt and dust torn up and flying in the faces of the archers. This is often where they had casualties. The desire to stand and retreat from the powerful horses was generally so strong that men would rise too early as the cavalry pushed through them. A clip from a horse's armored shoulder or steel shod hoof was enough to crush bones and kill. But this time the men held their ground, no one moving until the signal, two short horn blasts. Then they rose and moved smoothly backwards, careful to keep the gaps between them open. One quick blast, followed by two short ones, signaled the spearmen to move forward. With practiced precision the TorLite spearmen moved through the gaps in double time, stopping behind the still moving cavalry and forming a strong shield wall, their silver tipped spears angling forward. In a real battle, the spearmen would defend the archers from any enemy that made it through the cavalry, moving steadily forward and killing anyone who survived the onslaught of the Danite warhorses, which was generally very few.

They had performed the maneuvers expertly and Theron and the Danite cavalry peeled off in two directions, leaving the training field and returning to their commanders. On this day, Lord Rane was watching, mounted on his white stallion that contrasted sharply with his flowing gold cape, the edges lined in ice hound fur. Beside him was Commander Garn, the field commander of the TorLites, as well as Egrit Stollin, Commander of the Danite Corps. His official title was Warden Stollin and there was always some debate on who outranked whom. Commander Garn led the entire TorLite army, which numbered between fifteen and twenty thousand men. Warden Stollin led several thousand at best, but they were the Danite Corps, the deadliest warriors in all Urotha.

Commander Garn was the epitome of a military officer. He was lean and strong, his face aged and hard, as if it had been carved from stone, then weathered by wind and sun. But Warden Stollin was simply impressive. There was no other word to describe him. The man was huge for an Hiskani, with wide strong shoulders and a thin waist that made his shoulders even look more impressive. Where Garn was handsome in a rugged sort of way, Warden Stollin looked as if he perpetually sought conflict, his face a constant scowl while his black eyes seemed to glisten like wet stones. He constantly flexed his massive fists, his intense eyes scanning everything around him as if he were looking for something to crush. He seemed eager for violence. Despite this outward appearance, Theron had never known the powerful warrior to be cruel or unjust. In fact, he respected the man. He was the most skilled fighter he had ever seen, and he carried an aura of command about him that all seemed to feel.

Theron and the three other captains turned their steeds towards them as the rest of the Corp rode to the back of the field. As captains, they oversaw five hundred men each, basically ten vors. Each vor and ban, the smallest unit of twenty-five men, also had officers. Every ban would be led by a Second Spear, while a vor, which equaled two bans, was led by a First Spear. Theron, being from a noble family, as well as being a skilled fighter, rose through the Danite ranks quickly. The Core dismounted and began to practice spear and shield work, their shields always strapped behind their backs. The Danite Corps were seldom idle.

Theron and the other captains rode before the three horsed men. Lord Rane eyed them each but said nothing as he waited for the commanders to speak. Warden Stollin nodded at them, his face hard and unreadable. "Nicely executed. Remember, once you engage the enemy, keep your formation tight. The left flank was spread a little wide. Anything else Commander?" Warden Stollin asked, looking to Commander Garn.

Commander Garn pursed his lips, his eyes equally hard. "We do not know the terrain of Dral," he began. "Our cavalry may be obsolete if the land is indeed covered in deep snow and ice as our writings suggest. We cannot rely on our cavalry. I suggest we practice infantry maneuvers with the Danite Cops leading the wedge."

It was hard to tell but Theron felt as if he were trying to minimize the influence of the Danite Cavalry, perhaps attempting to make his own forces seem more necessary. But Warden Stollin said nothing, both of their eyes flicking to Lord Rane.

Lord Rane nodded. "See to it. Set the archer's markers at five hundred paces. Lead with four volleys dropping to one hundred paces, then attack with the annwil offensive."

Commander Garn nodded and rode off to ready his infantry, passing the orders down to his officers as well as the signal bearers. Warden Stollin nodded and looked to his captains. "See to it."

Theron and the others rode off without a word, passing orders do their own subordinates so they could ready their vors for the training maneuver. It wasn't long before a black flag was raised at the army's center followed by a burst of short horns, signally the annwil attack.

A thousand TorLite archers lined up in the rear, the Danite Core before them stacked in three lines. Behind them was a reserve line of Torlite infantry and flanking both sides were nearly six thousand more, each warrior holding a long spear and shield, a short infantry sword strapped to his waist. The maneuver they were about to practice was called the annwil offensive as eventually they would form a shape that looked like the horns of the dangerous mountain hunter. It would start with the archers firing a five hundred pace volley at the enemy as they advanced. As they moved forward to meet the enemy the archers would fire three more volleys, each one's distance dropping to four hundred, three hundred and finally two hundred paces. The danger, and difficulty, was that they were advancing forward while the archers were shortening the distance of their shots, allowing the men to get closer to the target range. The timing and accuracy had to be spot on to prevent the front line from being hit by their own archers. As the main line pulled the enemy in, the flankers would arc around and hit them form the side, forming the horns of the annwil. When executed correctly, it was an impressive maneuver, especially if the terrain allowed them to mask the actual position of the flankers.

At the start, a thousand long bows were raised at the sound of another horn burst. Seconds later a long horn blast signaled the arrows to fly while the center pushed forward at the double step. The arrows struck the ground in a neat line directly at the marker. Theron lifted his shield and the others followed suit. The sound of two hundred elite warriors lifting their shields echoed across the clearing, their spears' wood shafts resting on the edge, a groove in the shield designed for just that. It wasn't long before the next horn signaled the second volley of arrows. This time the main line sped up slightly as the second volley landed closer. Theron glanced back and forth across the line and saw that his men were in perfect position. He knew that the other two rows of Danites behind him would also be in straight lines, their spears tilted up and at pace with the front line. Again, the third horn sounded, and this time Theron doubled the speed. In a real battle they would likely be assaulted by enemy arrows. But if they stopped the damage could be more severe. They had to hope that their shields would protect their torso while their helms defended their heads. It was at these moments where inexperienced troops often fell apart. The next few moments were the most dangerous. The last horn sounded, and Theron angled his spear forward, its weight still resting on the edge of the shield. As the last horn ended its long note, Theron and the rest of the Danites were at full charge. He didn't dare close his eyes, but he wanted to. He knew the arrows were in flight, but he had to put trust in his instincts as well as the archers he fought with. Suddenly a thousand arrows slammed into the ground thirty paces away. It was perfect. The enemy would be in complete disarray, at which point they would smash into them with spears and shields, destroying whoever was left. As they ran past the last row of arrows Theron slowed the charge, angling his spear back up to signal the stop. As he did, he saw the thousands of men curve in towards the "enemy" flank, forming the horns of the annwil. Looking around, he experienced some satisfaction at the skill they had just shown. On the other hand, he wanted to vomit. Soon that very skill would be used against them. The Order would be marching towards the capital in less than a year.

***

Kith stood along the tree line, the Eskeli and Lathronin standing to either side, all three gazing out at the expansive water. Kith had never seen the ocean before, the vastness of the acid waters hard for him to comprehend. They stood above the beach, the dark sandy edge stretching north and south as far as he could see, the land peppered with spires of black and gray rock. A gentle descent through boulders and rocks of assorted sizes would see them to the beach below.

"The boat is below?" Kith asked, glancing at the Eskeli.

"It's been nearly six years, but I hid it well. See those two rock formations?" the Eskeli said, pointing to two black rocks jutting from the gray water like huge teeth. "I hid the boat in the brush straight off those rocks."

"And the boat will see us to Seebras?" Kith asked, his tone skeptical. He had never been on the waters surrounding Urotha, but he had heard many cautioned tales about the treaturous acidic seas. Few creatures lived in its dark depths, and the ones that did were generally quite dangerous. Boats could survive two or three days in the waters, but seldom longer.

"Yes. It was designed specially by the Dar-dan to survive the waters. We will be fine."

"If it's still there," Lathronin whispered.

"Let us look," Kith added, eager to get to the ancient ruins of the Dar-dan.

Together they carefully picked their path down and through the intricate network of rocks. Then they followed the Eskeli as he led them north along the dark sandy beach. Kith was in awe of his surroundings. He had never seen anything like it. The long stretches of dark soft sand sloping into crashing waves of dark greenish water seemed like a foreign landscape to him. It was cold but the snow that had plagued them their entire trip was nowhere to be seen. When Kith had asked about it Lathronin had told him that it was always warmer along the coastline. In the heart of winter there would be snow here, but now it was barren and cold, the sky covered in pillows of gray.

They found the boat buried under a pile of debris that the Eskeli had used to hide it. They uncovered it and dragged it to the edge of the beach. The boat appeared to be made of wood, in the shape of a typical long fishing boat, except for the fact that the exterior was black, covered in some strange glossy coating. The Eskeli said that it was the coating that offered the boat protection from the dangerous waters. It was nearly nighttime, and they had no desire to travel the waters at night, so they hunkered down and built a large fire in the sand. There was plenty of wood and their location was quite desolate. They weren't worried about being seen.

Their rations were running low and once they got to Seebras they would have to find more food. But they had enough for another week or so and this night they simmered a pot of water, adding salt, dried meat, potatoes, and onions. They ate the hearty soup with stale bread and washed it down with cold water.

"Why are the oceans acid?" Kith asked as he sopped up the last of his soup, tossing the moist bread into his mouth.

"I do not know," Lathronin replied. "Our knowledge at Tor'athian speaks little of the waters surrounding us."

"They were not always so inhospitable," the Eskeli said. Both young men looked at him with interest before he continued. "Deep below the surface of the oceans, great fissures cracked open and have been spewing poison gases into the water."

"How do you know this?" Lathronin asked.

"The Dar-dan. They knew many things."

"How long has this been happening?" Kith asked, having a challenging time comprehending the Eskeli's words.

The strange creature shrugged his shoulders. "For as many years as you see grains of sand. I do not believe even the Dar-dan knew for sure."

They were silent as their minds digested the creature's words. The vastness of the oceans was something Kith could not understand. Nor could he picture these cracks in the ocean's bottom that were spilling forth such enormous amounts of poison.

"Where does this poison come from?" Kith asked, still confused by the concept.

"The core of your world is melted rock and gas. It is so hot and volatile that occasionally the heat breaks through the surface. It has done so continuously for a very long time, destroying your once clean waters."

"I have heard that Mount Iradon has done something similar," Lathronin explained. "We have books that tell of a time when the mountain exploded and destroyed the people living below. But that was so long ago there are no traces of the event."

"But there are," the Eskeli countered. "The very rock formations along the coast of Urotha, the ones you see here, are all melted rock from the explosion. It dried and cooled, forming the Urotha that you know today. Even Seebras, the islands we visit tomorrow, were formed from the mountain."

"I am having a difficult time grasping what you are saying," Kith murmured. "It seems so..."

"Big," Lathronin interjected.

Kith looked at him. "Yes, that is it."

"You are not alone young Kith Caren," the Eskeli said reassuringly.

Kith looked at the Eskeli. "What is your world like?"

The Eskeli looked into the fire. "Its vast and green, with trees and vegetation so large and thick that one could easily get lost in it. We have rain and many rivers. It is beautiful."

"Did you have family?" Lathronin pressed.

"They all died. We lived in what you might call tribes. We fought continuously over our beautiful lands. We fought just to prove our strength. Skill at arms was the focus of our society. It led to our downfall. When the Dar-dan found us, there were few tribes left, and the few that were still strong hunted down the others."

"Why?" Kith asked.

"To kill. To prove their strength. We could," the Eskeli paused as he tried to formulate the best words. "We could have nothing without kills. To prove one's worth one had to kill." He looked up from the fire. "We were destroying ourselves."

"And the Dar-dan stopped you?"

"Yes. They showed us another way. It took many years for us to change."

"So, you left with the Dar-dan, leaving your world behind?"

"I did. I had nothing. I volunteered to go with the ship."

"Ship?" Lathronin asked.

"It floats in the air. Its large, bigger than a city."

"And the ship took you here?" Kith asked, amazed at the story.

"It did. Other Dar-dan stayed behind."

"So, there are Dar-dan still on your world?" Lathronin asked, equally engrossed in the story.

"I assume so, yes. Although the Dar-dan are always looking for more worlds, so perhaps they have left mine, as they did yours."

"I did not know there were other worlds," Kith said in wonder.

"Look up," the Eskeli said. Everyone looked up to the sky that was now clear, the dark clouds having drifted south, leaving behind a black sky peppered with twinkling stars. "See those lights. Those are all potential worlds, and there are many more out there that we cannot see."

Kith sighed. "My head hurts."

Lathronin chuckled as he threw another log into the fire. "I feel like an ant."

"The sentiment is fitting," the Eskeli added as their minds drifted to their own private thoughts.

The next morning they were on the water bright and early, the sun's rays already warming the chilly winter air. It was a clear day, the waters calm, unlike the turbulent feelings Kith was experiencing. He was heading to the ancient city of the Dar-dan to be tested in a way for which he wasn't sure he was ready. But he had to be. He was physically and mentally stronger than he had ever been. And the Eskeli said he was ready. He had to succeed.

Trying to get his mind off the task ahead of him, Kith looked down into the deep gray water as the Eskeli rowed them smoothly towards a series of islands that were just visible on the horizon. "If I were to fall in, would the waters kill me?"

"Not right away," the Eskeli responded. "Your skin would feel irritated, and if you got out immediately you would just have a red rash. If you were to stay in for a hundred oar strokes, your skin would start to burn. By five hundred strokes it would blister, but you could survive. After a thousand strokes the burns would be bad enough that you would likely die."

"And things live down there?" Lathronin wondered.

"Some. There are creatures that have adapted to the waters, surviving where most could not."

"What do they eat?" Kith asked.

"Others that have adapted. The stronger ones win in that world."

"It is not a world I want to visit," Lathronin murmured.

"No, it is not," the Eskeli emphasized.

Half a day later they could see the tall black rock of the islands rise before them. There was one in the distance that clearly had manmade structures, the black stone of the Dar-dan spires rising high into the sea air. That island was larger than the others, the massive spires dwarfed by the huge rock formations that formed the island. The Eskeli rowed in that direction.

Soon they were floating in deep waters just off a small inviting cove, ringed by dark gray sand.

"At one time there was a dock here, a place for boats to anchor," the Eskeli explained. "It rotted away to dust long ago. There is also a secret entrance into the lower levels of the city. It's through that narrow opening," the Eskeli said, pointing to a black cave in the rock face. The water was crashing against the rocks, pouring into the opening with each wave. It was not terribly wide, barely large enough for their own boat.

"Looks dangerous," Lathronin added.

"At high tide it is. On the outgoing tide one can leave the city through that opening in a small boat."

"An escape route," Lathronin figured.

The Eskeli nodded as he rowed closer to the beach.

Kith wasn't really listening, his eyes staring up at the huge towers that rose higher than anything he had ever seen, the shadows of the structures casting the entire area around them in shade. The stone looked smooth and the spires were connected by a black wall twice as tall as the one that surrounded Daswin. The entire structure, at least the part he could see, was built along the water's rocky edge. If one were so inclined, one could leap off the wall into the deep waters that surrounded them.

The Eskeli guided them into the cove where they carefully disembarked and pulled the boat higher onto the sand. Once they secured the boat, the Eskeli led them up a series of stone steps that switch-backed up the rock face. It looked as if the steps had been carved right out of the rock, the edges now worn from thousands of years of wind and turbulent weather. At the top they entered a flat part of the island that stretched for at least four arrow shots in all directions before converging into rocky spires and peaks that rose higher than the towers of Seebras. The land around them was covered in lush thick grass, patches of which peppered the rocky landscape. Small trees with purplish leaves were scattered throughout the area. They looked to be a version of the bandra tree.

Before them stood Seebras. The Dar-dan city was three times the size of Daswin, the entrance marked by a set of huge steps made of the same black stone leading to a set of stone doors that were cracked open. On either side of the doors were two statues, both the size of five men. As large as they were, they still only rose half way up the wall that surrounded the city. As they neared, Kith was able to make out the details more clearly. The doors themselves were impressive, carved from some gray stone as thick as a man's arm. From his distance, he could just make out a carving of a strange design that covered the expanse of both doors. But it was the statues that caused Kith to gasp. They were both black, formed from the same black stone all around him. The one on the left looked like the black statue at Daswin. He stood tall, his hands resting on a sword, the point stuck into the ground. His body was covered in a cloak like the one worn by the warrior in Daswin. Now that he thought more about it, it looked like the same cloak the Eskeli wore, the material made from many strands of cloth that always seemed to flutter in the air. Kith made a mental note to ask the Eskeli about the cloak. The statue was so expertly carved that it seemed to be alive. Kith remembered feeling the same sense of awe about the statue in Daswin. Theron had told him that it was an Ar'kan warrior, and he could only assume the statue before him was one as well. The statue on the right was equally impressive, also tall and covered in a cloak, his hood casting his face in shadow. He wasn't wearing armor but held one hand high into the air while his other crossed his body over his waist. As they ascended the massive steps, Kith could make out more of the details and was amazed to see the man's skin was covered in intricate sigils and designs. They looked like the marks he saw on the Drann priest and Eradicator he had fought. It was just a statue, but Kith was stunned by its details. The statues seemed so lifelike, except for the fact they were all covered in a layer of grime, dust, bird droppings, and whatever else you could imagine would accumulate over thousands of years.

The Eskeli caught him staring at the statue. "It's a Drann, one of the past protectors of your world."

Lathronin sneered. "Not anymore."

"No," the Eskeli agreed. "But we are here to rectify that." He looked at Kith, his eyes telling the young warrior the importance of their task. "Follow me."

They entered through the crack between the huge doors and followed the Eskeli into a massive courtyard, the entire expanse littered with debris built up over a very long time. The floor was paved in huge flat stones, their light gray color in contrast with the black stone that surrounded them. Many smaller spires rose up around them, dwarfed by the exterior ones but still impressive, their height expanding way beyond the exterior wall. There were paved roads in all directions but the main path from the gate led to a second pair of statues, both forms much smaller, but their detail equally impressive. The Eskeli led them down the main path and as they neared the statues Kith realized they were Eskeli. He stopped at looked up at one, marveling at the artist's skill. They both wore cloaks and armor, holding long spears, their faces covered in their strange masks.

"It's you," Kith ventured.

"Yes."

"How many of your kind were here?" Lathronin asked.

"There were four trainers at any one time," the Eskeli responded.

Kith's brow scrunched up as he tried to do the math in his head. "But I've been told that the Dar-dan were here for thousands of years. How did you live that long?"

"There were one hundred and three of us that volunteered to come with the Dar-dan. They kept us in long sleeps and woke us in small groups to live out our lives as trainers."

Again, Kith had a hard time grasping the Eskeli's words. "How long do you live?"

"Four hundred years is long," the Eskeli replied. "Most live less. I am now two hundred and fifty-five years old. It was a good life."

Kith looked up at the warrior, his use of the past tense not going unnoticed. He knew the Eskeli did not have much longer to live. The energy that worked the mask would soon dissipate, and then he would die. "I am sorry," Kith added lamely.

The Eskeli looked down at Kith. "As I said, it was a good life. And now, being here with you, I am content. You are as strong as any Ar'kan I have ever trained, Kith Caren. If my last task it to forge a warrior who can save this world, then my life has been well lived. Come, let us move on."

The Eskeli moved forward and they followed, Kith's mind holding onto the confidence in him that the Eskeli had just voiced. It was rare to hear such words from the creature, and Kith knew he would need the confidence in the trials to come.

As they followed the main road into the ruins Kith had a hard time visualizing it as a once populated city. Everywhere he looked was dirt and debris...and emptiness. There was nothing left that would indicate that at one time someone, or something, lived here. Anything made of wood or fabric had long ago crumbled to dust. The wind and elements had worn down much of the stone, and although many of the buildings were still intact, they were poor remnants of their former glory. Walls were streaked with endless years of bird dung and there were areas of the structures crumbling, the stone worked loose and worn away, exposing dark holes.

The main road was wide and paved in the same gray stone. It was a long walk before they stood before a huge structure, the entire façade covered in intricate carvings and statues, designs they had never seen. The building reminded Kith of the Drann temple at Daswin, but in this case it was much larger. Spires rose up on each corner and the middle was a square tower that rose so high that they could not see its roof. And that was just the front of the building. Kith could not see it entirely, but it looked as if the building extended further back. The entrance was marked by a set of wide stairs ascending to two stone doors, each side flanked by more cloaked statues.

The Eskeli didn't pause, ascending the steps with purpose. As they got to the doors, Kith noticed that the statues, which were twice his size, were different. They were simply cloaked, their faces hooded and covered in shadow. Compared to the other statues, they looked plain and unadorned.

"Who are they?" Kith questioned.

"They are the Dar-dan," the Eskeli said as he reached the door.

"They look so...plain," Lathronin interjected, voicing Kith's feelings exactly.

"Yes, they were humble. And they hid their bodies behind cloaks. Few ever saw their forms."

The Eskeli reached up and put his hand into an impression on the door. There was a flash of light around it and the door opened, the grating of stone on stone vibrating under their feet. Kith raised his eyebrows in wonder and glanced at Lathronin. The priest looked equally transfixed. The Eskeli looked back at them. "You are about to enter the OrnThonin, the training facility of the Ar'kan. Follow me."

Lathronin and Kith gave each other a furtive glance, their expressions a mixture of anxiety and excitement, and together they followed the Eskeli into the building.

They entered a large cathedral-like room, the ceilings tall and everything made of thick black stone. There was less debris here, the locked doors keeping the elements out. There were no windows but as soon as they entered sconces along the walls flanking them lit up and cast a bright white light.

Kith paused but the Eskeli didn't break stride. "Do not worry, it is Dar-dan magic."

Lathronin's expression was one of awe and Kith couldn't help but feel similarly. Everything they were witnessing was beyond what each had ever experienced. But they tucked away their amazement and quickly caught up to the long legged Eskeli. The massive hall was fifteen paces wide and completely empty. Whatever had filled the room in the past was long gone, turned to dust and scattered across the gray pavers that made up the floor. The hallway opened into a room that was even larger, its size stretching perpendicular to the hallway. Together, the hallway and room made a T shape. Kith noticed various passages along the walls, the dark entrances open, their doors crumbled from time. But as soon as they entered the large room, everyone's eyes were drawn to a huge set of stairs that descended into darkness. More sconces flashed to life around the perimeter of the room but none of the white light could penetrate the dark opening. The base of the stairs was wide enough for ten men but as they stepped closer to the dark hole, Kith could see that they narrowed the deeper they went. A railing of gray stone surrounded the back and sides.

"It is here we must go," the Eskeli said reverently. "You are about to gaze upon the Alltree."

"What is the Alltree?" Kith asked.

"It was the source of the Dar-dan power."

"Does it still have power?" Kith wondered.

"Yes. The tree draws power from your world. It is made from your field stones and acts similarly. It is the Alltree's power that will guide you through the Change."

"You make it sound like a walk through a field of wheat."

The Eskeli turned to look at Kith. "Make no mistake, it will be nothing like that."

Kith knew the Change would be extremely difficult, so he said nothing in response, his eyes already looking into the darkness. "Let us see this Alltree."

The Eskeli nodded and stepped onto the first step. When he did more sconces lit up and cast their light into the darkness. Together, they followed the Eskeli down the stairs.

They descended for many paces, much longer than Kith had expected. As they progressed deeper more sconces flashed to life to light their way. Finally, they reached the bottom and they stepped onto another floor, but this one was black and smooth. More sconces flooded the area with light and Kith's breath caught in his throat. Immediately he felt a sense of power, like a gentle reverberating throughout his body. Lathronin must have felt it as well as he glanced over at Kith, his expression telling all. The room was colossal and looked more like a cave. But they spent little time inspecting the perimeter as their eyes were pulled to a dazzling sight. The center of the room was marked by a huge black tree that grew from the ground, the tall form growing high and branching off into many directions. The trunk was as wide as two men laying down and as it rose higher it split several times into equally impressive branches. Thousands of small blue lights twinkled from its countless branches like glowing grapes. The lights blinked on and off at various times, creating a dazzling and beautiful picture. Where the branches reached the tall ceiling, they grew straight into the rock. There were four stone beds arranged around the tree but other than that the room was empty. Kith noticed that the ground around the tree was covered in a network of roots that stretched from the tree and grew up the beds, the ends buried into the stone.

"This is the Alltree," the Eskeli whispered.

Kith's eyes were wide as he gazed up at the massive structure. It wasn't really a tree, Kith noticed, but something made of a strange material resembling a leafless tree. "What is it?"

"It was made by the Dar-dan long ago, the material unknown to me. The lights that you see are field stones. They power the tree and everything else."

"What else?" Lathronin asked, just as enthralled as Kith.

"They ran the entire city, the lights, as well as the power to harness the Change and create the Ar'kan weapons and armor." Kith looked up at the Eskeli as if he were speaking a foreign language. "It will make sense in due time."

"This is incredible," Lathronin whispered. "I can feel the power all around me."

"In two days' time you will go through the Change. When you succeed, we will enter the last phase of your training."

"I thought the Change marked the end," Kith queried.

"No, there is still much to do. You must get become accustomed to your new power and speed, as well as your weapons." The Eskeli looked to Lathronin. "While this occurs, I have a task for you."

"What is it?"

"We will need food. The islands will provide the bounty. You will need to hunt. There are many birds that live here as well as a sea creature called a calwill. They are large but slow out of water. Their skin is thick and fatty. If you are lucky you will see them along the shoreline early in the morning. If not, then you may have to go to the mainland to hunt."

Lathronin nodded. They both had tasks, but for now, they could do nothing but stare up at the Alltree, its glimmering lights mesmerizing in the shadows of the cave.

***

Arim looked at Bos and the big warrior smiled, gripping his two-handed axe harder as he glanced back to the road. The supply caravan should be lumbering around the bend at any time. Arim's bow was nocked and he was comforted by the fact that three other bowmen were nearby, with at least that number of bowmen on the opposite side of the road concealed in the dense brush. Not to mention his big friend's presence had a way of calming his nerves. After all, there were few as strong and fierce as Bob, his abbreviated name for Big Old Bos. It was a silly nickname, which was likely why it had stuck. Cos's entire vor was hidden away around him adding to his sense of confidence. Along with the barrel-chested commander, they were accompanied by Carthen, Bear'lon, who was Carthen's shadow, and Lykin, the bowman. But despite their skill, numbers, and element of surprise, Arim was still nervous. They had been raiding the Emperors caravans now for the last six months, and Arim, and the others, had noticed that the supply lines were becoming increasingly better protected. The Order had been collecting as much food and supplies as possible. They would need it when they joined forces with the Kelic. An army marches on its stomach, and without food and supplies, they would not get very far. But Arim was becoming increasingly worried about their raids. Perhaps this time they would have a Drann priest accompanied by Black Watch soldiers. He sighed, trying to conquer his stress. After all, he would find out soon enough. There was no sense dwelling on it.

Suddenly the sounds of rolling wagons and horses found them, followed shortly by the appearance of the caravan. Peeking around the tree, Arim did his best to ascertain the enemy's numbers. So far, from what he could see, it looked like a traditional caravan. There were roughly six covered wagons, supposedly, according to their spies, laden with food and other goods, all heading from Lampure to Akari, Urotha's capital. It looked to be guarded by forty or so Torlites. With the element of surprise, they could defeat that force easily enough.

Arim readied himself as Bos looked up and smiled, his eager anticipation somehow easing Arim's tension. The horsed guards moved past them and soon the wagons lumbered by.

They would attack on Carthen's que, which Arim figured would be soon.

Suddenly one of the horsed men jerked and fell from his horse, an arrow quivering from his throat. In a flash the scene was in chaos. Arim rose and shot his first arrow, quickly following the shot with two more. The other archers did the same and within moments the horsed guards were down, most dead and a few screaming as they crawled for cover behind the wagons. The Torlites had quickly formed two hurried lines on both sides of the wagons, their shields up and swords drawn. Arim and the other arches fired into their midst, but many were blocked by their steel shields. It happened quite quickly, so fast actually that it seemed to Arim that they had been expecting the attack. Bos and the others around him roared and ran through the brush, striking the shield wall with their own shields, weapons coming together in a cacophony of steel on steel.

Arim dropped his bow, drew his sword, and readied himself to join the others when something happened that caused his heart to stop in his chest. The back flaps of the wagons suddenly burst open and dozens of men jumped from the backs, quickly joining the Torlites. But they weren't ordinary men, they were Danites, easily identified by their red capes and black glossy armor. There were at least thirty Danites, and when they pushed their way into the Torlite line things began to look very bleak.

Arim caught sight of Carthen, Bear'lon, and Lykin as they ran from the brush with the other members of the Order around them. They cut down five Torlites before a handful of Danites made their way to the front of the column. Arim glanced to Bos and saw that he was already in trouble, his axe not the ideal weapon for close quarters. The two comrades that flanked Bos were already down, killed by the skilled Danites. And now Bos faced two of the fearsome warriors by himself. The only good thing about fighting them alone was that now he had room to use his axe to its full potential.

The Danites crashed into Carthen and the others. Within moments the fight was a scene of frantic combat as the skilled warriors sought each other's deaths. Carthen's blade flashed through the air as he ducked and pivoted, his blade parrying attacks and adding his own ripostes faster than Arim could follow. Bear'lon and Lykin were impressive in their own right. Even against the mighty Danites, Arim felt they might prevail.

Arim made a quick decision and ran towards Bos, just in time it would seem as Bos was barely able to deflect several sword strikes, his own attacks blocked by the warrior's shields. Bos was able to keep the swordsmen at bay by sheer power and the length of his awesome weapon, the heavy steel blade moving much faster than the Danites thought possible for such a cumbersome weapon. But few were as strong as Bos and he maneuvered the axe as fast as Arim could a sword. The second Danite came at Bos's flank and had already delivered a cut across the big man's thigh when he was poised for a killing strike. Arim was there in a flash, his blade swooping in and deflecting the Danite's killing stroke. The Danite growled in frustration and engaged Arim. Arim knew he was in trouble. He didn't have a shield and despite his many years of training he knew immediately that he was outmatched. Frantically, Arim deflected the Danite's attack, trying to look for an opening of his own. He could hear Bos growling like an enraged animal as he brought his weapon down again and again on the Danite's shield. The sound was deafening but Arim had no time to see how his friend was faring. Arim was already bleeding from a shallow cut on his forearm and it was all he could do to avoid a killing stroke. Suddenly Arim's fears were realized as the Danite swordsman deflected a clumsy attack and rammed his shield forward in a vicious shield charge. Arim had no other way to block the attack so he raised his knee to try to keep the swordsman away. The powerful strike hit his knee and pain shot through his leg, launching him from his feet where he landed hard on his back. He tried to scurry to his feet but the warrior was already in the air with the point of his blade angled towards his chest. Arim screamed and whipped his blade across his body, the sharp edge catching the man's blade, the steel tip just missing him and burying deep into the ground, so close to him that the razor-sharp edge scraped across the steel of his cuirass. The Danite's weight was on Arim's torso and in a blink he had his blade up again, the point moving down towards his throat. This time Arim knew he was done for. The sparkling tip was only two hand spans from his neck. He would be dead in a fraction of a heartbeat.

Suddenly the man's head snapped to the right, so violently that his helm ripped free and his body was catapulted to the road a full pace from him. Bos was standing behind him, his axe bloody and held in both hands. Arim leaped to his feet to see the other Danite dead nearby, his shield a mess of bent steel.

"Thanks," Arim said as he frantically took in the scene around them. Bos nodded and did the same. It did not look good. Most of the Torlites were dead, but only a handful of Danites could be seen amongst the bodies.

Arim looked to the front of the column and saw Carthen kill the last of the Danites before him. The old warrior looked up and saw Arim and the other survivors. He ran to them with Lykin, Bear'lon, and one other man. Arim recognized him as Vorlarin, a skilled swordsman in his own right. The others were dead, killed by the Danites.

"We have to get out of here!" Carthen said. "It was a trap!"

"Where's Cos?' Lykin asked, his expression grim.

"There," Bos rumbled as he pointed to a column of men still fighting. The man was a blur as his twin hand axes buzzed around him. Even the two Danites fighting him seemed at a disadvantage.

"What should we do?" Arim asked frantically, knowing that if they left that the men that were engaged would die, or worse, be captured.

"We cannot save them all," Carthen said, stating the obvious. There were too many Danites, and every moment they pondered their choices, another member of the Order was cut down. Likely, they had just moments before they were all dead. "Get yours bows," Carthen ordered, his mind made up.

Lykin ran back to the front where he had dropped his bow. Arim did the same, rushing into the brush to pick up his bow and quiver. Six heart beats later they were standing next to Carthen again. But this time Cos had killed one of the Danites, but two more members of the Order fell around him, forcing another Danite through to engage Cos.

"Take out the Danites near Cos," Carthen ordered. "We grab who we can and run for it."

Lykin didn't question the order. His bow came up, an arrow already nocked. Arim hesitated, not sure if he could hit the Danite's through his own men.

At full draw, Lykin's hard eyes glanced at Arim. "Nock and aim," he ordered. "Now."

Arim blinked, his heart pounding as he did as he was told. Sighting a Danite, he released the air in his lungs. Just then Lykin released, followed shortly by Arim's arrow. They each fired two more arrows before Carthen and Bos ran forward to grab their men.

Lykin's aim was true. Two Danites fell back, one dead with an arrow through his throat, the other momentarily out of the fight, an arrow jutting from his shoulder. Arim's first arrow struck a Danite in the helm, the bolt deflecting off the steel. But it had given one of their men the reprieve he needed to ram his blade into the unprotected gap at the man's stomach. His second arrow found another Danite's arm, the sharp point ripping a hole through his bicep. Howling, the man leaped back as another Danite filled the gap, only to find an axe swooping down. Bos roared as he brought his axe down like a logger splitting wood. The Danite lifted his blade but the power of the strike pushed through his defense, the edge of his axe creasing the man's helm and cutting into his face. He fell to the ground like a sack of rocks.

"Let's go!" he yelled as he grabbed one man, a second following just behind him. Carthen had pulled Cos away just as five more Danites killed the remaining two warriors. Behind the five Danites were ten more.

They ran with all haste towards Arim and Lykin, both of whom had already nocked another arrow, their shafts flying by them, some dangerously close as the archers did their best to keep the Danites at bay and give them to time to escape. Two of the Danites went down and the others stopped their pursuit, quickly forming a well-executed shield wall. Lykin and Arim's arrows flew at them with great speed, the sharp steel tips ricocheting off the steel shields. But at this point they were just hoping to keep the deadly warriors at bay while their own men lengthened the distance between them.

As Carthen and the others neared the old swordsman never stopped. "Let's go!" he yelled. "Into the woods."

"I'll find you!" Lykin yelled as they ran by. Arim looked at Lykin, not sure what to do. "Go!" the scout ordered. "I'll find you."

"What are you going to do?" Arim asked as he fired two more arrows at the shield wall.

"Slow them down," Lykin replied as he continued to fire, his movements smooth and practiced, each arrow aimed to keep the Danite shield wall up and the dangerous warriors rooted in place. "Now go!"

Arim reached into his quiver and pulled out a handful of arrows, ramming their tips into the ground at Lykin's feet. He still had at least ten shafts and figured Lykin would need them. Arim nodded at the archer, then he ran into the woods, following Carthen and the others.

FOUR

Theron stepped into the large stone building and was immediately assaulted by the stench of it, the wretched odor nearly making him vomit. It was comparable to that of the battlefield after the fighting was over. Theron put his hand to his nose, but it did little to minimize the smells of the diseased, aged, and dying.

He passed two Danite guards and they respectively put their fists to their chests. One looked at him knowingly, "You get used to it, sir," he said.

Theron nodded. "I'm not sure I want to," he mumbled as he stepped further into the building. He recognized both men but did not know them by name. Neither were members of any of the vors under his command.

At one point the building was a storage bunker for Lord Rane's army, but Princess Morwin had convinced her father to turn it into an infirmary for those in the city who could not afford to pay for healing, or simply needed a place to die in relative comfort instead of a dirty alley somewhere. It was not Lord Rane's altruism that eventually led to his decision to grant his daughter's wish. She knew he cared little for the sick and dying, but she influenced her father's decision by reminding him that sickness and death were no good for the city. The nobility did not want an outbreak of the red fever, or the black rash, and no matter how far, or tucked away the poor corners of the city were, the smell of death and sickness always spilt over to the parts of the city where the higher ranks of society lived. It was in all their best interests to see to the sick and dying and to keep the streets as clean as possible. At least that was how she sold it to her father.

At one point the huge rectangular building would have been filled with crates stacked high of food, supplies, and even weapons. But now the room was filled with hundreds of beds, most of them full, and nearly thirty blue robed healers milling about seeing to their many patients. The infirmary was one of several Lady Morwin had pushed for and Theron knew that she visited them often. Today he was hoping to find her here.

An aged healer walked by, his face grim. "Pardon me, sir," Theron questioned, "is Princess Morwin here today?"

The old man glanced at Theron and his expression seemed to sour. Clearly, he was not a fan of the Danite Core, although, Theron thought, that made sense. Why would someone who had devoted their life to healing care much for someone who had devoted their life to killing. Theron could understand the man's resentment. "She is here, Captain," the man said, recognizing his cloak clasp and rank. "Look for her in the back. Last I saw the Princess she was in the storeroom in the back looking over supplies."

Theron nodded and walked down the aisle that was created between the many rows of beds. A few of the healers looked up at him, but most were too busy to even notice. The smell was still overwhelming but at least it had gotten no worse. He saw two more Danites next to a door that must have led to the storage room. Both saluted him with their fists to their chests as he walked through the open door. He saw her immediately. She was standing before a series of shelves lined with healing supplies. It looked as if she were counting the items and checking them off a manifest.

"Don't you have people to do that for you?" Theron asked.

She turned and smiled. "I suppose so," she shrugged, "but it's a nice excuse to get out of the castle." Princess Morwin had her hair pulled back into a single braid. She wore simple soft spun gray leggings and a white blouse under a dark gray wool cloak lined with white fur. She was definitely not dressed like a lady, let alone a princess. She caught Theron glance at her garb. "What? You've never seen a lady wear leggings? You know it is quite the fashion," she quipped.

"Maybe with the commoners," Theron replied.

She shrugged again. "I prefer to blend in."

"I can understand that."

"What are you doing here?" she asked.

Theron stepped closer, forcing her to look at him. "I enjoyed our time the other night. I would like to see you again."

She chuckled lightly. "Really? You enjoyed being attacked."

Theron smiled. "Well, if I recall, it was you that was attacked."

She laughed but her smile quickly faded. "That is true. And I must say the event has left me ill at ease."

"Is that why four Danites are accompanying you?'

"Yes, my Father's idea. But I must admit I feel better with them around."

Theron nodded. "And you should. So, how about a second shot? Perhaps we can have an evening together with no death and blood."

"That sounds so romantic when you put it like that," she replied with a mischievous twinkle in her eye. "What do you have in mind?"

"There is a night of musicians at a tap room in Mid-City. I think you would enjoy it."

"You want to take a Princess of Urotha to an ale hall?" She asked, her frown clearly forced.

Theron could tell that the idea appealed to her, so he pressed the point. "You can come as you are. No one will know your identity."

"And you? Will you arrive as a Danite Captain?"

Theron bowed mockingly. "I will come as a plain man, after all, a Danite Captain would never be seen with such a common lady."

She shoved him in the shoulder and laughed. "Do you always speak with such flippancy?"

"I'm afraid I was born with joyful confidence. It is a curse that plagues me," he added with a wink.

She suddenly frowned. "My father will not let me go out without a Danite escort."

"Do you always do what your father says?" Theron asked.

He had struck a nerve as her face turned hard. "No, of course not."

"Besides," Theron added. "You will be with a Danite Captain. I will be your escort."

86

She pursed her lips in thought. "Okay. When is this night you speak of?"

"Two nights from today."

"I will meet you at the Drann Statue at dusk," she agreed.

The Drann Statue was a creation of the Dar-dan, carved thousands of years ago to replicate the Drann ancients. It was three times the size of any man and located at the courtyard near the West Gate. It was made from the same strange stone as the Ar'kan statue at Daswin. Everyone knew the location of the statue. Theron bowed low at the waist. "I look forward to seeing you again."

She smiled as he turned on his heel and left.

***

Kith was lying on his back when the Eskeli stepped next to the stone bed. Kith wore no clothes, his body completely naked, the cold stone beneath him doing nothing to reassure him.

"Kith Caren, you are about to go through the Change. I want you to know before we begin, that you are as physically and mentally prepared as any I have taught before you, even more so. I have had little time to prepare you, and yet you have performed in an exemplary manner. Have no doubt, for it is doubt that will leave you vulnerable to failure."

Kith had to admit that he was nervous. But the Eskeli's words did indeed calm his heart some. He *was* confident. It was just the unknown that nagged at him. He had worked extremely hard, but so far, all his tasks were tangible. But now he was unsure what was going to happen to him. "What will the Alltree do to me?" Kith inquired, hoping to get some answers before they started.

"The Alltree will probe your flesh. It will be extremely painful. As it does so, it will fuse your body with the energy of the field stones. It will take your blood, and together, with the material of the Alltree, it will form your armor and weapons. You will be connected to all in a way that you cannot imagine. The stronger you are, the more the Alltree will test you. The pain will be immense. Use your mind to search for shelter from it. Whatever you do don't rise from the table."

"What will happen if I do?"

"You will likely die, your mind destroyed. If you survive the Change, your trial is still not complete. There are rare cases where survivors suffered physical and mental ailments after the Change, but if they don't occur during the process, it is unlikely they will occur after, especially considering you are a Stone Blood."

"What do you mean that the stronger I am, the more the Alltree will test me?"

"Not all Ar'kan are equal. Some come out of the Change with no Ar'kan weapons, although they are granted more speed and power from the field stones. Others are given a blade, or spear. There are few strong enough to earn armor along with weapons. The Alltree will know your strength and will test you accordingly. Now, Kith Caren, are you ready?"

Kith took a deep breath, his mind searching for any other questions. But there were none. Part of him just wanted to get it over with. "I am ready."

"Good, now, begin the mind dance."

Kith took a deep breath and his practiced mind instantly found the gentle rhythm of the dance, the beat slow and precise as his mind worked through the many sword forms. He concentrated on the images in his mind, shutting off all connections to the world around him. He was not aware of the Eskeli as he moved to the front of the stone table. It was here that a flat piece of black stone rose higher than the table, like a headboard to a bed. Black root-like tendrils snaked from the raised stone and meandered around the table, finding their way across the cave floor to the base of the Alltree. The Eskeli placed his left hand on the flat stone, the impression there barely discernable. Instantly light danced across the glossy stone and the Eskeli then placed his right hand next to the other. Blue light flared around them both, pulsing three times before the Eskeli removed his hands and stepped away.

A glowing blue light began to pulse down the black tendrils following the roots to the Alltree, then disappearing into its thick base. Within a few moments all the field stones twinkling from the tree began to glow brighter, their soft flickering light turning to a solid bright blue that shed the room in a moon-like brilliance. A few heartbeats later the Eskeli saw blue light pulse from the tree, this time racing across the tendrils to the bed where Kith was lying.

The Eskeli looked down knowingly and saw new black root-like structures break from the thicker branches that swarmed around the bed's base, rising like snakes up the edges of the bed. They moved with purpose, many branching around the stone slab angling towards Kith's feet and head. They grew to the bed's surface, the ends of the roots now like a woman's fingers whose ends were as sharp as needles. Without pausing they shot forward, breaking into Kith's skin and burying themselves into his shoulders and ankles, narrowing further as they entered his flesh.

Kith's mind dance was momentarily interrupted as the pain ripped through his concentration. His body jolted involuntarily as the black roots dug deeper into his flesh, blue light pulsing through them into Kith's arms and legs. Forcing his mind to the dance, he made its rhythm grow louder as he tried to mask the pain, the sound of the dance and the sword forms the focus of Kith's mind. But he could not hold back hkis screams as fiery pain rocked his body. Picking up the speed of the mind dance, Kith's mental body moved through the forms with power and authority, driving the pain deeper into his subconscious.

He screamed again, the pain breaking through his concentration. His mental body stumbled as his mind tried to deal with the intense agony. It felt as if his body were melting from the inside. His eyes blinked rapidly, releasing a river of tears. Arching his back, he screamed again as more pulsing blue energy stabbed and bolted through his body. His heart was pounding so hard that Kith thought it would explode, his legs and arms convulsing in the same shuddering rhythm. His howls of pain finally turned to a deep growl as he regained his focus, forcing his mind to pick up on the dance as his corporal form continued through the many sword forms with such intense purpose that his body finally stopped shaking and went rigid as a board, his muscles flexed and tensed as he gritted his teeth. It was as if the harder and faster he hit the positions, the easier it was for him to ignore the pain. So he moved through them with more intensity than he thought possible, the mental dance turning to a blur of deadly strokes, parries, and ripostes. After what seemed like forever, somewhere in his subconscious he recognized the pain lessening, replaced by a soft warmth in his hands and ankles, the pain now becoming a dull ache throughout his entire body.

The Eskeli was looking down at Kith, its expression unreadable. And although one would not be able to tell, the creature felt a sense of relief when blue energy began to materialize around both hands. He watched as thin black tendrils, like veins, grew down the length of Kith's arms, breaking through the flesh around his hands, the bleeding minimal as the roots knowingly evaded all veins and arteries. Kith's body was shaking subtly, his eyes closed in concentration as he fought against the pain. The Eskeli did not count them, but it looked as if six to ten black appendages had broken through, dancing like snakes before converging past his hand, blue energy dancing through them as they formed a straight black line along the edge of the bed. Within moments the shape of a sword materialized, blue energy pulsing down the glossy black blade. The same was happening on the other side, the black form much longer, the shape of a spear soon materializing stretching the length of the bed, the top of the weapon resting in the nook of Kith's arm pit, the black tip well past his head.

"Now we see your true strength," the Eskeli whispered.

The blue energy that was pulsing around his hands suddenly dissipated as more began to flash across his entire body. The worm-like appendages that had snaked down his arms were gone, the thicker roots buried in his shoulders sending more across his body. The Eskeli watched as black worm-like roots dug through Kith's flesh, the black veins arcing across his shoulders, chest, stomach, and thighs. The light across his body flashed brightly and at the same time the many thin black roots broke through Kith's flesh like worms wiggling and weaving across Kith's body.

Just as Kith began to feel the worst was over, a sudden blast of fiery agony lanced through his body. He screamed, the pain feeling like his blood was burning molten rock. The rhythm of the dance vanished, and Kith's corporal form fizzled away, replaced by the searing pain across his physical body. His eyes bolted open and his body shook violently. It was all he could do to stay on his back. Every part of his will wanted him to jump up and run from the Alltree, to distance himself from the very thing that was causing him so much pain. Kith's frantic eyes found the Eskeli and he screamed. "The pain! It is...overwhelming! I can't..."

"You can!" the Eskeli said forcefully, stepping closer to Kith. "The Alltree knows you are strong enough! You must believe that you are! Find your center again! You can do it!"

Kith shut his eyes again and flexed his muscles, his entire body rigid as he fought against the pain. By this time the root-like appendages had branched into hundreds of tiny black veins, each the thickness of a hair, those veins branching into thousands more, all of which were weaving across his body. Plates the color of gray charcoal began to form as blue light continued to dance across his body. Searing agony permeated his body, feeling as if he had been immersed in molten rock, creating a pain so constant and overwhelming that he thought he was going to lose consciousness. But for some reason he knew that was not a good thing. Again, using his mind, he created an image of himself standing in gray armor, intricate sigils etched into the strange material. He was holding a sword and spear and his entire body glowed a luminous blue. Yet pain continued to grip him, apparations of flaming red energy forming gaping maws filled with razor teeth and raking talons. Kith's body danced, his weapons a blue glow as they kept the burning monsters away.

As he fought the pain in his mind, his armor began to take shape. The thousands of tendrils wove a dark gray cuirass, the chest plate formed to fit his body perfectly. Charcoal gray sheets of material covered his stomach and more tendrils wove his cuisses that fit his thighs perfectly. Simple pauldrons took shape across his shoulders and it wasn't long for the worm-like appendages to weave vambraces across his forearms. Lastly, blue light seemed to coalesce around the cuirass.

"Yes," the Eskeli whispered with as much excitement as possible for such a creature. He stepped closer, careful to not touch him. As he watched, the blue light flashed brighter and small tendrils formed an impression in the armor, a black stone with blue veins materializing soon after. The light flared so much brighter that the Eskeli was forced back a few paces. He watched as Kith's body glowed blue, rising to a bright flash. The Eskeli covered his eyes and stepped back even further. The light held its intensity for a few heartbeats and then vanished.

Kith had no idea how long he had been fighting the pain; the agony having manifested itself as teeth and claw. He ducked and spun, attacked and defended, his black spear spinning and cleaving through the fiery pain. He fought and fought, the creatures he killed disappearing in flashes of orange fire, only to be replaced by more. But then suddenly they were gone, and he was surrounded by darkness. His temporal body dropped to his knees, his consciousness retreating. He needed to rest, and with that in mind, his body slumped to the ground, and he fell asleep.

The Eskeli's vision was still blurry from the intense flashes of blue light, but when its clarity finally returned, Kith was lying still on the table. There was no more blue light or black tendrils, the appendages having returned to the thicker roots at the base of the table. Kith's body was covered in charcoal gray armor. It appeared to be much lighter than regular plate, its surface etched with swirling sigils and patterns, some the Eskeli recognized from the Dar-dan language. Laying next to Kith's right hand was a black sword, the handle more gray than black with blue veins like topaz spider-webbing across the hilt. In the pommel was a field stone encased in black, the stone still swirling with blue energy. Near Kith's left hand was a six-foot-long spear, the long tip black and the handle made from the same material, veins of blue, like the handle of his sword, spiderwebbing across the entire shaft. Near the base of the spear was another field stone, the end cap encasing the softly glowing stone.

The Eskeli stepped next to Kith and was relieved to see him breathing, his chest gently rising up and down. Despite his ordeal, his face seemed calm. Below the surface of each hand the creature could see the gentle pulse of field stones, and glancing down to Kith's feet, he could see the same thing. Each stone pulsed softly, the blue glow just visible below the surface of Kith's flesh. He looked at the stone encased in the center of his cuirass and saw light flash through the blue veins, matching the soft pulsing rhythm of the stones. "Well done, Kith Caren," the Eskeli whispered.

***

Arim's chest heaved up and down, but they had trained hard for many years and the long and frantic flight through the dense forest was well within their skill range. Even Bos was able to keep up, his large form bringing up the rear as they ran like deer through the shadowy forest. At first, they had heard pursuit, but hours later they seemed alone, running from shadows as Carthen pressed on.

Arim was amazed at the old man's endurance. No one really knew how old he was, so perhaps he just looked older than everyone thought. He was sinewy and covered in lanky muscle. He moved with the grace of a dancer and Arim had never witnessed anyone best him with a blade. Even Cos and Bear'lon looked at him with undisguised reverence. His short hair and beard was mostly gray, with smudges of dark still fighting against the years. But it was his leathery skin that made him seem older than his martial abilities implied. He had the look of an aged piece of meat, and he was just as tough.

Finally, Carthen pulled up short, breathing heavily as sweat dripped from his face. Moments later everyone stopped around him, pausing briefly while everyone caught their breath.

"I think we are clear," Bear'lon stammered between breathes.

Carthen nodded, his expression grave. Everyone Knew they had lost a lot of good men, many of them friends. And it was likely that Carthen blamed himself. "Where is Lykin?" he asked, not seeing the archer present.

"He stayed behind to slow them down," Arim replied.

Carthen swore.

"He'll be fine, he always is," Cos countered.

"How did they know about the ambush?" Bear'lon asked. "Is your man in Lampure compromised?"

"Not possible," Carthen replied, his tone adamant. "Likely they simply guessed based on our previous attacks. They got lucky."

"We lost close to fifty men," Vorlarin muttered. "What are we going to do now?"

Carthen's eyes bore into the swordsman. "I know how many men we lost," he snapped, his tone sharp like a sword.

"What if they captured some?" Arim asked as he looked around at the men. They were all thinking the same thing. If any were captured, they would likely be tortured. But would they give up the Order's secrets? Would they divulge the location of their bases to ease their pain?

"We have to trust in our men," Carthen insisted.

"Not a single man would give us up," Cos agreed, but his expression didn't reflect his confident words.

"What now?" Bos asked, always eager to waylay conversation for action.

Suddenly a noise alerted them to their left. They turned towards it as blades slid from their scabbards. It was Lykin who appeared through the brush, his face a mask of exertion. He was carrying his bow and Arim noticed that he only had three remaining arrows. "We must move, and now! They have trackers!"

"They are still following?!" Carthen asked incredulously. He was clearly having a hard time imagining anyone able to keep pace with them.

"They are Danites, not so easily averted," Lykin added as he caught his breath. "I was able to slow them some, but they are not far behind."

"How many?" Bear'lon asked, his hands tightly gripping his axe.

"I killed two and wounded three more. My guess is there are at least ten tracking us now. They are fast. I am not sure we can outrun them. Eventually they will find us."

"Then we should pick a place to confront them," Cos suggested, "a location of our choosing."

"Ten Danites against seven," Vorlarin murmured, his tone showing his concern.

Carthen smiled, which was rare. "Doesn't seem fair, does it." But his smile was more malicious than humorous. He was looking forward to the confrontation. He wanted to kill them, to cause them pain after what they had done to his men.

"We need to set up an ambush," Lykin suggested. "They won't' be expecting that."

Carthen nodded. "Lead the way," he ordered, addressing Lykin. "We run hard," he hissed, his voice stern as he glanced at all the men. "This is why we train so hard. When we find a suitable spot, we stop and lure them in." No one said a thing, and moments later Lykin ran into the woods, the rest of the men following.

They ran for another bell before Lykin slowed, stopping the men as they emerged from the thick forest onto an open river bed. Smooth river rocks and downed wood debris littered the landscape. The crystal-clear river flowed gently through the forest opening before cascading down thick boulders. The turbulent waters were surrounded by steep sides of moss-covered rocks, the trees growing right up to the rock faces that had been carved by the river. The open area was a good spot to cross. It was also a good spot to set up an ambush.

The men stopped next to Lykin as Carthen scanned the area. Lykin already had a plan forming. "They will assume we crossed here," he said, thinking out loud. "We can hit them as they cross the river after us."

Carthen nodded his head as he quickly looked around. "There," he said, pointing to a thick mess of logs on the other side of the river. "I want you and Arim there with your bows. The wood will give you adequate coverage and you can target them when they cross."

"And you?" Lykin asked.

"I will be here hiding in the brush. They will not expect us to split our forces, keeping one on the other side of the river."

"Because it's risky," Lykin added. "You will be stuck on..."

"War is risky," Carthen interrupted, his tone all business. Lykin shook his head, knowing it was futile to argue.

"Bear'lon and Vorlarin, you will attack with me. Cos, you and Bob will stay with Lykin and Arim. If any make it across the river you will need to engage them. We need to capitalize on Arim and Lykin's arrows." Cos nodded. Carthen looked at their quivers. "How many arrows do you have?"

Arim counted his. "I have eleven."

"Three," Lykin added.

"Split them up and make them count," Carthen ordered. "Let's go."

"You three should enter the water with us," Lykin suggested. "Then move down river and cross back onto the rocks. We need the trackers thinking we all crossed here."

Carthen nodded in agreement and without further discussion Lykin, Bos, Cos, and Arim ran to the narrow portion of the river and began to cross to the other side. Carthen, Bear'lon, and Vorlarin joined them. Once in the water they carefully moved down river and emerged onto a thick bed of river rock. The others were halfway across by that time. The water was moving slowly and only made it to their knees. They crossed easily and picked out suitable locations on the far side. Carthen was right. The wood debris was thick and made for good shelter. They could hide behind the piles of logs and easily rise to fire their arrows into the approaching Danites as they slowed crossing the river. They would be easy targets.

Carthen and the others looked for hiding places on the other side. The old warrior looked at Bear'lon. "I want you and Vorlarin to attack their right flank. I will handle the left. Do not attack until you see me do so. Find a spot as close to the river as you can but far enough from the crossing point that they will not see you." The men nodded, Bear'lon's eyes holding Carthen's before he nodded and ran off with Vorlarin.

Both groups were careful to run on the thick smooth rocks and not make any prints. Vorlarin and Bear'lon found a spot upriver where the forest grew to its edge. It was good cover and it was an arrow shot away. They could cover that ground fairly quickly.

Carthen found a spot a bit closer. Just down river was a large pile of huge rocks, each boulder the size of a wagon. He climbed up the rocks and found a good elevated position behind a moss-covered boulder. He figured he could leap down the boulders and engage the Danites within fifteen heartbeats. Now they just waited.

It wasn't long before Carthen saw the first scout emerge from the forest. The second scout appeared close by, both men cautiously entering the open river bed, their vigilant eyes scanning the terrain around them. They were not Danites. They were Torlites trained as scouts, part of Lord Rane's regular infantry. They wore hardened leather and carried short recurve bows and short swords. They talked quietly as they inched further into the river bed, inspecting the ground as they went. Carthen saw one scout move close to the river, and when he saw the tracks, he called the other scout over. They talked quietly as they inspected the footprints and Carthen felt pretty secure in their ruse. His heart skipped a beat when he saw one man inspect the ground down river, looking for any spot where their prey might have backtracked, using the water as coverage. He squatted down to inspect some rocks not more than a stone throw from his position. Carthen nervously watched as the scout carefully inspected some stones near the river. It was midday and the sun was shining brightly. The old warrior hoped that whatever tracks they had created by emerging from the water was now dry on the warm rocks.

After a few tense heartbeats the scout rose and looked around, his eyes scanning the very rocks Carthen hid behind. With a sense of relief, the soldier turned and walked back to the other scout. Just then the Danites entered the clearing.

"Damn," Carthen swore softly. There were twelve of them. The men fanned out as they joined the scouts near the river bed. They had a brief discussion before one scout started across the river, the warriors moving in behind him. They had spread out along the shallow crossing point so as not to make an easy target. Carthen expected nothing less from the well-trained warriors.

Carthen already had his blade drawn as he inched closer to the edge of the boulder, readying himself to scurry down the rocks like a mountain goat and attack the men as they crossed. The old warrior knew that Lykin knew his business and would likely wait for a handful of the men to reach the other side before he rose and loosed his arrows. The goal was to catch most of the Danites in the water, killing the men on either side of the crossing before they knew what had happened. They had to reduce their numbers and increase their odds.

Three men had reached the other side when Lykin rose from his concealed location, Arim a blink after. By the time they had released their first volley, six Danites were still in the water and three more were on Carthen's side of the river.

As soon as Carthen saw the attack, he rose and quickly made his way down the boulders, running silently with all haste towards the surprised men. Bear'lon and Vorlarin burst from the brush on the other side, their weapons held at the ready as they ran silently. There was no battle cry. They raced towards the enemy, their silence more unnerving than any war chant.

The three Danites near them turned when they heard the attackers' race across the rock-strewn river bed. The officer who was in the water shouted orders to defend their backs. Two other Danites who were in the slow-moving current ran through the shallow water and joined their comrades, weapons drawn to face the charging men.

One man in the water went down, Lykin's shaft quivering in his throat before he fell back into the water. Arim's arrow struck another man in the meaty flesh where his shoulder connected to his muscular neck. The man would probably survive, but he was likely out of the fight. The three men who had reached the far side charged the archers, knowing that if they did not, they would be picked off one at a time. Lykin and Arim kept up their assault while Bos and Cos jumped from their concealed locations to meet the Danite charge.

Carthen's sword came high, but it was a ruse as he reversed his attack at the last minute. Catching the surprised Danite off guard, he whipped his blade past the soldier's defense and parted the flesh at his throat. Without stopping, he unleashed a display of swordsmanship that few had ever seen. Blocking another Danite's blade, he settled into a smooth dance as he fought two of the skilled men.

Bear'lon and Vorlarin had engaged the Danites on the other flank and by the time their blades met the enemy, two more Danites had run from the river to meet them. One took an arrow in the back of the thigh and went down into the water.

The other warrior came at Vorlarin's exposed flank as he desperately defended against a hulking Danite swinging a broad sword as if it were a mere stick. Vorlarin defended the attacks expertly, using his speed and skill to lessen the impact of the impressive strikes, the clashing steel sounding like a blacksmith hammering his metal. But when the other Danite's sword flashed towards his flank, he knew he was in trouble. He frantically whipped his sword across his body, diverting the Danite's attack, but the other muscle-bound soldier snapped his foot out and caught Vorlarin in the chest. He saw it coming and tried to spin away from it, but just wasn't fast enough. He grunted in pain as the kick snapped a rib. Stumbling backwards, his foot slipped on the wet rocks and he fell to one knee. He managed to block the other Danite's sword, reversing the parry and trying to catch the big Danite's blade as it came crashing towards him. The broad sword struck his own blade so hard that it pushed it down, the thick blade of the Danite's heavy sword striking Vorlarin in the side of the head, cutting his ear off and slicing deeply into the base of his neck. Roaring in pain and desperation, Vorlarin used his strong legs to launch himself up towards the surprised warrior, releasing his pinned sword in the process while drawing his hunting knife at his side. As he struck the huge man it felt like he had hit a stone wall. But the warrior was so taken aback by the attack that his footing was off, and he stumbled backwards, Vorlarin following his body to the rocks. By the time they struck the river rocks, Vorlarin had already driven his blade into the gap between his armor at his waist. His own blood gushed from the wound at his neck and as soon as they hit the ground, he felt a sharp pain in his back as the other Danite lanced him with his blade. With one last push of strength, Vorlarin stabbed the man below him again, ripping his blade across his belly. His vision blurred as he fell to the side, coughing as his lungs filled with blood. Lying on his back he looked up at the bright sun and smiled, knowing he had mortally wounded the huge Danite. He coughed again, tasting the blood that spilled from his mouth, the sounds of the battle around him slowly fading as he began to lose consciousness. The little pain he now felt dissipated quickly as the other Danite plunged his sword into his flesh a second time, the sharp steel cleaving his heart.

Carthen screamed in rage when he saw Vorlarin go down, his eyes quickly returning to his task. He faced three Danites and even their confidence and skill seemed to falter under the killing rage in the swordsman's eyes. Silver flashed in the sun as his blade cut, slashed, and blocked, his body in constant motion. One Danite stumbled back as blood gushed from a deep cut on his thigh. Another, thinking Carthen had overcommitted that attack, lunged forward with great speed, hoping to skewer him like a hunted boar. But Carthen spun like a top as the man's blade whistled by, all the while his own sword flowed with his movement, catching the man in his exposed shoulder, wounding him so bad that he dropped his sword grunting in pain. But the pain didn't last long as Carthen's sword reversed direction, the razor-sharp edge parting his throat like a sack of grain. The man's eye's widened as he futilely tried to stop the flow of blood. He fell backwards, crawled a few feet, and dropped face first into the edge of the shallow water. The pristine clear water turned red with his blood.

Bear'lon had killed his first Danite after Vorlarin had fallen. Growling like a rabid gar, he attacked the man who had killed Vorlarin. They exchanged blow after blow, but in the end even the skilled Danite couldn't keep pace with the power of Bear'lon's attacks. Finally, his axe smashed through a weak defense, nearly cutting his arm off. A few slashes later and the man was down, blood dripping from Bear'lon's axe.

Cos had already killed one Danite, but he had suffered a shallow cut across his forearm while fighting another. The man was good, his sword moving nearly as fast as Cos's axes. They fought across the smooth rocks as Bos, who was fighting off his right shoulder, blocked a downward chop from another Danite no more than a few paces away. Shoving the blade aside, Bos kicked out with his foot hoping to catch the man in the hip and knock him off balance. But the man was also skilled, as to be expected, and he saw the attack coming, jumping back at the last minute. But he never stopped, reversing direction like a leaping cat he sprang forward with his sword leading the way. His speed nearly cost Bos his life as the big warrior was pressing the attack. Bos tried to turn away from the attack, but the blade caught him on his pauldron, the sharp edge skimming across it before dropping and inflicting a shallow cut on his upper arm. Enraged, Bos released his axe and snapped his fist out with incredible power, striking the equally surprised warrior in the nose. Blood splattered into the air as his nose crushed under the impact. Stumbling back, Bos pressed the attack with a downward chop of his axe. The heavy blade struck the man where his shoulder met his neck, the cut so deep that it cleaved his ribs and sliced his heart. The man dropped like a sack of rocks, Bos's axe falling with him as the blade was wedged tight in the gruesome wound.

Lykin and Arim were now emerging from their hiding spots, their bows held high as they continued their attacks, all the while maneuvering to get better angles on the surviving men in the water. Lykin's arm flashed with incredible speed, releasing arrows as he moved with steady precision to his comrade's flank.

Arim followed, his hand speed not as great but his skills impressive, nonetheless. Reaching back, he nocked his last arrow and released it. The shaft struck one man in the chest, the close range enough to drive the steel tip through the Danite's gloss black armor. But their armor was so strong that the tip barely cut into the man's flesh. The warrior's eyes glared with rage and seeing that Arim had no more arrows ran at him in eerie silence. Arim dropped his bow at the water's edge and drew his blade. He saw that besides one other man, the warrior charging him was the last one standing in the water. In his peripheral vision he knew there was still fighting going on around him, but he had little time to ponder that as the man was nearly upon him. Suddenly the warrior jerked to the side, an arrow jutting from the side of his neck. He fell at the water's edge and didn't move.

Lykin was next to him in a flash. His arm was already up, his last arrow nocked. Standing in the water no more than ten paces away was the last man, an older warrior, the edges of his black hair tipped with gray. He stood at the ready with his long sword held low. Everything about him exuded confidence. Lykin released the shaft and with lightning speed the man's blade flashed across his body. The pinging sound of the steel meeting the shaft seemed to echo in the clearing and Lykin's eyes widened in surprise at the mean's speed. He too dropped his bow and drew his blade.

"No!" Carthen growled. "Do not attack him, he will kill you," he added as he stood calmly on the other side of the river. Danite bodies lay sprawled in death around him. Vorlarin's body was clearly visible amongst the dead. The old warrior looked every bit the deadly swordsman. He was covered in his enemy's blood and his eyes boiled with adrenaline. By this time Cos and Bob had killed their men, coming away with a few shallow cuts. They joined Arim and Lykin at the river's edge, their chests heaving up and down from the exertion of the intense battle.

The Danite in the water turned sideways so he could see Carthen. His eyes looked at him for a few moments before widening in recognition. "It can't be," he whispered.

"Captain Carvathian, it's been a long time," Carthen said. Bear'lon stepped away from his last kill to stand next to Carthen.

"It has at that," the warrior commented. "I was at your funeral. We thought you had died years ago."

Carthen shrugged. "That was the point."

The Danite looked around. Even though he was surrounded and the last Danite standing, he seemed unconcerned by his predicament. "So, what happens now?" he asked calmly.

"You die," Carthen replied.

The man shrugged. "I assumed. But by whose hands? Would any of these pups put up a fight?" he sneered.

Bear'lon stepped forward but Carthen put a restraining hand on his shoulder. "No, he is beyond you." Bear'lon's eyes narrowed but he took head, halting his advance. "Come," Carthen suggested as he used his bloody blade to indicate the near shore, "get out of the water. Let us fight on level ground."

The edge of the man's lips rose in a subtle smile as he made his way through the shallow current to stand at the rivers edge five paces from Carthen. Sensing the confrontation, Bear'lon stepped away from the swordsman. Lykin and the others waded across the shallow crossing to stand next to Bear'lon.

Carvathian swung his sword from side to side, readying himself. "I hope I survive," he mused. "It would be wonderful to see Lord Rane's face when I tell him that the famous Terwyn Gar is alive."

Arim's eyes widened and he looked at Lykin. The archer looked at him and shrugged. Clearly, he already knew Carthen's true identity. Bear'lon showed no sign of surprise. His eyes bore into the Danite captain with undisguised hate.

"I too would like to see his expression," Carthen admitted. "But you will die, and Lord Rane will remain in the dark about my identity." He said it with a casual confidence that was unnerving.

Carvathian shrugged. "Perhaps. But I must admit, it will be a glorious death, to die by the blade of Terwyn Gar. A warrior can only dream of such a death."

"I have more dreams than death in battle."

"Clearly so," the captain acknowledged. "Perhaps I will land a lucky blow. Maybe you will slip on the wet rocks. There are many uncertainties in battle. You know this more than any of us. But it matters little. I will die today. Even if I were to win, these men would cut me down soon after." He sighed and raised his blade. "You ready?"

Carthen lifted his blade and nodded. Then he charged.

They both shot towards each with great speed, their steel kissing and ringing loudly as they danced across the rocks. Attacks and parries went on for twenty tense heartbeats, their silver blades a blur as each sought the flesh of the other.

Arim was transfixed with their speed. He had seen Carthen fight before, but just glimpses. This was something completely different. He was watching a dazzling display of swordsmanship from perhaps two of the finest warriors he would likely ever see.

Suddenly Carvathian grunted and leaped back, blood dripping from a shallow cut on his forearm. Arim didn't even see the attack. But Carthen was relentless, leaping forward and keeping the Danite Captain in a defensive retreat. They went on like that for another hundred heartbeats, their bodies never stopping as they turned, ducked, and pivoted. Several times Arim thought that the Danite had the old man, but every time he evaded the attack and launched one of his own.

And then a blink later it was over.

Carvathian, likely hoping to end the fight with a desperation move, lunged forward, his long arms delivering a lightning fast jab. Somehow, the old man had swayed to the side, the Danite's sword slicing a narrow line across Carthen's arm. But it mattered not as Carthen's blade flashed up and sliced deeply into his exposed armpit. Not stopping, Carthen reversed his blade and brought it down on the man's neck as he stumbled by, severing his head in one clean stroke.

Carthen wiped the blood from his blade using the dead Danite's cloak. He then stood and moved before the group, looking at all the men before holding his gaze on Arim and Bos. "My name is Carthen," he said calmly, although his eyes revealed still a raging hurricane of emotion. It was as if the old man had been holding the man known as Terwyn Gar back, beneath the surface of his fake persona, and now, amongst the carnage and death, the deadly swordsman's real identity was trying to resurface. "You will say nothing of my true identity. Am I understood?"

"Yes," Arim replied quickly.

"Yes, sir," Bos added.

Carthen pursed his lips and nodded. "Let us bury Vorlarin and see to our wounds." The old man turned and made his way to their fallen comrade. Bear'lon and Lykin joined him. Cos looked at the two men, his stern eyes driving home Carthen's order before he walked away.

Arim looked at Bos, and for the first time he was speechless.

FIVE

Kith slowly woke, the sounds of water crashing on rocks nudging him from his deep sleep. Fluttering open, his hazy eyes took in the morning light, a strong cooling wind blowing around him. He was lying nearly naked except for thin cotton leggings, on a stone ledge, a thick wool blanket under him, his head resting on a soft pillow.

"How do you feel?"

Kith lifted his torso off the blanket and saw the Eskeli sitting cross legged behind him. The stone ledge they were on looked out to the turbulent sea, the dark green water crashing against the rocks twenty paces below. There was no rain, but the sky was filled with dark pregnant clouds. Likely it would come soon.

Kith analyzed his body. The last thing he remembered was agony, an immense amount of pain. But now it was gone. "I feel warm...really warm."

"It's a side effect of the energy that now flows through you. That is why we put you on the ledge, in the wind, to cool your body. You will get used to it. Your body temperature will always be higher, enabling you to survive in much colder weather than most."

Kith sat up and faced the Eskeli, sitting cross legged as well. "So it worked?"

The Eskeli nodded. "It did. You have surpassed my expectations Kith Caren."

"Well, I'm glad I'm not dead," Kith pointed out.

"Kith, the Alltree felt your strength and rewarded you with power I have not seen in any I've previously trained."

"Did I get a sword?" Kith knew that not all candidates survived the process, let alone were gifted with a sword or armor. At first, he was simply hoping to survive. But the hope of being gifted a blade was always there.

"Yes, and a spear and armor."

105

Kith's eyes lifted at that. "You're serious?" Kith knew that was a stupid question as the Eskeli did not joke, ever. "Where are they?"

"Inside. You shall hold them soon. But first, dig deeper, how do you feel?"

Kith took a deep breath and closed his eyes. He felt the power immediately. Warm energy was humming in his hands and feet, the power pulsing through his body in smooth rhythmic beats. Then he realized with surprise that the rhythm matched that of his heart. He also felt hot, really hot, like his skin had been burned under the sun days before. Kith figured the sensation would fade, or at least he would get used to it. There were epicenters of warmth and power in his hands and feet. Opening his eyes, he held his hands before him. He could not see the energy, but he knew it was there, beneath the surface of his skin. There was something else, something he could not put his finger on, like a connection to the world around him. His senses seemed heightened. There were so many smells and sounds. He was having a tough time processing it all.

The Eskeli saw the look on his face. "You are now connected to your world in a way others will never feel. The energy of the stones binds you to the world around you. You will hear, smell, and feel so much more. The energy pulsing inside you is not independent of the energy around us. It is connected to everything; thus you are as well. You are not wearing your armor, but when you do you will feel the binding of the Catalyst Stone. It will help you focus what you are feeling now."

"Tell me about this Catalyst Stone."

"The stone is not natural like the field stones. It was made by the Dar-dan to better harness the energy of the stones. It directs the energy flowing from the stones throughout your body."

"I don't understand."

"If you jump off a high wall, the Catalyst Stone sends energy to your legs to help you brace for the impact."

"How does it do this?" Kith queried, already excited by the prospect.

"The stone is linked to you. It responds to your thoughts."

Kith was having a challenging time processing such a thing. "So if I'm not wearing my armor, I am not as strong?"

"You still have the power of the stones flowing through you. You will always be stronger and faster, but it is the Catalyst Stone that allows you to direct the energy where it's needed most. You will always be more dangerous wearing your Catalyst Stone. It is why few Ar'kan, at least the ones gifted with it, ever take off their armor. It is also how the Ar'kan travel through the gates."

"It is the Catalyst Stone that opens the gates?"

The Eskeli nodded. "Yes. I shall teach you the words necessary to activate the gates, but it is the Catalyst Stone that connects you to them. Without the Catalyst Stone in an Ar'kan's possession, the gates will not work."

"Then how is Lord Rane opening the gates?"

"I can only assume that he has Bandlor's Catalyst Stone, the fallen Ar'kan warrior he dug up years before."

"But he is not Ar'kan."

The Eskeli paused. "I've been thinking a lot about this and have made an educated prediction. I believe that Lord Rane is a Stone Blood, like you."

"Really? What are the odds of that?"

"There are likely very few left. But it makes some sense. By all accounts there is no Drann more powerful. His natural connection to the E'lear would make him quite formidable. It is the only logical answer."

Kith's body was restless, the energy flowing through his body eager to be used. Kith rose smoothly, his body actually lifting two paces in the air. He landed with a shocked expression.

"You will have to get used to your new strength," the Eskeli responded.

"I see that," Kith responded, his surprised expression turning to a smile. "I am eager to begin the next step of my training."

The Eskeli stood. "Then let us start."

***

Lathronin readjusted the small deer over his shoulders as he walked across the dark sand to the boat that he had dragged ashore the day before. He had tired of hunting the islands, the game not the best table fare in his opinion. He craved the rich meat of the forest deer, and luckily, he had brought one down a few hours earlier. But the reality was he was getting bored on the island. Kith had woken from the Change three weeks ago and had been training with the Eskeli ever since. Lathronin had stepped into the ring a few times but learned quickly that even he could not keep pace with Kith. He was now simply to fast. The Eskeli's speed and strength allowed him to spar with Kith, but even he could not keep pace for long. So, to occupy his days, Lathronin had decided to venture to the mainland. He was glad he did, the deer, although small, would be a nice supplement to their meal this evening.

Lathronin set the deer carcass into the boat, along with his pack and bow. Grabbing the rope on the bow he began to pull the boat across the sand to the waters edge. The work was difficult and he was already tired from the overnight hunt. He had a few hours of rowing and he wanted to make sure to reach the islands before dark. Putting his head down, he readjusted his grip on the rope and pulled harder.

The young priest had no idea that he was being watched. A dirty hand reached out and pushed aside the tree branches, giving the man a better view. The hooded observer watched the gray robed hunter drag the boat to the water's edge. The man was a hunter himself, his woodland clothing making him nearly invisible along the forest edge.

"What do we have here," the man whispered. Besides selling the hides and meat from the game he killed, the hunter supplemented his income by scouting for Lord Rane's garrison in Lampure. Not everything he saw was sellable information for Lord Rane, but the hunter knew that a gray robed man dragging a strange boat into the water adjacent to Seebras, the ancient city of the Dar-dan, would likely be something they would want to know. They would pay good coin for such information. The man smiled, his yellow teeth barely noticeable in the shadows of his cowl as he backed away from the coastline.

***

Kith faced the Eskeli. He wore his armor and carried his sword at his hip, his long spear held casually in his right hand. He had been practicing with the weapons for many days and was still amazed by them. They were light, razor sharp, and unmarred despite weeks of constant use. The armor looked like gray steel, but it was nothing like typical plate. It was light and slightly warm to the touch. It did not hamper his movement like normal armor did. When he wore it, the world seemed to come alive, the energy flowing through it connected directly to the Catalyst Stone. He could feel the stone move power throughout his body depending on where he needed it the most. He could execute strength moves that would normally be impossible, the stone directing enough power to various parts of his body enabling him to do feats impossible for even an elite swordsman. His blocks and attacks were equally enhanced by the stone.

The Eskeli stepped closer, a blade in one hand and a whip made of what looked like links of silver in the other. "One thing you must learn is how to face an opponent who can wield the power of the E'lear. A Drann priest can bring the power to bear in many forms, but once you learn to cut through that power, you will be able to defend against it regardless of the form they choose."

Kith nodded to the whip. "What is that?" Although he knew it had something to do with his training.

"I cannot wield the E'lear, and we have no Drann here to help you with this part of the training," he said as he held up the end of the whip. "One of the more common Drann attacks is an energy whip. They can also throw super-heated balls of energy that will pass through steel, bone, and flesh as if they were nothing more than warm butter. Your weapons and armor will negate that energy, but if your flesh is struck, the attacks will harm or kill you just as anyone else."

"So I need to..." But Kith never finished his words as the Eskeli leaped forward, the whip flashing back and forward so fast that he barely had time to bring his spear to bare. The whip struck his spear, wrapping around the shaft and flashing towards Kith's face. Kith released the spear with one hand and dropped low, spinning on one heel and coming up near the Eskeli's exposed flank. It was a move he never would've been able to accomplish before the Change. The whip just missed his face and Kith pulled his spear away, the whip retracting as the Eskeli jumped back, turning to face Kith once again.

"Your armor, when struck with an E'lear attack, will dissipate the energy, rendering it harmless. That is an advantage as the Drann priests alive today likely know very little of what an Ar'kan warrior can do." The Eskeli attacked again, his sword flashing in a deadly arc as his other hand brought the whip back.

Kith leapt back from the blade, his eyes already following the arc of the whip. Barely avoiding the tip of the sword, he jabbed his spear forward, purposefully missing the Eskeli's wrist that held the whip. Pivoting, Kith snapped the spear sideways and struck the creature's arm with the flat of the blade. The silver whip was knocked off course and its deadly metallic end missed Kith by a half a pace. Without stopping, Kith lunged forward, the blunt end of the spear shooting between the Eskeli's legs. He turned and tried to trap the creature's legs between the spear shaft, pushing forward with the hopes of tripping him. The move was impossibly fast and well executed and the Eskeli was not able to retract his legs in time.

As the creature fell, Kith realized his error. He was so focused on the move and its results, that he failed to pay attention to the whip. As the Eskeli was falling, he snapped his hand out and forward, the silver whip flashing forward again with lightening speed. Kith saw it at the last moment. But he could not entirely avoid the attack. Leaning back and away, he tried to turn from the weapon, but the end caught him in the side of the face. The blunted steel stung as it left a raised red welt. He silently admonished himself as he stepped back, the Eskeli easily rising to his feet.

"If that had been a Drann whip, you would likely be dead."

"I am not used to facing such a weapon," Kith realized.

The Eskeli nodded. "This is why we train. Ready?"

Kith nodded and the Eskeli attacked again.

After practicing most of the day, the Eskeli led Kith to explore the ruins of the ancient city. The creature continued to teach him various Dar-danian words he may need to know, telling him stories of the ancient race as he guided him through the desolate city. It was clear to Kith that the Eskeli had a destination in mind, noticing he was leading him closer to the Alltree. He knew there were a few rooms that branched off that main chamber and Kith was hoping he was being led there. He was intrigued to learn more of the Dar-danian secrets.

He voiced his interest when they descended the steps to the tree. "Where are you leading me?" he asked.

"I am showing you the armory," the Eskeli replied casually, although the creature's voice always sounded casual.

Kith was excited, but he said nothing more as the creature led him past the Alltree to a large black double door. It was still standing, as if it had been built yesterday. Kith figured the door was not made of wood, as all the wooden doors were now nothing more than dust.

The Eskeli saw Kith touch the door and seemed to read his mind. "The door is not wood but made from a similar material as your armor, which has enabled it to withstand the tests of time."

They entered the large room and blue glowing lights lit up the interior. Kith was amazed at what he saw. All along the walls were piles of weapons scattered about. He saw spears, bows, arrows, swords, and even various pieces of armor that seemed to be made from the same material as his own. There were also shelves cut into the stone wall that housed other objects that Kith could not quite see in the shadows.

"What happened here?" Kith asked, looking around at the weapons. They were all made of the same material as his own weapons, although the markings on them were different.

"They were once all organized on racks, but unlike the door, they were built of wood. They no longer exist, but the weapons, like the door, still do."

"Are these weapons like mine?" Kith pondered as he picked up a spear. It was light and felt perfectly balanced.

"They are not, although the material is the same. Your weapons are linked to you specifically, and they are able to draw upon the E'lear flowing through your body," the Eskeli explained. "These weapons were made for those not strong enough to create their own weapons during the Change. They are so strong they never need to be sharpened. Besides your own, they are the best weapons in the Five Lands."

Kith inspected a few more weapons before his eyes were drawn to a nearby stone shelf carved into the wall. On it were three round metal objects, evenly spaced, and each as big around as an infant's head.

He picked one up and looked at it more closely. He was just about to ask the Eskeli a question when the creature intervened. "You should not touch that," he said, his voice more of an order than a warning. "It is dangerous."

Kith carefully set it back on the shelf as the Eskeli joined him. "What is it?"

"It is a very powerful device," the Eskeli warned. "When the top is turned it activates and releases a massive amount of energy."

"How does it work?" Kith was mesmerized by such a concept.

"I do not know," the creature said. "They are the same devices the Drann used to bring down the mountain on the gate so long ago. All I know is that there is a strange configuration of field stones inside. They collect and store a very large amount of power that is somehow kept in transition through a power loop. When the top is twisted, the loop is disrupted, and the power is released."

"Incredible," Kith whispered.

"It is," the Eskeli agreed. "Come, I have more to show you."

Kith looked at the strange objects one more time before he turned his attention to the Eskeli. There was still so much to inspect.

***

Theron sat opposite Princess Morwin. The ale house was full and boisterous, the evening crowd drinking and getting excited for the musical entertainment. It was an open session, so anyone could get up and play. The crowd was known to be ruthless judges however, their approval or disdain clearly noted by applause or lack thereof. It was not uncommon for the unruly patrons to throw food at players who, by their account, were not worthy of the stage.

Princess Morwin wore a soft spun blue cotton dress cinched tight around her small waist with a brown belt. A yellow shawl draped over her shoulders. The clothes were clean and well made, and she could've fit in with any common lady of the city who put on her best clothes for the night. Theron wore black leggings and a light gray tunic, his black sword belt and dark gray cloak finishing off his evening attire. Like the princess, his clothes were clean and well-made. He looked every bit the dashing swashbuckler.

"So," Morwin said as she leaned closer across the table, "are you excited to be going to Dral? Father said his army will leave in less than a month."

Theron frowned. Dral was the home of the Kelic. It was a frozen land filled with danger and mystery. No Hiskani had set foot on the continent for thousands of years, ever since the Dar-dan had left and shut down the gates. Theron was unsure why Rane wanted to conquer that land. It seemed to him that it would have nothing of value to make the cost worthwhile. "Not really. I do not see the purpose. What could a frozen land possibly have of value."

This time it was Morwin's turn to frown. "Father needs nothing more than conquest and power as a reason. He is a ruthless man."

"Have you ever been close to him?" Theron ventured. He had been feeling her out ever since they met, trying to decipher if she hated her father enough to turn against him. She could be a valuable ally for the Order.

"I rarely saw him when I was younger." She shrugged her shoulders in thought. "I did not have much of an opportunity to develop a relationship. As I grew older, I saw what a despicable man he was. Sometimes I think the Order should win. Urotha would be better for it." Theron raised his eyebrows at that, trying to play the role of a loyal offended subject. Morwin blushed some, but her expression turned hard. "I mean it. My family has no redeeming value."

Theron leaned back in his chair. "You seem to counter that very argument."

She blushed again, this time much deeper. "Thank you."

"The classic nature versus nurture argument."

Morwin laughed. "There was no nurturing going on in my family."

Theron was just about to respond when the crowd started to hoot and holler. They were sitting close to the stage, one of the perks of being a Danite Captain, and they saw a young man step onto the stage holding a three-stringed instrument called a bandalore. Clearly the crowd knew who he was and were eager to hear him play. Theron smiled as Morwin turned her chair to better view the stage. She seemed excited to hear the music and Theron was enjoying her company, especially now that the Princess clearly sympathized with the Order. There was some hope in turning her, and for Theron, that made his heart skip a beat. Perhaps he would be able to spend more time with her after all.

The young man turned out to be an incredible musician, the best of the first four that took the stage. His tune was one of his own and neither Theron or Princess Morwin had ever heard it. It started off slow and melodic, and built up speed and power, his hands a blur as they danced over the strings. Theron felt moved by the performance and by the looks of it, Morwin was equally impacted. The other three that followed were very talented, but after the first performance, they left them wanting more.

There was a break in the entertainment and Theron ordered an ale for himself and a glass of wine for Morwin. It was her second glass, but she seemed well in control. Theron thought that it might be an appropriate time to probe her further about her feelings regarding the Order.

"I am still thinking of what you said about the Order," Theron began.

"Oh," she said, leaning closer. She was smiling and Theron could not tell if she was toying with him.

"What would your father say if he heard you speak in such high regard about the rebels?"

"I'm sure he would think little of it," she responded. "He does not think highly of me, or my abilities. He would likely think my words nothing more than whining from an insolent child." She sipped from her wine and leaned in even closer, her eyes twinkling. "Why so interested in the Order?" She smiled. "Are you a spy Captain Falconan?"

Theron returned her smile with one of his own, leaning closer to her. She was obviously just teasing with him, but he thought he might push it some. They were so close that he could smell her hair, the hint of roses and jasmine stimulating his senses. "What if I said that I was."

She turned her head and raised her eyebrows but did not withdraw from his closeness. "I would say that my Father would be quite upset."

Theron nodded his head. "I suspect that would be the case."

Then she leaned back, her expression changing to curiosity. "Are you serious?"

"I am. I have always been. I was hoping that you would be interested in joining us." Theron was a bit nervous voicing those words, but there was something about her that pressed him to do so. She seemed so sincere about her feelings, and although it was a risk, Theron felt confident that even if she was not interested in joining, that she would at least keep his secret safe. After all, he had saved her life, and was clearly was not a fan of her father.

It took a while for her to respond. "What is your mission for the Order?" she asked, her voice quiet as she digested his words.

"I am a spy. I send valuable information to the Order."

"Then why did you kill the men when they attacked me?"

Theron reached his hand out and placed it on hers. "I did not want to see you hurt. I was not aware of the attack and although I knew little about you, I did not believe that your political sentiment mirrored your fathers. And based on what I've heard you say, I was correct in that assumption."

She slowly moved her hand out from under his, her expression thoughtful as she leaned back in her chair. "And what would you have me do for the Order?"

"Much the same," Theron added. "We need information. Your knowledge and connection to your father would be extremely helpful to our cause."

"And to what purpose?"

"We will overthrow your father and free Urotha from his Tyranny. Don't you want to be a part of that?"

"And you could protect me from suffering his fate?"

"Only if you join us. If not, your fate may mirror your fathers, although I will do all I can to make sure that does not happen, even if you say no to my offer."

"You trust me with this knowledge?"

"I do. I have a feeling about you."

Morwin sighed and drank the rest of her wine. "You have given me much to think about, Theron Falconan." She smiled and stood up. "I need to use the lady's room. Let us speak more of this when I return."

Theron stood and smiled. "Of course. Would you like some more wine?"

"I would. Difficult decisions should always be made over wine," she added with a wide smile. She walked by him and her body brushed against his, her hand gently touching his arm as she strode by.

Theron felt relieved. She had not said yes, but just the fact that she was joking eased his worry. If anything, he felt more secure than ever that she at least would not divulge his secret.

Theron drank from his cup, enjoying the bitter ale. The crowd was excited and talking loudly, clearly eager for the next performances. Suddenly Theron noticed a few of the patrons close to him look at him sidelong, the busy clatter of conversation suddenly dying down. It was then he felt the touch of cold steel on his neck. A few blinks later and three Danites stepped from around the table to stand before him.

Theron's heart sank. The man in the front was First Spear Tolbin, a veteran officer who had been in the core for a very long time. Theron did not know him well but knew he was loyal to a fault. The cold steel resting on his neck cut into his resolve and he began to panic, although he tried his best to not show it. The two Danites flanking Tolbin held loaded crossbows aimed at him, and he was sure there were more than just the lone swordsman behind him.

Tolbin's jaw flexed as his tense eyes bore into Theron. "I thought it a waste of time to come here tonight, but Lord Rane was adamant." The old warrior shook his head in disgust. "You have betrayed the Core."

Theron was just about to speak when Princess Morwin stepped from around the table, her playful persona all but gone, replaced by a wry smirk, her sparkling eyes hard and impassive. The change was startling. "Captain Falconan, did you really think I would betray my family?" My father has been suspicious of you for a long time. Our meeting at the party that night was not happenstance."

"You set me up," he whispered, his eyes looking around for a possible escape.

"It wasn't so difficult. Although," she added, "you threw us for a twist when you killed those men protecting me."

"A decision I now regret."

First Spear Tolbin saw his hand inch towards his blade. "Don't. You will be killed in seconds."

Theron shrugged. "Better than being tortured."

Tolbin shrugged. "One is so finite. The other, well, you never know what will happen. Now get up," he ordered. "Lord Rane will want to see you."

Theron looked around and saw that he had little choice. He could try to bring his blade to bear but knew he would be riddled with crossbow bolts before his blade left its scabbard. The tap room patrons were deathly silent, not wanting to get involved with Danite business. Theron stood slowly. "Lead the way." He tried to sound confident, but inside his heart was pounding. He was as good as dead. Worse actually, they would surely torture him for all that he knew about the Order.

The sword behind him nudged him forward and Theron made his way towards the exit. They left through the main door, everyone in the bar watching with wide eyes, their mouths shut in silence. Outside it was dark and they were greeted by five more Danites, each warrior carrying a torch. Their hard eyes narrowed as they saw Theron, but they quickly averted their gaze to their surroundings as Theron and the others stepped in behind them.

"Wait!" Tolbin said. Theron stopped and turned, seeing for the first time the men behind the Danite officer. The soldier that carried the sword kept the tip near him as Tolbin stepped before him. There were two others with loaded crossbows, the silver tips aimed at his chest. That made five crossbowmen in total. Princess Morwin stood casually behind them, her sardonic expression making Theron's blood boil. Tolbin held out his hand. "Your sword."

It was then and there that Theron decided his next move. He knew he was going to die. The question was, would he perish under a torturer's bloody tools, or die holding his own sword in his hand. His decision made, he slowly reached for his blade, his leather boots adjusting subtly, his weight shifting to the balls of his feet as he readied himself to die. He vowed he would take a few of them with him in the process.

Theron's hand tightened around his sword hilt, and just when he was going to draw it and attack, the two crossbowmen before him jerked as arrows slammed into their throats. One man pitched sideways and fell to the ground. The other's hand jerked on the trigger as he stumbled to the side, his bolt slamming into Tolbin's shoulder causing the warrior to grunt and spin away.

The scene erupted in chaos and Theron had no time to see what was happening, the Danite warrior near him whipping his sword towards Theron's hip. Theron's blade was halfway from its scabbard and he would not be able to bring it to bear in time. So he shot forward inside the man's reach and struck him in the face with his elbow, lessoning the impact of the warrior's blade as the sharp steel sliced a shallow cut across his thigh. Stunned, the man fell back, and Theron whipped his blade free, the silver steel arcing across his throat. Blood sprayed from the mortal wound as the man fell to the ground, his lifeblood drenching the dirt around him.

Theron whipped around and saw Tolbin struggle to his feet. Theron's gaze flitted to Morwin's and he nearly smiled when he saw her expression, her arrogance now replaced with fear. Suddenly an arrow struck her in the side and she gasped, falling to the ground. Tolbin rose and moved to attack, but he too took an arrow in the chest, the close-range of it piercing his armor. He was dead before he hit the ground.

It was then that a number of cloaked men erupted from the shadows and converged on the Danites. The crossbowmen had already been taken out by arrows, and the five remaining men formed a line of steel. There were at least ten men in dark cloaks and after a brutal onslaught, the remainder of the Danite's had been cut down by their superior numbers. Four of the cloaked men were killed, and one exceptionally skilled Danite swordsman was skewering a fifth while he himself was riddled with arrows from the five bowman who had now emerged from the shadows of the alleys north and south of them.

A dark-haired man holding a short sword ran to Theron's side. "We must go! And now!"

Theron recognized the man as the spy he had met after the attack on Rane's family.

"Wait!" he said as the man turned to leave. Theron ran to Princess Morwin who was trying to crawl away, the arrow in her side leaving a trail of blood in the dirt. Theron knelt and flipped her over.

Blood dripped from her mouth, but her eyes were defiant. "You will never win," she spat.

"Perhaps," he hissed. "Too bad you won't live long enough to see." And with that, he rammed the tip of his blade into her chest. Her eyes widened in surprise, blood erupting from her mouth. She blinked once, and fell still.

The spy grabbed Theron by the cloak. "Let's go!"

Theron rose quickly, his wrathful expression unnerving. "Lead the way," he growled.

They ran frantically through a winding series of alleys and dark roads, Theron following as the dark cloaked men led. He had no idea where they were going or how they would get out of the city. The alarm would be called in moments, and then the city would be locked down. All gates and exits would be closed. But he had to believe that the men of the Order would have a plan.

Suddenly the men in front turned into a narrow alley and they all bottlenecked near an old wood door. The man Theron recognized had it open in a blink and was guiding half of the men into the dark opening. The leader said a few words to the others and they departed back the way they had come, disappearing into the shadows like wraiths.

Theron was the last one. "Where are we going!? The alarm will sound soon!"

"Under the wall!" Suddenly a loud horn blew, followed by a series of short notes.

"That's the alarm," Theron cried.

"I know! Now go!" he urged, pushing Theron through the door.

Once inside they were cast in lantern light. It was a small room and the five remaining men, including Theron, were crammed in tight. There looked to be three lanterns amongst the men and the room was empty except for layers of dust and old straw.

"Follow me," the man said, grabbing a lantern from one of the men. Theron followed as did the others.

The spy led them through an opening and down an old stone hall, the ceiling barely tall enough for the men to stand. Fifteen paces later they entered another room, this one filled with old wood barrels. The spy didn't have to say anything as three of the men, guided by the lantern light, moved a series of barrels aside, revealing a floor covered in more dust and straw.

Kicking the straw aside, they uncovered a trap door, the wood new, the door well-built and in stark contrast with the dilapidated building around them. They opened the door and with no hesitation one man with a lantern climbed down the ladder. Two men quickly followed leaving Theron, the leader, and a third man behind.

The man nodded at Theron. "Go, I'll follow."

Theron didn't hesitate and quickly descended into the darkness. The spy was right behind him and the man brushed past him in haste. "Follow me." Theron reasoned the third man stayed behind to cover the trap door and remove any sign of their escape.

They made their way through a narrow tunnel, the ceiling just tall enough for them to walk without hitting their heads. The tunnel was supported by wood rafters and supports, and although it looked to be hastily made, it seemed sturdy enough. Theron reasoned they walked the distance an arrow could travel before they came to the end, where another ladder lead to the surface. The men before him had already climbed from the tunnel and Theron and the spy wasted no time in joining them. The ladder took them through another wood door, but this one was much more confining. It was smaller, barely large enough for Theron to pull himself through, and once at the surface, Theron smelt dirt and the fresh smell of the forest. He was kneeling amongst thick shrubs and brush, a soft lantern light ten paces away guiding him. He crawled through the dense brush until he entered a small clearing in a copse of trees, the rest of the men silently waiting for them. There was only one lantern still lit offering just enough light to guide Theron and the other spy to the clearing. Clearly, they were being cautious. They might be outside the city, but they were not safe. They could easily be spotted by guards along the city wall.

The leader joined Theron as they all huddled close. Even in the dim light Theron could see that the man was angry. "What you did was reckless," he whispered.

Theron narrowed his eyes. He was not used to anyone talking to him like that. "I was trying to turn her," he replied, his voice low. "Her addition to the Order would've been invaluable."

The man shook his head in frustration. "She played you. We should've killed her that night at the party. Lucky for you I saw the danger and followed you this night."

"In hindsight, you are correct. But it was worth the risk."

"Tell that to the men that died in saving you."

Theron clenched his jaw in anger. "I thank you, and your men," he added, glancing back at the others, "for saving me." Then he stepped closer to the man, his face no more than a handspan away. "But do not lecture me on loss and the dangers we face. I have been kissing Lord Rane's ass for the last six years. I have killed men for him. I have bled for him. I have lived in the den of that tyrant for over five years, all for the Order. I have sacrificed my own life for the cause, and I was prepared to do so tonight. I regret the loss of those men, but they knew the risks, just as I do. Now, we must leave. What's the plan?"

***

It was during the fourth week on the island when the Eskeli took Kith and Lathronin to Seebras's library, or what was left of it. The massive building was located west of the OrnThonin. It wasn't hard for Kith to imagine how stunning it would've been during its time of glory. But now it was empty, the huge cathedral-like building filled with debris, many of the windows broken, the glass scattered amongst the dirt and dust. It was midday and the sun's bright rays shone through the windows, the dust reflecting the light like smoke.

The Eskeli led them through an archway into a spacious room lined with stone shelves. He touched something near the door and sconces lit up immediately, casting a soft white light throughout the room. The stone shelves were empty except for a few that still held old tomes, their leather covers cracked like aged skin, the brittle pages beneath barely holding together, many turned to dust.

"Was this entire building filled with books?" Kith asked as they entered the smaller room, amazed at the main structures size.

"At one time, yes. The Dar-dan were collectors of knowledge. They had many books. But I am not here to show you the books," he added as he led them through another dark archway.

Again, he touched something near the archway and more lights came to life. This room was smaller, nearly empty except for what must have been the remains of tables and chairs. But now they were piles of dust. But Kith ignored the debris, his eyes pulled immediately to a painting on the far wall. It was expertly done, the soft light dancing off the faded colors.

They walked closer, following the Eskeli. Stopping before it, Kith was able to get a better picture of what is was. Even though large areas of the painting were faded, or damaged from moisture and time, Kith could clearly see that it was a representation of a great battle.

"It's incredible," Lathronin whispered.

"What are those things?" Kith asked, nodding towards a huge black creature, hundreds of smaller ones, each the size of a horse, behind the beast pouring from cracks in black stone.

"That is why I took you here. They are the Crawlers, black beasts who crave nothing but blood and death."

"And those are Drann and Ar'kan," Lathronin said, walking closer to the painting. Before the beasts were ten warriors, some wearing armor and carrying weapons, and others holding whips of fire and spheres of burning light.

"Yes. There was a great battle just before the gate in Skell. The men and women you see here defended the gate while others entered it to safety. But they all perished as they were trying to flee, and that huge creature took one in its mouth, the man's Catalyst Stone keeping the gate open just long enough for it and ten smaller ones to break through, appearing on the other side near Akari."

"The main gate?" Kith asked, remembering the Eskeli telling him that the gate in Akari was the hub to the system. It was where all other gates took you.

"Yes. Once there, they nearly killed everyone. Five more Ar'kan were killed, as well as six Drann."

"But they won in the end?" Lathronin asked, knowing the answer, posing the question out of sheer curiosity.

"Yes. Ten Drann used their power to drop the mountain on top of the gate while our best warrior, Bandlor, held off the remaining creatures. She was mortally wounded but managed to keep them near the gate so the Drann could work their magic. The creatures were killed, along with Bandlor, and all were buried with the gate under a mountain of rock."

"They look like lizards," Kith whispered, enthralled in the story.

"They are similar. They can run incredibly fast and scurry up a vertical wall. The only weak points on their body is their stomachs, which they keep protected close to the ground. Their bodies and long necks are armored with black scales and they have six legs, the front slightly longer than the rest. Even when they rear up on their back legs and attack with their longer arms, the under side exposed is similarly armored. Needless to say, they are hard to kill."

"How many are there?" Lathronin asked.

The Eskeli turned to look at them both. "Thousands, maybe more." And to drive his point home, he said, "you cannot let them break through the gate again."

"How would they get through without a Catalyst Stone?" Kith asked.

"We think the queen, although we are not sure if that is the proper term for the big one, is much more intelligent than a typical animal. There were some Dar-dan that believed the bigger one was not a queen at all, but a male. They were not able to learn much about the creatures before they decided to leave. Although they were not sure, the Dar-dan believed the queen, or perhaps the male, understood the power of the stone. They thought the creatures could feel it. The presence of a Catalyst Stone in Skell puts all the lands in peril. It was why they left. They would not risk the world for more field stones in Skell, and without the stones, there was no longer a reason to be here."

"So where did they go?" Lathronin asked.

"I do not know, although it is likely they went searching for another power source. The Dar-dan were afraid of the Crawlers and what they would do if they found the key to the gates. You must stop Rane before he opens the gate in Skell and puts Urotha in peril."

"I understand," Kith said.

"I do not think that you do. Skell is a wasteland. These creatures hibernate deep under the earth for hundreds, maybe thousands of years. During this time animal life grows again on the continent. When they wake, they ravage the land and kill anything living, only to go into hibernation once again. Over time, the land cannot bounce back from such destruction. The Crawlers want new land. If they get here, everyone will be killed."

"You talk as if they desire this death. Aren't they just animals?" Lathronin said.

"They are much more. The big ones lead the herd. We don't know how many of the large ones there are, or whether they are queens or just leaders. Unfortunately we know little about them. But we do know that their appetite for blood and death cannot be satiated. This Lord Rane will want the power of the Field Stones on Skell. But he does not know the dangers. You must stop him."

Kith nodded, the seriousness of the danger sitting heavy on his shoulders. "I will."

"And I," Lathronin added.

Together, they both stared up at the painting, dark thoughts of death and destruction flashing through their minds.

Finally, the Eskeli spoke again. "There is one more thing I wish to show you. Follow me."

The tall creature led them back through the library all the way to the lower chambers, home of the Alltree. No matter how many times he gazed upon the amazing structure he still felt a sense of awe, and now, his body filled with the flowing energy of the field stones, he felt something more akin to a deep emotional connection. He could not explain it, and he didn't try. The Eskeli led them from the tree to one of the walls of the huge room, the cave wall naturally rough. Looking more closely, Kith could see black roots from the Alltree embedded in the stone, the tendrils seemingly growing from the black rock.

The Eskeli stopped about ten paces from the wall, Lathronin and Kith doing the same. "Approach the wall," he said to Kith.

Kith looked at the wall and wondered what the Eskeli had planned. It looked simple enough, although looking more closely he could make out a strange pattern the black tendrils made against the dark stone. Kith stepped closer and when he was five paces from the wall the black tendrils suddenly flashed blue, more blue light setting off a subtle glow around the roots.

Kith paused as warm energy flowed from the Catalyst Stone on his chest to his appendages, his body subsequently feeling stronger. He looked back at the Eskeli, his expression one of wonder.

"The Stone is interacting with the gate."

"That is a portal?" Lathronin asked.

"It is. Step closer."

Kith looked back at the glowing root structure and stepped closer. He took two more steps before an area between the roots flashed blue and turned translucent. The portal was shimmering and flashing blue and white and looked to be about ten paces high and five paces wide.

"Where does it go?" Kith asked as Lathronin and the Eskeli stepped next to him.

"It is linked to the gate in Akari. The Dar-dan used it to travel back and forth during the Golden Age."

"If we walked through it, we would appear at the gate in Akari, the one that Lord Rane unburied?" Kith asked.

"That is correct, although it would not be wise. The gate there is in Rane's control and heavily guarded. It would be suicide."

"I imagine so," Kith whispered, still relishing the warmth flooding through is body.

"It could be useful at some point," Lathronin mused. "Is that a map?" he asked, moving to the right of the portal. It had not been there before, but now, glowing against the black rock, was what looked like a map of the Five Lands.

"It is," the Eskeli said.

Kith joined the priest near the map. It was clear from the glowing outlines that it was the Five Lands, but other than the size and shape in relation to each other, the maps themselves seemed useless. They could see no cities or mountains or roads. "What is the purpos..." Kith began, stopping mid-word as he looked closer. Each land had one glowing dot. "Those are the gates, aren't they?"

The Eskeli nodded.

"Each land has one gate only," Lathronin said softly as he looked more closely at the glowing lines and dots.

"Except for Urotha," Kith corrected, pointing out three glowing dots. One was clearly the gate in Seebras, the other, based on its location, was the main gate at Akari. But the third was centered in Urotha. "What about this gate?" Kith asked the Eskeli as the creature stepped closer. He did not think there was another gate in Urotha.

"That dot used to be the main gate," the Eskeli instructed. "It was built near the foothills as large amounts of field stones were found there. Its location in the middle of the continent also made it desirable. It could be easily accessed from all around. But there was a massive earthquake and a huge slide buried the river there. I believe it was the very same slide that formed the Rock Pass. The water backed up and formed a lake, burying the gate under the water. It is no longer accessible."

"I know that lake," Lathronin said. "It is quite large, and the waters so clear one can see far into its depths."

"Does that gate still work?" Kith asked in wonder.

"Yes, but one would have to find it. Also, once activated, water would pour through the gate until it was shut off. It would not be practical."

"That is when the Dar-dan built another gate at Akari?" Kith reasoned.

The Eskeli nodded. "There were veins of field stones in the mountains near the city. It was a good place for another gate. Let us go," the Eskeli added, changing the subject. "Our training for the day is not complete."

The Eskeli turned and left, Lathronin following. Kith slowly stepped away from the wall, the warmth suddenly diminishing as the gate flashed once and disappeared.

Six

Pornatious was glad to have been in Lampure when the scout came into the Drann temple with his news to sell. As an Eradicator, he had been out scouring the lands for any sign of the Idara, but the search had been fruitless, most now killed or pushed so far into hiding that they were unlikely to be found. Pornatious was growing weary of the hunt. He had returned to Lampure to rest, drink, and find a few buxom women to enjoy. He had had some fun the last few days, but this recent news seemed promising. The hunter could describe the man he saw at the coastline in great detail, and the gray robes and weapons he saw were a good sign that he had found an Idara priest. Why the priest was getting into a boat with a dead stag was unknown, but the deadly Eradicator smiled as he gripped the pommel of his horse tighter. They would find the answer to that question soon enough. There was a small coastal village less than a week away. They would commandeer a few boats there and sail to Seebras. Pornatious could think of no other reason as to why the Idara would be getting into a boat so near the ancient Dar-dan city. He must be going to Seebras. Glancing back, he made sure that the ten Black Watch warriors were ready, and seeing their determined expressions he nodded, nudging his horse forward. Together, they headed east, the Dar-dan temple of Seebras their destination.

***

Kith's skill with the drift cloak was developing quickly. The Eskeli had given him the Ar'kan cloak soon after he had gone through the Change. The incredible cloak was woven of thousands of strands of material, the likes Kith had never seen, the interior lined with what looked like a cotton-wool blend. And yet the fabrics were nothing like Kith had ever experienced.

He had no idea how the Dar-dan had created it, but the strands of fabric fluttered and danced, giving the wearer the appearance of movement that disguised his or her actual body position. In addition, the strands changed color, allowing the wearer to blend in to their surroundings. If one were so inclined, the Ar'kan warrior could reverse the cloak so it resembled a standard traveler's garb, allowing the warrior to blend in when necessary.

The Eskeli's spear shot forward and Kith easily avoided it, swaying to the side as his drift cloak fluttered around him. The Eskeli was wearing his own drift cloak and it had helped Kith study the creature's movements, noting the way he used the cloak to distract him. There were many times where his own spear missed the creature, the weapon harmlessly passing through the dancing fibers.

The Eskeli could no longer score a hit on Kith. They had been training on the island now for over a month. He was just too fast and strong, his enhanced physical abilities enabling him to move through the sword forms with such speed that even the highly skilled Eskeli could not match him in martial skill. Lathronin trained with him often, but the dangerous priest could barely give Kith a workout. Nonetheless, the constant training had honed his skills even further, his technique and moves having fully adapted to his new speed and power.

Their spears were a blur as they moved across an expansive smooth rock that edged one side of the island. It was Kith's favorite spot to train, the cool ocean breeze feeling incredible against his warm skin. The sound of wood on wood beat in a steady rhythm as they used the spears like staffs. They fought like that for half a bell, Kith scoring several more strikes before the Eskeli called a halt.

The tall creature stood before Kith. He was a bit slumped over, and for the first time Kith noticed that he seemed a bit tired. "There is nothing else I can teach you."

Kith nodded, apprehension beginning to enter his mind. "What now?"

"I do not have much longer," the Eskeli said. "I feel the mask waning. Soon, you will leave and contact the Order. You must stop Emperor Rane from crossing into Skell."

Kith was momentarily taken aback. He had known that the mask's energy was slowly depleting, but the thought of the Eskeli leaving him made Kith feel suddenly alone. The Eskeli voicing it made it seem so final. He had been with the creature for every waking moment for over a year, and although the Eskeli was not prone to making deep connections with any human, Kith had to admit that he would miss him. He didn't have many friends and the thought of losing one did not sit well with him. "Your absence will be missed, more than you know."

The Eskeli paused before nodding, the movement simple but somehow conveying something more, a reflection of a bond that he felt but could not explain. "You are the finest Ar'kan I have ever trained. I feel...good," he added, struggling with his words, "knowing that your spear, your sword, will be an extension of myself."

"Kith!"

Kith spun as he noticed Lathronin racing from the trail, the path lined with low lying shrubs. He was sprinting and his expression alarmed Kith. "What is it!?"

The priest stopped short of them. "Men are approaching. I was hunting the far coast and saw them. They are nearly at the city gates."

"Men?" The Eskeli asked.

Lathronin's expression said it all. "Rane's men," he hissed. "An Eradicator and ten Black Watch."

"Can we get to the city before them?" the Eskeli asked, his voice calm.

Lathronin nodded. "If we run."

"Then go." The Eskeli urged.

Lathronin whipped around and Kith followed, the Eskeli bounding behind them.

They made it to the front gates of the city just as the enemy emerged from the rocks along the coastline, the flat expanse before the city ahead of them. They were a thousand paces away but they could make them out clearly. The

Eradicator wore a black robe, the bottom portion split to allow quick movement. Red glossy armor covered his torso and strapped to leather belts were various weapons, a sword and several knives among them. His black hood was lined with red, giving the warrior an ominous appearance. The Black Watch soldiers wore all black, their armor similar to the Eradicator's, but glossy black. Kith knew that that armor was the best money could buy, coated with the resin of the bandra tree. Stronger than steel, it cost a small fortune. They were outfitted with small shields, swords, and spears, and running towards them at great speed.

"You must go," the Eskeli said, his voice still strangely calm.

Kith looked at the enemy who was quickly gaining on them. "We are not leaving you here."

The Eskeli reached up and put his strange hand on Kith's shoulder. "I do not have much longer, Kith Caren. This is where I die. I will buy you some time, although I will not be able to kill them all."

"I can't just..."

"You can. And you will. This world depends on you. You cannot die here. Remember the route I showed you to the underground water passage?"

Kith remembered it. The Eskeli had mentioned it the day they had arrived, and later, the creature had taken Kith and Lathronin to the underground exit. It was a corridor under the city that led to further tunnels that had been cut away for thousands of years by the moving water. "I remember."

"The tide is outgoing. Take a boat and leave," the Eskeli said as he turned to face the oncoming attack. They were standing just before the gate, which was perpetually cracked open, the hinges and operating mechanism long ago ruined with age and time.

Seeing the truth in the Eskeli's words, Lathronin urged Kith on. "Kith, we must go!" he shouted, pushing Kith away.

Kith growled in frustration, his hands gripping his spear tighter. "Thank you for all you have done!"

The Eskeli turned and nodded, before looking back to the enemy, crouching into a fighting stance. The enemy was now within spear throwing distance and two of the Black Watch soldiers, without breaking stride, pivoted and smoothly adjusted their bodies as well as their grips, arching back and throwing their spears with lightening speed.

Kith and Lathronin raced through the crack in the gate just as a spear struck the edge, the sharp point causing sparks to fly as it ricocheted off the dark stone. The other spear's trajectory was true, but the Eskeli pivoted, his own spear arcing and deflecting the weapon harmlessly to the side.

Kith and Lathronin ran as fast as they could, the sound of battle fading as they distanced themselves from the gate.

"We need our packs and bows!" Lathronin yelled.

Kith nodded, knowing the truth of his words. It would slow down their escape some, but they would not get far without their supplies. Luckily, the Eskeli had made their temporary sleeping quarters an empty building close to the underground exit. Kith now assumed that that was likely not a coincidence, and he silently thanked the creature, his friend, as they raced towards their gear.

Once there, they whipped on their packs, grabbed their bows and quivers, and ran back to the street. The escape exit was behind a series of doors near the western wall closest to the rocky coast. As they skidded in the debris filled street, Kith heard commotion further down the road the way they had come. Six men and the Eradicator were in pursuit.

Kith smiled grimly as he thought of the Eskeli killing four of the Black Watch soldiers. They likely had no idea who, or what, he was, and his martial skill would have been a complete surprise. That satisfaction, although fleeting in the shadow of his friend's death, made Kith smile, albeit briefly.

"Let's go!" Lathronin said, grabbing the edge of Kith's drift cloak.

Kith hesitated, his anger rising as he thought of the Eskeli cut and bleeding near the city's gate. "We can take them," Kith hissed, eager to use his new skill and power.

"Perhaps," Lathronin reasoned. "But it's not worth the risk. Don't let the Eskeli's death be a waste. You heard him. We must leave," he urged.

Kith remembered the Eskeli's words, his anger lessening some. The Idara priest was correct. Kith was confident that he and Lathronin could defeat the men racing after them. But unforeseen events could always happen in battle. Kith could slip and take a spear to the chest. The Eradicator, despite Kith's training, could kill him while he fought off the Black Guard. There were too many unknowns, thus too many risks. It wasn't worth it. Kith nodded and ran towards the west wall, the Idara priest doing his best to keep pace with Kith's enhanced speed.

They made it to the large stone building adjacent the west wall facing the water. The Eskeli had said it was a storage room, the secret door there leading to the catacombs below. Just as they entered the building, they heard the pursuit behind them.

"They are fast," Lathronin barked.

Kith nodded, expecting nothing less from Black Watch soldiers, the very best and deadliest of the Danites. "Let's go."

They ran inside and found the entrance, an opening in the floor against the far wall. At one point it had been hidden by a trap door, but now, the wood long turned to dust, it was a black pit in the ground, stone steps leading down. Wasting no time, they ran into the darkness, the strange Dar-danian lights along the narrow wall flickering on as they descended. Kith had no idea how they worked but he was thankful for the light.

The steps descended to a cave, the tunnel twice as wide as the steps and three times as tall. More sconces lit up as they entered the tunnel, which they knew from experience led to a larger cave complex filled with water as it poured in and out of the cliff opening.

They ran down the cave and came to a wharf, or at least what had been a wharf at one time. The stone had been carved into a level platform, the dock, when it was still standing, spanned the length of it, stairs dropping down to the wooden structure. Small boats would've been hanging from their support beams. No boat, even a Dar-dan one, could last long in the acidic waters. Typically, they were hung above it, lowered into the water when needed. But now there was no dock or stairs leading down to the water.

Looking to the back wall, they saw the two boats that had been placed there. By whom or when, they had no idea, but when the Esekeli showed them the area earlier they had inspected the four-man crafts. They were made from a strange material Kith had never seen, the same material the boat was made from that had taken them to the island. It showed no age other than slight wear on the bottom, likely from the toxic waters.

"How are we getting the boats down to the water?" Lathronin asked, looking back down the tunnel. He knew the enemy would be upon them in moments.

"We have no choice," Kith reasoned as he dragged one boat to the rock ledge above the water, Lathronin helping him. "We need to drop it."

"Then what?"

"We jump."

Lathronin didn't look too keen on that idea, but he had no time to come up with another plan as they sounds of pursuit turned his attention down the tunnel. Rane's men were running right towards them.

"Do it!" Lathronin yelled as he snapped his hand to the quiver on his back, an arrow nocked in a blink. Running a few paces to his left, his angle was better, and in two heartbeats had two arrows zipping down the corridor. One stuck a Black Watch pauldron and deflected off it, the sharp metal shooting up sparks as it ricocheted off the rock wall near him. The other hit a man in the thigh, the sharp point piercing his greaves a finger length. The man stumbled, righted himself, and continued his charge with barely a limp.

Kith used his enhanced strength to angle the awkward boat over the ledge, doing his best to position it so it would fall on its bottom and not capsize. When he thought he had it right, he let go, the boat dropping the five paces to the water below. The back end hit first, snapping the bow hard to the water. The boat shot forward some and Kith's heart skipped a beat when he saw the boat drift away.

"Lathronin, now!" he shouted, looking back. Lathronin fired two more arrows and ran back to Kith. Looking down he saw the boat slowly drift away. "Jump! I'll follow."

A spear shot past the priest, missing him by a hair. Needing no further encouragement, he readied himself, ran, and leapt off the ledge. Flailing his arms and legs, he hit the boat hard, tumbling to the front and nearly falling off. Looking back, his heart sank as he realized that his momentum in hitting the boat had caused it to drift even further away.

Kith spun as the men came around the corner. They were fifteen paces away. Without further thought, he turned, ran, and leapt with all his might towards the boat. He could feel the Catalyst Stone direct energy to his legs before he jumped, with more flooding his torso as he prepared to hit hard and likely have to brace with his arms.

Lathronin's eyes widened in surprise when he saw Kith's body fly through the air impossibly high. At first, he thought there was no way he could make a jump like that, the only alternative being a painful swim in the dangerous waters. But could he swim with the drift cloak and Ar'kan armor? He did not know, and hoped they would not have to find out. Following Kith's trajectory, Lathronin saw that he was going to make it, although barely. Scrambling forward to the back of the boat, the priest reached out just as Kith had landed. His force was so great that he nearly fell off the edge, capsizing the craft in the process. But Lathronin caught him, kept him from careening off the side, and dragged him backwards, where they both crashed hard against the sideboard. The tough Dar-dan material held, and despite a few bruises, they were surprisingly unhurt.

Regaining their balance, they sat up in the boat. The Eradicator and his men had just reached the edge of the wharf, and although they could see them, Kith knew they were now disappearing into the darkness of the cave, the outgoing tide pulling them towards the exit. But lack of visibility did not deter them from attacking. Kith saw a glowing ball of light appear in the Eradicator's hand, watching it slowly grow to the size of a child's head. Then he threw it.

"Look out!" Kith yelled as he whipped his sword from its scabbard and jumped forward, the glowing ball descending directly towards him. Energy flooded through his body and into his sword, the black weapon flashing blue light just before it struck the ball. The magical energy flashed bright. Two heart beats later it was gone. There was no explosion, no pain, no nothing. The energy had simply vanished.

Kith smiled as he looked back to the Eradicator, his expression one of anger and shock. One warrior threw his spear, but he missed, the weapon splashing harmlessly into the water near them. By this time they were deep into the cave's darkness, the only light visible a lightning bolt crack in the cliff face. The boat had picked up speed, the water funneling them in that direction. Kith picked up the oars and placed them in position. They were not safe yet. The men had come on a boat, and they had one still. They would not shy away from the hunt.

***

Theron and the four other spies had been running north all night, skirting the roads and moving steadily through the forest, taking advantage of whatever cover they could find. One man was a tracker and he swept front and back, covering their tracks as well as scouting ahead. He must have been exhausted, but he didn't let it show. Theron was impressed. All the men were tough, running for hours and stopping for short rests, not a word of protest or complaint from any of them. They had slept for four hours during the day, tucked away amongst thick trees and brush several clicks off the road. They were all exhausted and once their bodies had hit the soft mossy ground, they were asleep in moments.

Waking groggily, they rose and ate the last of their meager rations. Theron looked to the lead spy. "What is your name?"

The man looked up as he tossed the last chunk of bread in his mouth. He looked ragged, his eyes still angry. "You can call me Corvin."

"I need to get to my father."

Corvin picked up his light pack and cinched the straps tight. "We have no more food. That is our first task. Then we see about getting you to Daswin."

Theron nodded, knowing they wouldn't get far without food. He looked at the other men, his eyes finding the tracker's. "What is your name?"

The man stepped forward and pulled back his forest green hood. He looked to be a bit older than Theron, his black hair pulled tight and wrapped in a leather strap. "My name is Wilock, my Lord, but most just call me Wil."

Clearly the man knew who Theron was. "No need for formalities, Wil. Thank you for coming to my aid. How long have you been with the Order?"

"Ever since my pa was killed by Lord Rane's troops at Lampure. He was a hunter and three guards bought a plump deer he had killed. Except they never paid. When he complained, they got in a fight and they killed him. The officer at the garrison did nothing, and he laughed at me when I came for restitution."

"I see. I'm sorry about your father." The man nodded and stepped away. Theron turned to the other two. "I'd like to thank you both as well."

Both men stepped forward and offered their hands. One man was older, likely in his forties, streaks of gray already coming through his short hair. His name was Lannister and the other man, who looked to be in his late thirties, was Donnel. They all looked scrappy and tough, like a piece of dried meat that was too tough to chew. After Theron shook hands with both, he looked back to Corvin.

"Any ideas on where to find food?"

"There are homes scattered all along the main road north. We may need to steel it," Corvin added, his tone nonchalant.

"I have coin, that will not be necessary," Theron said.

"It would not be wise to leave witnesses behind," Corvin added. "Lord Rane's men will be searching these areas."

Theron realized what the spy was saying and shook his head in clear denial. "That is out of the question. We will take our chances." The other men said nothing but looked relieved. It was obvious that they would not have relished the killing of innocent country folk just to keep their passing hidden. Theron looked to Wil. "Lead the way. It is imperative I get to Daswin before Lord Rane's troops." Theron knew that Lord Rane had suspected Theron was spy, that he likely had the same feelings about his father. He would send his troops there and destroy the city. There was no doubt. He had to get there first to warn them.

***

Kith and Lathronin played hide and seek from their pursuers. Their boat was small and easily maneuverable, and instead of heading straight for the main shore, they immediately wound around the island to a smaller island just north. They hid their boat in a small cove, pulling the craft onto the beach and covering it with cut boughs from nearby trees. Lathronin stayed by the boat while Kith ran for a tall rock formation not too far off. He was able to move incredibly fast, the thrilling feeling of his newfound speed, strength, and agility still new and exhilarating. He wondered if he would ever get used to it. He bounded up the hill, quickly scrambling to the top where he lay flat and watched the waterway west of the big island, the tall peaks of Seebras visible in the distance.

He didn't have to wait long before he saw the sail of the bigger boat. His pounding heart slowed, and he let out a deep breath when he saw that the boat was heading west, obviously heading straight for the mainland. Clearly, they either thought he and Lathronin had headed west, or deemed they would never find them, the information they had for Lord Rane more important than sailing around aimlessly in the treacherous waters. Either way, there was a part of Kith that wished they had found them. He wanted to make them pay for what they had done to the Eskeli.

Kith returned to the boat and found Lathronin waiting anxiously. "They are heading to the mainland."

Lathronin nodded, his tense face relaxing. "Good. What now?"

"We need to get to Daswin and find out what is happening. Soon, the Kelic will be on the war march, heading south to meet Lord Byron and the Order. Emperor Rane will learn of Lord Byron's role in this insurrection soon enough. We need to know what is happening and how best to fit in."

Lathronin nodded. "Don't forget what the Eskeli said about Skell. We can't let Lord Rane open that gate."

"I know. I'm hoping the Order will have some information on that. I know they have spies in Akari."

"It's a half day rowing to the shore. Perhaps we should wait till the morning. Besides, it will allow more distance between us and Rane's men."

Kith nodded, thinking the same thing. "I agree. Let's set up camp."

They were off early the next day. Their plan was to head straight to Daswin, skirting the main towns and moving quickly, picking up necessary supplies from small villages and hoping to avoid any of Rane's men. They figured they could get there in less than a week if all went well. They had been in hiding, training and preparing for just under a year, and there was much they did not know. What was Rane's next move? When were the Kelic coming out of the mountains to join the fight? When will they be marching on Akari? One thing they knew was that the Eradicator that had seen them would surely be racing towards Akari to inform Rane of what he saw. Kith wasn't sure how he would explain the Eskeli to the emperor, or how Kith had dissipated his Drann magic, but he did know that the news would likely instigate a search for them, their presence a clear danger to their cause. Whatever happened, Kith and Lathronin were now in a much more precarious situation. They had to be careful.

***

Food was their first concern and on the second day heading northwest towards Lampure, they came across a small cabin surrounded by a clearing, the land around it tilled and growing the hearty root vegetable, a turbit. It was narrow in shape and often roasted to bring out its true flavor. The growing season was just starting and although the tops of the plants were green and bushy, the root would not be ready for another month.

"What do you want to do?" Corvin asked, looking at Theron.

"It is a single home," Theron mused. "They will not have much."

"And not likely any to spare," Wil added.

"We cannot all go," Theron pointed out. "If Rane's men question the families in the area it would be obvious we passed this way."

"Let me try to purchase something," Donnel suggested. "I know how to talk to farming families. Do you have any coin?"

"I do," Theron said, fishing out his coin purse. He dumped the coins in his hand. "I have nine silver tygs, eleven copper lods, and four gold crowns."

"More than enough," Donnel noted. "Give me a few silvers and coppers." Theron did and the spy tucked them in his pocket on his jerkin. He took off his sword belt and left it with the men. "I'll be back in a bit."

They didn't have to wait long before Donnel returned. He was carrying an old turbit bag over his shoulder that looked to be filled with something. He joined them on the edge of the forest and set the bag on the ground.

"How did you do?" Theron asked.

"Not bad actually. Luckily, they needed the coin. They had a little boy that was sick and wanted to take him to a healer. They were more than willing to give up what they could for the coin," Donnel informed as he pulled the food from the bag. There were two loaves of hard bread, a wheel of cheese, a jar of honey, two cured loral legs, a plump ground bird that lived in the forests all over Urotha. There were also five apples and a bag of various nuts.

"For how much?" Corvin asked.

"I got it all for a tyg and four lods."

Corvin shook his head. "That's a bit steep."

Donnel shrugged. "They will need all of it and more to heal their son."

"And we will need it...", Corvin started.

"That's enough," Theron interjected. "Well done Donnel. Now let's get moving."

Three days later they found themselves out of food and hiding in the dense brush along the main road as a small patrol of Rane's men rode by. They looked to be Torlites led by a scout. It was late in the evening and soon they would need to make camp.

Once the men rode by Corvin looked at Theron. "We are out of food," he noted, stating what they all already knew.

"We need to find a suitable spot to camp," Wil said, ignoring Corvin. Theron was thinking, his eyes looking back to the road. "What is it?" Wil asked.

Theron looked back at them. "There were only five men," he postulated. "Their saddle bags were filled with supplies and they will have to make camp soon just as we do."

"Are you suggesting that we attack the men?" Corvin asked.

Theron nodded. "I am. It was a small patrol. We can take them easily while they prepare their camp."

"It's not a bad idea," Lannister agreed.

"It's risky," Donnel added.

"Everything we do is a risk," Theron indicated. "But this is a calculated one that rests in our favor."

"I agree," Corvin said. "We can surround the camp and attack with bows, killing them quickly. Our chances of success are high. Let's do it."

The rest of the men agreed and took off at a fast pace, knowing that it would take them awhile to catch up to the men on horseback. They were hoping the patrol would settle in for the night along the side of the road sooner than later.

It was dark by the time they caught up to the men. Luckily, the night was clear, and the moon was out. They were forced to travel the road, the darkness of the forest, despite the bright moon, too thick to easily maneuver through. The dancing flames of a cook fire in the night led them to the camp. Making their plans along the edge of the road far from the fire, they agreed to converge on the camp from two directions.

Theron, Wil, and Donnel would attack from one side, while Corvin and Lannister would attack from the other. There were two bows among them. Wil would start the attack by shooting from his location, spurring Lannister to do the same on the far side. Then they would converge on the camp with swords and kill whoever remained.

It took them a while to get to their locations, their movements slow and precise as they inched through the dense forest on the north and south side of the road. Theron knew it would take Corvin and Lannister longer to reach their spot as they had to circumvent the entire camp to get to the north side. They could've tried sneaking across the road in the dark, but they didn't want to take the risk of being seen by the men, who were camped just off the side of the road.

The Torlites were sitting around the fire eating and drinking, their attention elsewhere as Theron, Wil, and Donnel hid in the brush no more than fifteen paces away. Wil had an arrow nocked and was looking at Theron. "You think they are in location?" he asked, his voice a soft whisper.

Theron nodded. "Go ahead," he said, his hand gripping his sword. Donnel readied himself as well, one hand holding his short sword and the other his hunting knife. Theron had witnessed the skill of the men the night he had been saved in Akari. Wherever they had received their training, they had done a thorough job. Theron knew that the Order had secret training camps throughout the mountains around Daswin. It was likely there where the men had learned to fight. But he was confident they could take out the Torlites with little difficulty.

Wil slowly sat up, rising above a thick bush. They were shrouded in darkness, the light from the cookfire not coming close to reaching them. Two men sat on logs, their backs facing them. He pulled back the arrow and his short recurve bow creaked in the silence. A heartbeat later he released and had another arrow nocked in a blink, the second arrow shooting across the clearing a moment later. Both arrows slammed into the backs of the two men. They grunted, the impact propelling their bodies forward into the fire. Ash and sparks shot up as they tumbled across the burning logs, their cries of pain cut off as they died quickly from the arrows.

Theron and Donnel burst from the brush, their silent attack accentuated by another man howling as an arrow took him in the back of the neck, the metal barb punching through the flesh. He managed to rise, his hand gripping the gruesome wound as blood gushed from around the wood shaft. He was met by Theron's blade, the sharp tip punching into his armored chest, nearly bursting from his back. Using his foot, Theron shoved the dead man off his blade as he looked around for another Torlite. A fourth man had taken another of Lannister's arrows in the back and the fifth had been killed by Corvin as he tried to rise and unsheathe his blade. They had killed them all in a few heartbeats.

"Well done," Theron said. "Let's get the bodies in the woods and take their supplies. I don't want to stay around here any longer than necessary."

The men went about their tasks and soon they had packs filled with food. They got back on the road and headed north towards Daswin. They would cover some distance before they themselves slept and ate for the night. Theron figured they still had at least four days before they reached Daswin. At least now they had enough food to make it there.

***

Kith and Lathronin made good time, pushing hard towards Daswin. Their honed bodies allowed them to run at a slow jog most of the day, stopping to rest and eat, sleep some at night, and continue on. Kith realized that he could've outdistanced Lathronin easily enough, his new-found speed and stamina still a shock to him. He could feel the energy flowing back and forth through his body, reflected off his Catalyst Stone in his armor to his legs, which tired the most as he ran. He was never cold, despite the chilly evenings, and his hunger was never as strong as it was before, even after such physical exertion. On top of all that, he woke from a few hours of sleep feeling as refreshed as if he had slept all night in a soft bed.

They stayed off the main roads as much as they could, but there were a few times where the forest was just too thick to make good time. Also, navigating through it was no easy feat. Lathronin and Kith were both skilled woodsmen, but they had little time and deemed the risk of traveling the roads necessary. They figured they could hide from any patrols. And if that were not possible, they knew they were capable of taking care of most threats.

On the fourth day they ran out of food. Lathronin had led them to a small town a few days north of Lampure called Byit. It was mostly home to the fishermen that fished the small river that flowed from the mountains into the acidic seas. It was the home of a hardy fish called the coowin, its firm white flesh quite appetizing. There were some loggers and farmers as well, mostly tough men and women who knew what a hard day of work felt like. It was a typical small village surrounded by a four-pace wall made of logs stuck into the ground and lashed together with rope. It was midday and the wood gate was open.

Kith and Lathronin hid in the brush along the main road that entered the city. "Should we both go in?" Lathronin asked, although his tone already indicated that he didn't think it was a good idea.

"You'll be recognized in your gray robes," Kith reasoned.

"I'm not so sure you'll blend in either," Lathronin added, looking at Kith.

"I can turn the drift cloak inside out and use my hood to cover my hair. If something goes awry, I will have a greater chance of getting out alive."

Kith was not boasting, just stating the truth. Lathronin was perhaps one of the best fighters in Urotha, along with his brother priests, but even he knew he would be no match for Kith. "What coin do we have?"

They had already consolidated the few coins they had, along with the ones the Eskeli had given them long ago. Kith dug into the coin purse and produced three silver tygs and twenty-one copper lods. "Plenty for food."

Lathronin nodded. "Get what you can and get out."

"Wait here for me," Kith said as he took his cloak off and turned it inside out, revealing what looked like a normal gray exterior. The cloak looked thicker than normal, as if it were lined with fur, but the dancing fibers could not be seen on the inside. He left his spear and bow with the priest and made sure that his rakian blade was covered by his cloak. Then he left for the gate.

Entering the small town, he looked down the main road for what might be a mercantile, or perhaps an ale house that might sell some food. The main road was lined mostly with small wood plank homes, a few side roads leading to more. There looked to be some sort of wharf along the river edge and Kith headed there. Most of the people about appeared to be farmers and women, the ladyfolk tending to their homes while the men were out fishing or logging. At least that's what Kith assumed.

A group of five Torlites emerged from a building down from him and Kith looked around quickly for a place to hide. He was near an alley, so he ducked down it and leaned against a side door. There was a woman just down from him dumping some debris into a wood barrel. She looked up when she saw him and frowned when he leaned against the wall. It was obvious he was hiding from something. She shook her head and went back into the door near her. Clearly, whatever was happening she didn't think it was any of her business.

Kith was glad she had minded her own business and glanced back towards the road. A moment later the Torlites walked by, oblivious of his presence. He let out a slow breath and removed himself from the wall, moving to the opening of the alley to see if it was clear. The guards were close to the gate when they turned down another side alley. He didn't know where they were going but wasted no time pondering the issue. Continuing down the main road he headed for the wharf. He passed a few townsfolk and they eyed him curiously, perhaps wondering why he was wearing his hood. But like the woman in the alley they minded their own business. Kith had a feeling that many of them, or maybe their husbands, were not fans of the law. It was likely that many of the tough loggers or fisherman were ex-criminals, or fugitives from the law, hiding in Byit to escape their previous transgressions.

The slow-moving river was as wide as Kith could throw a rock. The wharf was built next to a bank about an arrow distance in length, constructed of huge rocks that formed a wall against the water. From the bank a long dock was built with perhaps ten different docks reaching into the water, like fingers, each lined with small fishing boats. Most of the boats were out in the slow-moving river, and Kith reasoned within the next few hours many of the men would be returning with their catch. The air smelt of refuse and rotting fish and Kith didn't want to spend any more time there than necessary.

Looking around, he found a small ale house called, appropriately, The Wharf. The building was constructed of aged wood, the silver black color of the planks in contrast with the worn red door, the sign above it the same color. Kith wasted no time and entered through the door

The smells of sweat, fish, and stale ale assaulted him at once. The small room was dark, the meager light coming from hanging lanterns and a small smoldering fire at the far end, the old black rocks that formed the fireplace looking as if they had been there for hundreds of years.

But Kith's eyes were quickly drawn from his surroundings to a commotion at the bar, the red tunics of Rane's TorLites hard to miss. They seemed to be in some sort of conflict with two men at the bar, but Kith could not see them through the guards. The men he saw earlier must be part of this group, although why they parted ways Kith did not know. Perhaps they wanted to expand their search, or they reasoned that five TorLites were more than enough for a few rabble rousers. The soldiers had yet to turn around, so Kith stepped to the side and sat down quietly in a shadowed corner of the room. There were only a few men around, and they were clearly focused on the confrontation, not the newcomer. He thought about leaving, but he also needed supplies and reasoned that if the guards were focused on someone else that they might not pay him any attention. At least he hoped. Kith listened intently to the voices.

"Why are you buying so much food for two men?!" one of the guards said, his voice rising. The TorLites around him had surrounded the two men at the bar and several had hands on their short swords.

"I told you, we are buying for our family," one man said.

"Then why are they not here?"

"Our ma is sick," the other man said, his voice much deeper. "Our pa stayed with her at our cabin and sent us here."

"You two don't even look like brothers," the leader commented.

"We are half-brothers," the first man said quickly.

Even to Kith, it sounded like they were making up the story as they went.

"We are ordered on Lord Rane's request to arrest anyone who seems out of place. And according to the barkeep, he has never seen you. Not to mention, neither of you look like farmers. I'm going to have to arrest you until we can corroborate your story."

"Sir, you can't do that. We need to get back to our ma," the other man lamented, trying his best to sound sincere.

Something about the man's voice sounded familiar to Kith. Curiosity pulled him from his chair and he moved around to the other side of the room where he could get a better look at the two men. Leaning against the stone fireplace, Kith looked on as he tried to look inconspicuous. Glancing at the two men, Kith's heart suddenly stopped, his eyes going wide. It was Arim and Bos, Bos's big head rising above the guards. He had not seen his friends for over a year, but there was no mistaking their identity. Why were they here? They were clearly on a mission for the Order, and that alone meant they could not be captured.

Kith's hand went to his rakian blade and immediately he felt the Catalyst Stone react and send fresh energy into his limbs.

Just as Kith prepared himself, the lead guard reached for Arim. "You will be coming with us!" he ordered as he grabbed his arm. But Arim jerked away and drew his blade in one smooth movement. Bos, who was holding a canvas sack filled with food, simply charged the men, using his huge body as a battering ram.

Kith was on the guards in a blink, his black blade stabbing forward and skewering one man in the back. Never stopping, Kith's body was a blur as he drew his blade from the fatal wound and sliced it across the inner thigh of another, his humming blade cutting through his flesh and his femoral artery as if it were butter. Blood gushed across the dirty wood boards as the man fell, his body suddenly losing its will to move.

Bos barreled through two men before they could draw their blades. As the big warrior crashed through the surprised guards, Arim cut the leader across his extended arm and ran by him quickly, leaping through the hole created by Bos. Kith caught Arim glance at him, but he wasted no time to thank him as he followed big Bos out the door and into the street. Clearly, Arim could not see his features under the cowl of his hood.

Kith swore and followed Arim and Bos out the door, catching them easily in the street. "Arim! Bos!"

They both skidded to a halt and turned around, their faces one of panic. Kith removed his hood, his white hair causing their eyes to widen in surprise.

"Kith!" Arim exclaimed.

But they had no time for introductions as the three remaining Torlites, one injured, ran from the ale house and stopped ten paces away. Commotion down the street caught their attention and sure enough, the five Torlites that Kith had seen earlier were racing towards them. They were only twenty paces away and they covered the ground quickly. Kith's main concern was that two of them had crossbows. One looked to be loaded while the second man stopped his advance, his foot braced in the metal bracket at the front while he pulled the string back to the locking mechanism. It would be only moments before he had his bolt in place. They must have been returning when they saw the commotion. They looked uncertain, unsure of exactly what was happening, until they saw their comrades, their expressions grim, one with blood dripping from his arm, his sword held awkwardly in his left hand. They drew their blades and fanned out. The two men with the crossbows were in the middle. They were surrounded.

"You take the two behind me. I'll take these five," Kith said calmly, his bloody sword held casually in his right hand.

Kith didn't wait for a response. He was already hearing the beat of the mind dance and he moved towards the five warriors with a speed that they could not imagine. The crossbows clicked as both bolts flew towards him. Somehow, he was not worried, his mind in full concentration. His rakian blade spun and one bolt was nocked aside. The other bolt struck a glancing blow across his upper chest as he attempted to evade. Even with his great speed he was not able to avoid the bolt at such close range. There was a ping as it struck his Ar'kan armor. The material flashed as it absorbed the shock, the bolt careening to the side. Kith barely felt it as he attacked with a precision they did not expect. He was a blur as he shot past Arim and Bos, his black rakian blade moving with deliberate power and speed, the sword forms flashing through his mind as he adjusted his body to the attacks and defensive manuevers of the five men. Steel clanged and men screamed and grunted as they tried to stop the Ar'kan dance. But they could not, and soon, all five men were down, three dead and two wounded to the point where they could not move. Their pale expressions reflected stunned surprise having just witnessed a skill that no one had seen on Urotha for over a thousand years.

Spinning, Kith glanced over to see how Arim and Bos were faring. They had killed the two men, the injured third had run away. They stared at him, their eyes wide with shock, fear, it was hard to tell which.

"Kith, is that really you?" Arim muttered. Clearly, he was having a hard time processing what he had just seen.

"It is. We can talk later. Let's get out of here. Which direction are you going?"

"We have Carthen and others waiting along the river north of us," Arim answered.

Bos silently approached Kith. He placed his big hand on his shoulder. "It is very good to see you."

Kith smiled. "And you, my friend. Listen, I have a friend near the main gate. I will go to him and rendezvous with you along the river's edge."

Arim nodded. Then he smiled. "I don't think I want to call you milk anymore."

Kith chuckled. "See you soon. Stay safe," he added as he spun and ran towards the main gate, his body moving faster than any man.

"What the...", Bos began.

"Never mind!" Arim interjected. "Let's go. We'll get our answers soon enough." And with that, Arim ran up river, Bos close on his heels.

SEVEN

Kith found Lathronin and they hustled to the river's edge, moving quickly but silently, skirting the bank until they found them. Kith had reversed his drift cloak and as he led Lathronin into the small clearing he seemed to surprise even Lykin, who turned quickly at their sudden appearance, his hand moving to an arrow in his quiver. It was out of reflex and when Kith took off his hood, the bowman relaxed and offered him a smile and a subtle chuckle. They had been expecting him, but clearly his fluttering drift cloak was not what they expected.

"Kith, I can't believe it, it really is you," Lykin said, stepping forward to offer his hand.

Kith took it. "It is." Carthen was there, along with Bear'lon, Cos, and of course Arim and Bos.

Carthen stepped over to Kith, his appraising eyes taking him in. Even then they held little emotion, lacking the surprise on the other's faces. "It is good to see you," he offered, shaking his hand. "Are you heading to Daswin?"

"We are. This is Lathronin," he added, introducing the priest.

They all greeted the priest.

"Clearly, we have much to discuss," Carthen observed. "We are heading to Daswin as well. Let us get some distance between us and Rane's men before we have this conversation."

Kith nodded. "Lead the way."

They ran hard all day, finally stopping at dark. As luck would have it, they found an old abandoned cabin, the structure so aged and dilapidated that there were huge holes in the thatch roof. The cabin was far off the main road, which was why Kith had found it since they were staying off the main thoroughfares, running far ahead of the others and returning to tell them of his find. The plank walls were old, and many parts were rotten through, exposing large gaps. The floor was dirt, and even when the cabin was at its peak, they reasoned it would have been nothing more than a shack. But it would offer an adequate spot to camp for the night.

They risked a fire, reasoning that the walls of the cabin would hide the light and the thick darkness would mask any smoke. Someone would have to be literally walking ten paces from the cabin to see anything, and that was unlikely. As they prepared the fire and organized their evening meal, they made small talk, but once they had all sat down by the fire, their eyes expectantly went to Kith and Lathronin.

"Tell us what has happened to you," Carthen said, jumping straight to the point in his usual manner.

Kith was aware they knew that he had left with the Eskeli to train to be an Ar'kan warrior, but besides that they were ignorant of what had transpired over the last year. Kith wasn't even sure that Arim and Bos had been briefed on Kith's recent whereabouts. He had left so quickly with the Eskeli that he was not able to see his friends or say goodbye. Secrecy was cherished by the Order and Kith had no idea if his ban had been briefed on Kith's sudden disappearance or the fact that he was a Stone Blood and what that entailed.

So he started from the beginning, explaining his training with the priests and the Eskeli, all the way to their travels to Seebras and what had transpired there with the Alltree. Everyone listened intently until he was done, ending with the recent confrontation with Rane's men.

They were all silent for a while, digesting Kith's words. Arim spoke first. "Are the scars on your eyes from when they stitched them shut?"

"They are," Kith paused, thinking back to those days, which seemed so long ago to him. "It was a difficult part of the training to say the least."

"You really are an Ar'kan warrior?" Bear'lon questioned softly.

"I am. The Alltree has granted me this honor."

"Tell me more about this Alltree," Carthen pressed.

Kith shrugged. "I do not know much. If the Eskeli were here, he could tell you much more. All I know is that the structure was built by the Dar-dan thousands of years ago to harness the power of the field stones. It somehow powers the portals, along with creating the Ar'kan warriors."

"How did it do this?" Lykin pressed.

Kith shuddered as he thought back to the pain. "I was on a table," he began, recounting the Change he went through. "The Alltree moved as if alive, sending black tendrils, like roots, into my body. The roots changed me, placing stones into my body, making me stronger and faster. Somehow the Alltree forged my armor and weapons, my own blood a part of them. The pain was the most grueling I have ever felt. I thought I was going to die."

"And you did not because you are a Stone Blood?" Bos asked, speaking up for the first time.

"Yes, that is my understanding," Kith replied. "The Eskeli thought that my bloodline had been created by two Ar'kan warriors long ago. Over time many Stone Blood lines have died out, but some, a few, remained strong, including mine. My blood has an affinity to the E'lear, the energy around us that the stones harness, and because of this I was able to withstand the Change."

"The amount of power passed from the Alltree to a Stone Blood, is directly linked to one's own will," Lathronin added, speaking for the first time. "Not all Ar'kan warriors are the same in strength and power. The amount of power the Alltree bestows upon them is linked to their own mental and physical strength. Some can only withstand the Change, but cannot suffer through the forging of the sword, or even more so, the armor or spear, thus not tapping the true power of the Alltree."

Everyone looked at Kith.

"And what of Kith?" Carthen ask, voicing everyone's interest.

"He has all three," Lathronin added.

***

Lord Rane whipped his fist over his other hand, drawing E'lear from the silver disk and pounding his fist down onto the table. There was a flash of light and a boom as the table cracked in half, caving in on itself.

"You will find him!" he stormed, his anger palpable. Word had reached him quickly of Theron's treachery and the death of his daughter. It was not accurate to say he loved his daughter, as he really loved nothing but himself and power, but he respected and trusted her, which were acolades he did not hand out easily. She was cunning and ruthless, a powerful confidant that he had planned to use to help rule his growing empire. And now she was dead.

At the table was Grand Weaver Thryn, Warden Stollin, commander of the Danite Core, Commander Garn, war leader of Rane's Torlites, as well as Rallin, Rane's bodyguard. The Kelic slave never left his side.

The men jumped back from the table as it broke apart beneath them. None of them moved as Rane unleashed his anger.

"I want all Eradicators brought in, their searches redirected to find that murderous wretch! I want the army prepared to march in three days! Do it now!"

"Where are we going?" Commander Garn dared to ask.

Rane's eyes swung to the commander. But the stern warrior did not flinch under his boiling rage. A few heartbeats later he answered. "Daswin," Rane sneered, his anger now more like a boiling pot than an exploding volcano.

"So we are delaying our plans to take the Kelic lands?" the commander confirmed.

"Yes, they can wait. I want Falconan's head on a platter."

None of them dared to ask which one, Lord Byron Falconan, or his son, Theron. They knew that it was likely both. If Theron Falconan was a member of the Order, then likely so was his father. They knew that Rane would raze the city to the ground.

"Sir, I have more bad news," Thryn said, trying to sound confident under Rane's wrath.

Rane looked at Thryn, the air thick with hostility. Finally Rane blinked and his rage seemed to lessen. "What is it?"

"Scouts arrived just this morning." Thryn gulped. "A Kelic army was seen descending from the Northlands. They were heading south."

Rane took a deep breath and stepped back from the table. "How many?"

"Our scouts estimated ten thousand. They are heading to Daswin."

Rane shot forward and backhanded Thryn across the face, nearly knocking the priest to the ground. "Of course they are going to Daswin!" he raged. "Do you think I am an idiot!?"

Thryn righted himself, using his hand to wipe the blood from his nose. His eyes briefly flashed with anger but quickly turned to fright, stepping back from his enraged Dumbasa. "No, Dumbasa. I am sorry, my Lord. I was just trying to be fastidious in my report."

Rane's anger cooled some and he stepped back. "How many men do we have?"

"We have fourteen thousand Torlites, as well as a conscripted army of six thousand Shyeem and Acku slaves," Commander Garn replied.

"And what is your estimation of their fighting capabilities," Rane asked, obviously referring to the slaves.

"They have been trained in basic marching and formation fighting. They will fight to live another day," Garn reasoned. "But they will not fight hard."

"How many Drann do we have with combat skills?" Rane asked, addressing Thryn.

"We have ten Eradicators and another fifteen Drann with combat skills."

Rane pursed his lips. It was clear he was trying to keep his anger at bay. Clearly, he knew that ten thousand Kelic warriors would be a powerful enemy.

"My Lord," Thryn added quickly. "I do have an idea. We have ten new Drann recruits that are doing quite well in their training. They have just recently been marked, but I believe they can control more power."

"But we don't have any more field stones," Rane murmured as he stared down at the destroyed table. "Correct?" he asked, looking up at Thryn.

"Yes, my Lord. Perhaps we should go to Skell. With more field stones, we can increase the power of our Drann. Their power will be needed against the Kelic."

Rane looked down again, thinking. The silence was tense, but finally he looked up at the men. "Warden Stollin. I want two hundred Danite ready to march tomorrow along with a crew of engineers. We head to Skell. When we return," he added, looking to Thryn, "how much time will you need to mark the priests?"

"As you know there are only a handful of Drann with the skill to mark." Rane's eyes narrowed and Thryn saw him struggle with his anger. Clearly, he did not want to hear a long drawn out dissertation about things he already knew. Thryn got straight to the point. "It will take us five days."

"You have three. After that, we march to Daswin."

***

Kith, Carthen, and the others made it to Daswin without further incident, keeping to the side roads and forest edge for most of the journey. Lykin had dropped a deer which had added meat to their dwindling supplies. They had come upon one of Lord Byron's scouting parties, a group of soldiers returning from the north. They did not know who Carthen and the others were but had agreed to allow them to travel with them to Daswin. Once they arrived, Carthen abandoned all secrecy typical of the Order and went directly to see Lord Byron. He figured the Kelic would soon be arriving and when they did Lord Byron's role in the Order would be discovered. Now was the time to act.

Kith was unsure of his new role and how to act around the lord. For one, he reversed his drift cloak and hid his hair under the deep cowl as they made their way to Lord Byron's estate. He knew his presence would cause quite a stir in the city and was unsure if it was the right time to do so. Once inside however, he reversed the cloak once again. They were brought directly to Lord Byron's palace and escorted to the main conference room. Chamberlain Lorn knew who they were and had brought them directly to the room, following up shortly with servants carrying trays of cured meats, cheese, bread and butter, and chilled wine.

Lorn's eyes kept finding Kith and finally he spoke to him. "Kith Caren, is that you?"

Kith smiled. "It is I, Master Lorn."

"What has happened to you?" he asked. "You are so different."

"A lot, too much to explain now."

"Very well, maybe another time," he said as he gave him a subtle bow before leaving.

Kith thought the deference strange. Somehow his knew bearing, or look, had demanded the respect of the Chamberlain. Did he really look that much different?

They were famished and dug into the food and drink with relish. It wasn't long before Lord Byron entered. He looked haggard, with tired, puffy eyes. "Please continue," he said, indicating the food as he sat down. "It is good to see you all, although a few I do not know."

"Lord Byron, this is Arim and Bos, trusted members of the Order," Carthen added, introducing them.

"Well met and thank you for your service. Now, who is..." Lord Byron began, looking at Kith. "Kith, is that you?" he asked, astonished.

"It is I, my Lord."

"What has happened to you? What are you wearing?"

"Sir, it is a long story," Kith said, unsure of where to begin. The last time he had seen Lord Byron was when he had attacked the Black Watch soldiers and the Eradicator before they were about to kill Master Torbin for being a spy. There was much the Lord did not know.

"Give me the abridged version," he said with undisguised curiosity.

So, Kith went about telling the story one more time, although cutting out chunks he thought not important at the moment. Lord Byron listened with wide eyes, asking a few questions here and there. His response to the information was one of shock, just as it was with the others.

"That is an unbelievable story. I must say that I am happy to hear that there is much truth to the legends of the Ar'kan. Your skills will give us an edge over Lord Rane," he added.

"Sir, if I may be so bold. Lord Rane's defeat, although important to me, is not my most important task. I have a more pressing mission, although the two may coincide."

Lord Rane's eyes narrowed some. "What can be more important than freeing our lands of his tyrannical rule?"

"My Lord, my task is to make sure that Lord Rane does not enter the lands of Skell. If his defeat aligns with that task, then so be it, but if not, I must focus on that goal."

"What is so important about Skell?" Lord Byron asked.

"Skell has more field stones than any of the Five Lands. The Dar-dan depleted the lands of most their field stones, except for those located in Skell. Long, long ago, they were forced from Skell, pushed out of the land by an evil so great that it nearly destroyed Urotha."

"You are referring to the gate that Rane unburied?" Carthen asked.

"Yes. They buried that gate to keep the Crawlers in Skell from crossing over and destroying everything. I cannot let that happen again."

"What are these Crawlers?" Lord Byron asked, his face now a mask of worry.

"Dark creatures that look like big lizards and live beneath the rocky mountains in Skell. There are thousands of them led by a queen, or some leader, so the Dar-dan thought. They hibernate for hundreds, maybe thousands of years. The Dar-dan believed that they somehow drew sustaining energy from the field stones why they slept, but they were never sure about that. They rise from the surface to feed, destroying anything in their path before returning to the ground, giving the land time to repopulate. The cycle continued like that for thousands, maybe millions of years, until the Dar-dan broke the cycle, using the gate to unite the lands. Unknowingly, they endangered the other continents by connecting them to Skell. That's why they brought the mountain down on the main gate, to seal Skell forever."

Everyone was silent for a long time before Lord Byron finally spoke. "And you think Rane will go to Skell to get more field stones?"

"Yes. He will need the stones for his Drann priests."

159

"How are the portals opened?" Bear'lon asked.

"You need a Catalyst Stone," Kith answered. "The Eskeli believed that Rane is using the Catalyst Stone left behind by the dead Ar'kan warrior that bravely died helping protect the gate so long ago."

"And you have one?" Carthen asked Kith.

"Yes, it is this stone," Kith replied, touching the black and blue veined stone embedded in his cuirass. The stone was so dark that it blended in well with the black armor, but when Kith touched it the stone glowed a subtle blue before fading.

"Are you saying that these creatures somehow crossed through the gate long ago and that Ar'kan warriors fought them, bringing down the mountain on top of them to kill the creatures and seal the gate?" Lord Rane surmised.

"Technically it was the Drann who brought down the mountain, but yes, that is what happened."

"Drann?" Carthen asked in surprise. "They are the enemy."

"They were not then," Kith added. "The Drann and the Ar'kan warriors worked together to protect the Dar-dan and help rule the Five Lands. It was a golden age of peace and prosperity. The Drann now have followed a different path."

"How did the creatures get through if they had no Catalyst Stone?"

Kith thought back to the story the Eskeli told them as they had gazed upon the old painted wall in Seebras. "A big Crawler, a larger version of the others, perhaps the queen, killed an Ar'kan warrior while the gate was open, carrying the warrior through the gate while a handful of its brethren followed. The Ar'kan warrior had a Catalyst Stone and it was that stone that kept the gate open."

"That implies premeditation," Carthen reasoned. "Are you saying that these creatures can think?"

"The Eskeli believed so, yes, at least the leader. They believed the Crawlers themselves were somehow mentally linked to the leader, and that the E'lear had something to do with this link. But there was much the Dar-dan did not know and they left before they learned the truth of the creatures."

Carthen let out a deep breath and leaned back in his seat. Everyone was silent as they thought about this new danger before them. As of a few moments ago, they had a single task, and that was to defeat Lord Rane. Now, besides that surmountable task, they now had to deal with a horde of demon-like creatures descending on Urotha and the Five Lands and destroying everything in their wake.

Finally, Lord Byron spoke. "What are we to do?"

Suddenly the door to the conference room burst open. It was so sudden that the warriors at the table quickly stood, hands moving to their blades.

A man moved with haste from the shadowed corner, followed by a frantic Chamberlain Lorn. At first everyone thought the stranger was attacking, but once they noticed who it was, their hands dropped from their pommels, their shocked expressions remaining.

"Father!"

It was Lord Theron Falconan.

Lord Byron was up and running towards his son. He gripped him in a strong hug before finally releasing him. It had been over five years since he had seen his son and he knew the danger he had constantly endured. Theron's presence now was twofold. Something was obviously wrong, but he was happy to see him alive.

"Son, what are you doing here!?" Lord Byron asked as he held him at arm's length. Theron was taller than his father and had a more powerful bearing. He had spent the last five years training and fighting with the toughest fighting force in Urotha, and it had changed the young man, molding him into a powerful warrior. Lord Byron sensed the strength in his son and released him, realizing he was no longer the untried young man he had sent away to become a spy for the Order.

"I have been compromised, Father. Spies from the Order helped me escape and we have been running hard to get here."

"So, they must know of me as well."

"Yes Father."

"Rane will be mobilizing. He will come here and raze the city to the ground. Come, we have much to discuss," Lord Byron said, ushering Theron towards the table and the others.

For the first time Theron noticed the men at the table, casting his eyes over all of them. He knew of Carthen, Bear'lon, and Lykin, although he had only met them in passing years ago. They were important to the Order, that much he knew. Then he saw Kith and his eyes widened, moving towards him quickly.

"Kith, is that you?"

Kith smiled, extending his hand. "It is."

"What happened to your eyes? And what are you wearing? You look like that statue in the courtyard."

"We have a lot to discuss, my friend," Kith said. "But first, let us deal with the immediate threats. Then we can talk. I think I am not the only one with a good story."

"I agree," Lord Byron confirmed. "These men that traveled with you...are they in good health? Do they need anything?"

"They are waiting in the library."

"Master Lorn, will you please make sure our guests are comfortable and well fed," Lord Byron ordered. "And have servants bring us drink and food. I think we will be here for a while."

"Very good, my Lord," Lorn said as he bowed and backed from the room.

Lord Byron introduced his son to everyone, meeting Bos and Arim for the first time. Then they sat, all eyes turning to Lord Byron.

"We have several problems that must be addressed," Lord Byron began. "One, now that Lord Rane knows that I am leading the Order, he will bring his army here to crush us. Secondly, we need to make sure that he does not enter Skell for fear of bringing those creatures to our land."

"What creatures?" Theron asked.

Lord Byron looked to Kith. "Kith, give him the short story."

Kith nodded and explained to Theron what he had just explained to the others. He left out some details, figuring he would explain them in more detail when he had time to talk individually with his friend.

Theron sat back in his chair and pushed his hair back from his face. "That is quite the story, my friend, and I must say I'm eager to hear the rest."

"The one good thing," Carthen added, "is that if Rane marches here immediately, then he will not be entering Skell."

"That is true," Kith reasoned.

Lord Byron looked to his son. "How long would it take Rane to mobilize and get his troops marching?"

Theron thought for a moment. "He had already been preparing to invade Dral. Now he will just change his target and head here. I think he will have his army marching in three or four days."

"So soon," Lord Byron muttered, clearly not happy with the news.

"How many men?" Carthen asked.

Theron looked up from his thoughts. "A thousand Danite, nearly fifteen thousand Torlites, as well as over five thousand slaves from Dareef and Bylor."

Carthen let out a deep breath. Then he looked at Lord Byron. "How many men can you muster?"

"Two thousand town guards," Lord Byron responded.

"We have been gathering our forces all year preparing for the Kelic. I can gather a thousand from the Order immediately, and maybe another two thousand from further outposts. But it will take nearly two weeks to gather that many."

"How long for Rane to march here?" Kith asked.

"Once he leaves," Theron answered, "a fortnight at the most."

"What about the Kelic army?" Bear'lon asked. "Will they reach us in time?"

"Our scouts show them several weeks out," Lord Byron answered. "It will be close."

"We need to slow Rane down," Arim interjected, his voice soft, lacking the confidence of the others. He was not used to talking with such esteemed people, and he nearly blanched when they all looked his way. "It's the one thing we can control," he continued. "If we can slow Rane down, then we can find the time to gather our forces and join up with the Kelic."

"What is your name again, son," Lord Byron asked.

"Arim."

"Your idea is sound," Lord Byron added, his eyes flicking to each person at the table. "Anyone have any ideas how we can slow him down?"

"I may have an idea," Carthen solicited.

***

"I can't believe it's you," Theron beamed, sipping a glass of chilled wine while Kith sat opposite him in Lord Byron's library. There were two large bowls of meat stew and hunks of fresh bread at the table. Both men were still hungry after their long trek and they dove into the food as they talked. The last time he had been in this room was over six years ago when he had been asked to join the Order. It seemed so long ago to Kith, like another lifetime. The group had discussed Carthen's plan for over an hour before everyone parted ways to prepare. Theron had dragged Kith away, so they could talk alone.

"A lot has changed, that's for sure," Kith responded as he ate the hearty stew. "I can't believe you are a Captain in the Danite Core."

Theron paused, his eyes serious. "*Was* a captain," he corrected. "It was the hardest thing I've ever done. And living in that viper's nest, let's just say, was difficult. But I'm sure it was nothing compared to what you went through. I wondered what had happened to you after the winds came. I'm glad the Order found you."

Kith wiped his mouth and leaned back in his chair, images of his training flashing through his mind. "Me too. They have been good to me."

"And that creature, the Eskeli, found you last year?"

"Yes, my Ar'kan training started soon after."

"And this threat from these creatures in Skell is real? I just can't believe it."

"It is."

"I know that Rane had planned on going to Skell after he took Dral, but now I don't know. The discovery that I was a spy might cause him to change plans."

"We have to stop him," Kith said adamantly.

Theron drank more wine. "Kith, he will not be so easy to stop. I have never seen anyone wield the E'lear with as much skill, and his swordsmanship is beyond anything I've seen. Can you really defeat him?"

"I don't know, but I must. This is all so new to me. I am not fully aware of all my abilities."

"What *do* you know?"

"I am stronger, faster, and do not tire as I used to. My armor and weapons have the ability to negate E'lear, although I've only tested it once."

"What happened?"

"We were found at Seebras by an Eradicator and his Black Watch soldiers. The Eskeli killed a handful of them and gave us time to get away. As we escaped in a boat the Eradicator threw a ball of white energy at us. I had seen one used before and knew that it would explode when it hit. It was coming right at us, so I just reacted, bringing my sword up to meet it. The ball was simply cut in half and the energy disappeared. There was no explosion, nothing."

Theron exhaled through pursed lips as he leaned back in his chair. "That will come in handy, there is no doubt."

There was something pressing on Kith's mind and he voiced it. "There is something I've been wondering. The Eskeli found me when I tried to intervene on an execution. There was an Eradicator and his Black Watch in town and they were executing suspected members of the Order. One of them was my friend, Torbin the Distiller. I could not let him die so I attacked forcing other members of the Order to intervene, including Carthen."

Theron swallowed the rest of his wine. "You attacked an Eradicator and Black Watch soldiers by yourself?"

Kith nodded. "It was a foolhardy thing to do, but I just couldn't sit there and watch Torbin die. Anyway, one of the Black Watch soldiers that I fought was Tallin. Do you know what has become of him?"

"So obviously you didn't kill that murderous swine," Theron snarled. "I had heard that he had become a member of the Black Watch. That does not surprise me. But no, I have not seen or heard what has become of him since."

Kith nodded and drained his glass. He did not like ale much, or most spirits, but he had to admit that he fancied the expensive sweet wines as they were served cold. And this wine, being from Lord Byron's own cellar, was quite exceptional.

"How were you found out?" Kith asked.

Theron's lip curled up into a playful smile. "I was trying to get in close with Emperor Rane's daughter. She seemed sympathetic to our cause and appeared to hate her father. Plus, I must admit, I liked her, and she was gorgeous."

"But..." Kith urged, thinking he knew the answer already.

"She was lying. Emperor Rane had suspicions about me and used her to bring them to the surface."

This time it was Kith who smiled. "A man who swoons the ladies being swooned by a lady." Kith chuckled. "What happened to her and how did you get away?"

Theron's smile disappeared. "I killed her. I only got away because members of the Order were following me. They never trusted the princess and as it turned out they had been right. I owe them my life. They intervened when she sprung her trap, rescuing me in the process."

"The men you came with?"

"Yes."

"It seems we both have been stuck in a storm of change. The Northbite race seems so insignificant now, and so long ago. So much has changed."

"Yes, I feel like I have aged twenty years in the last six."

"I know the feeling," Kith added, looking up at his friend. "I'm not sure I can support the mantle placed upon me. I mean, why me? Why was a simple orphan boy picked to be the last Ar'kan warrior to save our lands? Theron, I'm not sure I can bear that kind of pressure."

This time Theron's usual jovial smile returned. "Of course you can. Kith, you are one of the strongest people I have ever met. You walk the right road even when it's the most difficult path. You risk your life for your friends. There is no other person I would rather see in that drift cloak. Besides, you will not be alone."

"Thank you, my friend. It is really good to see you."

"And I you," Theron affirmed. "Now, what do you think of this plan?"

Carthen's plan was to bring their army out from behind Daswin's walls and meet Rane at the Rock Pass, a narrow stretch of road passing through a series of small mountains. He believed it would be folly to stay behind the city walls and be trapped, the city destroyed by his superior forces, or starved out while their supply lines were cut off. He wanted to take the fight to him, on territory of their choosing. Technically they were just hills that surrounded the pass, mostly formed from piles of rocks and giant boulders. The road cut through a narrow gap for about half a day's travel, the edges of the road comprised mostly of rising cliffs formed by huge rocks. It was the perfect spot to spring a trap.

"The plan is sound, but the element of surprise is key," Kith added. "But it will be difficult to get our troops into position without his scouts seeing us."

"Not to mention, will the Kelic get here in time?" Theron questioned.

"I hope so, they are quite formable. If we can hold them off at the pass until the Kelic arrive, we will have a chance."

"You say that as if you've fought one," Theron queried.

"I have."

Theron's eyes lifted from the last bite of his food. He paused as he finally put the spoonful in his mouth. "I should've known," he chuckled through a mouthful. "Tell me about it."

Kith told Theron the story of their adventure through the mountains to reach the Kelic, explaining the annwil attack as well as his fight with the Kelic to determine if they would send their warriors to help them fight Lord Rane.

Theron listened intently and when Kith finished, he simply shook his head and smiled. "You have been busy, haven't you?"

"You could say that."

"You climbed a frozen wall with an Idara priest and killed two annwil. Then you defeated a Kelic warrior, all the while the pressure of their alliance sitting on your shoulders. And you now worry about whether you can carry the burden of the only Ar'kan warrior. Humility is typically a virtue but yours is starting to irritate me." Theron was smiling and clearly not angry. He had made his point.

Kith smiled. "I will do better to hide my insecurity."

"That is wise. Besides, if I can give you advice as a military leader. No one wants their hero to be unsure. You must exude confidence, whether you feel it or not."

Kith could see the wisdom in Theron's words. "I shall take your advice."

Suddenly the door to the library opened and Chamberlain Lorn entered, bowing to both. "I'm sorry to interrupt, but your father would like to see you in the council room immediately. You too, Master Caren."

Kith had never been called master, and he didn't like it, but he was unsure if he should say anything. He opted to be silent as they both stood from their meal.

"Thank you, Lorn," Theron responded.

They followed Lorn to Lord Byron's council room, the very room they had left just hours before. The night was going to be busy and they would be lucky to get a few hours of sleep before the sun rose the next day.

When they entered the room, it was empty except for Lord Byron and Carthen. They were looking over maps and talking quietly when they approached.

"Good, you are here. Please have a seat," Lord Byron offered.

They sat as Carthen spoke as he remained standing. "Tomorrow we are holding a town meeting, requesting all able-bodied men to leave their homes and fields to fight, to protect their lands. Riders are out now spreading the word. Kith, I want you with me when I announce my true identity. We have decided that now is the time."

Kith was confused, and he looked at Theron for an explanation, but his expression was equally unsure. Lord Byron interjected. "Carthen is not his real name. He has been with us since the beginning and we have kept his identity hidden for his safety."

"My name is Terwyn Gar."

Theron's eyes widened, and Kith's thoughts went immediately to the painting he saw in the market so long ago. The warrior known as Terwyn Gar fighting against a mass of enemies. He had not known who Terwyn Gar was at the time, but since then had learned of the warrior that most spoke of as a mythical swordsman whose skills were unmatched. Kith had doubted that he had actually been real. Turns out he was wrong.

"I thought you had died in battle over fifteen years ago," Theron muttered, hardly believing what he had just heard.

"Yes, that's what I wanted Lord Rane to believe. I have been fighting against him ever since."

"Why do you want me with you, sir?" Kith asked, unsure of the role they wanted him to play.

"Kith, whether you like it or not, you are a beacon of hope for everyone here, just as I am. We need to play the part. We," he said, indicating Lord Byron, "plan to use your new identity, and mine, to conscript as many able-bodied fighters to the cause. What more can instill a sense of righthousness, can cause men to dust off their swords and join a worthy cause, than an Ar'kan warrior of legend?"

"Besides," Lord Rane interjected, "we will likely have some difficulties with the local Drannn priest. He is loyal to Rane and he will definitely intercede."

"You plan to kill him?" Theron asked.

"That is not my intent, but he may very well attack us when he learns who we are and what we plan to do. We may not have a choice. We need you with us for more than just recruiting efforts. If Legatis, the Drann priest, attacks us, you will be needed to defend against his magic."

"I understand," Kith said, acknowledging his reasoning. "I will be there."

***

It was midday when Kith and Lathronin met with Lord Byron, Carthen, Theron, and some of the other members of the Order, like Bear'lon, Lykin, Bos, Arim, and the team that had rescued Theron. They stood behind them, their vigilant eyes scanning the massive crowd that was forming. Several thousand townsfolk filled the central square and more were pouring into the gate as they waited. Nearly two hundred soldiers stood like sentinels around the square keeping an eye on the proceedings, while many others and their officers were preparing to march towards the Stone Pass.

Kith saw the Drann priest immediately, his white tunic and cape marking him as a third rank priest. The only tattoos Kith could see were on his hands, and he knew that energy coalesced there constantly. Kith could feel the E'lear around him. The man's eyes were alert and wary. He was surrounded by five Torlites, their expressions showing their nervousness as they scanned the crowd for danger. It was obvious that they did not know what was happening, but that something was amiss. It was too soon for any message to have come from Akari uncovering Theron's treachery, but they were about to discover the truth soon enough.

A quarter of a bell had passed before Lord Byron strode to the edge of the stage. The crowd quieted to a soft murmur as his aristocratic eyes scanned the crowd, drawing their attention to him. "Townsfolk of Daswin, I am here to inform you of a secret that I've kept hidden for many years, the consequence of this secret bringing danger to our town. Events have recently unraveled that have forced the truth to rise to the surface." He paused to let his words sink in. "I have no love for Lord Rane. He is a despot who has no qualms about stepping over the corpses of his own people to climb the hill of power."

Kith looked at Legatis and saw his eyes widen, the Torlites around him settling their hands on the pommels of their swords as they looked at the Drann for orders. No one ever openly ridiculed emperor Rane, especially within the earshot of his Drann minions. Kith readied himself but thus far the Drann priest did nothing, his eyes narrowing as he listened to Lord Byron.

"As a conquered vassal, I have been reluctantly following his orders," Lord Byron continued, his eyes glancing at Legatis and the Torlites. "But below the surface, I have been fighting him ever since he usurped my lands. He has murdered his own people, your own families. He has taken our men, some so young they can barely lift a sword, to fight for him. They are now likely dead, their blood drenching the soil of some far-off land. He has burdened us with unfair taxes. You all know these truths!" Lord Byron paused. "I am the head of the Righteous Order! I am the tip of the spear that will destroy Lord Rane!"

The crowd was deathly silent as they looked around with uncertainty, unsure if they heard their lord correctly, even though his voice carried over the crowd easily enough. Lord Byron was taking a gamble. He knew that nearly everyone had no love for Lord Rane. But he also knew that Rane's fear tactics had subjugated the people of Urotha into submission long ago. He was hoping that his openness, his bravery in speaking the truth, would break through the shackles Rane had on his people.

There was suddenly a shout. *Down with Rane!* Then more shouts joined that one...*For the Order!* And within moments the crowd was shouting and cheering.

But it didn't last long, a huge flash of light and an explosion in the air caused the crowd to move away from the light, their shouts and screams quickly dropping to frightened murmurs as Drann priest Legatis moved to the front of the stage, his Torlites surrounding him. He stood below the stage, over fifteen paces away from Lord Byron, just below where his explosion of light had caused a gap in the crowd.

"You speak words of treason before a Drann priest! How dare you!" Legatis stormed.

Lord Byron was calm as he looked expectantly at the priest. "It is not just I," he said, "but many others. My second in command in the Order," he continued, using the opportunity to point to Carthen, who stepped forward, his hand resting casually on his sword, "is none other than Terwyn Gar!"

"Lies!" Legatis spat. "Terwyn Gar died years ago! I was at his funeral!"

"Many were at my funeral!" Terwyn shouted. "I wanted Rane to think I was dead. I hated fighting for him. I refused to do it any longer. We," he said, looking at Lord Byron, "formed the Order to destroy his murdering tyranny. We are asking for your help!"

Someone shouted from the crowd. "How do we know you are who you say you are?"

Then another responded, this voice closer to the front of the stage. "May I speak!?"

Kith looked to the many men at the front of the crowd looking for the owner of the voice. It sounded familiar.

"You may speak," Lord Byron said, gesturing for the man to join him on the stage. Kith watched as a man walked up the steps to join them. His heart soared when he saw who it was. It was Master Torbin, the distiller.

Torbin smiled and winked at Kith before joining Lord Byron. "I was on this stage nearly two years ago," he began, addressing the quiet crowd. "Some of you remember that day." There was a murmur as the townsfolk whispered amongst themselves about that horrible day. "I was to be executed for being a member of the Order, which I was not. I was rescued by a friend, along with Terwyn Gar and members of the Order. This man," he said, pointing to Carthen, "defeated an Eradicator and helped save my life. Who else but Terwyn Gar could do such a thing? I may not have been a member of the Order then, but I will join now! I will no longer live under the despotic shadow of our emperor! Who will join me?!"

"The word of one man, a spy at that, means nothing!" Legatis yelled, trying to bring the crowd under his sway. "Any man or woman caught, or even admitting to being a member of the Order, will be executed for treason!" Then he moved his hand over one of the silver disks and pulled glowing E'lear energy from it, forming a ball of white light about as big around as a child's head. "Anyone who stands against this order will die by my hand!"

"I don't think so," Terwyn Gar said, glancing back at Kith. Kith took his que and moved forward, his drift cloak fluttering around him, energy from his Catalyst Stone pulsing in his limbs, ready to explode with power if need be. "Beside me is Kith Caren, the very same man who saved Master Torbin." Terwyn Gar looked at Legatis. "Look at that statue!" he yelled even louder. "And look at Kith Caren! What do you see!? Your power does not hold sway over us anymore."

Legatis laughed, although it seemed a little forced as he looked at Kith more closely for the first time, his eyes glancing to the huge black Ar'kan statue in the middle of the courtyard. "And why is that?!"

Kith took the lead, drawing his sword. "I am an Ar'kan warrior! I weild the power of the ancients! I am here to help defeat Lord Rane!"

The crowd was deathly silent as they watched the confrontation. Some of the townsfolk were looking intently at Kith, their eyes glancing to the black statue in the center of the courtyard and back. The resemblance was startling.

Legatis laughed. "There have been no Ar'kan warriors for thousands of years. Let me prove your words lies! I hold you all guilty of treason! A crime punishable by death!" And with that he flung the glowing ball of energy directly at Kith.

Kith reacted faster than anyone thought possible, his body leaping off the stage, his drift cloak fluttering in a mesmerizing dance. Without even a running start, the E'lear energy allowed him to jump two body lengths high, meeting the glowing ball of energy in mid-flight, nearly five paces above the transfixed crowd. His sword, now held in both hands, swung down and met the ball of E'lear, cleaving through the energy. There was a blue flash of light as his sword dissipated the energy, then nothing. The ball simply vanished as Kith continued his arc, landing just before the Drann priest, his sword resting on the priest's neck. Kith had jumped impossibly far, over fifteen paces, and, in a blink, had his blade nicking the Drann's flesh near his jugular. The Torlites around him didn't even have time to draw their blades, their expressions full of shock.

"If you draw your blades," Kith said casually, "you will all die."

The men looked at Legatis, their hands frozen to their pommels. Legatis's eyes were wide as he looked frantically at Kith. "How did you do that?! That's impossible!"

This time Kith raised his voice, ignoring Legatis's plea. "I *am* an Ar'kan warrior! We need your help! All able-bodied men must pick up their steel to defend Daswin! Lord Rane is marching his army here to destroy us!"

"Is this true?" someone yelled in the crowd.

"It is!" Lord Byron answered. "In two days we are leaving the city to meet his army! We need your help to defeat him! Join me, join Terwyn Gar, join our Ar'kan warrior, defender of our lands! If you do not, Emperor Rane will raze the city to the ground, killing everyone in his path! What say you?!"

Kith thought it interesting that Lord Byron had left out anything regarding the army of Kelic descending on them from the north. Perhaps he deemed the information unnecessary, or perhaps it was simply he did not know how the people would react to an army of Kelic joining them. Of course, many were staring at him in astonishment, but it was hard to tell if it was due to his white Kelic hair or that he had just jumped impossibly far and defeated the magic of a Drann priest.

There was a long pause before someone finally responded. *My steel is yours!* More shouts of support came from the crowd. Then more choruses of support joined in. Within moments the entire crowd was shouting for Rane's end.

"You are all going to die," Legatis growled at Kith, his voice just a whisper.

Kith subtly shifted his blade, the razor-sharp edge drawing a little more blood. "Perhaps, but death finds us all." His eyes flashed blue as he emphasized his point.

Legatis clamped his mouth shut.

EIGHT

For the second time Emperor Rane stood before the portal ready to enter the lands of Skell. Beside him was Rallin and Thryn, as well as Warden Stollen, two hundred red caped Danites behind them. At the rear was a team of twenty engineers and miners ready to find and remove enough field stones from Skell to mark their Drann priests in training. They would need as many wielders of the E'lear as possible when they confronted Lord Byron's make-shift army, although it wasn't the Order he was worried about, it was the ten thousand fierce Kelic who were joining them. Rane was furious that the Order was able to unite with the Kelic, pulling them from their secluded home in the Northland. Thus far, Rane had allowed the Kelic to live at Dungrin undisturbed, their isolation more of a deterrent to Rane's forces than their warriors. But now they were marching south, and although their alliance with the Order infuriated him, he was also eager to finally rid his lands of the cold loving giants and the Order all together, crushing them under the boots of his army. They had no way to defend against the power of the Drann. They would all die, their corpses littering Urotha.

Rane had already uttered the word *Skell* in the Dardanian language and the portal had reacted as it had previously, a shimmering translucent opening appearing. They had already entered the lands once before, but other than quickly scouting the area around the portal, they knew very little of the terrain they were entering. The Skell portal was located in the mountains, black rocks jutting up all around them. During their previous brief exploration, they had found a few natural paths, probably animal trails, that led to huge cliff faces, all overlooking heavily forested lands below. The climate was like Dareef, the air warm and the terrain littered with black mountains and rock formations, the rest seemingly covered in green foliage. But where Dareef was warm and wet, Skell seemed much less humid, the heat less overbearing. The good thing was that their engineers had said that the field stones could likely be found in the mountains that surrounded the gate. Rane was hoping they would only be gone a few days.

Without looking at his men surrounding him, Rane entered the portal first. The others followed just behind.

As they appeared on the other side, Rane felt the warm air first. Looking around, the scenery looked just as Rane remembered. The portal was nestled in a wide clearing with plenty of room for the two hundred warriors. All around them were jutting black peaks. The boulders and craggy stone surrounding them were peppered with gnarly short trees that managed to grow straight out of the dark rock.

The creature's heart thudded in its massive chest as it felt the pulse of the portal, the white shimmering opening causing saliva to drip from its black fangs like a gar facing down its prey. It had not eaten in thousands of years, the yearning to do so was nearly overwhelming. Its children had spread out around it, their black shapes blending in perfectly with their surroundings. They had been frozen in the same position for weeks, waiting for their orders. But weeks were like the blink of an eye to the Crawlers. Having spent the last thousand years dormant had allowed them to hold their lizard-like bodies still, their minds linked to their leader, the large Crawler waiting patiently for its prey. For it knew the bags of flesh and blood would come. Memories of times long ago flashed through its mind as images of battles and warm flesh fluttered in its mind. It had not been present so long ago, but the memories of its predecessor were seared into its mind, linked through energy shared by the field stones that filled their land. The ancient battle fought so long ago with the creature's predecessors and this strange two-legged prey was like a dream, shared through mindlinks and passed on, like stories told to younger generations. The beast knew things it should not. It knew of new lands filled with more prey. It knew the portal was the link to get there.

Although the leader had no accurate sense of time, it had been weeks since it had been awoken, the disturbance in the E'lear when the gate had been used drawing the creature to the portal. It had not moved since, its huge black body curled around the rocks surrounding the portal, its hard exoskeleton blending in perfectly to the rocks around it. The creature, and its children, were bred from the very land, and millions of years of evolution had formed the Crawlers into perfects killers.

The warm four limbed bodies filled the clearing, the Crawlers hiding all around them. The leader felt its children's hearts quicken, their desire to feed like a wave crashing down on its senses. Its black eyelids opened, and yellow-orange eyes peered at its prey, the men fanning out into the clearing below. It felt the heat of the E'lear pulsing from one of them, make that two, but one in particular was noticeably stronger. It wanted to crush the life from it but knew that that would have to wait. Somehow, from memories passed on, it knew that that particular prey would have to be pushed away from the gate. The goal now was to get through the portal, and that meant it had to remain open. The leader's eyes seared into its prey, the signal to attack emanating from it in a pulsing wave of hate.

Rane was just about to start giving orders when the rocks surrounding them began to shift. He blinked and the shifting turned to movement. Blinking again he realized that massive black shapes were attacking, lizard-like creatures propelling themselves across the rocks with incredible speed. He had barely gotten his blade from its scabbard before the first screams began.

"Protect your liege!" Warden Stollen shouted as the closest Danites surrounded Rane, their spears angled out just as the creatures hit them. Steel tipped spears deflected off their black exoskeletons and within moments the clearing was filled with screams and spraying blood.

Everything had happened so fast that Rane had had no time to observe the attack through a strategic lens. He barely had enough time to draw his blade and bring forth a whip of E'lear energy before a creature leaped off a rock towards him, black claws and fanged mouth aimed for him. Rane dove sideways and snapped his whip across his body. He had glimpsed the effect the Danite spears had had on the creatures and hoped that his Drann magic, or his Rakian blade, would prove more effective. The creature reached for his diving form and missed by a hair, Rane's whip wrapping around its limb at the elbow. The beast howled as Rane rolled, pulling the whip tight at the same time. Coming to his feet Rane saw the creature roar in pain as it scrambled awkwardly to face him, its arm missing, the limb twitching on the ground.

But the beast didn't even pause, hurling its body forward again, its huge maw snapping shut as it sought Rane's flesh. A large form jumped between them, Rallin's foot snapping out and hitting the creature in the side of its head. The Crawler was as big as a horse, but longer, and its head was heavily armored. But the great Kelic was stronger than any Hiskani, and although the kick did little damage, the power stopped its advance and snapped its long neck to the side. Rallin followed up by driving his blade down while it was stunned, its steel tip punching through its eye and into its brain. It shuddered violently and died.

"Cannot pierce armor," Rallin said as he panted heavily. He was covered in blood and his right arm suffered two lacerations, likely from their claws.

Rane nodded and took their quick reprieve to assess the situation. Many of the Danites around him were dead, but strangely only a few of the creatures could be seen battling the remaining fifty or so men. He was sure he had seen many more descend upon them. "Rallin, can you see the gate?"

Rallin turned towards the portal, peering above the battle. Then he jumped on top of the dead beast and looked again. "The creatures are swarming through the portal," he said as he looked back at Rane. Rane was worried as the Kelic's eyes uncharacteristically shown with worry.

"It's a diversion while they enter our lands. We must get to the portal!" Rane shouted above the battle. Obviously, the stories they had heard about strange creatures living on Skell were true. Rane had never really doubted it, but he had never expected that they had the ability to lay an ambush and to think through plans strategically. The Crawlers had been waiting for him. In the past, the gate had always stayed open until Rane had purposefully closed it, which could only be done near the gate. Or he could put some distance between himself and the portal, which in the past had caused the gate to close automatically. The portal *had* to be closed, the question was what was the best way to do that? If he ran, the distance between his Catalyst Stone and the gate would likely close it. Then he could wait and enter the lands safely. Of course, the danger was that more and more of the Crawlers would get through the longer he waited.

Making up his mind, he looked at Rallin. "We need to cut a line to the gate, pass through, and close it!"

Rallin nodded and jumped down from the carcass. Warden Stollin was still alive and directing the Danites, the elite fighting men having formed a shield wall around their liege, the front-line angling swords through the gaps while the back line shot their deadly spears above, most of the steel tips bouncing off the Crawler's hard exoskeletons. The wall was holding, but barely. Men were ripped from the wall and torn to pieces. Soon, there would not be enough men to close the gaps in the wall.

Suddenly there was a bright white flash and one of the Crawlers nearby catapulted over the remaining fighting Danites and landed in a heap next to Rane and Rallin. The beast had a huge gaping hole through it, the massive wound smoking. Thryn emerged through the gap, his face a mask of sweat and blood. His eyes were wide with adrenaline. "My liege, what are we to do?!"

"We must get to the gate and close it!"

Thryn nodded as the battle commenced behind them. The elite Danites warriors fought with all their skill, their shield wall doing its best to protect them as their spears shot out, looking for gaps in the creatures' defenses. But there were few weaknesses, and strong clawed arms whipped in and ripped shields away, exposing the warriors to more attacks. Teeth, claws, and tails lashed in, slicing and crushing as the Danites backed up, closing the gaps as more and more men died. But it was obvious to anyone watching that within moments the last of the Danites would be overrun.

"We must close the gate!" Rane said as he looked at Thryn. "You and I will blow a hole through the line! Warden!" Rane shouted. "When we move, form a V formation and cut through the hole we create. Once we are through the gate, we must close it!"

Thryn nodded.

"What of the creatures that have already made it through the gate?" Warden Stollen asked as he disengaged from the shield wall.

"We can deal with that *if* we survive this!" Rane shouted as he looked at Thryn. "Ready your E'lear!"

Thryn and Rane drew power from their sigils, balls of energy forming in each of their hands as they moved to the front of the shield wall. Rallin stayed close to Rane, his huge sword held at the ready. Rane looked to Thryn. The priest's eyes were wide with fright, but he nodded his readiness.

Warden Stollen stepped next to Rane, the wall of Danites before him wavering under the brutal onslaught. He was just about to give the order to *gap*, or to create a hole in the line, but it turned out to be unnecessary. A black spiked tail shot over the wall and struck a spearman in the head, launching him sideways. Clawed hands snaked in and ripped two other men from the wall, their bodies disappearing in the black mass of scaled flesh.

The hole in the wall was just before them.

"Now!" Rane shouted as he jumped through the gap, two glowing spheres of energy flying before him, his rakian blade leaping to his hand. The balls exploded as they stuck a Crawler, the power knocking the beast backwards and injuring other beasts that were close. Thryn's two spheres followed and white light filled the gap as two more creatures were thrown back into the throng of attacking Crawlers. Rane, Warden Stollen, and Rallin pushed through the gap.

"Follow!" Warden Stollen shouted over the chaos of battle. "Spear formation!"

The dying Danites heard the order and pushed forward, using their shields, swords, and spears to push the Crawlers back. Most of the Crawlers were entering the gate and little did the men know that there were only twenty or so of the beasts holding the line.

Rane fought with all the skill he could muster. His blade spun and sliced, E'lear from his sigils flowing into the blade and cutting through their exoskeletons where normal swords could not. In his left hand he formed a shield of translucent E'lear, the energy shimmering in a circle that protected his torso from the Crawler's attacks. He used the shield as a weapon as well, directing burning energy through it whenever it struck an enemy. It was not enough to kill the Crawlers, but it was sufficient in stunning them so he could push closer to the gate.

Behind him Thryn held a huge ball of E'lear between both hands. As he moved forward, he directed bolts of energy that shot from the ball into any Crawlers that got close. The E'lear's energy managed to pierce the beast's exoskeleton causing the creatures to howl in pain. Some died from numerous wounds, other simply moved away, looking for an easier kill. Rallin and Warden Stollen were there to finish off any stunned beasts, angling their blades for their eyes, mouths, or softer underbelly, resulting in the path before them opening as Rane and Thryn cut through the creatures. They were like a rock in the middle of the river, the Crawlers pouring around them like water.

Finally, they reached the gate but before them were more Crawlers, the smaller ones entering the portal as a large one stood before it, the beast turning to the face them. There were only twenty Danites left and the few remaining Crawlers whose job was to keep them from the gate swarmed in around them. They were now surrounded.

Rane knew he could not stop or they would all die. He had to get through the gate and then close it. To do that, he had to defeat the big Crawler.

He looked at Thryn. "Focus your energy on the big one!" Then he glanced at Warden Stollin. The man was covered in blood and suffered a wound at his hip. But his eyes boiled with adrenaline and he still had fight left in him. Rallin looked the same, his tall form near his master. "Protect us why I kill this creature."

They both nodded.

Rane closed the energy to his shield causing it to disappear in a flash. Drawing more, he formed a long spear of glowing E'lear, and without hesitation he launched the weapon just as the large Crawler reared up, its huge body attacking quickly, long clawed arms reaching for him. Most of the lizard-like creatures were as big as a horse, but this Crawler was four times that size. Its head alone was as big as Rallin and it had a maw capable of ripping a man in two in one snap of its jaws.

The spear struck the beast in its long neck, snapping its head back in a white flash. The thing howled in pain and stopped its charge. Two bolts of E'lear from Thryn flashed and struck the beast in the chest as Rane raced forward, his small body like a bug looking up at the boot that was going to crush it.

Rane darted from one huge leg to another, his rakian blade cutting deep gashes in its flesh, the E'lear flowing through the blade and cutting through the hard armor as if it were normal flesh. Claws tipped in black talons slashed, looking for him, hoping to rip him to pieces. But he evaded the attacks like a fly buzzing around a striking hand, all the while his sword cutting into the thing's legs.

More bolts flashed from Thryn, striking the beast in the chest and neck and keeping its full attention from Rane. Danites fought all around them as the Crawlers closed in on them. Warden Stollin and Rallin were also there to protect their flanks. The only thing blocking them from the gate was the big Crawler.

The massive beast roared in pain as more searing bolts struck it. Howling in anger, it snapped its huge tail around its body, the spiked end brushing aside a handful of Danites before striking Thryn in the side. Three spikes, each as long as a sword, punched through the priest's body. With a flick of its tail it lifted Thryn into the air and with a snap, launched the Drann thirty paces where he stuck a rock wall with a sickening crack. It mattered little as he was already dead.

Rane drew more E'lear and formed a long whip of sizzling energy, simultaneously ramming his blade half way into the creature's lower chest. Looking down, the Crawler shifted back from the attacker and snapped its huge head down, its massive jaws open for the kill.

Rane did a flip backwards, narrowly missing the deadly jaws. Never stopping, he snapped the whip forward, the long strand of energy whipping around the creature's thick neck just as it retracted the attack. Rane knew he could not let go or the connection to the energy would be severed, the whip doing little harm. So, he gritted his teeth and held on as he was yanked from the ground like a stone thrown from a catapult. Holding onto the glowing whip, he swung around and smacked hard into the creature's back, a sharp spike on its spine ripping through Rane's side. He couldn't tell, but it felt like it missed anything important and grazed the muscle and flesh above his hip. But he had no time to ponder the seriousness of the wound. Holding on with all his strength, he channeled a huge amount of energy into the whip that was still wrapped around the thing's neck. The Crawler howled louder than anything they had thus far heard, shaking his head violently. Rane was ripped from the thing's back once again, but still he held onto the whip, pushing more E'lear into the weapon as he roared defiantly. Suddenly the connection to the beast was severed and he was flying through the air. He retracted the whip and landed near the remaining Danites, rolling to his feet. Pain lanced through his side, but he ignored it. The big Crawler was thrashing about, its headless neck spasoming like a worm on a hook, blood dousing everything around it before it crashed to the ground dead.

"We must go!" Rane shouted as he ran to the portal. Rallin and Warden Stollen were still alive, as well as ten Danites. The remaining Crawlers seemed confused, and did not attack, unsure of what they should be doing now that their leader was dead. Using the reprieve, the surviving men pushed through the portal, Rane closing it behind them in a flash.

***

It was late morning the following day when Kith was finally able to get away from the meetings. Lord Byron was having a difficult time with some of the nobles and Kith's presence was requested to instill a sense of fear, and hope, for many did not believe the stories they had heard of the Ar'kan warrior of legend. He had sat through various councils and had done his part, although he was often unsure what his part was to be. He was no actor, nor was he a politician. Lord Byron knew all this and helped guide him in the proceedings, giving him subtle clues as to when he should reflect strength or just stand nearby and show his presence. Kith knew that the backing of the nobles was important in securing as many forces as they could muster for their growing army. But despite the importance of the mission, a few nobles, those in the back pocket of Rane, left their holdings with their men and belongings. It was clear they saw Lord Byron's defeat as a forgone conclusion and did not want to align themselves with the losing side.

They were leaving early the following day and Kith had a few things he wanted to do. He had his cloak reversed and his hood pulled over his long white hair as he meandered through the bustling town. He had never seen the town so energized. There was a strong sense of anxiety in the air. Some people were packing their things and heading for the countryside, deeming it safer than staying in a city that was now Rane's target. Others prepared their homes for the possible attack, while still some, young and old men alike, prepared themselves for the battle to come.

Kith found the mercantile easy enough, the familiar old sign hanging above the weathered door. Entering, he immediately noticed a change. Many of the shelves that lined every inch of the store were almost bare. He could actually see through one wall of shelves to another.

"I'm sorry, we are closed," a familiar voice came from the other side of the shelf before him. He caught glimpses of RuAnn loading some of the goods lining the shelf into a burlap sack. Kith moved around the shelf as RuAnn looked up, her face tired, her expression perturbed at the interruption. Kith removed his hood and her expression shifted quickly, moving from annoyance, to surprise.

"Kith, is that you?"

"It is."

She ran to him and hugged him, holding him tight before releasing him. "I thought you were dead," she said as she kept her hand on his arm. "What has happened to your eyes?"

"It is a long story." Kith reasoned that RuAnn had not been in the town square when he had attacked the Drann priest the day before. Consequently, she was not privy to what had happened to him. Although his martial display would've just raised more questions. Kith was glad she was absent from the town gathering. "I was hoping we could talk before I leave. Are you leaving?"

"We are. My mother and I are leaving the city and we are trying to salvage as many goods as we can. Our wagon can only hold so much."

"Where are you going?"

"My mother has a cousin that lives near Lampure. He owns a tap room called The Wanderer. He will secure us work for the time being."

"Good," kith said. He did not want to see RuAnn caught up in the violence, which was part of his reason for coming to see her. The other, well, he just wanted to see her again. He was not sure if he would be returning, the dangers ahead being all too real. "That is why I am here. I wanted to warn you and urge you to leave. Make sure you don't travel west of Lampure. It may not be safe."

"Kith, what happened to you? After you attacked that Eradicator, I thought for sure that you had been killed."

"We escaped. I was not able to tell you then, but I am part of the Order. And now, well, I am something else."

"What do you mean?"

"You know that statue in the town square?"

"Yes."

"Well, I am that," Kith said lamely.

RuAnn's face scrunched up in confusion. "I thought that statue depicted one of the ancient warriors."

"It does." Kith sighed in frustration. It was simply not something you could explain in passing. "Do you have time to discuss this further?"

As if on cue, RuAnn's mother yelled from the back door just before she entered. "Ru, where is that bag?" She stopped when she saw Kith, her expression wary before recognizing him. "Kith?"

"Yes, ma'am."

"What has happened to you?" she asked, looking him up and down. The changes from when they saw him last were clearly startling. Kith had to admit, the ordeals he had suffered had changed him, not just mentally, but physically as well. His bearing was strong, like a predator, and he moved like a dancer. His shoulders had grown wider, and his face had become more chiseled, like stone. The scarring surrounding his piercing blue eyes signaled a strong warning to others that he was not to be trifled with, like a rattle on a poisonous snake. He simply looked dangerous.

"We were just discussing that. It's not something I can explain in a few words."

"I'm sorry, Kith, but we are leaving in a few hours," Marne said. "I want to be on the road before dark."

"I understand," he said softly, not sure what else to say, glancing uncomfortably at RuAnn.

Picking up on his unease, Marne looked at her daughter. "Finish up and meet me in the alley. We still need to pack the wagon." Then she looked at Kith. "I am glad to see you alive, young man. I hope you will be careful," she added, as if she knew that his future would be filled with danger.

"You too," Kith replied. "Do not take the road to Ronis. It will be dangerous."

Marne nodded and glanced at RuAnn before turning and leaving them together.

RuAnn stepped closer to Kith once again, her hand gripping his. "I'm sorry we cannot speak further. You will be careful, won't you?"

Kith nodded. "The road before me will be dangerous. I just wanted to see you and make sure you were safe before I left."

She picked up the bag at her feat and slung it over her shoulder. Looking up at Kith, she reached out and touched his neck, pulling him close as she kissed him softly on the lips. "Be careful, Kith Caren. I am hoping to see you again." Then she turned and walked through the back door leaving Kith alone in the room.

Kith felt a mix of emotions, although he could not easily define them. His mind was focused on his emotions as he made his way towards the business district. He was angry, or was it frustration at his inability to live a simple life, to be able to get into the wagon with Ru and her mother and ride off to safety. No, it wasn't that, he thought. It was fear. He was afraid he could not live up to the mantle placed upon him. He was afraid that people like RuAnn would be crushed under Rane's black boot because he could not defeat him, or worse, keep the Crawlers from entering Urotha.

Dark clouds had boiled up from the grayness of evening, shadowing the sun early and casting an ominous feeling over the city. It was fitting considering the recent turn of events, as well as Kith's dark emotions. He was still thinking about his interaction with RuAnn when his senses, ever alert, picked up on nuisances that he never would have detected before his Ar'kan training. The smell of stale sweat and tobacco found him, the odor as strong as cat urine. There was a shuffle of feet on dirt, the subtle sound echoing in Kith's trained mind. The E'lear flowing through him thrummed, sensing the intent of someone's focused mind. No, more than one mind.

He had taken the back allies, eager to stay away from the crowds. As he reached a cross in the path, the alley continuing straight, left, or right, he knew the attack would come. Although he could not see them, he knew the assailants were hiding behind trash barrels to his right, and a dark entry marking a door on his left. He had left his spear in his room in Lord Byron's palace and all he now carried were his zyths and his rakian blade. But he doubted he would need to draw any steel.

Sudden movement came from behind the barrels on his right as two forms jumped out, the lead attacker aiming a thick club at his head. Simultaneously a man leaped from the dark entry on his left, the flash of silver warning Kith of the knife he carried.

Kith moved with the grace and speed that the ruffians were not prepared for. Spinning by the descending club, he gripped the man's arm in an iron grip and whipped him around, all the while using his foot to snap kick the man with the knife in the face. There was a crunch as his nose broke. His head rocked back so violently that he dropped like a sack of bricks. Kith silently swore, hoping he had not killed him.

Never stopping, Kith used the first attacker's momentum and flipped him in the air, his body striking the third attacker and knocking them both into the barrels. He stood calmly as the men scrambled to their feet, one nursing his shoulder where Kith had jerked his arm and flipped him. The other drew a long knife from under his dirty over coat. They were clearly street ruffians' intent on robbing him.

"If you want to live, put the knife away," Kith said calmly.

The man with the injured shoulder glanced at the man on the ground. "Did you kill him?" he stammered.

"If I did, it was not my intent."

The man with the knife stepped closer to Kith and spit at his feet. This thief was bigger than the others, his demeanor telling Kith he was the leader. Suddenly Kith recognized him, the jagged scar on his face bringing back unpleasant memories. It was Lightning Jax, leader of the Bone Squad. He looked the same, just older, a lot older, like every year in the streets had equaled five. "You don't give the orders here! I do!" he said, jabbing his knife towards Kith.

Kith looked around confidently. "Are you sure? I will say it again, put the knife away if you want to live." Kith didn't really want to kill the man, but he also knew that Lighting Jax was a leech on society and had probably killed handfuls of people for less than a few coins. His death would quite literally save lives. Kith was not naive enough to think that someone else wouldn't take his place. But Lighting Jax was obviously quite resourceful, having survived in the streets for so long. The Bone Squad may dissolve with his death, or perhaps another, one less violent would take over. Either way, Kith would not lose sleep if he was forced to kill him.

The man on the ground began to groan in pain and slowly get to his knees, his hand moving to his bloody nose. He was wobbly, but eventually was able to stand. "You broke my nose," he groaned, his voice as shaky as his legs.

"I am glad," Kith replied. "I had thought I broke your neck."

"Bane, stick that shit eater!" Lightning Jax yelled.

Kith laughed. He had not heard that nickname for quite some time, and now, as events had taken a full swing from when he was fifteen, the absurdity of the situation was suddenly comical.

"What's so funny?" Lighting Jax sneered, stepping a little closer to Kith.

"You don't remember me, do you?" Kith asked.

"Naah, why should I?"

"Six years ago, you and your gang attacked me in an alley. I stabbed one of your friends and an old man came to aid me, defeating you as easily as a man sparring with children." Kith narrowed his eyes. "You were going to kill me."

Lightning Jax froze and his jaw tightened as he thought back to the event. "I remember dat," he hissed. "But you'ze hair was black, not white."

"True, but it was me," Kith continued. "And now it seems I have been given the chance to right a wrong."

"I don't think so," Lighting Jax said as he shot forward, his knife lunging for Kith's chest.

Kith reacted with precision and speed, his body swaying slightly to the side and both hands working in unison. One snapped out and struck the ruffian at the elbow of his attacking arm, forcing it to jerk back towards his own body. Kith's other hand had grabbed Lighting Jax's knife hand as it was forced back towards his face. With a quick jerk Kith rammed the knife directly into his throat, angling it out, he sliced through the right side of his neck.

Spinning away, Kith avoided the spray of blood and Lighting Jax stumbled into his crony, spraying his body crimson. He fell to the ground, his blood covered compatriot looking at Kith with stunned eyes. If you blinked, you would've missed the move.

"Now," Kith said calmly. "I will allow you to leave, or you can stay and die."

Kith barely finished his words when the two thieves ran off into the night.

Kith continued towards the business district and found that the attack had actually angered him. With all that was happening in the city these thieves still deemed it necessary to kill and steal. Kith knew he was no saint. In fact, he had stolen many times when he was homeless and living in the streets. He was painfully aware that sometimes it was necessary if you wanted to survive. But he never stole from those who were poor, and he never resorted to violence to get what he needed. He didn't hate thieves, he just hated thieves that had no morals.

After walking for half a bell, he finally made it to his destination. Standing before the thick wood door, he took a deep breath, pulled his hood off, and knocked. He had not spoken to Master Torbin for over a year. Prior to the other day, the last time he had seen him was when he had attacked the Black Watch soldiers before his execution. He had no idea what had become of him since.

The door swung open and Torbin greeted him, immediately recognizing his long white hair. "Kith!" Torbin blurted. "In Dar-dan's name, its you! Come in, come in," he said, hastening him inside. Kith shut the door behind him as Torbin cleared off a space at the main table. Kith had been there a handful of times, but it looked different now, a bit more disheveled. "Please, sit down," he urged. "I'm sorry for the mess but I'm packing. I'll be leaving in the morning."

Kith sat. "That is probably a good idea."

Torbin paused as he looked at him more intently, his dark eyes appraising him in more detail. "Even though I saw you the other day, I still can't believe how much you have changed. I am glad you are here. I have wanted to thank you for quite some time." Kith tried to wave him off but Torbin ignored him. "You saved my life, young man. You acted when no one else would, and because of those actions I am alive today. I don't know how I can ever repay you."

"It is not necessary. You have done much for me. You looked after me when I had nothing." Kith paused, feeling a bit uncomfortable. "It is what friends do."

Torbin laughed. "I have no friends that would attack an Eradicator and his Black Watch soldiers. Kith, you could have died."

The corner of Kith's lips curled up in a knowing smile. "The thought did cross my mind."

"Which makes your actions even more heroic. Whatever you need, I will provide. I owe you everything."

"I need nothing. I just came to see you. I wanted to make sure you were okay and to warn you that perhaps you should leave the city."

Torbin nodded. "Yes, that is my plan. I hope the Kelic army will arrive on time."

Kith was not aware that anyone knew about the Kelic army, and he voiced his confusion. "How do you know about the Kelic?"

Torbin smiled. "I know that yesterday I had made it sound like I was joining the Order. But the reality is I have been a member of the Order for years, even before I met you. I am no fighter, so I will be helping the Order in matters of logistics in the trials to come."

"I wondered about that."

"And I know you are as well," Torbin added. "Lord Byron and I have had numerous conversations about you. He has filled me in on who you are and what has happened to you. I cannot believe it. It seems so..."

"Impossible?" Kith queried.

"Yes."

"Trust me," Kith acknowledged, "I feel the same way."

"So, what will you do?"

Kith shrugged. "I will make sure Rane does not open the gate to Skell, and hopefully kill him in the process."

Torbin looked at him with concern. "And you have the power now to accomplish this?"

"I hope so."

"Be careful son," Torbin pleaded. "You are carrying a heavy burden."

Kith nodded but said nothing, the weight of his words true enough.

They shared a glass of cold wine together and talked for another bell or so. After Kith left, he felt better about seeing his friends. At least he knew they would be away from the fighting. He made his way back to Lord Byron's palace, the guards recognizing him easily enough. They bowed to him as they let

191

him in, which of course felt quite strange. He was no lord, or even a noble. He didn't like it, but he realized that he was now playing a role that he had not expected. People looked at him with hope, and despite his awkwardness, he would do his best to make sure their faith was not misplaced. It was late, and he was tired so he went straight to his room. He planned to be on the road when the sun rose the next day. He needed the rest and hoped sleep would come. If it did, it would have to fight back the turbulent thoughts swirling around in his head. Kith wasn't sure sleep would win.

***

As soon as Rane and the survivors burst through the gate onto the other side, he knew they were in trouble. There were nearly forty black Crawlers looking straight at them, their orange-red eyes burning with rage. All around them was carnage. Torlite bodies lay everywhere, ripped apart, blood splattering the rocks surrounding them. There was always at least a vor of men guarding the gate. There were none now.

The Crawlers started to attack as soon as they saw them, but stopped in their tracks, burning eyes flashing in confusion, some looking around as if they were unsure what to do. Simultaneously Lord Rane felt a wave of thoughts crash into him, the onslaught dropping him to one knee. The cognitive pressure felt like a huge boulder on his head and he swooned, dizziness nearly overtaking him as he forced himself to stand, pushing back the mental onslaught. He had never felt anything like it, but for some reason he knew it came from the creatures. He could sense that much.

More images flashed in his mind, and although it was hard for Rane to make sense of them, they seemed to be heavy with uncertainty. He picked up images of the big Crawler he had killed, and as the seconds progressed so did the anxiety he felt from the creatures wash over him. He realized that they did not know what to do without the big Crawler. How he could sense that he had no idea.

"Why are they not attacking?" Warden Stollen whispered, his voice strained, his long sword and shield held before him. The warrior was covered in black blood and his dark hair was drenched in sweat and stuck to his head. The others looked no different.

The men were looking at Rane, who was clearly having some reaction to the beasts. Grunting away the pain in his head, his thoughts began to form a rationalization as he focused his mind on the huge amounts of E'lear flowing through his sigils, the power humming in the disks at his hands. He could feel that the creatures were somehow linked to the power.

And just as he realized that, the creatures began to advance once again, although quite slowly, as if the draw to feed on the sacks of flesh and blood before them was not as strong as previously. Rane growled as he wrestled with the mental onslaught as well as the power within him, finally overcoming it with his will. He willed them to stop, and surprisingly they did.

Rane straightened as he slowly began to gain control, the swirling anxiety from the creatures lessening some as they sensed the colossal amount of E'lear behind Rane's will. "They sense the E'lear in me," Rane hissed. "I willed them to stop."

"And they listened?" Warden Stollen questioned incredulously.

Rane nodded and blinked a few times to clear away the dizziness. The mental pressure had lessened to a dull humming as the Crawlers seemed to look to him for guidance.

"Are you saying you can control them?" Warden Stollen asked.

Rane stood up straight, the edges of his lips curling up into a wicked smile. "I believe so."

***

The sun's ambient light was barely peaking over the mountains the next morning as Daswin's army continued its preparations. Some residents were fleeing the city, long lines of wagons, their lanterns dangling, could be seen from the city walls. Others were hunkering down, joining the fight by helping with provisions, collecting water, and preparing weapons. There was much to do to be ready for a siege. No one knew for sure what was going to happen. The only knowledge they were privy to was that Emperor Rane would soon be marching the most powerful army Urotha had ever seen to their city. People were scared.

Kith slung his pack over his shoulder, cinched the straps, and grabbed his spear. Lathronin and Theron were next to him, their packs and weapons ready. Each also carried a woodsman's axe tied to the back of their packs. Likely they would be needed where they were going.

They were near the main gate and Lord Byron, Carthen, Arim, Bos, and Bear'lon were there to see them off.

Lord Byron hugged his son. Then he quickly released him and kept him at arm's length, gripped his strong shoulders. "Be careful, son. I don't want to lose you again."

Theron nodded, his face stern, his casual boyishness no longer apparent. His strong jaw was set, his eyes registering a man who had seen violence. "You too, Father. I'll see you at the Pass."

Carthen stepped over to Kith. "We need to know what we are dealing with. The information you bring us will be vital."

"I understand," Kith replied, making eye contact with everyone. "Be safe."

Before they could leave, Lord Byron addressed Kith directly. "If you cannot find the sunken gate, will you return?"

"I do not know," Kith admitted. "Likely I will continue on by myself. I can cover the distance to Akari faster on my own," he added as he saw Theron about to interject. "Your skills," he added, looking at his friend, "will be needed with the army. But I believe we will find this gate."

The idea about finding the sunken gate near Rock Pass had come to Kith the other night, but they had had little time to discuss the details. The plan was to use the gate to go to Akari. From there they would spy on the army and return with valuable information. Kith had discussed his plan with Theron and his friend had insisted that he join him. Theron had also added to the plan by suggesting they try and destroy whatever siege engines Rane was likely bringing with him. The last thing the city needed was trebuchets and fortified ladders at their gate. If they could destroy them, they could use the portal to return to Daswin before Rane arrived at Rock Pass.

"But will the portal even work?" Carthen asked.

There were many holes in their plan. Would they even find the gate, let alone be able to use it? And if they did, would the gate at Akari be guarded? Likely it would. Their best plan for success was to use it at night and to keep their numbers small, which was why the only other warriors with him were Lathronin and Theron. Hopefully they could evade whatever guards were stationed there. Everything was a risk, but, marching to Rock Pass and fighting with Daswin's men did not seem like the best use of Kith's skills. He would be fighting soon enough. But deep down, he knew there was more he could do. He just hoped that Theron and Lathronin, despite their martial skills, would not slow him down. Though he had to admit, he was thankful for their company. And if anyone could keep up, it was them.

"The Eskeli said the portal should be functional," Kith responded.

Carthen nodded and shook his hand.

Everyone said their goodbyes and before the sun's full light rose above the horizon, the three warriors were clicks away, running at a rapid pace past the long line of wagons.

NINE

It took the trio three days to make it to Rock Pass. It must have been a record on foot since they had run all day, taking only short breaks for water and food, sleeping no more than four to five hours each night. Kith had led at a blistering pace, and he mused that there were likely few people besides his two companions that could've kept up. The E'lear flowing through his body protected him from exhaustion, but he knew that his companions did have such luxury. Yet, despite the grueling pace, it was manageable for the other two warriors, their difficult training hardening their bodies beyond what most could hope to achieve.

It was late evening on the third day when they arrived at the lake, the trail through the Rock Pass steep and difficult. Even Kith was drenched in sweat despite the chilling evening air. They stood upon a huge rock, the edge of it careening over the crystal-clear lake four paces below. For as far as they could see, the landscape consisted of large rocks, with trees and grass intermittently growing amongst them. It was obvious that a huge slide and created everything around them, the elements of time softening the terrain to form a beautiful landscape of contrasting hard stone with lush green vegetation.

"This is quite beautiful," Theron pondered, wiping the sweat from his face as he reached for his water bag.

"Where shall we look for the gate?" Lathronin asked.

"The Eskeli said the gate had originally been built in the town. If we can find the remnants of the ruins, we should be in the right area," Kith guessed.

"It's going to be dark soon," Theron reasoned, looking at the sun as it began its nightly slumber. "Start the search in the morning?"

Kith was eager to get started. But snooping around in the dark would do them no good. Nodding to the others, he took off his pack. "This is a good spot to camp."

The others agreed, and it wasn't long before they had a fire going and all three were sitting on their wool blankets, eating salted beans and rabbit.

Lathronin had been staring out into the water when he turned to Kith. "I've been wondering...if we find this gate under the water, how will we reach it?"

Theron swallowed a mouthful of beans as he looked at Kith, clearly contemplating the same issue.

Kith shrugged. "Depends on its depth. I am hoping the gate will be along the lake's edge, where the water is shallower." Pursing his lips, he looked poignantly at his companions. "Then we sink to the bottom while I activate the gate."

Theron looked concerned, and his eyes darted to Lathronin, who looked equally uneasy. "You want us to tie a rock to our feet and sink to the bottom of the lake?"

"If it is shallow enough, I believe it will work, although a rock shouldn't be necessary, your armor will suffice," Kith replied.

Even though Theron had not worn his plate armor, his chainmail would easily do the job. "But what if the gate does not work?"

"When I get close, the gate should respond to me. I will know if it will work before we have to sink to the bottom."

"That is reassuring," Lathronin replied, his typical stolid expression replaced by one of open sarcasm.

"I hate to poke holes in the plan," Theron interjected, "but if the plan is to come back the same way, how will we rise to the surface wearing our armor?"

Lathronin looked even more apprehensive, Theron's words adding to his unease.

"Let us deal with one issue at a time," Kith suggested, smiling faintly. "It will work," he added, with more enthusiasm, trying unsuccessfully to ease their apprehension. "Let us just find the gate first, then we can contemplate the dangers of using it."

The next day they began their search for the city ruins as soon as the sun's light made it possible. The terrain around the lake was rocky and lined with huge boulders and cliffs. It was difficult work. About mid-day, Lathronin hollered and everyone joined him near the west side of the lake. He was staring at a flat wall of stone, boulders and scree piled up all around it. Grass and other foliage had grown over the ground, the green growth creeping up the exposed wall. It stood out from the rock around it as it was flat and square, the edges cut so they fit perfectly together. Clearly it was made by man.

"Looks like a piece of an old wall," he pointed out.

Kith agreed and moved towards the water, the ground sloping into the water's edge. There were some small trees and shrubs growing there, but where there were just rocks and scree, they could get right to the lake shore. Looking around, Kith could see far into the clear water. The other's joined him.

"Doesn't look too deep," Theron added hopefully.

"Let's get those axes out," Kith said. "We need a raft."

They had planned to build a raft, so they had brought axes and plenty of rope. It was nearly dark by the time they had a crude raft built, timbers lashed together, with smaller ones on top to form a make-shift deck. It was not pretty, but they tested it in the shallow water and it did indeed hold their weight. They agreed it would make no sense floating around at night, so they built their camp near the rocky shoreline, their bedrolls laid out among the tuffs of soft grass. The sky was clear, but the evenings had been cold, so they built up a large fire to wait out the night.

"Do you think Rane is on the march?" Kith asked after a long moment of reflection looking into the flickering flames.

Theron pursed his lips in thought. "I would assume so, yes. He was already preparing to invade Dral. Mobilizing his forces would not take so long."

Kith tossed a stick into the fire. "Do you think we have a chance?"

Theron sighed. "With the Kelic, yes. Without," he shrugged his shoulders. "I'm not so confident."

"Are the Danite really so fierce?" Lathronin asked.

Theron nodded. "They are. The rigorous training weeds out all but the very tough. But it's the drilling that makes them so deadly. Constant training...cavalry, foot, you name it, they are experts at it. A Danite is just as good fighting in groups as they are individually. I would not want to face a Danite charge."

Kith looked up from the fire. "Good thing you are here, with us. Your knowledge of their ways will help defeat them."

Theron shook his head in doubt. "I hope so."

"I've been thinking," Kith said, looking at Theron. "When I activate the gate, do you think water will rush through, carrying us with it?"

"Its likely," Theron replied. "You'll have to make sure you shut the gate quickly when we pass through to the other side."

"There seems to be a lot risk in this plan," Lathronin said. "You sure it's worth it?"

"I think so," Kith answered. "I see no other way where we can cover the distance to Akari fast enough to get intelligence and return before Rane's forces get to Rock Pass."

"And we still plan to try and slow him down?" Theron asked, somewhat eager.

"If a way presents itself, then yes."

All three of the warriors stood on the wobbly raft, looking down into the clear water with trepidation. Luckily, they had found the gate easily enough. It was fifty paces to the left of where they had launched their raft and not so far out. Blue glowing sigils hummed with power as they had floated over it. It was impossible to miss in the waning sunlight, the shadows of night creeping in quickly. But that had been their plan all along, to use the gate and appear on the other side at night. They figured if there was anyone guarding the gate that they would have an easier time eluding them at night. At least they hoped so.

Kith had swam down to inspect it and estimated it was roughly twenty feet under the surface. There were several large stones blocking half of it but there was still plenty of room for the three of them to enter. Now they stood above it staring down into the water.

Theron looked at the rope that was hanging over the edge. "You think it will hold while we are gone?" He looked skeptical.

"It's all we can do," Kith replied. They had attached one end of a rope to a large rock and tossed it overboard as an anchor. Their reasoning was that if they were going to be coming back through the gate, that they might need the raft close by. They wore their packs but figured they would have to dry most of the contents. Some of the food and their tinder boxes would be ruined, but they could find more tinder, and hopefully more food.

"I'm not really liking the idea of sinking to the bottom in my armor," Lathronin lamented. His armor was light, mostly hardened leather, but still, combined with his weapons and pack, he would sink quickly. Theron and Kith even more so. "And coming back the same way seems worse."

"You saw me swim to the bottom and back with my armor on," Kith replied. "When we return, you both will remove your armor and wrap it in a bag. I'll carry it to the surface."

"You sure you're strong enough for that?" Theron asked. They had not tested that theory.

Kith nodded. "It will work. You ready?"

Lathronin let out a deep breath and nodded.

Theron smiled. "Let's have some fun."

"Remember," Kith warned. "If we meet resistance when we come through, our plan is to evade and run. We have more important things to do than fight guards."

The two warriors nodded in understanding and gripped their weapons.

And then Kith jumped into the water, the other two following. They sunk quickly and landed just before the gate. Blue sigils were glowing all along the smooth black rock, reacting to Kith's Catalyst Stone. Part of Kith's training was to learn various Dar-danian words, especially the ones used to activate the gates. He spoke the word for Akari, and even though it was underwater, the gate reacted, a shimmering flashing across the entrance.

And just as Theron had predicted, all the water around them was sucked into the gate. The vacuum was so intense that Kith lost his bearings as he was sucked through rapidly. He could feel the power of the gate hum but had no idea of his surroundings. He was tossed around for a few heartbeats and then suddenly he found himself tumbling onto hard ground, the power of the water behind him so strong that it pushed him across the rocky terrain. It felt like he was in a river.

He felt he must be on the other side of the gate and as the water cascaded around him, he struggled to find his friends. Seeing them thrash about in the cascading water, he yelled the word to shut the portal. Suddenly the power of the water was gone. As the water around them dissipated into the rocky ground he was finally able to stand and get his bearings. Theron and Lathronin were close by, looking equally disheveled. Looking around quickly, Kith prepared himself for an attack. But none came, and as his water drenched eyes adjusted to the near dark surroundings, he realized they were alone.

"There is no one here," Theron said as his vigilant eyes scanned the shadowy surroundings.

"Either of you injured?" Kith asked. His armor had protected him, but he knew the rocky ground could have caused them some injury.

"A bit bruised and battered," Lathronin answered as he moved closer to them, his spear held at the ready.

"I'm fine," Theron said as he began to look around, Kith and Lathronin joining him. It only took them a few moments to see the bodies. They were scattered all around the portal. It was hard to see in the waning shadows, but it looked to be nearly fifty dead Torlites. "What happened?" Theron said as he knelt to inspect a Torlite corpse. His chest had been ripped open as if his leather armor had been paper. The smell of rot was present, but not as strong as Theron had experienced on the battlefield. He reasoned they had been dead no more than a few days.

Kith knelt by another body. The man's head and left arm had been ripped off, huge chunks of flesh torn from his torso where his head had been. "I don't know, but they clearly died a horrible death."

"By teeth and claw," Lathronin asserted, looking over a third body. The man was intact, but suffered massive lacerations across his legs and face, the width and depth indicative of three sharp talons.

Kith stood. "We need torches. I want to inspect these bodies."

Theron frowned. "Everything is wet. We wouldn't be able to get them lit."

Lathronin rose from the body and joined them. His expression was dour. "Kith, do you think this was done by the Crawlers?"

Kith looked worried. "I don't know. I have never seen anything like this." He looked around. "The fact that they were killed by some creature while guarding the gate does not bode well."

"But if that is the case, where are these beasts?" Theron asked.

"I don't know. But without further evidence I suggest we stay with the original plan. We need to find Rane's army," Kith added.

"It's nearly dark," Lathronin pointed out. "Tomorrow morning, I can check the tracks and see if we can get an indication as to what happened here."

"I don't like the idea of camping near the gate and all these bodies," Theron protested.

"Nor do I, but what choice do we have?" Kith pointed out.

"We could hike up and come down in the morning," Lathronin reasoned.

"It's at least a couple clicks out of this hole," Kith added.

"Well worth the hike," Theron said, his expression clearly indicating that he had no desire to sleep amongst the dead men.

"Okay, let's go," Kith agreed.

The next morning, they decided it was not necessary to venture back into the deep pit. There were enough tracks around for them to get a sense as to what had occurred. Kith was a good tracker, but Lathronin was by far the more skilled. Together they had ascertained that something with claws had crawled out of that pit. There were human prints all around but the foot traffic near the pit was so heavy that it was impossible to determine any details. Tarite tracks were everywhere, mostly heading back and forth along the make-shift road that led into the pit. The massive beasts of burden were likely used to pull the huge amounts of rock and dirt from the excavated hole. It had taken Rane and his slaves' years to unbury the gate. So long that there was a small deserted town built at the top of the pit to house the slaves and overseers. Everything was now old and rundown.

"There was *something* that came out of the pit. I can make out human and tarite prints everywhere. But these are different," he added pointing to strange prints in the dirt. It was pretty obvious that they were made by something that had long sharp claws. "They seem to be heading south."

"Towards Akari," Theron said, his voice showing his concern.

"We need to move fast," Kith said. "Let's follow the tracks."

The others nodded, and Kith started to run, his pace brisk but steady. Theron and Lathronin joined in behind him, but he didn't hear the steady thump of their booted feet. His mind was whirling with the possibilities that Crawlers had already gotten through the gate. The thought unnerved him to say the least.

They ran hard all day, taking a few breaks to eat and drink. Kith was impressed with their stamina, neither of them having field stones constantly feeding them energy as he did. Knowing that, Kith kept his jog at a reasonable pace. It was near dark when they came to a small village nestled in the thick forest along the main road to Akari. Theron told them it was a logging community called Landor and it was just a few hours east of the capital. The population was no more than a few thousand, but the inn and mercantile was always busy as the town was built just off the main road. It was quite likely that someone in the small village would know the whereabouts of Rane's army. After all, you can't move thousands of men and horse without people knowing. And, if Rane's army was heading east to Daswin, they would've had to pass the small village.

"I must say I'm relieved," Kith said as he looked down at the village from the side of the road. It was not yet dark, but the grayness of dusk was settling in. From their vantage point on a gentle hill overlooking the town, it seemed to look normal. Lantern and candle lights shone from the buildings and hazy smoke drifted from the chimneys as the townsfolk went about their evening routines. "I was afraid I'd find a destroyed city, and everyone brutally killed like the men near the gate."

"The creatures did not come this way," Theron agreed. "Everything looks normal."

"We need information," Lathronin said, voicing the obvious.

"Why don't I go down and see what I can see," Theron suggested. "Neither of you will blend in, if you know what I mean." Lathronin's attire clearly marked him as an Idara and Kith's long white hair would be hard to hide.

"Is it possible that anyone there will recognize you?" Kith asked.

Theron shook his head. "No, unless there are Danite there, but that is unlikely."

Kith nodded, knowing it was the best plan. "Get some supplies while you are there. We'll meet you back here."

Theron nodded and started walking towards the town.

The village had no surrounding wall. It was not necessary; the small town being located so close to the capital allowed for a small garrison of nearly twenty men. Also, it was rare for bandits or thieves to raid a town of its size, especially one only a half day's ride from the capital. Theron had been to the village before and went directly to a popular taproom called the Stumbling Gnome. It was known for clean rooms with fair prices and a large selection of ales. There were a few people about as they made their way home for the evening. Besides a few furtive glances, they ignored Theron.

Pushing open the stout wood door, Theron walked with purpose to the bar. The taproom was made up of two rooms. The main room was large and spacious, the log walls covered with a dozen or so mounts of various animals found in Urotha. There were wide antler racks from mountain spars, four legged beasts the size of horses that roamed the upper reaches. There were horns from the light footed urgin, a small hoofed creature found in the praires all around Urotha. One wall even boasted two six-foot horns that came from a huge sea creature called a malimom. The beast was well over twenty feet long and very rare. There were pelts from ice hounds and gars, one of which was so large it looked like it could cover a bed made for four people. Besides the bar on the far wall, there was an open stone fireplace in the middle of the room, the top covered with a metal chimney that rose to the ceiling. Theron had seen the fantastic structure before, but still marveled at its construction. Word was that the owner of the taproom had once been a blacksmith and had designed and built the chimney himself. It was one of a kind and Theron had never seen its equal.

The other room was cut off by a half wall on either side, the entrance open to a smaller room. Where the main room was simple and strong, the furniture stout and sturdy, this room was more elegant, two large leather sofas facing a huge low table adjacent to a stone fireplace against the wall. There were a few other small tables about, the chairs covered in soft fur covered pads. Stairs led up to a series of rooms available for rent. That particular room was reserved for those staying at the Stumbling Gnome, and presently, Theron glanced a lone couple drinking wine near the fireplace.

Theron ignored the ten or so patrons and made his way to the bar. A tall skinny man with was pouring two mugs of ale. His had jet-black hair had strands of gray that sparkled in the lantern light. "Evening sir, what can I do for you?" he asked as he set the mugs on a tray.

"I'm heading to Tobin and was hoping to get a cold ale and supplies for a few days."

The barkeep glanced at Theron more closely, his appraising eyes fluttering around him like a humming bird before making eye contact once again. "Tobin is a day from here. Will you be needing a room or do ya plan on traveling at night?"

"I'll be back on the road after the ale," Theron answered, shrugging as he said, "I'll likely just camp on the side of the road for the night."

The barkeep nodded as he grabbed a mug. "What ale would you prefer?"

Theron glanced at the six kegs and his eyes were drawn to one called *Gorrum's Black Eye*. "What's that one," he asked, pointing to the placard hanging from a nail pounded into the keg.

The barkeep smiled. "That's like a meal in itself. It's a dark ale aged in burnt barrels and infused with crystalized palit sugar. Its thick, a little sweet, and goes down smooth."

"Sounds good, I'll take a pint of that."

The barkeep nodded as he poured the ale. "As far as rations, I can get you bread, cheese, some cured fish, and some salted spar. How many days did you say?"

Theron didn't want to invite suspicion, but he needed rations for three people, not just him. "Well, I'm only staying in Tobin for a day, then I'm heading back to Daswin. Would you have enough to outfit me for a week?"

The barkeep pursed his lips in thought just as a serving girl rushed to the bar, picked up the tray with the two mugs, and dashed off again with little more than a glance at Theron. "I believe I can accommodate you," the man replied as he set the mug of dark ale before him. "I'll get the order in, but it will be a little while before we can get everything together. I'm short on staff today but if you sip your ale slowly, I'll have everything ready by the time you're done."

"Much appreciated."

"Oh, by the way, I'd be careful heading back to Daswin," the barkeep added as an afterthought as he gripped the door handle that presumably led to the kitchens. "Emperor Rane marched his army through here just yesterday."

Theron pretended to be surprised. "Really!? Where are they headed?"

The man shook his head. "I'm not sure, but it was his entire army. I thought at first that he was heading to that portal he found, although I still don't believe it. But he turned East. I've never seen so many men. Rumor has it that he is marching to Daswin, although I'm not sure why. Just wanted to warn you," he added, as he opened the door to get his order ready.

"Thank you," Theron added as he thought about what the man had said. It was great news. They were not far behind, and at their pace they could likely reach the army by tomorrow.

As Theron was thinking and sipping his ale, two men entered and made their way to the bar. They were both tall for Hiskani, but a few fingers shorter than Theron. Theron sensed their presence immediately. They moved with purpose, their postures tall and straight, their vigilant eyes casually scanning their surroundings. When Theron glanced their way, one of the men was looking right at him. His eyes narrowed for a moment, before he nodded in greeting and turned his gaze back to the kegs on the wall.

There was something about them that Theron did not like. They were warriors, at least the swords they wore and their confident bearing suggested that was true. He could always tell someone was a fighter when he saw one, like two predators standing next to each other, each one knew the other was potentially dangerous.

Theron turned and put his back to the bar, pretending to peruse the occupants of the room. As he did so, his eyes caught a poster on the near wall flanking the two men. Returning to the poster, he nearly blanched when he analyzed it more carefully. It was a wanted poster for him, his name written in bold words above a drawing that looked eerily like himself. Clearly, whoever had drawn the picture, had seen him many times, which wasn't terribly strange considering he had been a Danite Captain. There was a reward of a thousand crowns, which was an astronomical amount for a bounty.

Just then the man at the bar furthest from him noticed the poster and moved closer, reading it over. "Hey, Balt, have you seen this?"

The man closest to Theron glanced over and looked at the poster. "No, must be new." When he noticed the bounty, he whistled. "A thousand crowns! That's a king's hoard. This Theron fella must have done something really bad."

"Probably banged the emperor's wife," the other man said, laughing at his own joke.

Balt laughed and looked at Theron. "Can you believe that bounty...a thousand gold!"

Theron glanced over quickly before looking away. "That's a lot of money for sure."

"I'd like to get my hands on that guy," Balt added, looking down at Theron's sword. "Fancy blade, you know how to use that?"

Theron shrugged. "Some. Its my fathers and he taught me a little before he died. He had been a Torlite for most of his life."

The man nodded. "I'm Balt and this is my friend Tagit."

"Well met," Theron added as he shook Balt's hand, nodding to Tagit in greeting.

Just then the barkeep came back from the kitchens. "Shouldn't be much longer," he said, addressing Theron.

"Thank you," Theron added, trying to keep his face away from the two men as best he could. He was increasingly nervous and wished the barkeep would hurry with the provisions.

The barkeep moved to his two new customers and took their orders, pouring them two cups of ale and setting them before them. They each took a large gulp before Balt addressed the barkeep.

"Hey, what do ya know about that bounty?"

"Came in three days ago. Word has it that the man was a Danite Captain who betrayed the Emperor."

"See," Tagit laughed, "he stuck the queen with his sword, if ya know what I mean."

"My name is Balt and this is Tagit. We are caravan guards looking for work in Akari. We've been known to do bounty work here and there. You got any more information about this man?"

The barkeep shrugged. "Read the fine print. There is more information on the poster," he said as he moved away to address an issue with the serving girl.

Balt did just that and walked to the poster, reading it more carefully. Theron glanced his way but tried to look inconspicuous. Was something else written there that might give his identify away? Unconsciously, his hand moved to his blade for reassurance.

"What else does it say?" Tagit asked.

"It says," Balt answered, leaning close to read the fine print, "that his sword has a silver wire handle and a gold pommel in the shape of..."

Theron's heart pounded like a drum as Balt stopped reading the poster. He turned slowly to look at Theron, his eyes appraising him in a new light.

Tagit picked up on his friend's unease and glanced at Theron before looking back at his friend. "What is it, Balt?" Balt was eying Theron, his hand slowly moving to his sword.

"Our friend here," Balt began, looking at Theron, "is carrying a blade that fits that exact description. And look at him," he said, his voice rising in excitement, "he looks just like 'im."

Theron moved off the edge of the bar but didn't reach for his sword. "Now hold on there," he said, "just cuz I look like em doesn't make me him. Why would I hang out in a taproom with a wanted poster of myself?"

Balt ignored Theron and looked around the room, a few of the patrons already sensing the confrontation. "Folks!" Balt said, raising his voice for all to hear. "This man before me looks just like our man in the poster! And his sword is an exact description! Are there any sword wielders here interested in splitting a thousand gold crowns?"

The room was deathly silent, but three heartbeats later two men rose from a far table, one wearing a sword and the other a knife and hand axe. They wore leather armor and were likely mercenaries looking for work in Akari. Both men moved to flank Theron.

One of the men with a missing tooth and aged skin, said, "We'd be interested."

Balt smiled, looking back at Theron. "Now friend, we can either take you alive, or dead, the choice is yours. The bounty is seven hundred gold if you are dead, but either way, we are going to be rich." He drew his blade and the other three followed, the sound of steel scraping from their scabbards poignantly loud in the tense room.

Theron's eyes narrowed, and he slowed his beating heart. He had been afraid that they would find him out, but now that they knew, he was deathly calm. His black eyes found each man, his gaze tense and somehow able to project steadfast confidence despite their drawn blades. "If I am indeed the man on that wall, then you know what I'm capable of. If you move that raised steel any closer, you will all die."

"We are four, and you are one," the man wielding the axe and knife said. His tone was not as confident as his words, however.

Theron looked at the man. "I am a Danite Captain. There is no chance of victory for you."

Balt shook his head. "Sorry, but the golds worth it."

"Worth dying for?" Theron added, his tone cool and controlled. As he spoke, several of the patrons that were nearby moved away, sensing the confrontation. Two even left through the door. Great, Theron thought. They would surely inform the soldiers at the garrison in town. He had to force their hand and get out quickly, one way or the other. "I'm leaving. If you try and stop me, you're going to get hurt, or worse," he added with emphasis, "you'll be dead."

Theron turned towards the door to leave just as Balt lunged at him. He had been expecting it and sidestepped the attack, whipping his blade from its scabbard at the same time. By the time Balt retracted his blade, Theron was already attacking, his body moving towards the man with great speed, his blade flashing and scoring a deep cut along the man's left shoulder.

Balt screamed and fell back as Tagit swung his own blade towards Theron's exposed flank. Theron kicked out with his left leg and struck the man in the side of the knee, thwarting his attack as he stumbled into the side of the bar. He righted himself quickly only to meet Theron's fist, the same fist holding his blade. Blood splattered across the bar as the man's nose was crushed, the power and weight behind the attack forcing him to drop like a rock. He hit the ground hard and didn't move.

Theron leaped back as he sensed the attack from behind. A hand axe struck the bar where he had been and embedded itself deep into the wood. Theron's sword whipped around and came down on the man's arm as he tried to yank the axe free. More blood sprayed the counter as the man's arm was severed at the elbow. Screaming, he fell back, turning the wood crimson.

The third swordsman stood transfixed, staring at Theron, his alleged friend on the ground near him bleeding profusely. He slowly backed away from Theron, his wild eyes taking in the scene as his friend howled in pain.

"You best leave," Theron said to the man, "or you will fare no better."

The man needed no further encouragement and turned and ran, leaving his friend behind. Theron looked to the barkeep behind the bar. "Get me that food! Now!"

The man stood stark still, his wide eyes staring in fright at Theron, blood from the injured men dripping from his face. "I-I..."

"Now!" Theron yelled again. "Just get me what you have!"

The man broke from his fright and ran through the door. Theron wiped his blade on the unconscious man's shirt and sheathed it. Balt was groaning on the ground, his hand trying in vain to stop the flow of blood from the deep cut on his shoulder.

"Best get that stitched or you'll bleed out," Theron said, tossing a bar rag to him. "Keep pressure on the wound."

The barkeep ran back in and set a canvas bag on the blood splattered counter, stepping back without saying a word. Theron reached into his coin pouch and tossed the coin onto the counter. "Sorry bout this." Then he grabbed the bag and ran out the door.

Theron found them quickly and it only took one glance from the others for them to know that something was wrong.

"We have to go!" Theron urged.

"What happened?" Kith asked. "What did you find out?"

"There was a wanted poster of me and a bounty of a thousand crowns. A few men recognized me."

"And?" Kith pressed.

"Let's just say I didn't kill them."

"Are those rations?" Lathronin asked, indicating the bag.

"Yes, although I'm not sure how much. I had to leave in a hurry."

"Did you find out about Rane's army?" Kith asked.

"He is a day ahead of us. We can catch him easily."

Kith smiled. "Good. Let's go, the guards will be after you soon."

They ran hard for another few hours, hoping to distance themselves from any pursuing garrison guards. But it eventually got too dark to travel safely so they camped far off the main road. Evidence of Rane's army was everywhere. The road and surrounding brush had been trampled, thousands of boots, horses, and wagons turning the smooth dirt into a churned-up mess. A patrol of guards arrived a few bells after they set up camp, but the trampled road hid their passing and the town guards rode by, their torches flickering in the distance as they disappeared into the night none the wiser. It wasn't long before the guards came back, obviously giving up on finding Theron in the dark. They took turns keeping watch and then fell right to sleep, exhausted from their constant running.

The next day they were off before the sun was up, moving at a steady but strong pace. Everyone was tired by now, except Kith, but the knowledge of Rane's army so close was like wiggling an apple in front of a horse. They wanted to see what they would be up against, and were hoping to wreak some havoc on the army, slowing them or destroying some of the siege machines, hopefully doing both. Anything to weaken Rane's army before they met sword to sword at the Rock Pass.

Kith had run ahead hoping to find the army before dark. And as luck would have it, he came across Rane's troops a few hours before dusk. His drift cloak was wrapped around him and he was moving quickly through the forest just off the main road. Like a wild animal, he raced between trees and leaped over downed logs, his drift cloak fluttering behind. To anyone watching, he would've looked like a blur as the cloak changed hues to match his surroundings. They would have seen something...but discerning what, would have been difficult. It was likely they would think it nothing more than the play of the last of the day's light against the forest trees.

Racing to the edge of the forest, he stopped just behind a tree before a wide meadow. The terrain was mostly forest, but occasionally the thick trees and brush opened into expansive grasslands, interspersed with hills and rocky terrain.

The meadow before him was huge, spanning from the road in both directions. It was a great spot for an army to camp, which was why Rane had picked it even if they did have a few hours of marching light left. They would likely find no better spot before dark. From his vantage point, Kith could see thousands of men moving about their evening tasks preparing camp, erecting tents and setting cook fires.

Kith figured he had an hour before Theron and Lathronin caught up to him. He wanted to use that time to scout the edge of the camp and see what he could see before darkness set in. Slowly, he moved from tree to tree like a shadow, his drift cloak making him nearly invisible. He knew it likely they would have perimeter guards, so he took his time, stealthily moving around a man he had spotted near the forest edge. As he made his way around the large clearing, he stared in awe at the sheer size of Rane's forces. There were thousands of men and hundreds of carts and wagons laden with food and supplies. He was about halfway around the camp when he saw a ring of forty huge wagons draped with thick canvas. Strangely, he could see the canvas on many of the wagons flutter and move, like something alive was hidden inside. Kith noticed that there were no guards close by, which he thought strange if they were indeed carts filled with supplies. A good military commander, even in one's own territory, always guarded their supplies. Without them, the army was more or less useless. So why were their none about? Tucking the thought away, he continued around the encampment. He didn't have to go much further before he saw the siege machines. Rane had two huge tower ladders, each one nearly as tall as the trees around him. They were clearly built to position near a city wall, using the system of stairs inside to traverse to the top. A team of men were unhooking the oxen that had been pulling the huge structures. They were so large that it took six oxen per ladder. He also saw six trebuchets, two oxen pulling each one. There were plenty of men about, mostly the oxen handlers who were now unhooking the strong beasts and leashing them to the trees around them. Kith stopped ther e and decided to head back, hoping to catch his companions before they got near the camp.

Running back the way he had come, Kith intercepted his friends soon enough. Informing them of his find, Kith led them directly to where the siege machines were being housed. By now it was nearly dark and they could easily see thousands of cook fires, their flickering light penetrating the evening darkness.

The three of them had positioned themselves on an expanse of rock just back from the edge of the forest. In was a clear night, and despite the faint glow of the moon, there was little to no chance that they could be seen through the trees before them, the shadows of night thick like oil. From their vantage point, they had a decent view of the camp as it sprawled out below them.

"There must be twenty thousand men down there," Lathronin whispered.

"Maybe more," Theron added softly.

"Any ideas about those huge wagons?" Kith asked.

"They are big cages used to transport the tarites," Theron answered. "But I've never seen them covered in canvas. The tarites don't like that," he added.

"Why have carts to transport tarites when they could just walk? Kith asked.

Theron shook his head. "They are huge creatures and very strong. But not good for long distances. Rane uses the wagons to carry them from various mines all over Urotha."

"Maybe we should get a look inside one," Lathronin added.

"I agree," Kith said. "What do you think about the siege machines?"

"I don't see many guards," Lathronin pointed out.

"I'm sure they are not expecting any threats so far from Daswin," Theron mused. "Likely their scouts are ahead, not behind."

"I don't think I would have a problem sneaking in there," Kith suggested. "I could look in those wagons as well."

"You still want to burn those machines?" Lathronin asked.

"I think the risk is worth it," Kith said.

"I agree," Theron added. "It will likely slow him down. He might stop and have his engineers build more now, rather than wait until he gets to Daswin."

"How long to rebuild something like that?" Kith asked.

Theron pursed his lips in thought. "He has a lot of men, but even so, it would likely take four to five days to rebuild what I see below."

"Based on our information, that would give the Kelic time to reach us," Kith acknowledged.

Theron nodded, his eyes perusing the camp below. Then he looked at Kith poignantly. "You think you can get in there, light the fires, and get out, without being seen?" His tone didn't sound so confident.

Kith nodded. "The drift cloak conceals me well. The trick will be lighting eight fires quickly without being spotted."

"What about dousing each one in oil, moving from the nearest to the farthest," Lathronin said. "Then lighting the one further away first and moving back towards the forest, using a torch to quickly light each fire before disappearing into the trees."

"They would never be able to find me in the forest at night," Kith said.

"What about us?" Theron asked.

"I think it best that you position yourself far away from camp, at a rendezvous spot, and I will find you after I set the fires."

"You want to do this tonight?" Theron questioned.

"If we wait another day then we will have to follow the army in the morning," Kith answered. "That means more risk of being seen, not to mention it puts us further from the gate in Akari, which means a longer trip back. I say we do it tonight."

"We are exhausted," Theron warned, "and you are asking us to run more tonight with little rest."

Kith looked seriously at his friends. He knew he was pushing them hard. They did look exhausted. "What if we find a rendezvous spot and you two get four hours of sleep. Then I hit them, and we make a run for Akari. Can you do it?"

Theron sighed deeply. "I can."

"I as well," Lathronin added. "The sleep will help."

"Good. Let's get ready."

Kith pulled the drift cloak around his shoulders and settled the large hood over his face. Taking a deep breath, he moved from his concealed spot behind a tree, silently moving into the clearing and the thigh high grass. He snuck quietly through the meadow, heading directly for the train of covered wagons. He still thought it strange that there were no cook fires or guards about. Normally, wagons would be guarded. But these were not. It made no sense.

As he neared the closest wagon, he saw the canvas flutter, a low rumble emanating from it. He stopped instantly as he looked closely at the wagon. Again, something inside moved, followed by a clicking that ended in a strange hiss. Suddenly Kith's heart was pounding, and he wasn't sure why. Clearly, there was something alive in the wagon. Taking a deep breath, he moved closer, getting within an arm's reach before stopping again, another eerie clicking sound freezing him. Looking closely, he saw a black claw emerge from under the canvas, the sharp tip tapping on the metal frame.

"It can't be," Kith whispered, his voice trembling. Whatever was behind that canvas was emitting a sense of fear that Kith had not experienced before. He wanted to back away into the night and leave it to his imagination. But he could not. He needed to know what was in that cage. Was it a Crawler? Were they all filled with Crawlers? If so, how?

Kith stepped closer and reached out for the canvas flap. Slowly he gripped the thick material and eased it slowly open. Black scales shifted and the creature inside hissed louder, its body banging on the steel bars. Kith nearly dropped the canvas and ran, but he pushed the fear away and opened the flap further. Something black swirled inside and suddenly a lizard-like head crashed into the opening, its black scales banging on the bars and teeth like sharp pieces of shale gnawed viciously at the steel bars. Orange eyes flared in the darkness as the creature hissed and growled, trying in vain to break through the bars and rip into Kith's flesh. Kith dropped the canvas and involuntarily jumped back.

"Crawlers," Kith swore softly. Somehow Rane had captured them. Could he control them? Looking around, he tried to get an idea of how many wagons were in the clearing. Moving through the shadows he counted forty-one. Now it was clear why there were no men around. No one wanted to get close to the deadly creatures. And they surely needed no guard.

There was nothing he could do about the Crawlers, so with great concern he left the wagons and headed towards the siege machines. He needed to concentrate on the task at hand, but the fear of what the creatures were capable of gnawed at him as he zoned in on the nearest machine. There were various fires all about, but the darkness and tall grass, combined with the power of the drift cloak, made Kith no more than a glimmer as he drifted towards the first trebuchet. Most of Rane's men were sitting around fires talking and relaxing after marching all day. There were a few perimeter guards about, but Kith easily avoided them as he knelt next to the first machine. Taking off his pack, he withdrew the first bag of oil. They had taken three bags each for just such an occasion, and Kith has stuffed six into his pack. As quietly as he could, he dumped the content all over the lower wooden legs of the machine. Corking the bag, he put his pack back on and made his way to the other machine which was only five paces away. Just as he neared it he saw the shadow of a man step from around it, the soldier tying the string on his pants. He had been relieving himself in the shadows and Kith had not seen him.

Kith froze and slowly lowered his body to reduce his silhouette. But he had nothing to hide behind and he was no more than four paces from the man. Trusting in his drift cloak, he lowered his head some, keeping his body as still as a statue. He was confident in his cloak, but he was concerned about his pale face and white hair in the darkness. The man looked his way and yawned, seeing only darkness and shadow before walking away towards the nearest fire.

Releasing the breath he didn't know he was holding, Kith made his way to the next trebuchet and followed the same procedure, pouring the contents of a second bag onto the wood. He continued on, moving deeper and deeper into the enemy camp. But the guards were few and far between and when he did see them, he simply ducked low and waited for them to move away. There was no way they would see him with his cloak wrapped around his body.

He was able to douse every machine without further incident. Squatting low next to the last big ladder, Kith readied his torch. This is where things could go awry. He had to hope that the enemy would be so preoccupied with the burning engines that they would not notice the torch moving away towards the safety of the forest.

Taking a deep breath, Kith readied himself. "Here we go," he whispered, as he struck the flint across the metal on the tinder box. Sparks flared, and the tinder caught on the first try. That was a good omen, he thought, as he used the burning tinder to ignite the oil-soaked torch he had brought with him. Without pausing, Kith used the torch to light the oil on the huge piece of equipment. And then he was moving, a silent shadow racing through the night, the only evidence of his passing was his illuminated shadow created by the meager torch light.

Ten heartbeats later and three more engines were afire, the camp waking as the flames licked at the darkness. Men yelled in the chaos as Kith moved to the last few engines. He ignited a trebuchet, looking around frantically for anyone noticing his passing. Something to his left caught his attention and he spun, a lone Torlite running towards him.

"Hey, what are you doing?" the man said as he drew his infantry sword. Kith bolted towards him like a crossbow bolt. He was so fast that the man barely cleared his blade before Kith, having drawn one of his zyths, flew by him, the razor edge of his weapon parting the flesh at his neck like a sack of grain. Kith was ten paces away before the man even blinked, his sword dropping to the ground as he tried in vain to hold back the blood spurting from his neck. Kith lit the last trebuchet on fire before the man fell to the grass.

Racing along the perimeter of the meadow, Kith used the meager moonlight to guide him. One of the things he noticed was that he could see much better in the dark than his comrades. The Eskeli had advised him that the powers of the field stones were many. They were engrained in his body in such a way that some of their gifts would be subtle, and possibly grow with time. If he could have looked upon himself now, he would have seen the slight blue glow of his eyes, like those of an animal that hunted at night.

Silently thanking the Dar-dan, he ran hard, dodging trees and leaping over downed logs. He headed towards their rendezvous point with great haste. He knew Rane's men would be after him. They had to get away and get the news back to Carthen and Lord Byron. Kith was happy in what he had done to the siege machines, but his accomplishment paled in light of what he had discovered. The presence of the Crawlers created a sense of forboding that consumed his thoughts. What were they going to do? He didn't have any answers.

***

Emperor Rane stood before the burning towers, twenty of his elite Danite guards standing behind him. Thousands of men were back further still, looking up at the billowing flames as they ate away his siege engines. The fire was so acute that Lord Rane could feel the heat on his face, the intensity of the flames matching his malevolent glare. The light shed from the burning machines lit up the surrounding meadow.

After a few moments Rane strode towards the Crawler's cages, his Danite guards following silently behind him. Rallin, Rane's Kelic body guard, walked just behind, his intense blue eyes ever vigilant. Commander Garn and Warden Stollin were also there. They were clearly concerned, Rane's silence unnerving, wondering if they were to be blamed for the lapse in security. These types of mistakes under the leadership of Rane could lead to one's death. It would not be the first time someone under Rane's power died from a mistake. Whether they were responsible was irrelevant. Rane would likely punish someone. It was this unknown that caused the two men great anxiety, but to their credit, neither showed it as they followed their emperor to the massive cages.

Rane stopped near the cages and focused his attention on the E'lear that was swirling through the sigils that covered his body. Immediately he felt the thoughts of the Crawlers, their minds connected to the E'lear in a way that Rane did not yet fully understand. In fact, he had learned that he could not stay close to the beasts for long as their thoughts pounded into his consciousness. They were looking for his guidance. Presently, images of hunger assaulted him, their minds intent on blood and death. They had not eaten since they killed and fed on the Torlites that had guarded the gate. They were eager for fresh blood. Rane pushed those thoughts away and searched deeper, looking for any clues as to who may have lit the fires. If they did not see something, which was unlikely due to the heavy canvas that covered their cages, then perhaps they heard or smelled the culprit. If so, perhaps Rane could sense who may have done the deed. It was a longshot, but Rane's anger needed to be satiated.

It was not long before a fresh thought jumped to his consciousness, images of a man in a strange swirling cloak dancing in his mind. The image was so strong that Rane nearly fell over from the mental assault. Touching his temple with his left hand, he used his prodigal mental will to hold the image, zeroing in on the creature that sent the visual. The cage was nearby, and once he found it, he pushed all the other swirling thoughts away, focusing on that creature alone. It was a difficult task, and anyone besides Rane attempting it would likely have fallen over unconscious. Rane grunted and put both hands to his temples. Rallin stepped closer but Rane held out his hand, holding him back.

Again, he focused on the creature's thoughts. He could see the man in his mind's eye, but his face was covered in shadow and his form was a blur, the cloak he wore making him look like a shadow in the night. But other thoughts came to him, one he could not clearly understand, although the intent was clear. The Crawler had his smell. The creature wanted the man's blood.

Rane looked back at Commander Garn. "Open that cage," he said, pointing to the wagon holding the Crawler.

Commander Garn looked concerned. "But my Lord, will the creature not attack?"

"Open the door," Rane growled, his voice sharp with barely contained fury.

"Yes, my Lord."

Commander Garn moved forward and issued the order to a Torlite who was standing off to the side, the man's face pale with fear. He had the keys to the cage and was obviously concerned. The young soldier stepped to the cage and put the key into the lock, his hands shaking. The canvas fluttered with movement but then stopped, like a breeze had ruffled the fabric in passing. After a pause, he turned the key and the lock clicked open. The man moved back quickly as the door slowly opened a finger's width.

"Remove the canvas," Rane ordered, his mind still focused on the mental link with the Crawler in the cage. He sent images to the beast of what he wanted, using his will to subdue the creature. Although he did not show it, Rane was concerned that he would not be able to control the beast. So, he took the colossal amount of E'lear he was controlling and pushed it all to the two sigils at his hands, ready to deploy it if necessary.

The young Torlite ordered a few other men to remove the straps that tied down the canvas. Then he stood back, holding one edge, and pulled hard. The canvas slid off and immediately the door opened, the Crawler emerging like a snake from a hole. The creature's body was bigger than a horse and long, with four back legs and two more longer ones in the front. It crawled out like a lizard, using its clawed hands to easily climb the cage, pausing on top, its back four legs gripping the iron cage while it rose up, its front arms extended, its long neck snaking down and facing Rane. The beast's mouth opened, and it hissed, exposing long black teeth as long as a man's fingers.

Rane felt Rallin behind him tense, but no one moved, their eyes on Rane as he stared down the beast. The creature was ten paces away, but Rane held no doubt that it could cover the distance in one leap and be on him in a blink. He readied himself as he pushed his will out, sending images to the creature. Communication was difficult, and he was unsure if he was able to pass on his orders in a way that the creature could understand. The creature sent back images of it ripping the man to pieces, one more Crawler standing behind it. The thought meld seemed to be working.

So it wanted help, Rane figured, interpreting the creature's thought. Rane thought that interesting, figuring that any normal man would be no match for the creature. But clearly, the Crawler had sensed something in the man, something that smelt of danger.

"Unlock one more cage," Rane ordered, his eyes never leaving the creature, his thoughts unwavering.

The Torlites, feeling a bit more confident that they were not going to be eaten, did as ordered, releasing one more of the beasts. Once released, the first Crawler leapt off the cage and landed with ease, the other Crawler joining it. Rane felt them communicating, their orange-red eyes flicking to him and back to each other, hissing and uttering deep rumbling growls. All the while he continued to push his E'lear laced will into the two creatures, making sure they understood his orders and that he was not to be trifled with. They seemed to sense his power, and for whatever reason viewed him as the alpha, as the leader, taking the place of the big Crawler he had killed.

And then in a blink, they were gone, racing into the blackness like silent death. Rane suddenly felt a release, like a weight lifted off his mind, as the creatures ran off into the woods. He turned to Commander Garn. "We will rebuild our machines in the morning."

The commander nodded. "Where did those beasts go?"

The corner of Rane's lips lifted slightly, the thought of what the creatures would do to the strange cloaked man assuaging his anger at losing the machines. "I sent them on a hunt," Rane answered as he walked away, Rallin following like a shadow.

TEN

Kith had caught up to the others, and after a brief discussion of what he had seen and done, continued west towards the gate in Akari. It was dark, but the ambient light of the moon was enough to guide them, especially since they had decided to stay on the Imperial Highway leading to Akari. They figured that Rane would send trackers after them, and the faster they could distance themselves from Rane's army, the better. They had valuable information to get back to Lord Byron.

They hadn't gone more than a few clicks when Kith, who was leading, heard something behind them moving quickly through the thick forest that flanked the road. It was subtle, but to Kith's enhanced senses it was clear that something was fast approaching.

"What is it?" Theron asked as Kith skid to a halt, the other two, panting heavily, stopping just behind him. Kith had not taken his spear when he had entered the enemy camp, keeping it with Theron and Lathronin. But now he spun it at the ready and faced the brush behind him, listening intently.

"Something is following us," Kith whispered.

"I don't hear anything," Lathronin said, moving his spear to the ready.

Kith heard it again, moving fast. Then he heard something on the other side of the road, his head whipping towards the new sound. "Prepare..."

But his warning was cut short as a black form burst from the brush, the creature moving on six legs impossibly fast, leaping at the last moment towards Lathronin who was nearest. Kith lunged forward and threw his spear with great speed, spinning away and drawing his sword, drifting towards the other side of the road. He knew another attack was coming.

Lathronin's eyes widened at Kith's speed, his spear sailing past his head and just missing a hand span. But the warrior could not match the Ar'kan warrior's speed, or the attacking creature, and as he tried to spin away from the beast, he felt fiery pain rip across his shoulder. Pivoting, he turned like a top, his spear leading as it spun across his body. As he turned, he saw the lizard-like creature. It had landed where he had been, Kith's spear jutting from his shoulder. His own spear raked across the thing's black exoskeleton doing no harm to the beast.

Theron had drawn his blade and attacked the thing's flank, his sword hitting it harmlessly across its armored back. But Theron had no time for another attack as the creature turned and launched at him, its body moving with such speed that Theron could not hope to match it. Long front claws flashed, scoring one long gash across Theron's leg. Luckily, he had danced back and the red grooves across his thigh were shallow. Grunting away the pain, he resumed his attack as Lathronin did the same.

The second Crawler burst from the other side of the road, its charge led by a head and neck twice as long as a horse, its mouth gaping, exposing two rows of razor-sharp teeth. The Mind Dance found Kith quickly, his body reacting on instinct honed from years of training. His left hand found the zyth at his hip, unclipped the snap, and flung the weapon side handed, all the while his body dropped low and spun sideways, his right hand snapping his sword forward. Kith felt the Catalyst Stone push currents of energy to where it needed to go, causing his body to react with speed, precision, and strength that should not be possible.

His zyth struck the creature in its open mouth and instantly the thing howled, clamping its jaw shut as it sailed past Kith. Kith's sword ripped across the thing's flank, blue E'lear energy bursting from the weapon and cutting a deep valley down its side. Black blood splashed from the wound as it landed, spinning around angrily to face the deadly swordsman. Howling loudly, the beast shook its head violently with its mouth open and the zyth flew free, black blood spraying the road.

As the dance pounded in Kith's mind, he let his body flow, moving forward again for the attack. But the Crawler, although hurt badly, was not done yet. Surprising Kith, the creature dropped low and scurried forward like a lizard, its speed throwing Kith's timing off. Kith's sword was angled high when the Crawler spun at the last moment and flicked its spiked tail across Kith's legs. E'lear surged through his legs and he jumped high, the tail missing his knees by a hair. But as his body descended, the beast reversed the momentum of its tail, catching Kith in the side of the leg just as his feet touched the ground. The armor plate covering his thigh flashed blue, the black spikes deflecting off its smooth surface. But the impact was enough to knock Kith's legs out from under him. But with speed and power only an Ar'kan could possess, he caught his fall with is right fist, his hand still gripping his sword. His feet touched the ground just as more energy surged into the arm holding him up. Using the power, he surged upwards and his body righted itself, his sword arcing across his body to protect his flank from the attacking Crawler.

The creature's mouth was open and lunging forward, trying to clamp Kith's shoulder and arm in its iron grip. The beast was not prepared for Kith's ability to arrest his fall and turn it into a counter attack. Instead of meeting flesh and bone, Kith's sword, flashing blue again, zipped past its dagger-like teeth, slicing through its jaw so deep that the thing's mouth was not able to open or shut. Kith jumped back as the creature howled, rearing up and roaring in agony, its lower jaw hanging straight down and flopping around uselessly. Kith wasted no time, lunging forward and ramming his blade into its belly just below its armored chest. Pushing down, Kith's sword sliced through the creature's abdomen the length of his forearm. Ripping the blade free he spun away. The Crawler howled even louder, rolling away as it spasmed in death, its black blood and glistening entrails covering the road.

Theron and Lathronin attacked the creature with all the skill they possessed, striking its flank when it turned to attack the other. Despite their skill and teamwork, the Crawler managed to break through their defenses. Lathronin was bleeding badly from the three gashes across his shoulder and he was beginning to tire. The beast saw Theron as more of the threat and changed its tactic, attacking him with renewed vigor.

Theron backpedaled but he could not keep the beast at bay. Swatting aside Theron's blade, the Crawler leapt high, its front claws coming down on Theron's shoulders, its great weight dropping Theron to the ground like a rock. Landing on top of him, Theron felt the claws squeeze and try to pierce the chainmail protecting him. The beast's weight was pressing down on him and he could barely breath.

Lathronin had remembered the story the Eskeli had told them about the Crawlers, that their one weak point was their underbelly. The Idara priest was staring at the creatures armored back and knew that it would not take long for the killer to rip Theron's throat out. He also knew that his spear would do little harm to its back. Thinking quickly, Lathronin dove forward to the creature's flank, landing on his injured shoulder and rolling to his feet. Pain shot through his left side, but he ignored it as he came to his feet next to the creature's side, the tip of his spear already angling towards the Crawler. The point struck true and drove deep into the side of the creature's underbelly. Roaring in pain, the beast released Theron with its two front claws and used them to swat at the spear.

Theron growled, the weight of the creature on his torso nearly unbearable. But once his arms were free, he yelled in anger and fear and brought his sword back with both hands. Then he rammed it with all his strength into the thing's belly. His blade sunk in half way and black blood gushed from the wound, more spraying his face as he pushed the blade down a hand span. The Crawler shook and cried in pain. Theron felt the thing convulse as its weight left him, pushing away from the blade that was deep in its belly.

Tumbling away it came to its feet. Blood poured from its mouth and as Theron scrambled to his feet, he saw a purple bulge push through the hole in the thing's belly. Kith's spear was still dangling from its shoulder. Kith joined Theron at his side, Lathronin just behind them. The Crawler was growling and shaking its head, as if it didn't know what was wrong with it. Then suddenly the purple bulge burst though the gaping wound and part of its innards struck the ground. It swayed for a few moments before stumbling and falling to the ground, black blood pooling around it like oil boiling from the earth.

Kith looked at Theron, his eyes wide with the frenzy of battle. "Are you hurt?"

Theron blinked as if he did not know, the shock of the battle still with him. He looked over his body, feeling around his shoulders where he felt the pain the most. "I'm beaten and bruised," he said, "and I have a shallow cut on my thigh."

Lathronin looked pale. "I'm afraid I'm losing a lot of blood," he said, his left arm hanging loosely at his side, blood dripping from the deep gashes on his shoulder.

"We need to see to your wounds," Kith said, looking around. It was dark, and despite the moonlight, there was no way they could properly inspect the injuries without a fire. He took the moment to get his spear and find his zyth.

"We will need a fire and rest," Theron said, voicing Kith's thoughts.

"They might send more of those things," Lathronin whispered, his voice strained.

"Or trackers and a contingent of Danites," Theron added, his tone somber.

"It's a risk we have to take," Kith replied, retuning to them. "But let's not do it here. We need to get into the woods and put some distance between us and these creatures." He looked at Lathronin. "Can you travel a short distance?"

"If we wrap my wounds," he strained, but then he just nodded, his exhaustion taking away his energy to speak. He would do his best, Kith knew that.

"If you falter," Theron said. "I will carry you. You saved my life."

Lathronin shook his head. "We saved each other's lives."

Kith helped the priest take off his pack, digging out the bandages and healing salve they had brought with them. Kith ripped Lathronin's shredded shirt off at the shoulder, exposing the cuts. It was dark but even in the dim moonlight they could see the wounds were deep and ugly.

"You ready?" Kith said as he took the lid off the salve. "This will hurt."

The priest nodded.

Kith used his fingers and dug out the thick green paste, smearing it into the deep cuts. Lathronin flinched but said nothing. Once done, Kith wrapped the bandages around his arm and tied them tight, hoping to stop the bleeding. Immediately they soaked with blood. But it was the best they could do at the moment.

"Let's go while I still can," Lathronin groaned.

"I will take his pack," Theron said.

Kith shook his head. "No, I can carry it easily. Save your strength if we need to carry him."

Theron nodded. "Lead the way."

Kith moved off into the dark brush, Lathronin staying just behind him. Theron brought up the rear, and together they slowly disappeared into the shadowed forest.

An hour later and Kith called a halt. He had found a clearing of soft moss, downed trees and large boulders surrounding it giving the spot some natural protection from their firelight. Lathronin dropped to the soft ground with a groan. Theron took off his pack and went to him, using the soft part of his pack to lift his head.

"I'm so tired," the priest said.

Theron looked concerned. "We need a fire."

Kith was already on it. He had dropped both the packs and was quickly scrounging for dry wood. While he was preparing the fire, Theron removed the blood-soaked bandages on Lathronin's shoulder. Fresh blood seeped from the wounds and Theron swore.

"It's still bleeding," he said gravely.

"It should have slowed by now," Kith replied, preparing to use his tinder box to light the fire. He had created a circle of rocks, piling small tinder and larger sticks around it.

"It's something from the beast," Lathronin whispered. "Some infection from its claws. I can feel it."

Kith stopped what he was doing and looked at Theron. "What about your wound?" Kith was clearly worried.

Theron looked at the cut on his thigh. It was still bleeding, but little. The wound was quite shallow in comparison to Lathronin's. It did sting. "It stings," he said. "Its bleeding some still, but I don't feel sick."

Kith nodded and went about striking the flint across the box. Several sparks later he lifted the pile of tinder and softly blew on it. Once the dried sticks burst into flame, he settled them in the middle of the rocks and quickly stacked smaller sticks over the flames. Soon he had a small fire going and he piled some of the bigger sticks on the growing flames. He would need to search for more wood.

"We need hot water to clean the wounds," Theron said.

Kith was already on it. He went to his pack and removed his metal cook pot. Filling it from his water skin he put the lid on and set it next to the fire so the flames were licking at its edges. Then he pulled more clean bandages from his pack and wet to Lathronin's side.

"I'm thirsty," the priest groaned.

Kith grabbed his water skin and poured it down his throat. He gulped several times before Kith pulled it away. "Better?"

Lathronin nodded his head, a faint smile breaking through his pain.

"We need to close his wounds," Theron said. "I can try stitching them."

"You know how?"

Theron nodded. "It was part of our training. I brought my kit."

"What about trying to cauterize the wounds?" Kith asked.

"The pain may be too much," Theron reasoned. "If it was a hole created by a sword or spear thrust, then yes, that might work. But these cuts are long and deep. The pain would be intense."

Kith nodded. "Let's clean the wounds and repack them. Then you can stitch him up. We need to do the same with yours."

Theron nodded, and they went about preparing the materials. After turning the pot several times, the water was near to boiling. They used a piece of clean cloth from an extra shirt to dip in the water and clean the cuts. All the while Lathronin had a piece of leather from a belt in his mouth that he could bite down on. Once the wounds were as clean as they could get them, Lathronin had passed out, whether it was from the pain or loss of blood they could not tell. But it was just as well as Theron was able to stitch the wounds without the priest twitching from the pain. Once they finished, they rewrapped his wounds with the last fresh bandage, saving some for his own wound. His cut was red and irritated, but it bled very little. He cleaned it, covered it in a salve, and wrapped it tight to hold back any fresh bleeding caused by the cleaning.

It was late into the night by the time they were done. Theron was exhausted and Lathronin was still sleeping, his breathing shallow but steady.

"I will watch over us. Get some sleep," Kith said as he grabbed his spear that was leaning across a nearby log.

"Do you not need rest?"

"I can go long periods without sleep," he replied. "As long as I have food and water, the E'lear energy flowing through me will keep me functioning. Don't worry," Kith added. "I will be guarding you from the darkness."

Theron was not worried. He had absolute faith in his friend's ability to protect them. He smiled and laid his head down, sleep finding him instantly.

Kith woke them at dawn. They had to help Lathronin stand. He was still pale, and he could barely hold his head up as he sat on a large rock.

He was shaking his head, his eyes grim. "I cannot walk to the gate," he acknowledged. "You need to leave me."

"That is out of the question," Theron interjected quickly. "I will carry you."

Lathronin shook his head slowly. "I have lost too much blood. Even if I could walk, by the time I made it back to the gate, I would likely be dead."

"We are not leaving you here to die alone," Kith said, his tone adamant. "We will take turns carrying you. At least that way you have a chance. Leaving you," he added, shaking his head, "there is no chance."

"We are warriors," Lathronin whispered. "This is how we die."

"You are not dead yet," Theron snapped. "Enough talk." He looked at Kith. "We need to make a sling."

Clearly, Theron's training had been extensive. He showed Kith how to make a sling using his cloak. Ripping it into pieces, they fashioned two slings, each one tying around his shoulders and dropping to loops at his waist. Kith helped Lathronin onto Theron's back, both of his legs pushing through the loops. That way, the weight of his body settled on his shoulders and all the priest had to do was focus on keeping his arms wrapped around his neck. If he lost consciousness, they could even tie his arms around his torso.

Kith led at a slow pace, Theron following just behind. They decided that it was best to head back to the Imperial Highway. Traveling through the dense woods was too difficult while carrying the priest. They would risk being spotted by Torlite patrols, but they really had no other choice.

They took turns carrying Lathronin, Kith enduring most of the burden. There was no way Theron could match Kith's strength and energy levels. But the pace was slow. Several times, Kith directed them off the main road while people passed. His hearing was so acute he picked up on their comings before they could see them. Most were simple travelers, but they did manage to avoid a patrol of Torlites just before the sun began to set. Towards the end of the day, they were forced to tie Lathronin's hands around their necks. He simply didn't have the strength to hold on.

Setting up camp a short walk into the woods, they risked building a fire. Lathronin was still pale and cold, his breathing shallow. They laid him next to the low burning fire. Theron inspected his leg and found the wound tender and inflamed.

"I think Lathronin was right," he acknowledged grimly, inspecting his leg. "This wound is not healing as it should."

"Do you feel infection setting in?" Kith asked, clearly worried.

"No, there is no smell. It stings some, but other than that it feels like the salve is working." Theron looked up. "I think I was lucky," his solemn eyes looking to the priest.

Kith sighed. "What should we do?"

"We will continue to carry him," Theron said adamantly.

"Yes, we will. But when we get to the gate, we will need to swim to the surface of the lake. Lathronin is unconscious. I do not know how that will work."

"Do you have the strength to carry him to the surface?"

"I believe so. But its his breathing I'm worried about. If he in unconscious he will not know to hold his breath."

Theron looked into the fire. He had no answer to their predicament.

After a long pause, Kith stood up from the fire. "Get some sleep. I will watch over you."

"You have not slept in two days," Theron contended.

"I will be fine." Kith turned and disappeared into the forest shadows.

They were up and moving by dawn the next day. Kith figured they had most of the day to travel before they reached the gate. He also reasoned that the closer they got to Akari the more patrols they would find. Fortunately, they made it past the logging town of Landor and arrived at the gate several hours before dark. They had continued to take turns carrying Lathronin, stopping for short breaks to eat and drink water. Even Kith was tiring, the constant strain on his body and lack of sleep starting to take its toll. But the E'lear flowed through him when he needed it the most, allowing him to push through. He knew he would need to sleep soon. But he was more concerned about Theron. The warrior was utterly exhausted, and he had no E'lear to keep him going. Kith knew that the man was surviving on a steadfast will to carry him through their predicament. He was impressed with his friend's constitution. Lathronin came to several times, and they took those brief moments of consciousness to give him water and food, the latter going down slowly and with some difficulty.

As they made their way through the old slave quarters erected at the top of the pit, the portal deep below them, Kith heard the familiar sound of horses in the distance. Stopping, he looked back the way they had come. His fear was realized as a patrol of Torlites, twenty in number, rode over the gentle crest of the hill they had just descended. Seeing them standing near the pit's entrance, they urged their steeds forward.

Kith, carrying Lathronin, silently swore and looked down the long path they had to traverse. They would never make it.

Theron drew his blade and looked at Kith, his eyes wild with fear. "We will never make it to the gate," Theron growled, stating Kith's thoughts.

"Drop me!" Lathronin said, waking for the first time in hours. His voice was strong, which gave them both pause. "Now!"

Kith lowered him quickly and Lathronin stood on wobbly legs. "Where is my pack!? Hurry!"

Theron was carrying it and tossed it to Lathronin. The priest reached into the pack and dug deep for something. After a few tense moments, he drew forth of small black bottle with a wax cork. Kith recognized it immediately.

"You can't!" he said. "We can still make it."

"We cannot, and you know it," Lathronin said, breaking the seal on the top. He looked around at the entrance, which was marked by strong stout logs embedded into the ground, the opening to the pit about five paces wide. On either side were tall rock cliffs. There was no way to enter the pit other than through the opening. "I will hold them here," he said, drinking the liquid quickly.

"I don't understand," Theron said, his wild eyes looking back towards the fast approaching patrol.

"I do not have time to explain," Lathronin said. "You must go! Now!" Suddenly his body went rigid and his tired eyes snapped wide open. "Gooooo," he growled, as something took over his body. In a blink his body was alert and tense, ready for explosive action. With speed and dexterity they did not think the priest possessed, his weakness gone instantly, he procured his bow and stuck a handful of arrows into the ground. His sword and spear were near him, having been carried by Theron.

The patrol was an arrow shot away.

"We must go!" Kith stormed, already moving away from the focused priest.

Theron joined him with apprehension. "What!? We cannot leave him! He will die here!"

"He is already dead!" Kith stormed. "I will explain later!"

Lathronin broke from his trance and looked back at the duo. His eyes were wild with energy, and behind his tense gaze was something else, perhaps satisfaction, or glee, they could not tell. "It is a warrior's death!" he yelled, a faint smile cracking through his intense gaze.

Both of the warriors nodded, then turned and ran. As they descended deep into the hole, they heard the cacophony of fighting above. Kith did not think they had time for Theron to take off his armor. Despite Lathronin's skill and newfound energy, he could not stop twenty men on horseback. The best they could hope for was a reprieve, so they could get through the gate. As if on cue, they heard the pursuit of horses above. Some had gotten past the priest. Lathronin was likely dead.

"When we get to the gate, you will not have time to take off your armor!" Kith yelled as they reached the bottom of the pit.

"I will drown," Theron yelled back.

"I will carry you to the surface."

Theron said nothing, the very idea of emerging at the bottom of the lake wearing his chainmail as frightening as taking on the remaining horsed soldiers. But he was exhausted, and he doubted he had much fight in him. This was their best chance of survival.

By the time they reached the gate, eleven horsed men made the final turn at the bottom of the pit. They would be on them in ten heartbeats.

Skidding to a stop, Kith took several slow deep breaths, trying to slow his breathing. He would need to be calm when they entered the water. He looked at Theron. "Take off your pack," he ordered. Kith did the same. "When we enter the gate, drop your gear at the bottom of the lake. I will carry you to the surface and return for our packs and weapons." Theron nodded, too afraid and tired to say anything. "Take a deep breath when we enter."

Kith heard the pounding of horses behind him as he let out a deep breath, saying the Dar-dan word for the old ruined city. The gate activated, blue sigils slowly lighting up, a translucent shimmering flashing across the opening. He looked at Theron who nodded back, taking a deep breath. Then he stepped through the gate, Theron just behind him.

The frigid water struck Kith like a hammer blow, his reaction almost expelling the breath he was holding. Holding it in, he looked around frantically for Theron. Luckily the sun had not quite set, and enough light was penetrating the clear water for Kith to spot Theron struggling near him. E'lear ignited in him and his arms and legs pumped, propelling him through the water like a fish. He grabbed Theron and spun him around, holding him by his chest. Theron calmed some and allowed Kith to pump his arms and legs, driving him straight towards the surface. They burst through the water and they both drank in the needed oxygen. Kith's legs were moving quickly, fueled by the energy flowing through his body. Looking around, he thanked the Dar-dan that the make-shift dock was still floating nearby, anchored to the land by their rope. Pulling Theron through the water, Kith swam to the crude raft. Theron grabbed the edge and pulled himself up.

"I'll get the rest of our things," Kith said, huffing from the exertion.

It wasn't long before Kith had their packs and weapons piled onto the raft. They paddled the raft to the lake's edge and jumped onto the dry ground. Theron immediately sat on a boulder nearby, his head held low. He was exhausted, and the ordeal with losing Lathronin had drained him further.

Kith dropped the packs and gear on the ground. They were both exhausted and it was nearly dark. They needed a fire, food, and sleep. Luckily, they had thought ahead and had wrapped their tinder box in an oil skin bag. Hopefully it was still dry.

Kith collected wood and piled it in a clearing near the lakeshore. Theron, shaking from the cold and his wet clothes, helped him, retrieving the tinder box from the dry bag. Luckily, it was still dry and it wasn't long before they had a big fire going. Kith's core body temperature was much higher, the energy from the stones keeping him warm despite his wet clothes.

"You need to take off your clothes and dry them by the fire," he said.

Theron nodded and went about it, stripping down to all but his cotton under clothes. He dragged some downed trees closer and used them to drape his clothes near the fire. It wasn't perfect, but if they kept the fire roaring, it should do the trick. Theron huddled close to the flames while Kith prepared a meal of beans, cured ham, and an apple each.

"So what was that?" Theron finally asked, looking up from the fire.

Kith knew what he was talking about. "It's called Droslonick. It's a Dar-danian word that translates to *warrior's death*. All priests who make it through the training carry the elixir."

"But what's in it?"

"I don't know. It's a carefully guarded secret. It is so powerful that it can bring you back from the brink of death, with the energy of five men. But once it runs its course, it kills you."

Theron slowly shook his head in anger. "We might have made it."

"Maybe. But against twenty horsed men, it is likely you would not have survived. And Lathronin, he knew he was dying. He gave us time to get away. He died a warrior's death."

"He saved me in life, and in death."

Kith nodded solemnly. "He was a friend to me."

Theron looked at his friend. "Those creatures, how many did you say they had?"

"Looked to be forty or so."

"How can we defeat that many?"

"I don't know. But we must find a way."

"What if Rane brings more through the gate?"

Kith was staring into the fire. He looked up, his eyes blazing. "I'm going to kill Rane."

***

Lord Byron and Carthen stood on a pile of boulders looking down at the Rock Pass. Piles of rocks surrounded them, as high as several trees, making a natural funnel to the path below. According to their histories, long ago there had been a massive earthquake that shook the nearby mountain, causing an avalanche of rock, earth, and mud of epic proportions. It was so severe that it blocked the river, causing it to back up and flood the town that was there. The people suffered greatly. Those that survived the initial avalanche were then likely to drown from the rising waters. But the mudslide was even more massive, creating a natural wall along the northside of the Imperial Highway. The Rock Pass, as it came to be known, was about twenty clicks long, one side dominated by tree covered rolling hills with intermittent rock walls, and the other a wall of boulders and mud, now, a thousand years later, covered in tall straight trees that somehow were able to grow along the steep cliff. It was the fastest way for an army to get across Urotha.

"This is a good spot," Carthen said, looking at their surroundings with a military eye.

Lord Byron was nodding. "Good cover for our archers and spearmen."

The plan of course was to try and use the natural bottleneck of the pass to slow down Rane's army. They only had fifteen hundred men, not enough to face them openly. The plan was to fall trees at precise locations, the archers all the while ready to pepper the enemy with arrows as they were forced to stop. They hoped to do this as many times as possible, slowing Rane down while they waited for the Kelic to arrive. The last they had heard the Kelic army was still six days away. If Kith and the others failed to slow Rane down, they figured his army would arrive at their location in two days.

Lord Byron looked up to the rocks and cliffs rising behind them. "I believe the lake is nearby, perhaps just behind us."

"I believe so," Carthen acknowledged. "You think they found the gate up there?"

"If not, I think we would've heard from them."

"That's good news," the old warrior added.

"Let's hope so."

***

The next morning Kith and Theron were off early. Theron had slept all night, and even Kith, feeling secure in their location, slept for a few hours. Despite the E'lear flowing through him, he needed to rest his eyes. It had been over three days since he had closed his eyes for any substantial time.

They skirted the huge lake, jumping and climbing from boulder to boulder as they began their descent on the southern side. Kith stopped on top of a huge boulder, the crystal-clear lake behind him. Rocks and dirt were piled high, like a wall, and yet trees managed to grow from various locations. But below them the terrain dropped quickly, descending to the Rock Pass. There were small streams that formed as water from the lake broke through gaps in the rocks and boulders that formed a natural dike on the south side of the lake. Kith looked back at the lake, then to the pass below, his mind suddenly processing a thought.

"What is it?" Theron asked, jumping from a boulder to stand next to him.

"The wall of rock and dirt we are standing on is holding this lake back," Kith mused softly.

"I think the river used to cascade down from here," Theron replied, still unsure what Kith was getting at. "What are you thinking?"

"Just an idea," he said, dismissing it quickly. "Let's get going."

Kith found the Order's army easy enough. They were not too far from the lake. They had actually found some scouts, two members of the Order who were keeping an eye out for Rane's own scouts. The men directed them to the main army. Once they hit the Imperial Highway, they headed east, knowing they would find the army in a few hours. They came across a crew that was preparing several huge trees to fell across the road. They were informed by the crew that that the main army was further back. Continuing on, they came across two other work crews, preparing more trees to drop across the road.

When they found the army, the first officer they encountered instructed them that Lord Byron and the other officers were scouting a nearby wall of rock that spanned the length of the road. Pointing them in the right direction, Kith and Lathronin found them with little difficulty.

Lord Byron, Carthen, Bear'lon, Lykin, and to Kith's surprise, An'thryne, were all standing on the edge of an expanse, a hill of rocks, boulders, and scree, spanning out before them, all funneling down to the road below. Scattered across the steep drop were various trees, some tall and straight and others short and bushy.

"Father," Theron announced, traversing the make-shift path to join them. They turned, their eyes showing their surprise.

"Son," Lord Byron said, moving from their position to join them. He smiled and gripped him in a strong hug, releasing him after a moment to clasp Kith's hand. "It is good to see you both."

The others joined them and after quick introductions, An'thryne spoke the words that Kith was dreading. "Where is Lathronin?" As soon as he asked, he knew the answer.

"He didn't' make it," Kith said. "He died Dros-lonich."

An'thryne pressed his lips together and sighed, nodding in understanding moments later as he processed his comrade's death.

"Perhaps we should reconvene in my tent," Lord Byron suggested. "We clearly have much to discuss."

Lord Byron's tent was large but simple, the center dominated by a command table. There were a few chairs, his bed in the corner, and another table presently filled with pitchers of water and plates of bread, dried meat, cheese, and sliced fruit. The table was covered with various maps, some showing Urotha and the Imperial Highway, others much more detailed drawings of the Rock Pass. There were not enough chairs for everyone, so they all stood around the table.

"Tell us what happened," Lord Byron instructed.

So they did, informing them of all they saw at the portal in Akari, Rane's army, the monsters from Skell, as well as what happened to Lathronin. There were a few intermittent questions, but for the most part, they let the two tell the tale.

"Lathronin saved my life twice," Theron said, needing to acknowledge the warrior's heroics.

The other's nodded in silence. There was nothing else to say. They all knew that Lathronin's death would likely not be the first.

"He died as he should," An'thryne added.

After a moment, Lord Bryon looked at Kith. "These creatures," he began, "Do you have any idea how Rane was controlling them?"

Kith shook his head. "They were in cages built for tarites. But two were sent after us. How he did that I have no idea."

"Do they have a weakness?" Bear'lon asked.

"They are heavily armored by some strong exoskeleton," Kith answered. "Regular weapons do little to them, unless you can get to their underbelly, which is not so easy."

"But your weapons can penetrate their armor?" Carthen asked.

"Yes."

Lord Byron sighed. "Kith cannot kill them all."

"Let's focus on what we know we can do," Carthen suggested. "You damaged their siege engines, which will either buy us time now, or later. Hopefully our scouts will return soon with Rane's location. With any luck, he will build his engines now, giving us time to prepare our attacks. Your quick actions may give us the time we need to properly prepare a defense."

"When we came down the mountain, we saw the work crews," Theron interjected. "By the looks of it, you plan to drop trees across the road. I'm assuming you will attack from an elevated position at the same time."

"That is correct," Carthen answered. "But we will not stay long, moving to a second position. We will do the same thing twice more, trying to kill as many of Rane's forces before we depart back to Daswin. We need to reduce their numbers, allowing us a fighting chance when the Kelic arrive."

"But what do we do about the Crawlers?" Bear'lon asked. "By the sound of it they could easily attack us from our elevated positions. What chance do we have against such an enemy?"

No one said anything as they digested the big warrior's words. They knew the creatures were a problem. They could scurry up the rocks and rip into their forces with ease, their own weapons doing little to stop them. As was mentioned earlier, Kith could not kill them all.

After a long pause, Kith spoke. "I may have an idea." He pursed his lips in thought before he continued. "There is a huge wall of rock and trees that are holding the lake back. If we could destroy the wall, we could flood the pass with water from the lake."

Everyone was staring at him as if he were crazy. After they realized he was serious, Lord Bryon spoke first. "How would that even be possible?"

"That lake is massive," Lykin said, speaking for the first time. "I've scouted it many times. It can take an entire day to hike its shoreline. And I know the wall you speak of. If you destroyed five cities and piled all the stone in one spot, it might be the same size. I'm sorry, Kith, I just don't see how your plan would even be possible."

"It's not possible," Kith said, "at least not with what we know. But the Dar-dan have the magic to accomplish such a feat. At least I think they do."

"But the Dar-dan are gone," Theron responded, wondering where Kith was going with his plan.

Kith nodded. "They are, but their magic is not. While I was at Seebras, the Eskeli showed me some of their weapons that still exist there." He paused as he looked around the room at the faces looking back at him. "They have devices, magic devices, that can explode with great power. They are the same devices that they used to bring down the mountain on the gate thousands of years ago."

"There is really such a weapon?" Lord Byron asked.

"I saw them," Kith affirmed. "But there is one problem. I am unsure if I can use them properly."

"Let's just say you can," Carthen contemplated. "Do we know they are powerful enough to accomplish such a feat?"

Kith shook his head, letting out a deep sigh. "I'm sorry, but it's just an idea. I'm afraid the plan raises more questions than answers."

"But if they worked," An'thryne added, "then the Pass would be flooded with so much water that it would destroy Rane's army."

"And perhaps even the Crawlers," Theron interjected. "I must admit, I have little desire to fight them again."

Lord Byron let out a deep breath as he thought. He looked over the map of the pass one more time before he spoke, looking up at Kith. "How long would it take you to get the devices and bring them back?"

"I can take the gate directly to Seebras. I can be back by tomorrow."

"In that case, I think it is worth the try," Lord Byron said. "When can you leave?"

"I'm going with you," Theron jumped in.

Kith shook his head. "Not this time, my friend. I can travel faster by myself and it is unlikely I will encounter any trouble. Stay and rest."

"What about you?" Theron said. "You've slept only a few hours the last three days."

Everyone looked at Kith in surprise. He looked around at the men staring back at him. "I can go without sleep for long spells," he said. "But you are right, Theron," looking back at his friend. "I will take a few hours of rest before I leave. I'd like to get to the gate before dark."

Lord Byron nodded. "Very good."

ELEVEN

Kith tumbled across the black stone floor, a river of water catapulting him forward. Shouting the words to shut the gate, the water receded immediately, and he picked himself up off the wet floor. Instantly his eyes were drawn to the Alltree. He could feel the energy emanate from it as the thousands of field stones drew energy from the magnetic field around them. They pulsed and twinkled like stars on a cloudless night. His body felt alive as it vibrated with the energy of the tree.

He had little time to waste so he quickly found the weapons room the Eskeli had showed him months ago. It looked exactly as it did before. Rakian blades, spears, armor, and bows were scattered across the floor, the wood that formed the racks long ago disintegrated with time. But he paid them no heed, moving with haste to a small alcove against the wall, an insert forming a shelf carved from the very stone that surrounded them. Nestled on the shelf were three oval objects, each one about the size of an infant's head. They were black and smooth, with veins of blue E'lear flickering across the surface. Kith was not completely sure how they worked. All he had to go on was what the Eskeli had told him. Now he wished he had asked more questions.

Thinking back, he remembered the Eskeli had told him that they were self-charging, the alignment of stones inside having drawn in as much power as they could hold. The stones inside were specially manipulated to draw in more energy than typical, the alignment directing the energy into some sort of energy loop, although Kith had been lost early in the explanation. It was more Dar-danian magic that Kith did not understand. He was trying to recall how to trigger the device, his careful eyes inspecting one he had picked up. It was warm, but not overly so. There were some rough edges that circled it near the top, under the edge, a small crack that wrapped around the egg-like device. Suddenly he remembered, a smile cracking through his concentration. When he had held the egg months ago, the Eskeli had warned him not to twist the top. That was it, you twist the top and it activates the device, the energy loop interrupted, releasing the huge amount of E'lear in one massive explosion. Then his smile disappeared as he remembered they had never discussed the time frame. How long did one have before the explosion? Clearly there must have been some sort of delay. The question was, how much time did one have to get away once the device was activated?

Pushing the troublesome thought away, Kith took all three devices and put them in his pack. He needed to get back. They had much to do.

***

"Good news," Lord Byron said, looking around at the warriors in his tent. "The Kelic are two days from Daswin."

Kith had returned with the three devices and immediately Lord Byron had called a meeting. The three metal objects were sitting on top of his table, the faint E'lear glowing like pulsing spiderwebs over their surface. Everyone eyed them with skepticism, their expressions showing their doubt. Could such small things really hold such power?

"That means they can be here in four," Carthen added.

"What of Rane's forces?" Kith asked, having been gone for the original briefing.

Carthen looked at An'thryne. The priest had been out scouting and had returned early that morning. "They are two days out, marching hard." The priest paused. "And they have more siege engines."

"That was to be expected," Lord Byron continued. "Kith," he inquired, Looking at the strange oval shaped balls, "what do we know about these weapons?"

Kith sighed. "I'm afraid, my Lord, not much. I know they are quite powerful, being the same devices that brought the mountain down on the gate thousands of years before. I also know you activate them by turning the top. But I'm afraid that is the extent of my knowledge."

Lord Byron let out a deep breath.

It was Theron who spoke. "So, we have two problems with the devices. We do not know their power. And we do not know how long, once the weapons are activated, one has before they release their power."

"That is correct," Kith agreed.

"So, we need three volunteers to activate the devices," Bear'lon whispered.

"I will activate them," Kith said firmly. He looked at all the men. "It was my idea. It is my duty."

Theron was already shaking his head. "You cannot activate all three. Our engineers have already located the prime positions for the devices. They are digging them out as we speak. They are too far apart."

"Not for me," Kith said. "I can cover the distance faster than you think."

"Perhaps you can," Theron acknowledged. "But the risk is too great. If one releases its energy before you get to the others, then it might not be enough to destroy the damn. It would all be for nothing. We need this to work. The risk is too great. I will activate the second."

"You will not," Lord Byron interjected. "You are the heir to the throne. What is the point of all this if there is no one to pull us from the rubble? You will be that person," he added, his tone leaving no room for argument. Then he looked at everyone else. "I will activate the second. As Kith said, it to is my duty."

"Sir," Carthen interjected, "we can't lose..."

Lord Byron held up his hand and Carthen stopped speaking. "If I am lost, Theron is more qualified to lead than I ever was. And he will have you, the most skilled commander to ever walk Urotha." Then he smiled, glancing at Kith. "Besides, I have an Ar'kan warrior to watch my back."

"I will activate the third," Bear'lon said.

No one said anything, all knowing the dangers and the risk the three were taking. Lord Byron nodded to Bear'lon, accepting his offer.

Finally, Lord Byron spoke. "We need to set the first two ambushes, as well as prepare the devices. We have much to do. Please, take your leave, and good luck."

***

Two days later Kith found himself standing on the edge of a huge boulder, the expansive crystal-clear waters of the lake behind him. Lord Byron and Bear'lon were next to him, each man holding one of the devices. It was mid-morning and they had been waiting since sunrise.

"The horn should be sounding soon," Lord Byron said, his eyes scanning the rocks and trees below them. Somewhere to the west their ambushes had likely been triggered. Huge trees had been downed, blocking the road, and hundreds of spearmen and bowmen lined the pass, most hiding along the steep cliffs on the lake side. Their goal was to rain down steel tipped shafts upon Rane's army as they bottle-necked at the blockage, retreating quickly to do it again further east. Their objective was to kill as many men as they could, running further away and luring Rane's army to the location below the lake.

Bear'lon looked at the three wooden tubes embedded into the rocks, spread out several stone throws from each other. "You think they will work?"

The engineers had dug holes into the rock and rubble at locations they deemed adequate to destroy the dike. The wooden tubes were embedded in the holes, and the devices, once activated, would be dropped into them, rolling down into the holes, hopefully before releasing their power.

"We'll know soon enough," Lord Byron answered.

As if on cue, a horn blast shattered their conversation, three long bursts marking the signal. Even though they were waiting for the signal, the three men were startled, the sound alarming. They had no idea what would happen when the devices were activated. If they survived the devastation the ancient weapons released, then what would happen to the dike and the lake? What direction would the water travel, and would it strike the enemy as they hoped? There were so many unknown variables that it was hard to plan for each possible outcome. But all they could do was follow the plan step by step, reacting to the inevitable outcomes the best they could.

"Remember!" Kith shouted as they all jumped for their target locations. "Get to the high ground as fast as possible!" There was one suitable location to flee to once the devices were triggered, and it was five hundred paces west of the lake. There was a tall rock structure that looked out over the water. If they could reach it, they could not only hide behind the structure to protect them from the power of the explosion, but they could climb it easily enough to observe the flow of the lake as it cascaded down the mountainside. But they had to get there first.

Kith bounded down the various boulders like a mountain goat, reaching his location first, which was the furthest from the rock face and safety. The others had agreed to his location, recognizing they could not match his speed. Holding the device in shaking hands, Kith watched the other two as they made it to their locations. Lord Byron lifted his hand high before dropping it. It was the signal.

Kith gripped the rough edges around the top of the device and turned it. It turned easily, clicking once. Kith stopped, his heart pounding, ready to drop the device into the hole. Just as he was poised to drop it, Bear'lon's baritone voice shattered his anxious thoughts.

"Keep turning it!" he shouted.

He readjusted his grip and continued turning. To his surprise the top turned, clicking a second time, and a third, before coming to a halt. Then he dropped it into the tube and started to run.

He bounded up the rocks, E'lear flooding through his legs as he jumped ten paces at a time. He cleared the wall of rocks and boulders and started to sprint along the lakes edge, the huge mountain of rock before him begging him to run faster. Bear'lon and Lord Byron were just in front of him, but Kith would be past them in a few heart-beats, his pace so much faster. His heart was pounding in his head, matching the rhythmic beat of his legs. Joining the other two, he slowed as he urged them on, the protection of the rock two hundred paces away.

"Run faster!" Kith urged, glancing back and half expecting the devices to ignite.

They pushed harder, the only sound in the serene setting their panting breaths. They were a hundred yards away when suddenly the world lit up with an intense white light.

They were not looking towards the explosions, but it mattered little. The blasts were so bright that the white light flooded the world around them. Ear shattering sound hit them soon after, following in a blink a concussive wave of power that lifted them off their feet, tossing them forward like leaves in a wind storm. The air turned from cool and brisk, to burning hot in less than a heartbeat.

The three warriors tumbled to the ground, kith popping up moments later. Lord Byron and Bear'lon were not so quick to recover, standing up slowly as smoke rose from their seared clothing. Luckily, besides a few minor burns and bruises, they were not seriously injured. The location of the devices forced the power of the explosion outward, showering the hillside with rocks and debris powerful enough to rip trees from the ground.

Although they suffered some minor burns, they were not concerned about their injuries. Instead, their attention was drawn to the dike and the lake. The rumbling of stone and rock echoed off the peaks around them. It sounded like a massive earthquake, followed shortly by the roaring sound of cascading water.

"Did it work!?" Bear'lon shouted above the din of the water.

The others could barely hear him above the raging sound of the water. And although they could not see the water ripping through the dike, they could make out the current as the weight of the entire lake pressed in on the shattered dam before them.

"It must be!" Kith shouted back. "You can see the current of the lake change."

"We should inspect it!" Bear'lon suggested.

"No, look!" Lord Byron yelled, pointing towards the dam. "It is not safe!" Sure enough the power of the lake water was ripping through more of the dam, tearing away sections of dirt and rock that had built up for over a thousand years. Trees were torn from their roots and tossed down the mountain as easily as a feather drifting down river.

"In the name of the Dar-dan," Bear'lon whispered, although no one could hear him.

"Let's go!" Lord Byron ordered. "We need to join the fight!"

Kith nodded, although it was unclear who would be left to fight. They had no idea where the water and debris were flowing. With any luck, it would soon crush the Crawlers and the head of Rane's army. But there was always the danger of the cascading water doing as much damage to their own forces as the enemy, although their engineers predicted they would be safe. They had picked the spot of the ambush for just that reason.

It didn't take them long to make it down the crude trail, and when they reached the first vantage point, they all stopped in shock. Standing on the edge of a rock, they could see the Rock Pass below, or at least what was left of it. The cacophony of the raging mudslide drowned out the remains of the battle being fought below. Nearly two clicks away, a massive river of water, mud, rocks, and trees, ripped down the mountain. The wall of water and debris was so high that it crashed over the rocky walls on the far side of the pass. But much of its power had been diverted down the pass, a wall of brown water as tall as the city walls of Daswin stormed down the road, the walls of rock and hills channeling most of its power towards Rane's forces. Whatever army had existed beyond that point, did not exist any longer.

Once they had taken in the devastation, they inspected more closely the battle raging below. There were still nearly six thousand of Rane's men, along with what looked like twenty or more Crawlers. Despite the devastation of the flood, it looked like it had missed the head of the army, destroying only the rear of Rane's column. The Crawlers were scurrying up the rocky sides that flanked the pass, ripping into their men with ease. The defenders' arrows and weapons did little damage to the creatures, and soon the rocks were splattered with the blood of their men.

"Some of the Crawlers still live," Kith growled. "We need to get down there."

"Lead the way," Lord Byron ordered, his jaw set, determination etched across his face.

They moved quickly, weapons already drawn, eager to join the fray. As they descended, Kith caught movement to his right just before they reached the main trail that switchbacked for a hundred paces to the pass below. Moments later two Crawlers appeared climbing over the edge of a cliff. They were only twenty paces away.

"To me!" Kith yelled as he pivoted towards the threat.

Lord Byron and Bear'lon had not heard the creatures and whipped around suddenly, their eyes wide as they flanked Kith.

"Your weapons will do little harm," Kith warned. "Aim for the eyes, mouth, and underbelly."

One beast shot towards them like lightening from the sky, the other roaring mightily, its dragon-like mouth opened wide as the ear shattering shriek struck them.

Kith wasted no time, stepping back he lunged forward with his spear so fast that his movement was barely discernable. The weapon shot forward with precision, striking the roaring beast in the open mouth. Its head jerked back with enough force to nearly snap its neck, the spear burying deep in its brain. It snapped its jaws futilely several times before falling backwards off the cliff.

By that time the other Crawler was on them. Kith leapt forward to meet it, his blade materializing in his hand, blue E'lear sizzling across its surface as he dodged the beast's swiping claws, the blade a blur as it cut through its exoskeleton protecting its longer front legs.

Roaring in pain, the Crawler shot its long neck forward, its powerful jaws snapping at Kith's torso. Bear'lon's axe came down hard on the beast's shoulder, the power of the strike barely moving the creature, the razor edge sliding off its carapace leaving little more than a scratch behind.

But it was enough to draw its attention from Kith, its long head whipping around and striking Bear'lon square in the chest. Several of the spikes on its head cut into his flesh before he flew backwards to his back.

It was all the time Kith needed as he expertly spun his blade, angling the tip into the side of its head just below what looked like an ear. It was a narrow opening in the side of the thing's neck, and Kith's rakian blade penetrated it like it was warm butter, the full length of the blade driving deep into the Crawler's brain. The beast spasmed once before dropping dead to the ground.

Kith put his foot on the beast's head and ripped the blade free.

Lord Byron was helping Bear'lon to his feet.

"Are you injured?" Kith asked.

Bear'lon growled, his hand touching a puncture on his shoulder and a shallow cut across his cheek. He was bleeding, but not profusely. "I'll be fine."

Lord Byron was staring at Kith with obvious shock. "I've never seen someone move so fast."

"The Change has given me extraordinary power," Kith acknowledged.

"Good thing," Bear'lon muttered, picking up his axe. "How are we supposed to fight those things? My axe did nothing."

"We must prevail," Lord Byron said, trying to sound more confident than he clearly felt.

"Let's go," Kith said, feeling a bit vulnerable without his spear. He would eventually retrieve it, but he had no time to do so now.

They covered the switchback trail as quickly as they could, Kith leading the way. Nearing the bottom, the chaos of the battle hit them hard. Their own men were hastily trying to form defensive lines as Crawlers leapt amongst them, ripping and shredding, breaking apart their lines just as fast as they formed. Drann magic lit up the sky as spheres of energy landed with deadly force, scattering their men with explosive power. Men screamed, and Crawlers roared, the fighting quickly turning into pockets of melees.

"Look!" Bear'lon yelled, pointing to the front where the fighting was the most intense. There was a wall of defenders holding strong, shields and spears angled out, barely keeping a handful of Crawler's at bay. "It must be Carthen!"

The big warrior didn't wait, racing towards the front line. Kith and Lord Byron joined him, Kith easily outdistancing them both. All three engaged the enemy, cutting through handfuls of Rane's men as they worked their way to the front.

Suddenly a Drann priest stood before them, a long whip of energy flashing through the air, the crackling power cutting one of the defender's in half before reversing the whip towards Kith. Bodies surrounded the priest, most missing limbs, or worse, the power of his magic unstoppable. The man's rictal grin widened in glee as he saw the whip soar towards Kith, expecting it to do the same damage to him as it did the others. Quickly though, his smile disappeared as Kith's blade flashed, cutting through the power with ease, the whip vanishing in a blink. Kith barely slowed, his hand releasing a zyth at his side, throwing the weapon side armed towards the priest. The sharp spikes struck him in the neck forcing him to stumble backwards. As the man fell backwards in death, Kith buzzed by him, his hand flashing out and taking the weapon back before he even hit the ground.

He then fought his way to the front and saw Carthen holding the center of the line, his sword moving with expert precision, destroying any of Rane's men who got too close. He could see Bos's big body next to him, a shield held strong as he worked his axe faster than should be possible for such a heavy weapon. He had no time to see if any of his other friends were nearby, the onslaught of Rane's Danite's rushing them with renewed force.

But Kith cut through the enemy as if they were children, working his way to Carthen's side. Bear'lon and Lord Byron followed in Kith's wake, and soon they were all fighting side by side. They cut and killed, trying to hold the line as more of Rane's warriors crashed into them. Kith wondered where the famous Danite Calvary was, hoping that perhaps they had been destroyed when the wall of water had struck. Both sides were fighting with little control and Kith figured that their plan had worked, destroying and disrupting Rane's superior forces. It looked now to be a battle fought by pockets of remaining men, each man simply trying to survive.

But where was Rane?

Kith had little time to ponder that question as an Eradicator and three Black Watch warriors suddenly broke through the enemy line. The Eradicator, dressed in his black cloak and red armor, was carrying a glowing war hammer, the entire weapon made from E'lear energy. The Black Watch warriors carried shields and swords and were guarding the man's flanks.

Without pausing, the Eradicator roared and swung his hammer straight at Lord Byron, who, out of instinct, raised his sword to block. The hammer crashed through his defenses with ease, striking him in the shoulder so hard that those nearby heard the crack as it snapped his shoulder and clavicle, the E'lear energy of the hammer causing more damage as it shot through him like fire. Lord Byron screamed in pain and fell back, Carthen leaping in to protect him.

The Eradicator roared in anger and expertly pulled the hammer back, reversing his swing much faster than Carthen thought possible. Bos was engaged with the far Black Watch warrior, the black armored warriors always in their Eradicator's shadow. Kith moved in quickly to engage the nearest Black Watch, hoping to dispatch him quickly so he could take out the Eradicator and his devasting hammer.

Carthen barely dodged the hammer, his own blade snapping forward and catching the man on the wrist as he drew his hammer back again. Crying out in pain, the Eradicator took the injured hand off the hammer and shot it forward, pushing a wave of energy directly at Carthen's chest. The power struck him true and it looked like a Kelic warrior had kicked him in the chest, the power knocking him off his feet to his back. Stepping forward quickly, the Eradicator raised his hammer and brought it down with all his strength, the glowing head aiming for Carthen's face.

Kith's blade shot forward and the Black Watch warrior spun towards him, catching the rakian blade on the metal edge. The blade cut through the steel and narrowly missed the man's arm holding the shield. Kith's eyes widened, and he froze momentarily as he recognized the warrior. It was Tallin. He too recognized Kith. It was impossible not to, his white hair fluttering around him as he fought. There was no exchange of words, no banter, nothing. Kith graced the man with a slight smile before he attacked.

His sword stuck Tallin's shield several more times, literally cutting off pieces before Tallin decided to go on the offensive. Stepping back, he tossed his damaged shield at Kith's face, leaping forward with his sword. Kith spun as the shield flew past him, his drift cloak fluttering around him. Tallin lunged at Kith, his blade disappearing in the folds of the cloak. Tallin's eyes lit up briefly, thinking his blade had found his flesh. But Kith pivoted around the attack, his cloak flowing over the blade like water. Tallin tried to move backwards, but Kith was too fast, his rakian blade slicing across his bicep, parting the muscled flesh with the ease of a surgeon's knife.

Tallin cried out and dropped the blade, his arm gushing crimson. Kith never stopped, his body a blur, his cloak fluttering around him as he rammed his blade deep into Tallin's stomach and all the way through his back, and when Kith spun away, he ripped his blade through the warrior's side, nearly cutting him in half.

Tallin's eyes widened as his guts spilled from his body. Stumbling momentarily, he slipped on the gory mess at his feet and fell to the ground.

Carthen saw the hammer coming and tried to spin his feet under him in hopes that he could launch himself out of the way. But he knew he wouldn't be fast enough. Suddenly Bos was there, straddling him with his shield held high. The hammer crashed into the shield and nearly bent it in half, breaking Bos's arm in the process. Bos cried out and dropped lower in his stance, but still he held the shield above him as the Eradicator brought the hammer back for another strike.

But the hammer disappeared in a flash as a blue glowing blade burst through the man's chest. Crying out, the man fell sideways, dead before he hit the ground. Kith was there, and he helped Carthen to his feet as more of their men joined them to fill the line, giving them a brief reprieve.

Bos was pale, his shield arm held useless at this side, the destroyed shield laying next to him.

"It is good to see you, Kith!" Carthen yelled over the fighting. "Looks like the plan worked."

Kith nodded. "Where is Rane?"

"I don't know! He was fighting at the front when the water struck! I lost sight of him after that and have not seen him since!" Carthen looked at Bos. "You need to go the rear and see a healer. Your arm is broken."

Bos smiled, although it was clearly forced, as he lifted his huge axe with his good arm. "I can still fight."

Carthen looked quickly about, trying to discern the flow of the battle. Kith did the same, seeing a Crawler nearby pounce on an Acku warrior and rip into his chest. Rane had conscripted thousands of slaves from Bylor and Dareef, and now they were dying in a far-off land.

"The Crawlers are attacking anyone!" Kith yelled.

"We need to form a defense against them!" Carthen added.

Just as he said the words, a line of twenty fighters from the Order pushed through a mass of Torlites, men with swords and axes lined between them just as they had practiced. Kith had informed them of the Crawlers weakness, and they had a few days to work out a possible solution. Groups of spearmen would try to use the long weapons to raise the lizard-like beasts onto their back legs, while the other warriors maneuvered their blades towards their soft underbelly. They had little time to practice and everyone knew that the reality of fighting these powerful beasts would not go smoothly. But it was the best plan they had.

Two Crawlers, one of which had just finished off a Torlite, turned their fiery eyes on the men before them. They scurried at them with frightening speed, and as they came together the warrior's spears shot forward, aiming for their faces.

One reared up and swatted away the spears with its front legs. More spears shot forward and struck the thing's armored chest. The creature leaned back and whipped its tail around, striking a swordsman who tried to get closer. The spiked tail launched the man back into the line, taking a spearman with him. But still the spears jabbed relentlessly, one finding the inside of the creature's mouth. It howled and leaned back further, trying to avoid the painful silver tips. Two men ran forward, sweeping in low with powerful arcs towards its exposed gray belly. The unarmored section showing was perhaps a line about a hand's span in width, and the second strike from the axe wielder was true, cutting a deep gash. Black blood spewed from the wound. The spears continued jabbing high, forcing the howling creature back as one front leg swung down, its black claws ripping across one of the men's faces as he readied a second swing. The man spun away, his blood splattering the axe wielder across the face. But the second man continued the attack, one of his axes swinging in for another strike. Again, his aim was true, his blade cutting so deep that the Crawler's innards began to bulge from the wound. It screamed as it flipped over, swords and spears cutting into it until it was dead.

The other Crawler barreled into the line, shattering spears as if they were sticks. Kith was closer to this one and bolted towards the defenders, his drift cloak a swirling cloud around him. Two warriors went down under tooth and claw, while others swung their blades with little effect. Then Kith was there, his rakian blade pulling energy from his body until it was bright blue. Just in time as the creature sensed his presence and spun quickly, its lethal tail flailing towards Kith. He continued his momentum as he brought his sword up to meet the attack. His rakian blade cut the tail in half, the spiked end flying to the side. Black blood sprayed Kith and the men around him, but still Kith attacked. Leaping straight up, he came down on top of the creature's back, his agility keeping him clear of the spikes while he rammed his blade straight through its back. The beast jerked violently, and Kith leaped off, pulling his sword with him. Landing five paces away, he rolled and came to his feet. The creature was laying flat on its stomach, its body in its last death spasms.

"Kith, well done!"

It was Cos, his two axes held at his side, both dripping blood. Kith had been so caught up in the fight, that he did not recognize one of the warriors as one of his old leaders. Kith joined him near the dead Crawler. "Well met!" Kith said, looking around. There seemed to be a brief reprieve from the fighting, although the howls of the remaining Crawlers could still be heard as they fought nearby.

"What is happening?" Cos asked. "The flood seemed to work. Is Rane dead?"

"I don't know," Kith said. "The Crawlers are attacking anyone, so Rane's hold on them is gone. Either he is dead, or he left."

Carthen and Bos joined them. "The fighting is slowing," Carthen said, looking around. Sure enough, he was right. They could not see any more Crawlers, and the few pockets of remaining Torlites and Danites were no longer, either dead or having fled. Other than a few skirmishes in the distance, most of the fighting seemed to be over.

Suddenly a runner found them, his face covered in sweat and blood. His eyes were wild but seemed to reflect a glimmer of hope. "Sir," the young warrior said, "you are needed at the front."

"What is it?"

"The Acku are surrendering."

Carthen nodded and moved quickly towards the front, the others following. There were dead bodies everywhere, many their own men as well as Lord Byron's soldiers. But still, the enemy lay amongst them, as well as dead Crawlers. The battlefield reeked of sweat, blood, and shit. There was nothing heroic about it. Kith was appalled at the vast number of dead. The road was littered with thousands.

As they came to the front, there was a line of nearly two hundred defenders, some members of the Order and others were Lord Byron's men. Tired and splattered with dirt and blood, they still held their weapons strong, their eyes glancing nervously to a line of at least a thousand Acku tribesmen. The red skinned men looked fierce, but not one held a weapon. Carthen pushed his way to the front and Kith, Bos, and Cos joined him.

"Sir, they just stopped fighting and dropped their weapons." It was Arim who spoke, and Kith smiled happily to see his friend. He was holding an injured arm, blood dripping freely from a bad cut across his shoulder, just below his pauldron. He was limping as well, but despite his injuries he winked at Kith, quickly looking back at Carthen.

Carthen nodded and walked forward, stopping ten paces from the men. There was a tense pause before a man to Carthen's left stepped forward and walked towards the swordsman. He wore a hardened leather cuirass, his muscular arms bare. His black hair was braided in a long plait that was wrapped in turquoise cloth. He stopped before Carthen, his tense eyes looking the warrior over.

"Rane gone," he finally said, his Hiskani rough. "Rane enemy. You," he said, pointing to the fighters before him, "no enemy. We no fight."

Carthen nodded and reached out his hand. The man looked at it momentarily before grasping it, grip to forearm. "No fight."

TWELVE

The fighting was over, but they had a lot of work to do. The men that had survived helped bring the injured to the healers who had quickly set up tents several clicks east of the battle. But the healers were few and they could not keep up. More men died of their wounds as everyone struggled to help those who had a chance of survival.

After Kith retrieved his spear from the dead Crawler, he found Theron at his fathers' side. He had already seen to Bos and Arim, both of whom were injured badly. But luckily, neither of their wounds were life threatening. However, Lord Byron was not fairing so well. He was pale and asleep, his arm wrapped tightly in white bandages to keep it still if he woke. Theron looked up when Kith made his way to him.

"I'm glad you are well," Kith said, looking down at his father. "How is he?"

Theron was dirty, his face and armor splattered with blood. His long hair was a tangle of dirt and grime. He looked a mess, but they all did. "Not well," he said. "The healer said the bones in his shoulder are shattered so bad that even if he survives, it is unlikely he will be able to use the arm."

Kith nodded solemnly. Lord Byron's breathing was shallow and ragged. He didn't look good. "His breathing looks strained."

Theron looked away, his eyes rimmed in moisture. "It is. They said the strike was so powerful that it likely drove ribs into his lungs. They think it unlikely he will live. But they gave him a mixture of something to keep him asleep. They say the pain is minimal."

"I wish I could've gotten to him sooner."

Theron shook his head. "He was an Eradicator. Even Carthen struggled against him. It was a good thing you were there at all."

"Well, I hate to pull you from your father, but we are meeting in Carthen's tent. We need to talk about Rane. His body was never found and the Acku slaves said he retreated with several thousand warriors, most Danite. He used the slaves, Torlites, and Crawlers, to cover his escape."

Theron stood, his expression turning stoic. "Do we know where he went?"

"No, but it's likely he is returning to Akari. We cannot let him return to the city to bolster his forces for another defense. Nor can I allow him to cross over to Skell once again." Kith paused as he looked at his friend. "I need you with me. I have a plan."

Theron looked at his father, his mind reeling with indecision. Finally, he reached out and touched his arm. "Father, if you can hear me, I need to leave you. Our kingdom is still in danger. It is up to me to defend it." A few moments later he looked back to Kith. "Lead the way."

Carthen's tent was occupied by Bear'lon, Cos, and An'thryn, the exhausted leaders grabbing a hasty meal of dried meat, bread, and water, all the while discussing their next move.

As Kith and Theron entered, Carthen looked up from a stack of papers coming in from the officers who had survived. His tired bloodshot eyes were surrounded in shadow. They were likely assessing their death toll, as well as deciding what to do about Rane.

"Kith, Theron, good, I'm glad you are here. How is your father?" Carthen asked. He was clearly despondent, and Kith thought that something was wrong.

"Not well. They do not think he will make it."

The room was quiet, taking in the young warrior's words.

Kith finally noticed that someone was missing. Lykin should've have been here. "Where is Lykin?" Kith asked. But as soon as he did, he knew the answer.

Cos and Bear'lon looked down while Carthen's sad eyes found him. "He did not make it. He was fighting a Crawler and the beast had already killed five men. By all accounts, he held his ground all the while firing his bow as the beast charged him. His arrows finally found an eye and its open mouth before it crashed into him. As the beast was dying, he ripped Lykin's chest open." Carthen stopped as he blinked away the tears. Kith knew that they had had a strong bond, a friendship forged through steel and blood. "But we lost many. It has been a tough day."

"But one that could have been much worse if your plan hadn't worked," An'thryn added, looking at Kith. "I have never seen such destruction. The wall of water took out two thirds of Rane's forces, killing thousands and half the Crawlers. We lost many good men, but in the end, we won the battle. Rane is finished."

"Not yet," Kith said, his tone serious. "If he gets to the gate, he may try to bring back more Crawlers. I have no idea how he controlled them. But we cannot let that happen again."

"Even if we follow him," Bear'lon said. "We cannot reach him with a sizable force in time."

"How many men do we have here, right now?" Theron asked.

Carthen sighed, speaking up again. "I do not have exact numbers as they are still coming in, but it looks like we have maybe five hundred survivors. The Crawlers killed so many. It was a slaughter."

"When will the Kelic be arriving?" Kith asked.

"Scouts just returned," Cos said. "They will be here tomorrow."

"How many men?" Kith asked.

"When we sent the scouts, we instructed them to guide five thousand warriors here, leaving the rest at Daswin to protect the city," Carthen explained. "We figured we would be retreating and using hit and run tactics to slow Rane's larger army down. In the end, we were certain we would be defending Daswin. But your plan worked, which changes everything."

"But we still need to find and kill Rane," Theron said, his tone adamant.

"I have a plan," Kith said. "Now that the water is likely drained from the lake, I can lead men through the gate above to Akari. We can have an army of Kelic waiting for Rane by midday tomorrow."

The warriors all seemed to light up, their tired bodies energized with new hope. "Even if Rane moves quickly, it will take him and the remainder of his army at least six days to make it back to Akari," Carthen acknowledged.

"We would have time to set up an ambush for him before he even reaches his city," Bear'lon said. "We can end this once and for all."

"Exactly," Kith replied. "Who wants to join me?"

Kith was met by a room of eager smiles.

The next day the Kelic arrived around mid-morning. The battlefield was still a bloody graveyard and men worked in shifts to bury the dead. It was difficult work as they were on a road, the land flanking it lined with cliffs, steep hills, and dense forest. They had to load the bodies on wagons and take them to fields located a quarter day away. Everyone worked solemnly, in many cases carrying, transporting, and then cremating their friends. They had to remove the dead Crawlers and the enemy as well, but that was done with much less respect. They still had days of work ahead of them. But no one complained. They were just happy they were on their side of the shovel.

Kith, Carthen, Theron, and An'thryne, met the column of Kelic warriors. They were just as fierce as Kith remembered. Many of the Hiskani had never seen a full-blooded Kelic, and paused their grueling work to gaze at the impressive fighters. They seemed paler than Kith remembered. Perhaps it was the lack of snow and ice around them to lessen the contrast. But they looked like they were made of snow, their long white hair adding to their ghostly appearance. But it was their eyes that made most of the men stop and stare. Their irises were lightning blue, and where Hiskani eyes were white, the Kelic's were a shade of light blue, with veins of various blues spiderwebbing throughout.

Most had discarded their long fur cloaks, having tucked them away long ago in their packs. They wore armor of various designs, some hardened leather and others steel, while some still, mostly the war leaders, were made of annwil scales. They all carried long spears and swords, and many wore zyths at their sides. Some carried huge bows, so long that it would be impossible for an Hiskani to draw. Despite the chilly air, they wore short sleeved tunics exposing their huge muscle-bound arms, some of which were graced with intricate blue tattoos.

Kith was glad he didn't have to fight them.

The column stopped a good distance from the battlefield and the four Hiskani leaders moved toward them. As they neared, three Kelic stepped forward to join them in the middle of the road.

Kith recognized two of them. One was RosGard, one of the hunters that had found them on the pass years before. The other caused Kith's heart to beat faster. It was ThornGrun, RosGard's son, the very same warrior that he fought to guarantee their alliance.

The young warrior looked at Kith, his penetrating eyes twinkling. He nodded slightly as his father addressed them, his Hiskani rough. "Well met." He looked at the priest. "Clan Dungrin greets you priest."

Anthryne nodded but said nothing, looking to Carthen to speak.

"The enemies of Rane greet you, RosGard, hunter of clan Dungrin," Carthen said.

The big Kelic nodded and looked to his son. "My son, ThornGrun." The war leader glanced at Kith, his eyes piercing. Kith could not read the Kelic's expression, but it was unnerving just the same. "My," he continued, looking to the slightly shorter, but even more hulking warrior beside him, "...second," he added, struggling for the right word, "BarGandon."

"Well met," Carthen greeted. "You know An'thryn, order of the Idara, and I believe you remember Kith Caren." Then he looked at Theron. "This is Theron Falconan, heir to the Daswin throne."

RosGard nodded in greeting, looking around at the carnage. "Battle over. Our blades clean." He was clearly not happy.

"There is still fighting to be had," Carthen informed him. "Rane and his men escaped. We need your help to defeat him once and for all. Your blades will be red in three suns."

"This good," RosGard said, smiling, his canines erasing his mirthful expression. "We tire of marching." He looked around at the road. "We camp here." It was more of a statement than an order. But clearly there was no other place for his men to set up camp. In fact, their forces would extend far down the road, but there was nothing that could be done. The road was the only open space available.

Carthen nodded. "We have food to share."

The big warrior nodded. "We rest and eat." Then he turned and walked away, BarGandon right behind him.

ThornGrun paused and stepped towards Kith. He towered over him, and Kith thought he looked to have grown larger with even more muscle. He was an imposing figure. "You different."

"Yes, much has happened to me," Kith acknowledged.

"I hope we fight together."

"It will be an honor."

"This Rane. He warrior?"

"Very much so," Kith acknowledged. "It is said he has no equal with a blade. And he can wield powerful magic."

"I have heard this."

"I will kill him," Kith said adamantly.

ThornGrun nodded. "I will be beside you." Then he turned and walked away.

The next morning a small army of Kelic stood around the gate, with Kith, Theron, An'thryne, Carthen, and Bear'lon before them. It was incredible to see the lake all but gone, the water now a channel flowing slowly towards the cliff face where the dike had once been. Now it was a slow flowing river, water from the inlet streams collecting at the deepest portion of the old lake to flow downhill towards the cliff face where the wall of rock and earth holding back the lake had once been.

They stood on muddy ground, pockets of water and rocks and other debris that had been under water for hundreds of years now exposed. It was messy work to move over three thousand Kelic up the mountain side and near the gate, but luckily the gate had been submerged near the shoreline so the trek through the old lake bottom was minimal.

RosGard, ThornGrun, and BarGandon walked next to the Hiskani leaders as they stared at the strange black gate. Besides Kith, the only person who had used a gate before was Theron, and the others looked positively concerned.

RosGard looked at Kith. "We walk through," he said, gesturing to the gate. "Appear somewhere else?" His tone was doubtful.

"Yes," Kith said. He had already briefed everyone on how the gate worked and what it would feel like, but everyone was still reticent, and rightly so. "I will go through first and keep it open for you to bring your men through."

"Rane will be on the other side?" ThornGrun asked.

"We will have half a day's march to the Imperial Highway," Theron answered. "We will set up our ambush there."

ThornGrun nodded but said nothing, looking back at the gate with obvious trepidation.

"Ready?" Kith asked, looking to RosGard.

The big warrior nodded. "Lead."

Kith made his way closer to the gate, moving steadily through the mud. As he neared, blue sigils slowly began to glow around the gate's perimeter. There was a stirring behind him as the thousands of Kelic warriors shuffled nervously.

He spoke the Dar-danian word for Akari, and the familiar translucent wall fluttered across the opening. The nervous Kelic whispered amongst themselves but none shied away. The Hiskani leaders led by Theron joined Kith, and together they stepped through the gate.

***

"Sir, there seems to be no one following us," the scout said, sweat dripping off his face. He had been running hard all day, scouting the rear of Rane's column before returning with news. Over two thousand Danites and Torlites had escaped with Rane, and he had left more than that number behind, along with the Crawlers, to hold off the enemy while they had retreated. Luckily, he was able to pull three of his most powerful Drann away from the fighting to join them in their escape.

Rane nodded, sending the scout away with the wave of his hand. He was tired, his clothing and armor splattered with a combination of blood and mud. The first day of the retreat had been the worst. The wall of water and mud had destroyed the road, wiping out over ten thousand of his troops. The destruction was the worst he had ever seen. Wagons full of food, his new siege engines, horses and men, were swept away and bashed against the rocks and trees that lined the road that made up the Rock Pass. It was so bad that most of that day they had to make paths through the woods that flanked the pass, the Imperial Highway destroyed or blocked with debris and piles of bodies. It was slow moving; the only consolation being that if the enemy were following, they would be enduring the same conditions.

It was day two and the road was finally clear, allowing them to move much faster. They had stopped for a quick rest, eating a small meal. They were able to pull some supplies from a few wagons that had not been destroyed, but they would run out of food within three days. They needed to find more food.

The question now was what to do? He had lost most of his army. Would the enemy be following to try and end the war at Akari? If so, he had little time to build another army. He could get more men from his conquered lands in Dareef and Bylor, but that would take time. He was confident that he could hold the city with a small force, but if the enemy maintained a successful siege, they would eventually starve him out. He knew that Byron and the Order had suffered massive casualties, especially at the claws and teeth of the Crawlers. Would they be able to put together an army large enough to lay siege to the city and destroy him once and for all? He doubted it. But he was concerned about the Kelic. He knew they would be joining the Order soon. Would they to march to Akari with the rebels? Or would they tire of the game and head back home to the comfort and security of their frigid mountains? There was so much he did not know. He could try and reach the gate, go to Skell, and return with more Crawlers. But even that had risk. He was still unsure how he was able to control them. Could he do it again? The danger of attempting such a task may be too high, even for him.

Making up his mind, he turned to Commander Garn. "Ready the men. We need food so send out hunters. We make haste for Akari."

Commander Garn nodded and moved away to pass on the orders. Rallin stood passively next to Rane. He too looked disheveled, but the blood that splattered his armor was not his own. Despite his ragged appearance, his lightning blue eyes sparkled with intensity. He seemed eager for battle. But then again, Rane thought, he always was.

Rane had pushed his men hard, running at a moderate pace, stopping for water and to cook the game his hunters brought in from the forest. They had no feasts, but it was enough to keep the hardy warriors moving. Nearly a thousand of his men consisted of his famous Danites. Luckily for him, they were all at the head of the column when the wall of water had struck, destroying his forces. Still, most of his elite warriors had survived. They were strong, in both body and mind, and running for three days with minimal food was well within their skill range. The Torlites suffered more, but they kept up with the elite warriors. To do anything else was to be left behind, and no one wanted that.

Rane had sent out scouts to patrol the rear, but still there was no pursuit. He did not feel any need to scout the road before him; after all it would've been impossible for the enemy to get ahead of him. And he controlled the land. There was no danger to the west. It was this faulty thinking that led him into the ambush.

They had left the narrow confines of the Rock Pass days before and now they fast marched on a road that meandered through patches of hills covered in trees peppered with open grasslands. They stopped for a quick rest in an open field that was surrounded by dense forest. It was the same spot they had camped when their siege engines had been set aflame, the blackened and burnt husks of the machines visible against the tree line.

It was here where the attack came.

As his men spread out to rest in the grass, tall white forms suddenly emerged from the shadows of the thick forest, ghostly apparitions hurling themselves forward onto the grassy meadow. Some threw spears while others, who had formed a quick firing line, launched arrows from bows that were larger than anything Rane had ever seen. It was unnerving that men so large could move with such speed and stealth.

Shouts echoed in the clearing as Danites rushed to form defensive lines around their liege. Some of his men were struck by the enemy spears and arrows, tumbling to the ground as they died in the thick grass. But most made it, forming a wall of Danite steel, while the surviving Torlites rushed in to form flanking lines.

Rallin's blade was out, standing at the ready next to his master. The three Drann were also there. Rane could feel the E'lear flowing through their bodies. Warden Stollin and Commander Garn had drawn their steel, their expressions of alarm turing quickly to stoic masks as the energy of battle took over.

More arrows struck the front lines, the bows so powerful that when the arrows struck the men they were tossed backward like a child's doll. The line was already beginning to crumble under the Kelic onslaught.

After the third volley of arrows, RosGard ordered the charge, and Kith and the others, including a wall of Kelic, charged the front line. Carthen was fighting three men down from them, and flanking Kith was Theron and ThornGrun. The thundering feet of the Kelic sounded like a cavalry charge

A they struck the wall of Danite steel Kith's body was alive with E'lear. Swerving subtly, a Danite spear flashed by him, his drift cloak fluttering around him in a mesmerizing dance. Within seconds, his spear sliced countless throat as he cut holes in the enemy lines. Even the Danites before him could not avoid his deadly spear tip.

It was not long before the path before him was open, a dozen dead Danites littering the ground. Suddenly a ball of white light flashed before his eyes. He felt the E'lear from the attack and new he was in trouble. Without thinking, he spun the spear before him, the weapon striking a ball of energy as large as his head. Instantly the spear flashed blue as it dissipated the E'lear, the ball vanishing into nothing.

Without stopping, Kith pushed energy into his legs and leapt forward for the gap in the line, leaving his comrades behind. He felt the heat of another ball fly over him and hoped his friends behind him would not be stuck. Landing, he rolled and came up quickly, bolting towards a surprised Drann priest. He felt the concussion wave behind him as he attacked. Kith's spear shot forward and took the man in the chest. The E'lear was now flowing through his body like a raging river, giving Kith enough power to lift the man in the air, his body suspended by his spear. With a heave of both arms, the Drann priest was flung from the weapon and tossed ten paces away. Without stopping, Kith attacked the next opponent near him, a hulking Kelic.

Meanwhile, Theron dodged the white sphere as it flew behind him, striking a Kelic and rolling back another five feet before exploding. The expanding E'lear killed three nearby Kelic, the heat wave powerful enough to burn Theron's skin on his back and force him forward into the enemy Danites.

But they too had been knocked off guard, and Theron capitalized on that by attacking with new fury. Two more men went down by his blade just as ThornGrun struck a third so hard that his sword, cutting him from groin to shoulder, lifted him off the ground and catapulted him backwards. Using his massive size, the enraged Kelic shouldered an unfortunate Torlite backwards and leapt through the line, Theron following.

The line further down fell apart under the powerful onslaught of the huge Kelic. Carthen and the others expertly burst through, engaging any enemy that had broke from the formation to protect their liege who was in the rear.

Carthen ripped his blade from a Torlite, deflecting another warrior's attack with the flick of his blade and attacking with another flick that easily parted the flesh at his throat. In his periphery, he saw Kith engage a Kelic, who he concluded must be Rane's bodyguard that so many spoke of with great fear.

The dying Torlite fell away and Rane stood before him, a black rakian blade in one hand and a glowing whip in the other. "You!" he snarled, recognizing Carthen as the famous Terwyn Gar. "You should be dead."

Carthen smiled. "Something you will soon experience." Then he attacked.

Theron found himself facing his previous commander, Warden Stollin. The man looked as fierce as he remembered, and despite Theron's own skill, a wave of doubt washed over him.

"It saddens me I must kill you," Warden Stollen growled as he readied his blade. "You had so much potential."

Despite his nerves, Theron smiled. "That is funny, I could see the same about you." Then he attacked.

Their blades met and the rhythm of their steel was drowned out amongst the cacophony of the battle around them. Warden Stollen was every bit the swordsman as Theron, perhaps even better, but he had been running for days on little food and his sword arm was beginning to tire, his movements dragging ever so slightly.

But it was enough. Theron's blade met a desperate attack, his wrist turning slightly, angling his blade around the Danites and pushing it to the side. The experienced commander was simply to tired to reposition his sword in time, or to adjust his body for an appropriate defense. Warden Stollen's flank was open and Theron snapped his foot forward, striking the man in the side of the knee. Something snapped and Warden Stollen screamed, his right knee buckling. Theron's blade whipped around and struck the Danite commander in the neck as he fell forward, his scream cut short as his head was removed from his body.

Meanwhile, Kith deflected Rallin's first attack easy enough, his spear spinning the Kelic's blade away and coming back around. As fast as the warrior was, he could not totally avoid the speed of Kith's riposte, the tip of his spear catching the warrior on the side of the cheek as he leaned away, opening a shallow gash and forcing him to step back.

Suddenly a whip of energy snapped towards him from his left. Kith leaned back, incredibly far, the E'lear in his body allowing him to momentarily hold a position that would otherwise be impossible. He felt the heat of the whip narrowly miss him as he snapped back up, spinning on his heal away from both attackers.

Just then, ThornGrun leapt in, his huge sword angling towards Rallin as the big bodyguard pushed off his heel to resume his attack. Their blades met as Kith, seeing that ThornGrun had engaged Rallin, attacked the Drann, knowing his magic was more dangerous.

The Drann's whip retracted and spun towards Kith again. Spinning his spear in front of him, the whip wrapped around it and in a flash disappeared. The Drann's eyes widened as Kith kept the spear spinning, the tip angled for the priest's stomach. Thinking quickly, the Drann shot both hands out and white light exploded in Kith's eyes. It was so sudden and bright that Kith jumped back from it and his spear missed. But the light did nothing other than temporarily blind him. But Kith didn't need to see to be able to kill. He moved forward quickly as two Danites joined the fight, trying to protect the Drann. Kith's spear deflected their sword attacks, all the while his vision blurred with dancing lights. As he moved around them, his drift cloak flowed like water and the enemy swords flashed and jabbed, narrowly missing him as his own weapon found their flesh. He tripped one by taking his legs out with his spear shaft, quickly whipping the sharp end around and slicing through the other's throat. Never stopping, he flipped the spear around and rammed the tip straight down, impaling the man who had fallen. Sensing the displacement of air, Kith ducked low, the E'lear flowing through his legs allowing him to hold a balanced position as the Drann's energy whip just missed his head. Kith felt the weapon's heat as he turned on his heel, his body still low, his other hand retrieving a zyth at his hip and flinging it sided armed as his legs pushed him back to his feet. In a blink, the zyth struck the priest in the chest, the power of the strike causing him to stumble backwards, his eyes wide as he registered his own death.

ThornGrun heaved Rallin's sword away and attacked with the ferocity the Kelic were known for. Their swords met again and again as the two huge warriors moved around the clearing. Rallin deflected an attack and kicked out with his foot, trying to strike ThornGrun in the side of the knee. But the young Kelic was just as fast, turning slightly as he too kicked his foot out and deflected Rallin's kick. But Rallin was extremely fast, and ruthless. Moving forward, he reversed his blade and the razor edge whipped across ThornGrun's chest. The Kelic's armor was made from annwil scales and Rallin's blade slid harmlessly off the cuirass, but the edge of the blade caught his exposed shoulder as it slid across his body.

ThornGrun grunted as blood ran down his arm. The cut was not deep, but the dripping blood would eventually get to his hand, making his grip on his sword more precarious. Renewing his attack, he switched his sword to his right hand, swinging the blade across his body and forcing Rallin backwards. Simultaneously he drew a hand axe he carried at his side with his bad arm and followed his sword with a downward chop of his axe.

Ever since he had lost the fight to the white-haired half-breed, he had practiced with two weapons. Kith had caught him off guard with his ability to use the sword and zyth together. ThornGrun had promised himself that he would learn to fight with two weapons, and now it was going to pay off.

Rallin dodged the sword attack and blocked the axe, shoving the weapon away as he growled with anger and shot forward with a reverse swing of his sword. But ThornGrun used the two weapons with skill, blocking and attacking, forcing Rallin to be more defensive. Yet, even with ThornGrun's vicious onslaught, Rallin was able to keep the two weapons at bay, and even manage several attacks of his own. Neither warrior had any idea what was happening around them, their engagement consuming their full concentration. Each Kelic warrior knew that any break in focus could lead to disaster.

ThornGrun blocked a side attack with his axe, Rallin's heavy blade and power nearly shattering the strong wood handle. And it likely would have if the young warrior hadn't cushioned the blow, hooking the lower end of the axe on the blade's edge and driving it down towards him. He then snapped his foot out and struck Rallin's arm at the elbow. There was an audible snap as the warrior's elbow caved in at the joint. ThornGrun, never stopping, swung his sword backhanded, angling the blade up and across Rallin's body. The heavy edge scraped across his armor but the tip found the edge of his neck as it slid by. Blood poured from the wound as Rallin stepped back, his good hand cupping the side of his neck while he desperately shot his foot out, aiming for ThornGrun's midsection. The warrior was fast and as ThornGrun rushed forward to finish him off, Rallin's foot hit him squarely in the chest and launched him backwards. The kick hurt, but it lacked the power to do any damage through his armor. It was clearly a desperation move as Rallin tried to bring his sword arm up to protect his exposed body. But he could not, his arm flopping uselessly as his sword fell to the ground. ThornGrun recovered quickly and sprung forward, his axe striking the warrior on the leg as he desperately tried to push ThornGrun away. The blade cut deep and he used the weapon to push Rallin's leg away just as he rammed his sword up and into the man's stomach, the sharp tip angled up and into his lungs. Even in death, the powerful bodyguard reached down with his blood-covered hands and gripped ThornGrun's neck, squeezing with all his power. Blood oozed from his mouth as he squeezed, but he was losing strength and when ThornGrun growled and twisted his blade, he found his heart. Instantly Rallin's grip relaxed and his eyes fluttered, a hiss of air leaving his mouth. Then he slumped forward. The only thing keeping him from falling was ThornGrun's sword.

Carthen knew he was in trouble as soon as he engaged the Emperor. Despite his skill with a blade, he was much older than Rane. He was not as fast and strong as he used to be, and where his abilities had lessened, Rane's had improved. He also had no way to counter his Drann magic, which presently was the immediate danger. Rane's energy whip snapped towards his sword arm and Carthen dodged, barely avoiding the fiery weapon. But as Rane retracted it, the whip caught him in the shoulder, burning through his armor and opening up a painful wound. Carthen knew that to stop would mean his death, so he pushed the pain away and pressed the attack. Their blades kissed several times, their expertise clear to anyone watching. But again Rane flung the whip over his head and brought it down towards Carthen. Rane was so fast that the old swordsman again barely avoided the weapon, the end striking the grass where he had been. But it was just a ruse as Rane then lunged forward with incredible speed, catching Carthen off balance. His sharp rakian blade skewered him low in the left shoulder. He grunted and leapt back. But instantly he knew he was in trouble when he felt his lung tighten, likely filling with blood. He nearly stumbled and looked up just in time to see Rane's whip fly towards him. He had no defense for the weapon and knew that he could not avoid the attack, which would likely cut him in half. Suddenly a blurry form appeared before him, his raised spear catching the whip, which flashed once before dissipating.

Rane shuffled back, his fierce expression turning to shock as his E'lear evaporated in a blink. He had never felt the likes of this experience and did not think it possible. Standing before him was a white-haired warrior wearing a cloak that danced around him as he moved. Looking around, he noticed the fighting was over, his men dead all around him. Massive Kelic fighters circled him, their white skin and armor splattered in blood.

Theron, covered in blood, joined the others around the fight, his eyes tense with battle rage. But something else fluttered there, a sense of worry for his friend. He had seen Rane fight, and despite Kith's new powers, worried that he could not defeat the emperor warrior.

"Who are you?" Rane asked.

Kith looked back and saw Carthen lifted away from the fight. He did not know if the leader would survive, but he had other concerns at the moment. Looking back, his eyes caught Theron's. The young warrior set his jaw and nodded at him. The meaning was clear. Kith's focused eyes turned to Rane, the rhythm of the mind dance finding him quickly as he prepared himself for the fight he had trained so hard for. "I am Kith Caren. The man who is going to kill you."

"How did you do that?" Rane asked, ignoring his last comment.

"I am an Ar'kan warrior. You will pay for your crimes against the Five Lands."

The edges of Rane's lip curled up in a smile. He tried not to think about the fact that when he defeated the warrior before him that he was surrounded by over a thousand Kelic. First thing was to defeat the young warrior. Then he would figure out a way to escape. "You speak lies. There are no more Ar'kan warriors." Then he paused, remembering the story an Eradicator named Pornatious had shared with him about a warrior from Seebras who had negated his power. Rane thought the man had been lying and had him whipped ten times. As it turned out, the man had been telling the truth. "You were the warrior from Seebras."

"Yes."

Rane spat on the ground. "You will never defeat me."

"You are about to find the fault in those words." The beat of the mind dance was pounding in Kith's head and then he shot forward, his cloak a blur in the night.

Rane used a different Drann tactic, employing a glowing bolt of energy shaped like a spear that shot from his hand. The tip of the energy shot forward with such velocity, that Kith's body, even enhanced by the E'lear flowing through it, barely avoided it as it shot over his left shoulder. He could feel the searing heat from the bolt as it retracted to Rane's glowing hand. Then they crashed together, Kith's spear and Rane's sword spinning, deflecting, and attacking, all the while their bodies danced across the trampled grass. Rane employed the bolt several more times, the energy spear shooting forward from his glowing hand. Kith avoided a second attack, but the third struck him in the chest as his spear deflected Rane's blade. Kith's eyes widened in surprise, expecting to feel the weapon punch a hole through his torso. But he felt no pain. There was a flash as his armor took in the E'lear and dissipated it over its surface.

Rane spun away, staring at Kith with wonder, an expression that subtly turned to concern. "That is impossible."

"I told you, I am Ar'kan."

Rane growled and attacked again, his left hand drawing a long knife at his hip, both blades angling towards him. As the mind dance beat in his head, he moved into a focused rhythm, his spear working around him so fast that the observers had a difficult time following the two warriors. Kith's cloak floated around him and several times Rane thought he had him, his blades finding what he thought to be his form behind the cloak. But each time Kith's body moved away and Rane's blades found only the fluttering fibers of the cloak. One such time Kith spun on his heel so fast, that when he whipped his spear around the end caught Rane on the side of his head, knocking him off balance where he nearly fell to the ground.

Catching himself quickly, Rane pulled E'lear from one hand and flung a sphere of bright white light in Kith's face as he moved in to finish him off. Kith brought up his spear, but the ball flashed bright before disappearing. Kith realized it was not meant to do him damage, just to blind him, a similar tactic the other Drann had used.

Rane righted himself and shook off the dizziness. Then he flipped the knife around in his hand and flung it overhand as Kith backed away, his eyes opening and closing quickly as he tried to focus on Rane. Kith had been trained to fight blind and quickly projected his senses, immediately hearing the displacement of air as the knife flew towards him. He could only see blurry forms around him, but his heightened hearing and quick reflexes moved his body to react, spinning his spear before him as he backed up. There was a ping as his spear struck the knife, deflecting it to the ground.

But Rane did not stop, and as soon as his knife was in flight, he reached to his bandolier which held four small throwing knives. Two more were flying towards Kith before he deflected the first.

Kith blocked the second but Rane's speed was such that the knives were too close together, the third finding its target. The knife struck Kith in the arm; a sharp pain shooting through his limb as his hand suddenly felt paralyzed. Kith felt warm blood pour down his arm as he released the spear with his injured arm. He knew he could not wield the spear properly with one arm, so he dropped it and drew his rakian blade with his good hand. Shaking off the lights in his mind's eye, he glanced at his left arm. Rane's knife had hit him in the elbow and the blade had sunk in several inches before falling out. He could barely move it and his left hand didn't work.

Rane regained his full faculties, a red abrasion across his cheek, his nose bleeding. The emperor smiled when Kith looked at him, his expression one of pain.

Again they came together with the speed and skill that few had ever seen. Kith forced more E'lear into his body when he felt it drag, a surge of power strengthening him, the beat of the dance leading his body as he fell into a deadly rythm. Rane matched his speed at first, but it wasn't long before that became impossible. Kith's blade opened up a shallow cut along Rane's right leg, and a few heartbeats later sliced across his left upper arm, finding a gap of flesh in the man's red armor.

Rane cringed, deflecting another attack while drawing a ball of energy from his sword arm, flinging the super-heated ball side armed as Kith pushed the offensive. Rane moved back quickly, hoping the ball would find flesh, realizing that Kith's armor was somehow able to negate his magic.

Kith saw the ball in his peripheral vision, stopping his forward movement. His rakian blade whipped across his body, the edge striking the ball, causing it to disappear in a flash. Kith then angled his blade down and rammed it into the ground. His good hand now free, he dropped low, spinning on his knee as he drew a zyth from his hip, flinging the weapon as he used the momentum of his spin to increase its velocity.

The zyth struck Rane in the neck and his eyes bolted wide in shock. Stumbling, he tried to stand as he dropped his blade. Blinking several times, blood gushed from his mouth as his legs finally gave out. He fell to the ground with a thud.

Kith stood up straight, reached back and pulled his weapon from the ground, advancing towards Rane's body. He stood over him as Rane coughed a few more times, dark blood spitting from his mouth. His wide eyes found Kith as his body stopped twitching, his eyes glossing over.

ThornGrun stepped next to Kith, his blue eyes looking down at Rane.

"I told you I'd kill him," Kith whispered.

ThornGrun looked sidelong at him, his canine smile and blood-splattered face frightening in the shadowing evening. "I told you. I be at side." He paused as he looked back at Rane's body. "Well done, Kith Caren."

***

Two months later and Kith sat quietly in the corner of the Sloshing Keg, an ale house in Daswin, a glass of mulled warm wine cradled in his hands. Despite the two roaring fires on either end the air was chillier than normal, although the effect on him was minimal, the E'lear flowing through him keeping him warmer than most. He had taken his drift cloak off and had laid it over the chair next to him, his long white hair pulled back into a tail tied with a red strip of leather. His spear leaned against the wall behind him, along with his bow and quiver. At his waist was his rakian blade and both zyths. The room was half full and the furtive glances of the patrons did not go unnoticed. He knew his white hair pegged him as a half breed, and although most of the people of Daswin were now accustomed to seeing the huge Kelic, it was unlikely that their prejudices would vanish overnight. That would take time. Kith found it interesting that most of the stares were not full of hatred, but with something else. Was it fear? No, he didn't think so. He saw some people gesturing towards him as they whispered among themselves. They seemed to be more in awe of him, even admiring, which was a nice change from what he was used to, although he could not be sure.

He was too exhausted to care, having arrived in town just a few hours ago. After the battle at Stone Pass, Theron had spread the word of Rane's death. They had had a lot of work to do, and he requested help from Ronis, the closest town to the pass. It was a fairly large farming community with a small outpost of Rane's men. Once the soldiers learned of Rane's death, they threw down their swords without a fight. Recruiting thousands of workers, Theron worked on clearing the pass from the debris created by the flood. In the process, they worked diligently carrying away the dead and burying them. Even the Kelic army helped, although their presence had created quite a stir.

Lord Byron had died four days after the battle. Theron said very little, the task of putting things back together weighing heavily on him. Luckily, Carthen had survived. His experience and wisdom would help advise Theron during the trials that were sure to come. Theron had immediately sent Kith on a mission with five thousand of the Kelic warriors, the huge fighters eager to see more blood. It was a mission that only Kith could accomplish. The lands of Dareef had been conquered by Rane. And there were thousands of Shyeem and Acku slaves that wanted to return home. Kith, being the only one who could use the gates, took on that task, the Kelic warriors providing escort in case Rane's followers in Dareef would not listen to reason. There was some fighting in Dareef, but once Rane's supporters were killed or captured, the Dareef took back control of their capital city, Hamond. Dareef was hot and humid and Kith could not wait to depart.

His army of Kelic had arrived in Daswin hours ago, and instead of reporting to Theron immediately, he opted to rest at the Sloshing Keg. He was tired of traveling, preparing, planning, fighting, everything he had been doing for the last year. He simply wanted to sit by a fire with nothing to do other than drink a glass of warm wine. His minded drifted to what he would do next, the warmth of the fire like a warm blanket draped over his back. He had come a long way since the Northbite race. But now he wondered what his role would be. He was an Ar'kan warrior, the only person capable of using, and protecting, the gates. But he had no idea how he would fit into a world where the Dar-dan no longer lived. What was the purpose of an Ar'kan warrior in such a world? It was a question that Kith could not answer. Now that the war was over, what would he do? His only goal had been to protect the lands from the creatures in Skell and to kill Rane. Now that he had accomplished those goals, he felt out of place.

Sensing a change in the patrons' demeanors, Kith looked up from his wine and his deep thoughts. A huge Kelic had entered, and seeing Kith in the corner made his way towards him. The room was silent but for the tense whispers from its occupants. It was ThornGrun and he stopped before Kith's table, his stoic expression cracking as he exposed his canines in a smile.

"Father arrived, said you here."

Kith nodded and motioned for him to sit. "I needed to relax."

ThornGrun settled his huge body in one of the chairs, the wood creaking but holding. "What is *relax*?"

Ever since their fight with Rane and Rallin, the young Kelic warrior had formed the beginning of a friendship with Kith. ThornGrun had been quite angry with his father when he had been directed to stay behind to help Lord Theron and lead the Kelic remaining in Daswin. RosGard, his father, had wanted his son to learn what it was like to lead in war, and in peace. ThornGrun was furious, but did as he was told. He very much wanted to accompany Kith to Bylor and Dareef, but his father had not allowed it.

"You know the word tired?" Kith asked.

"Yes. It what you feel after long battle."

"To relax is what you do after long battle," Kith explained.

"So it is to be with woman," ThornGrun added.

"No...well, it..." then he noticed the Kelic smile again and realized he had been joking.

"Father told me you fight in far off lands. I wish I there to fight with you."

Kith nodded. "We did. Your father's men are quite impressive."

Just then a serving girl tentatively came to the table. She was clearly nervous and kept her eyes on Kith. But even that gave her obvious anxiety, her eyes downcast and her voice shaky. Kith noticed she was quite attractive, her bosom pushed up by a purple bodice, a necklace carrying a green stone tucked in her ample cleavage. "Can I get you anything?" She asked.

"Another mulled wine," Kith ordered. "ThornGrun?"

The big warrior looked at the young woman. "Pitcher ale."

She nodded and left quickly.

ThornGrun looked at Kith. "Your women ugly. They no muscle."

Kith laughed. "Some do, my friend, but I'm afraid they still would not be to your liking."

ThornGrun nodded. "What you do after relax?"

Kith sighed. "I was just thinking about that. I'm not sure what to do now that the war is over."

"There will always be fighting."

Kith shrugged and drank the last of his wine. "Perhaps. But there is no fighting *now*. What about you? What are you going to do?" Kith was prepared to take the Kelic to Dral, their ancient homeland, but he had been so busy with his other tasks that he had not entertained the idea until now.

"Some Kelic want to go to Dral, but most of us do not. I will stay here, in Dungrin with my father."

Kith was surprised at that. "You don't want to return home?"

"Home? My home is Dungrin. We know nothing else."

Kith nodded in understanding. The Kelic that had been left behind on Urotha when the Dar-dan left had been living there for thousands of years, most of those years filled with subjugation, murder, and war. None of them knew what it was like to live anywhere else. For them, Urotha was their home. "Will you honor the peace?" Kith knew that peace was not a word in the Kelic language. They lived for raiding and war and he was worried that he might be forced to fight the Kelic in the future.

ThornGrun picked up on his unease. "We not know peace. Friends now, enemies later, it is way of Kelic. But we will try. I find wife, make babies. But later," he added, shrugging his shoulders, "one not know."

"Lord Theron is a good man. I will always stand by him." He looked up at the warrior. "I do not want to fight you ever again."

ThornGrun smiled. "Nor I you."

The serving girl returned and set the drinks on the table, departing quickly. ThornGrun poured a cup of ale from the pitcher and downed it in one gulp, pouring himself another. "You not have plan, you find wife, make babies."

Kith smiled, the idea of settling down intriguing. But the thought felt like a dream, the idea of it seemingly impossible considering who and what he was. Kith was a weapon, he knew as much. Marrying, having children, building a home. Those ideas, although pleasant, were slick with oil. Every time he reached for them, they slipped from his mind. A perfect weapon should not hang above a fireplace mantle. It should be used.

But ThornGrun's suggestion directed his thoughts to a certain someone. He didn't know what his future held. But he did know he needed to see RuAnne. Kith raised his glass to the Kelic, who held his own up in response. He had learned the Hiskani custom of toasting and seemed to enjoy it, although Kith was pretty sure he just saw it as a good reason to quaff the entire cup of ale. "To a temporary peace and making babies."

They clicked their cups and ThornGrun smiled, draining his cup in another big gulp.

EPILOGUE

Kith had not been to Lampure since he was a kid. Most of his memories of the place were not pleasant. His mother had died there, although he remembered very little of her. He had been put in an orphanage, and the memories of those events so long ago remained seared into his conscious. He had not been treated well, none of the kids had. For those reasons he had run away when he was eleven and had been on his own ever since.

The town looked just as he remembered it, the images flooding back to him as he walked through the wooden gate. There was the Lyne River on the north side of the town, and the city walls, built of logs lashed together and driven into the ground, protected the southern side. The east and west sides were covered in tall rocky terrain, the east blending into a cliff wall facing the turbulent ocean.

It was dusk and the sun had nearly disappeared, casting shadows throughout the town. Most of the homes were built of wood and thatch, but some, near the center of town, were erected of stone with roofs of wood planks and shingles. It was in that direction that he headed. He had already turned his drift cloak inside out, his face tucked deep into the shadows of the hood. There were people about, most heading home from work and some heading out to frequent the various tap rooms. Most ignored him, and the few that did not, simply glanced his way before looking elsewhere. He was armed, his short bow unstrung and stored in his quiver, the end sticking high above his head. His rakian blade was hidden by his cloak but he held his spear casually as he made his way towards the business district. It was not uncommon to see a warrior in Lampure, but they would still draw the furtive glances of the farmers and fisherman that made up most of the town's population.

There were no Torlites about, Theron had seen to that. But Kith did see a few guards wearing the crimson colors of house Falconan. It would be a while before Theron and all the other leaders worked out the political mess created by Rane's death. His family had ruled all of Urotha for over two hundred years with an iron fist. Now that he was gone, they had to sift through the political rubble to determine how the land would be governed. Kith was glad he didn't have to be a part of the that, having already caught glimpses of the difficulties awaiting Theron and the lands' other leaders. He was not envious.

The first thing Kith did was secure a room at an inn called Morrells. It was a nice place with clean rooms. Kith paid five silvers for two days. He had plenty of coin. Theron had seen to that before he had left. The young lord had told Kith that there would always be more whenever it was needed. It was nice to not have to worry about that. But Kith had a feeling that he would be earning that coin in the years to come. The man at the counter, Lorik Morrel, was kind but seemed wary that Kith would not remove his hood. But Kith's silver was enough to keep the man's interest in check, and he gave him a key without voicing his obvious concerns.

Kith made his way towards the center of town, the likely place for the tap room called The Wanderer. Ru had told him before she left Daswin that their cousin owned the place and was going to put them up there. Keeping his face hidden, he moved through the throng of people that were heading in the same direction. He passed four guards wearing Daswin's colors and decided it would be faster to ask them the tap room's location. He didn't know any guards who didn't enjoy a few ales after a shift. They were standing along the road talking quietly, making their presence known as they occasionally eyed the people around them.

Kith stopped near one. "Excuse me, I'm looking for a tap room called The Wanderer. Do you happen to know its location?"

The man nearest him looked a bit perturbed at Kith's interruption, and his eyes narrowed with suspicion when they saw Kith keep his hood pulled low.

"I do," the guard said. He pulled himself from the post he was leaning on and nodded towards Kith's hood. "What's with the hood?"

Kith shrugged. "I'm cold."

Another guard stepped closer. "What's your name?"

"Kith Caren."

The man's eyes widened some, then he laughed. "Yeah, and I'm Lord Rane." The other guards chuckled and joined in on the joke.

Kith decided to speed up the process. He reached up and pulled his hood back, exposing his long white hair, the plaited tail laying over his right shoulder. "I *am* Kith Caren."

The near guard's hand went instinctively to his sword but the other guard grabbed his shoulder. "What are you doing?!" he said strongly. "Remove your hand." Obviously, he was in charge.

The guard looked chagrined as he slowly removed his hand from the pommel of his sword. "I'm sorry. He startled me."

The leader looked at Kith more closely, his wary demeanor turning to one of awe. "Are you really him?"

"I am." Kith didn't know that his reputation had preceded him. But it didn't surprise him either. Soldiers often passed on stories of battle exploits, more often than not exaggerated beyond the truth. "Now, about that tap room?"

By this time the other guards had joined the leader. The man was older than the others, gray hair brushed into his black beard. He looked rugged and battle hardened, a long scar cutting across his right cheek. "Yes, yes, I apologize for my friend's brashness. It is not often we see the white hair of the Kelic."

"I understand. But by my understanding, you will be seeing them much more. If I can give you some advice, never reach for your blade in their presence. It will not end well for you."

The man nodded, glancing at his subordinate to make sure his point was made. "Point taken. Now, if you head to the center of town, you can't miss it. It will be on your left, the sign above the door blue."

Kith nodded. "Thank you." He reached up and pulled his hood back over his face.

The man nodded, not sure what else to say. He was clearly in shock at seeing the famous Ar'kan warrior who had killed Lord Rane. Kith smiled beneath his hood and walked away. He had to admit, it did feel good to be respected. It was not something he had been accustomed to.

The guard had been correct, the tap room was easy to find, a handful of patrons entering before him. Shutting the door behind him, the boisterous noise of the bar's occupants hit him first, followed by the scent of roasting meat and ale. Kith was not a big ale drinker, but he did love the smell. Looking around, the tap room was a typical configuration. The bar was long and covered most of the length of the far wall. There were two fireplaces flanking him on the opposite walls and the center of the room was filled with stout tables and chairs. The walls were covered with various old weapons and shields, other spaces occupied by furs from various animals. The room was warm and comfortable.

Kith looked around for a table and spotted RuAnn immediately. She was serving ale and food to a table near the fire. There was an empty table in the corner of the room and Kith headed in that direction. He saw one other serving girl who was working the other side of the room. Kith figured RuAnn would find him soon enough. He removed his quiver and leaned it and his spear against the wall behind him. Sitting down, he kept his hood pulled over his face and scanned the room. The Eskeli had taught him to always be prepared, those instincts drilled into him for over a year. And now, even with the war being over, he still sent out his feelers, listening and looking for any possible threats. It was done instinctively. Sensing no immediate threat, Kith leaned back in his chair as RuAnn made her way to him.

Her eyes were wary as she noticed he still wore his hood. The room was warm so that likely seemed strange. "Good evening, sir. Can I get you anything?"

Kith reached up and pulled back his hood, smiling all the while. "I hope you can."

Ru's eyes lit up and she relaxed, her smile wide and welcoming. "Kith!" She clearly wanted to hug him but her hand held the tray and she was working. "It is so good to see you. I had heard what happened to Rane. People spoke of a white-haired man who had killed him. I just knew it was you."

Kith nodded as he looked around the room. He noticed the patrons glancing his way but he ignored them. "How are things here?"

"Great!" she beamed. "My mother's cousin, Farwin, owns the place. We live with him and I serve while my mother helps cook."

"That is good. Are you going to go back to Daswin?"

"I think so," she said. "But I am not sure when." She looked around at all the patrons and her smile disappeared. "Kith, I'm sorry, but I have to work. Are you staying in town?"

"I'm staying at Morrels."

"I would like to see you, so we can really talk."

"What time is your shift over?"

She frowned. "Not til closing."

Kith figured that was the case. "I will come back later."

"Really?" She asked, smiling again.

"Of course. You are why I am here."

Ru blushed and stepped back from the table, smiling. "See you later then?"

"Yes."

"Did you want something to drink?"

Kith shook his head and stood. "No thank you. I will get something when I come back later."

Ru smiled again. "Ok." She turned away and went to a nearby table, her eyes flicking to Kith several more times.

He caught her glances as he pulled his hood back, draping his quiver over his shoulder. Smiling at her, he headed towards the door.

Kith came back later and as soon as he opened the door to the tap room, he knew something was wrong. The typical raucous chatter one would hear in a busy bar was gone, replaced by concerned whispers as the patrons looked towards the main bar.

Kith saw a man wearing a black cloak holding RuAnn close, her posture pulled back from him as she struggled in his grasp. Two other men, both wearing dark cloaks and armed with swords, were laughing by his side. The trio was clearly drunk. A man behind the bar, likely Ru's cousin and owner, was trying to placate the group as the leader manhandled her.

Kith's eyes narrowed as he instantly found the mind dance, the rhythm pounding in his head. It was all he could do to not draw his blade and cut them down where they stood. Moving forward quickly, he stopped five paces from the trio.

"Release her!" Now!" he ordered.

The men stopped laughing and turned to face him. The one holding Ru pulled her even closer and Ru, unable to break his grasp, stopped struggling, her expression hopeful when she saw Kith. The other two men, seeing Kith's threatening stance, brought their hands to their blades.

"If you draw that steel you will die," Kith growled, his anger barely in check.

The men kept their hands on their hilts but did nothing more, their eyes darting to the leader.

"And who do we have here?" the man holding Ru sneered.

Farwin came from around the bar and got between them. "Now hold on. I don't want any fighting or bloodshed." Then he looked at the man holding Ru. "I'm asking you to release her and leave. If not, I will call the town guards."

The leader ignored him and continued to stare at Kith, his eyebrows raised in question.

Kith obliged him and pulled his hood back. "I am Kith Caren."

The man's eyes widened and he pushed RuAnn away. The other two men sensed his concern and readied themselves. It was then that Kith saw traces of tattoos barely noticeable on his neck just above his tunic, as well as Drann markings on his hands. He wore a sword and knife and looked as if he knew how to use them.

"You!" the man growled. "You escaped me once. You will not do so again."

Kith looked at the man more closely. Then it dawned on him. It was the Eradicator that had attacked him on Seebras. It was the same man who had killed the Eskeli. The other two men must be Black Watch soldiers.

"You killed my friend."

"That thing!?" Pornatious sneered, smiling. "Yes, I did. I nearly cut him in half."

Kith let the comment slide over him as he listened intently to the mind dance, his hands opening and closing, eager to hold his weapons. "Rane is done. I killed him. You have no authority here any longer. You have two choices. Lower your weapons and be tried for crimes against your own people, or die here, now."

By this time Farwin, Ru, and the patrons nearby, knew this was a confrontation that they had no control over. They had backed far away, watching intently as it intensified.

"A trial?" Pornatious mocked. "I was following orders."

"Orders that were given by a murdering despot," Kith added. "Following them makes you no different than he."

Kith could feel the man pull more E'lear from around them and readied himself. The two soldiers flanking the Eradicator sensed it as well and moved further apart, obviously hoping to flank Kith when the violence exploded.

"I will take my chances here!" Pornatious growled as he whipped his right hand across his left, drawing E'lear into a glowing spear. The Black Watch soldiers then attacked, their blades ripped from their scabbards in a flash.

Kith was ready, the mind dance pounding in his head like war drums. He shot forward so fast that the people watching simply saw a blur. His rakian blade appeared in his right hand and he drew a zyth with his left. The soldiers were not prepared for the speed of the violence directed at them. Kith's blade flashed right, the edge slicing through the man's stomach as he dropped under the soldier's sweeping sword. Springing up, he continued forward, his zyth catching the other sword between two of its blades. Pushing the weapon away, Kith spun around the man, his sword angled between his legs. Slicing his sword across the inside of the man's thigh, he cut through his femoral artery and continued his momentum around to face the Eradicator. It all happened so fast that Pornatious's eyes widened in surprise as he shot the spear of E'lear forward, his back pressed against the bar. Kith swayed away from the spear, the heat of the weapon burning the edge of his face as he smoothly launched forward and inside the man's reach. Pornatious's eyes widened even more as Kith's sword, now glowing blue with E'lear, punched through his chin and out the top of his head, the heat of the weapon cauterizing the fatal wound so that when Kith yanked the blade free and spun away, there was no crimson spray. The Eradicator coughed blood once and slumped down on the bar, his eyes glazing over in death.

Kith turned and saw the Black Watch soldiers twitching on the floor, their life blood pooling around them. He saw the same four town guards standing at the entry, their swords drawn, their stunned expressions staring back at him. They had witnessed the attack, but had barely registered his movements. The room was deathly still, everyone's wide eyes fixated on Kith.

Kith knelt and wiped his blade on the Eradicator's cloak before sheathing it. Standing, he looked at Ru. Her eyes were wide with fright. She seemed just as shocked as everyone else. It was at that point that Kith knew he would never be able to have a lasting relationship. He was a weapon. And weapons are surrounded by violence. She deserved better.

"I'm sorry," he said softly. Then he turned and left the room, the town guards parting as he pushed through the door.

"Wait!" Ru yelled as she followed him outside. Kith turned, his expression sad. But he said nothing. "Where are you going?"

"I don't know." He hesitated. "I came to see you. I wanted to see you. But," he shook his head, not sure what to say.

"I wanted to see you as well. Why are you leaving?"

Kith sighed. "Look around. I just killed three men in front of you."

"They were bad men. They attacked you first."

"Perhaps," Kith agreed. "But I cannot be the man you want me to be. I am not that man, no matter how bad I want to be."

Ru stepped closer and reached her hand out, touching the slight burn on his cheek. She looked up at him. "You can be anyone you want to be." She leaned in and kissed him softly on the lips.

Her touch felt good, really good, but Kith knew it could not be. He held her by the shoulders and gently pushed her away from him. "I'm sorry. I cannot. I am an Ar'kan warrior. That is what I am. I belong to the Five Lands now. That is my purpose." He leaned down and kissed her one more time. "You deserve something...different, I know that now." He paused, not sure what else to say. "But I will see you again."

Then he turned and left, disappearing quickly into the night.

THE END

Join Jonas in the Cavalier Trilogy!

Praise for the Cavalier

"This intensely written novel of fantasy and magic, good and evil, draws you into a rich tapestry; the world that author Jason L. McWhirter has created."
Fantasy book review (M.G. Russell)

"The writing is crisp and polished, and the narrative has a good level of description for a fantasy novel. Jonas is a sympathetic character who the reader immediately cares about…"
Sift Book Review

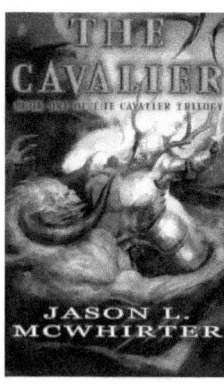

Are you a fan of Jonas Kanrene? Check out his new adventure in book one of the Shadow Knight Novels! Look for it at Amazon!

If you loved McWhirter's Steel Lord Series, then you must read Brant's new adventure, the Glimmer Blade. It promises to leave you feeling a gambit of emotions! Look for it at Amazon.

www.ingramcontent.com/pod-product-compliance
Lightning Source LLC
Chambersburg PA
CBHW070837250626
47159CB00003B/823